Livvy took a deep breath. Her hands were clenched into tight fists at her sides. "Don't you see? I've made my choice. I'm going to live forever. That's my choice. You want to stay home and see your boring friends and that boring geek Ari, and go to school like a nice girl and be a nice, boring person for the rest of your life. And I've made a different choice. That's all. So get out of my face, Dee. Go away and don't come back."

"I . . . don't believe you." Destiny let the tears roll down her cheeks. "You're my sister. My *twin* sister. And the two of us belong together. We—"

"We belong together? Okay!" Livvy cried. She let her fangs slide down over her lips. "You want to stay together forever? Fine. You stay with *me*."

She grabbed Destiny around the waist and started to drag her across the parking lot toward the woods.

"Hey—let go!" Destiny screamed, unable to hide her panic. "What are you doing?"

Livvy pressed her mouth against the back of Destiny's neck. "You and me—forever," she whispered.

Dangerous Girls

The Taste of Night

A novel by
R.L. STINE

Avon Books
An Imprint of HarperCollins*Publishers*
Parachute

Library of Congress Cataloging-in-Publication Data
Stine, R.L.
Dangerous girls : the taste of night / by R.L. Stine.— 1st ed.
p.   cm.
Sequel to: dangerous girls.
"A Parachute Press Book."
Summary: Livvy Weller wants her twin sister, Destiny, to join
her on the darker side as a vampire, but Destiny is determined to
restore Livvy to her human condition and bring her back home to
their family.
ISBN 0-06-059616-3 — ISBN 0-06-059617-1 (lib. bdg.)
ISBN 0-06-059618-X (pbk.)
[1. Vampires—Fiction. 2. Sisters—Fiction. 3. Twins—Fiction.]
I. Title.
PZ7.S86037Dap 2004   2004002151
[Fic]—dc22   CIP
                                                                AC

YA
Sti   occc 8/4/25

First Avon edition, 2005

For Susan Lurie,
still dangerous after all these years.

Contents

Part One: July

Chapter One: My Sister Is a Vampire 3

Chapter Two: "Can You Kill Your Own Daughter?" 9

Chapter Three: The Vampire Hunt 15

Chapter Four: "Good-bye, Livvy" 20

Part Two: One Month Earlier

Chapter Five: Livvy's Graduation Party 27

Chapter Six: Night Birds 35

Part Three: Earlier That Day

Chapter Seven: The Evil at Home 47

Chapter Eight: "The Monster Did It" 56

Chapter Nine: The Vampire in the Tree 62

Chapter Ten: Is Livvy in the House? 66

Chapter Eleven: Rip 72

Part Four

Chapter Twelve: Livvy's New Love **87**

Chapter Thirteen: A Surprise Reunion **93**

Chapter Fourteen: The Taste of Night **98**

Chapter Fifteen: "I'm Not Just a Vampire" **103**

Chapter Sixteen: Destiny Flies **106**

Chapter Seventeen: Trouble at Ari's House **113**

Chapter Eighteen: Who Is the Next Victim? **125**

Part Five: Two Weeks Later

Chapter Nineteen: "Maybe He's Just What I Need" **135**

Chapter Twenty: "Now You Think I'm a Psycho Nut" **145**

Chapter Twenty-one: Dad Might Kill Livvy **150**

Chapter Twenty-two: One Evil Dawn **156**

Chapter Twenty-three: "I Want to
Go Back to My Old Life" **164**

Chapter Twenty-four: A Death in the Vampire Family **172**

Chapter Twenty-five: "It Won't Be Pretty" **177**

Chapter Twenty-six: "I'd Like to Tear Destiny to Bits" **180**

Chapter Twenty-seven: Blood on Her Lips **184**

Chapter Twenty-eight: Livvy's Revenge **189**

Part Six

Chapter Twenty-nine: The Party Crasher 195

Chapter Thirty: Livvy and Harrison 201

Chapter Thirty-one: "You're Still
Connected to Your Sister" 204

Chapter Thirty-two: A Date with a Vampire 209

Chapter Thirty-three: Harrison and Livvy 217

Chapter Thirty-four: Destiny and Patrick 221

Chapter Thirty-five: An Evil Creature of the Night 227

Chapter Thirty-six: An Unexpected Murder 230

Chapter Thirty-seven: The Real Murderer 238

Part Seven: Night of the Full Moon

Chapter Thirty-eight: Harrison's Big Date 245

Chapter Thirty-nine: Destiny Surprises Patrick 250

Chapter Forty: Livvy Surprises Patrick 257

Chapter Forty-one: A Vampire Must Die 260

Chapter Forty-two: "One Last Kiss . . .
Before I Kill You" 263

Chapter Forty-three: Thicker Than Blood 268

Part One

July

Chapter One
My Sister Is a Vampire

As Destiny Weller made the turn onto Collins Drive, a light rain started to fall. She squinted through the windshield, through the tiny, shimmering droplets of water, and pressed her cell phone to her ear.

"I think it's going to get really stormy," she said, glancing up at the lowering, black clouds. "I really don't feel like going out tonight, Ana-Li."

Her friend Ana-Li May made disappointed sounds at the other end. "I know it's hard for you, Dee. But the summer is going fast, you know. You should try to have at least a *little* fun."

Fun? How could she be talking about fun?

Destiny clicked on the headlights. The wipers left a smear on the windshield glass. She kept forgetting to replace the blades.

Hard to think about things like that.

3

"You've been really great," she told Ana-Li. "I mean, all summer. You're the only one who knows the truth about Livvy. I mean, except for Dad and Mikey. And Ari, of course. And you've been—OH!"

Destiny let out a cry. The cell phone fell from her hand as she hit the brakes hard. Her tiny, silver-gray Civic skidded on the wet pavement.

Startled by the sound, the girl on the sidewalk whipped her head around. Her face came into view.

Destiny gasped. No. Wrong again.

A car honked behind her. Heart pounding, she lowered her foot on the gas pedal and fumbled for the phone.

She could hear Ana-Li on the other end. "What's wrong? Dee? Are you okay?"

"Sorry." She leaned forward to squint through the smeared windshield. The rain pattered down harder. "I keep losing it. Every time I see a girl with long blond hair, I think it's Livvy."

"That's why you've got to get out of yourself," Ana-Li said. "You know. Go out. We'll go to a club or something. Dance our asses off.

Maybe meet some hot guys. It'll take your mind off . . . everything."

"*How can I take my mind off it?*"

She didn't mean to scream, but the words burst out of her in a shrill, trembling voice. "Ana-Li, my twin sister is a *vampire*! She's out flying around, prowling at night, hungry for warm blood, killing—killing things. I . . . I don't know what she's doing. I haven't seen her in two months. Do you know what that's done to my family? To my dad? My poor little brother?"

"Yes, of course I know, Dee. You don't have to scream at me. I—"

"There's *no way* I can take my mind off it," Destiny continued. She made a sharp right, tires skidding again. She'd almost missed her turn. "I think about Livvy all the time. And Ross too. I still can't believe he went with her. Ana-Li, I . . . I want to see Livvy. I just want to hug her. I know it's impossible, but I want to tell her to come back to us."

There was silence at Ana-Li's end.

"Ana-Li? Are you still there?"

"Yeah. I just don't know what to say. You know, I'll be leaving for orientation. Yale is a long way from here. I thought maybe in the short time we have . . ."

Destiny pulled into a parking spot at the curb in front of the familiar, low redbrick building. The rain had slowed. The wipers left a thick, gray smudge as they scraped over the glass.

That's the way I see everything these days, Destiny thought bitterly. Through a dark blur.

"Listen, Ana-Li. I have to go. I'm here, at my dad's office. I have to pick him up because his SUV broke down again. He never takes care of it." She sighed. "He can't seem to take care of anything these days. Just stays in his lab twenty hours a day. Then he comes home too wrecked to talk or do anything."

"Sorry," Ana-Li murmured on the other end.

"No, *I'm* sorry," Destiny said. "Here I am, laying all this on you again for the hundredth time. I'm really sorry. Can I call you later?"

"Yeah. Sure."

She clicked the phone shut and dropped it into her bag. Then she took a deep breath while checking her short, blond hair in the mirror.

Ana-Li has been terrific, she thought. She's always been a great friend. After that horrible night Livvy and Ross decided they wanted to live forever as vampires . . . Ana-Li has always been there for me.

She slid out of the car and gazed up at the sign above the glass door: WELLER VETERINARY CLINIC. Yes, her dad still treated sick cats and dogs, spayed and neutered them, gave them their shots, washed away their fleas, and mended their broken bones. But he spent most of his time in his lab at the back of the building, reading, studying old books, mixing chemicals, working out endless equations, searching for a cure for vampirism.

Destiny made her way through the brightly lit waiting room, empty now, quiet except for the gurgling sounds from the fish tank in the wall. "Hey, Dad—are you ready?" Her voice echoed down the hall as she passed the empty examining rooms.

"Dad?"

She found him hunched over the worktable in the lab, surrounded by darkness, standing under a cone of light from the single ceiling lamp. His eyeglasses reflected the light. He didn't seem to hear her at first.

"Dad? I'm here."

To her surprise, he had tears running down his cheeks. He crumpled the papers in his hand, then furiously ripped them in half and sent them flying to the floor.

"Dad—?"

Dr. Weller turned to Destiny, his face flushed, his eyes hidden behind the shiny glasses. "I'm afraid I have very bad news," he said.

Chapter Two

"Can You Kill Your Own Daughter?"

*D*estiny's breath caught in her throat. "Dad—what is it?" she finally choked out. She hurried across the room and stood across the table from him, under the bright, white light.

He shook his head. "It's my work. It's going nowhere. I'm no closer to finding a cure than I was two months ago."

Destiny grabbed the edge of the metal table with both hands. "But you'll keep trying, right, Dad? I mean, you're not giving up, are you?"

His pale blue eyes stared at her from behind his glasses, thick gray eyebrows arching high on his balding head. "I don't know how much time I have." His voice came out in a whisper. His eyes didn't move from Destiny's. "I'm under a lot of pressure."

"Pressure? I don't understand, Dad."

He stepped around the table and put an arm around her shoulders. "A lot of pressure." He hugged her briefly, then guided her to his small office at the side of the lab.

He dropped heavily into his desk chair, brushing back the tuft of gray hair on top of his head. Destiny stood, tense, in front of the desk, arms crossed over the front of her blue T-shirt.

"You know I have chosen two roles," Dr. Weller said, gazing up at her. "I'm the Restorer, the one who can restore neophyte vampires to their normal lives, if they're not already complete vampires."

I know very well, Destiny thought with a shiver. You don't have to explain, Dad. You restored *me*, remember? I was bitten too, just like Livvy. But you restored me, and now I'm fine, perfectly normal. But Livvy . . .

"And I'm also the Hunter," her dad continued, breaking into her thoughts. "Ever since your mother died . . . killed herself because of a vampire . . . I . . . I . . . I've vowed to kill as many vampires as I can. To rid Dark Springs of this . . . this filthy plague."

He rubbed his chin. Destiny saw that he hadn't shaved for at least a day or two. "My two roles . . . curing and hunting . . . they don't always go together."

"What do you mean, Dad? Destiny lowered herself into the wooden armchair across from the desk. "What's going on?"

"I've been working so hard to find a cure," he said. "You know. A cure for Livvy. And for Ross too. And any other vampire who wants it. And I've been neglecting my duties as a hunter."

Destiny leaned forward, her hands tightly clasped. All her muscles tensed as her father went on.

"The vampires in this town . . . they've become an even bigger danger. There are too many of them. People are starting to become aware . . ."

Destiny swallowed. "You mean, that couple that was murdered in Millerton Woods last weekend?"

Dr. Weller nodded. "The police have been able to keep everything quiet. People in Dark Springs don't know about the vampires. Like your friends, Dee. Your friends all think that Livvy and Ross ran away together. They . . . they don't know the truth."

Destiny nodded. "Just Ana-Li knows. And Ari, because he was there that night. No one else."

Dr. Weller frowned, deep lines creasing his forehead. "Well, people are starting to guess. The police have been getting calls. Mayor Hambrick has been getting frightened calls. He wants to get the governor to call in the National Guard. I can't let that happen. Too many innocent people will be killed."

"What are you going to do?" Destiny asked.

"I have no choice. I have to get my hunters together. I have to hunt them down—and kill as many vampires as I can."

Destiny let out a sharp cry. "Kill them?"

She suddenly pictured Livvy . . . Livvy before this all happened . . . when their mother was still alive. Livvy in that sexy red halter dress she wore to the spring dance their junior year. Her hair all shimmering, cascading down her bare back. The bright red lipstick . . . her sparkly earrings . . . her smile . . .

Destiny shook herself to chase the picture away.

"You can't just go out and kill vampires," she told her father. "How will you find them?"

Dr. Weller leaned forward over the desk. He grabbed Destiny's hands and held them between his. "There's an abandoned apartment building across the river from the campus. It was supposed to be student housing, a dorm for the community college. But the construction company went bankrupt and the building was never finished."

Destiny narrowed her eyes at him. "And—?"

"We think several vampires are using that building. Sleeping there during the day. Living in the apartments. I have my hunters organized. We're going there. Going into those apartments and killing as many of them as we can."

Destiny pulled her hands free. She jumped to her feet. "When? When are you doing this?"

"In two weeks—the next full moon."

Destiny swallowed, her throat suddenly dry. "Two weeks!"

He nodded. "Yes. We'll go in at sunrise when they're all asleep. I wanted to warn you. I mean, if something happens to me . . ." His voice trailed off.

"But, Dad—" Destiny realized she was shaking. "What about Livvy? What if Livvy is in one of those apartments? You . . . you can't kill your own daughter. You can't!"

A sob escaped Dr. Weller's throat. "My daughter is already dead."

Destiny moved around the desk and grabbed her father's sleeve. "But she's not! She's still alive. You know she's not dead. You can't do it. You can't kill her—*can* you?"

"I don't know!" Dr. Weller hugged Destiny again and held her tight. "I don't know. I don't know! If I find Livvy in there . . . I don't know what I'll do."

Chapter Three
The Vampire Hunt

*D*r. Weller pulled the dark baseball cap down over his head and gazed up at the moon, full and low in the sky, pale white as the sun began to rise. Dressed in black, hats down over their foreheads, the hunters—twenty volunteers—gathered in a silent circle around him at the open entrance to the tall apartment building.

Dr. Weller heard the flap of wings high in the sky. He glanced up the side of the redbrick building, at the window openings, glassless and dark. A tall pile of concrete blocks stood near the front of the entrance. Boards of Sheetrock in varying sizes, wire, and rolls of cable were strewn across the ground. Signs that the construction had stopped abruptly, long before the building had been completed.

A thin arc of red sunlight rose in the distance. The hunters leaned on their wooden stakes, waiting for their orders.

Dr. Weller took a deep breath. "The vampires should be sleeping by now," he said, eyes raised to the window holes. "But this may not be easy. If they somehow got word that we were coming . . ."

"We can handle them," a young man said, raising his stake in front of him like a knight's lance.

"They might have set a trap for us," Dr. Weller said. "We need to take all precautions. As we spread out in there, we need to be in constant communication. Did you check your walkie-talkies?"

Some of them muttered yes. Some nodded. Some reached for the phones clipped to their belts.

"Make sure they're all set on the same frequency," he continued. "If you're in any trouble, just press the button and shout your location. We'll all hear you."

They nodded again. One man at the edge of the circle made a striking motion with his pointed stake, as if he were killing a vampire.

"Let's go," Dr. Weller said. He hoped they didn't see the shudder that ran down his body. He spun to the building and began jogging toward the entrance, raising his stake as he ran.

Livvy? Ross? Are you in here?

The thought of his daughter lying white and pale, asleep in this vacant building, made his stomach churn. He could feel the muscles tightening in his throat. A wave of nausea swept over him, and for a moment, he thought he was going to vomit.

Livvy?

Oh, Livvy.

Then he was inside the dark lobby, cooler in here, the smell of plywood and pine and plaster dust, and his stomach settled. Through his glasses, his vision grew sharp as he focused his mind. In the dim light, he could see the half-tiled walls, the opening of the elevator shaft.

He suddenly could hear every footstep of his hunters, hear their shallow breaths, even hear their *thoughts*! At least, he imagined he could.

Every sense alive now.

Alive. Yes, I want to stay alive. I don't want to die tonight in a nest of vampires.

A nest of the *undead*.

Undead. My own daughter . . .

A shaft of red sunlight poured through the open lobby windows. The day was pushing out the night. He felt as if he were moving through a dream, colors changing, darkness giving way to bright light.

Trying to force away all thoughts, he led the hunters to the stairs. And as they climbed, single file up the concrete stairway, shoes thudding and scraping the dust, Dr. Weller heard the moans. Soft at first, then louder as they stepped out onto the first floor.

A shrill animal howl somewhere down the long hallway. Open doorways to the left.

Stakes gripped against their sides, the hunters trotted toward the open doorways. Dr. Weller clicked on his flashlight and sent a beam ahead of them on the floor. He saw piles of trash, rattling and blowing from the gusts of wind through the glassless windows.

Sudden movement. An animal scampered out from under the trash. Dr. Weller stopped and motioned for his hunters to stay back, and then lowered the beam of yellow light to the creature. A fat raccoon.

The animal waddled away from the light, down the trash-cluttered hall, followed by four small raccoons, running hard to keep up.

Dr. Weller motioned for his posse to move

again. Stepping over the garbage and stacks of newspaper, they walked silently toward the dark apartments.

No doors on the apartments. They heard hoarse coughs. Loud snoring. Eerie moans and groans . . .

Yes, they're here.

Yes, they're asleep.

Yes, it's time.

Dr. Weller raised his wooden stake and pointed it down the hall. "Let's kill vampires!" he cried.

Chapter Four

"Good-bye, Livvy"

He stepped into the first apartment, wooden stake raised in his right hand, flashlight gripped in his left. He swept the light around the floor. It stopped on a figure sprawled on his back, arms dangling over a nearly flat mattress on the floor.

Heart pounding, Dr. Weller moved closer. A young man, asleep, his mouth open. And the dark stain on his chin . . . the dark stain . . . caked blood. Running down his chin onto his bare chest.

He must die. I have no choice. I have accepted this responsibility.

But yet Dr. Weller hesitated. Am I taking a human life?

No.

Not human. Not human any longer.

A scream of agony ended his thought, followed by another shrill scream from down the hall. The hunters had found their prey. Vampires were being slaughtered.

He set down the flashlight. He raised the pointed stake high in both hands.

Another scream of horror from another apartment.

The young man stirred in his sleep. Closed his mouth. Eyes still shut, he licked at the caked blood on his chin.

With a loud grunt, Dr. Weller arched the stake high, then brought it down with all his force. The point pierced the young man's chest, then sank deep into his body.

His arms shot up and his legs kicked. He opened his eyes wide and a scream of pain shattered the silence of the room.

Dr. Weller buried the stake deeper, pushing hard, gripping it with both hands. The vampire's eyes sank into their sockets. The arms and legs, still now, began to shrink. A rush of air escaped the vampire's mouth, and then he didn't move again.

Dr. Weller freed the stake with a sharp tug. It pulled out easily, no blood on the tip.

He grabbed the flashlight and lurched back out into the hall. Screams echoed off the plaster walls. Screams and howls of pain and shock, and the hard-running footsteps of the hunters as they invaded the open apartments to kill their deadly prey.

Dr. Weller stopped for a moment to catch his breath. Then he dove into the next apartment, the wooden stake trembling in his hand.

The light danced over the apartment floor. A small, square rug in one corner. A suitcase against the wall. A wooden table cluttered with bottles and tubes and jars of cosmetics.

Dr. Weller swallowed. A female vampire lived here. His legs suddenly felt weak as he moved toward the bedroom in back. The flashlight grew heavy in his hand. He took a deep breath. Held it. Burst into the room.

And saw her sleeping on a low cot.

He recognized her with his first glance. Livvy.

Oh, no. Livvy.

She had cut her hair as short as Destiny's. She wore a long, black nightshirt down over her knees. Her hands were crossed over her chest. In the trembling glow of the flashlight, her short, blond hair shimmered around her pale, sleeping face.

I can't do this, he thought.

I brought her into the world. How can I kill her now? I despise all vampires. A vampire murdered my wife, took away the person most precious to me.

I hate them. Hate them all.

But to drive a stake through my own daughter? That's asking too much of any man.

Images flashed through his mind, bright and clear as photographs. Livvy as a baby. Livvy and Destiny in their snowsuits building their first snowman. Livvy and her mom giving each other makeovers, bright purple lipstick shining on his wife's lips, sparkles in her hair.

Livvy . . .

I can't.

With a sob, he turned to leave. He stopped when she stirred, groaning in her sleep.

She's not my daughter, he realized.

It's not Livvy anymore. It's a deadly creature in Livvy's body. And I have no choice.

He moved back to the cot. Raised the stake high in both hands. Changed his mind.

One last kiss for my daughter. A good-bye kiss.

Good-bye, Livvy.

He lowered his face to her cheek.

And he let out a startled cry as her hands shot up. Her eyes opened wide. She grabbed him by the neck and tightened her fingers around his throat.

"Ohh—" he gasped.

She stared up at him, and the fingers squeezed tighter, tighter . . .

"NO!" he choked out, struggling to free himself from her grip. "NO! LIVVY—PLEASE! NO!"

Part Two
One Month Earlier

Chapter Five

Livvy's Graduation Party

"I love the blue eye shadow. It's so retro," Livvy said. She turned to her two new friends, Suzie and Monica. "How does it look?"

"Awesome," Suzie said. "But wait. You have lipstick on your chin." She dabbed a tissue over the dark spot on Livvy's chin. "There."

"Is that the cinnamon lipstick or the grape?" Monica asked. She shoved Suzie aside to get a better look at Livvy. "It's so hard to tell in this light."

A single sixty-watt bulb hung on a long cord from the ceiling.

Livvy took the tissue from Suzie and dabbed at her lips. "It's black. For nighttime. My favorite time."

Monica grinned at Livvy. "My favorite time too. Party time." She licked her full, dark lips. Then she picked up her hairbrush and began running it through her long, straight black hair.

"Hey, it's date night," Suzie said.

"Every night is date night," Monica said, "when you're hungry."

Livvy turned to Suzie. "Are you coming with us?"

"I think we should go out on our own," Suzie replied. "See what's out there. Check out the fresh meat. You know. And then we can meet later."

Livvy studied Suzie's face, so pale, nearly white as snow. Suzie had been an immortal for a long time, for so long Suzie didn't remember when she made the change.

One night when the moon was still high in the sky, and the three girls had fed well and were feeling comfortable and full, Suzie told Livvy and Monica her story. She'd had a tough time, chased from town to town, nearly caught by vampire hunters in a city near Dark Springs.

Her troubles showed on her face, Livvy thought. Suzie's pale, papery skin was pulled tight against her skull, so tight her cheekbones nearly poked out. Her hair was patchy and thin. Her arms were as skinny as broom handles, her fingers bony, almost skeletal. Her eyes had started to sink back into their sockets.

She tried to cover it up with loads of

makeup and by wearing trendy clothes, young people's clothes. And she stayed in the darkest corners of the night, swooping out only when prey was near. But Suzie was too far gone to hide the fact that she was an immortal.

That won't happen to me, Livvy thought. I won't let that happen to me.

Livvy tossed back her blond hair with a shake of her head. She had cut it short—short as her sister's—and she loved the way it felt now, light as a breeze. "Wish we had a mirror," she murmured.

Suzie laughed. "What good would that do? We don't have reflections, remember?"

The lightbulb over their heads flickered and went out. Livvy sighed. "The generator must have conked out again."

Some clever immortals had hooked up a power generator to the building across the street. The stolen electricity provided light for the whole building. But the generator was too small and kept blowing out.

"Wish we lived in a fancy hotel," Monica said, still brushing her hair. "Instead of this empty apartment building. We could send down for room service. You know. Dial the phone and say, 'Just send the waiter up. We don't need any food.'"

Livvy laughed. "Forget room service. I just want to live in a place where the lights stay on."

"Lights hurt my eyes," Suzie complained, furiously powdering her face.

"I don't mean *bright* lights," Livvy said. "None of us can stand *bright* lights. I just mean lights that don't flicker on and off every few minutes."

The three new friends had built their dressing table out of plywood and concrete blocks left by the builders of the unfinished building. They had set it up in front of the glassless window where they could sit and watch the sunset.

Livvy had found a cot in one of the downstairs rooms and dragged it up to her bedroom. Suzie and Monica shared an apartment downstairs but came to Livvy's room in the evening to do their makeup and get ready to go out.

Livvy liked them both. Monica was big and dark and sexy and had no trouble getting the guys. And Suzie had the experience. She knew everything they needed to know to survive.

"When's the full moon?" Monica asked, adjusting the top of her tank top.

"I think it's in a few weeks," Suzie said, gazing up at the darkening sky. A faint smile crossed her pale lips. "Warm blood under a bright full moon. Poetry, right? Does it get any better than that? I don't think so."

Livvy turned to her. "What about tonight? They'll be some hot guys out tonight. Why wait?"

Monica brushed her arm. "Hey, didn't they have graduation at your school this morning? I thought I saw some cute guys walking around in blue robes."

Livvy glared at her. "Why bring that up?"

Monica backed away. "Whoa. I didn't mean anything. I was just asking."

"Do I give a damn about high school graduation?" Livvy snapped. She surprised herself at how angry she felt. Was she angry at Monica— or at something else? "I don't give a damn. Trust me."

"Okay, okay." Monica raised both hands as if asking for a truce.

"I've already graduated," Livvy said, still feeling upset. "I've graduated to what I want to be." She stood up. "Hey, maybe tonight I'll celebrate my graduation. Maybe I'll have a little graduation party of my own."

"We'll all party tonight!" Monica said, licking her lips.

Suzie gazed out the window. She seemed to be in her own world. "You know," she said, finally turning back to them, "the better looking the boy, the richer the blood."

"No way," Monica insisted. "That's superstition."

"It's a proven fact," Suzie said, toying with a strand of her long hair.

"Who proved it?" Livvy asked.

"I did." Suzie grinned. "Listen to me. The hot guys have the hottest blood."

Monica stared at her. "No lie?"

"No lie."

Livvy sighed. "I get so high when the blood is fresh and warm. I mean . . . the way it feels on my lips and then on my tongue. I can feel it all the way down my throat. And afterwards, it's so wild. I always feel like I'm flying . . . just flying out of my body, into outer space."

"I always feel so warm," Suzie said, her eyes dreamy. She sighed. "Like a happy, contented baby. But then the hunger starts again. So soon . . . it starts again, that gnawing . . . that needy feeling."

"Let's keep it light," Livvy scolded. "It's my

graduation party tonight, remember?" She stood up. "How do I look?"

She had her short, shimmery hair combed straight back, pale lip gloss, light blue eye shadow covering her eyelids, a pink midriff top over low-riding, white jeans, lots of bare skin showing, three earrings in each ear, a glittery rhinestone in her right nostril.

She walked up and down the bare room, doing the model strut. Monica and Suzie made admiring sounds. "Whoa. I love the nighttime!" Livvy exclaimed. "I feel lucky tonight!"

She realized that Suzie was staring past her. "Hey, what's up?"

She turned—and saw a fat brown field mouse hunched near the open doorway, gazing up at them with its shiny black marble eyes.

Suzie spun off her chair and lowered her lean body into a crouch, eyes unblinking, locked on the mouse.

"Oh, no. You wouldn't," Livvy said. "It's so cute."

With a sudden lightning movement, Suzie pounced. The mouse let out a squeak as Suzie grabbed it, wrapped her fingers around its stubby brown fur.

Its last squeak.

Suzie tore off its head and tossed it out into the hall. Then she tilted the body over her mouth and squeezed out the juice.

When she had finished, dark blood trickling down her chin, she heaved the drained corpse into the hall. Then she turned to Livvy and Monica with a grin. "Appetizer," she whispered.

Chapter Six
Night Birds

Livvy transformed into a slender blackbird. She perched on the windowsill, gazing out at the purple night sky.

Her feathers felt stiff and scratchy, and it took a while to get used to the rapid pattering of her heart. Once she adjusted to seeing two views at once, her eyesight was sharp.

She raised her wings and lifted off the window. The cool air ruffled her chest feathers. She swooped higher, pale white stars blinking so close above her. What a thrill!

To fly. To be free of the ground. To swoop and soar like a wild creature.

I'll never get tired of this, Livvy thought.

And then she felt the hunger, a sharp pang that tightened her belly. She opened her beak and let the onrushing air cool her throat. The gnawing hunger was insistent, wave after wave, until she felt dizzy from the need.

I have to feed.

What will I find tonight? Who will help me quench my thirst?

The yellow moon loomed above her, wisps of gray cloud snaking across it. Livvy lifted her wings and floated, gazing up at the moonlight.

No one else can see the moon like this. I am so lucky.

But then she felt a ripple in the wind at her side and heard the flutter of wings. Livvy turned and saw another blackbird, more plump with a streak of white in its wings, soar beside her.

The two blackbirds flew together, side by side, wings touching. They lifted high toward the stars, then shot low above the shimmering trees.

Livvy landed softly in tall grass and felt the dew tickle her feathers. The other bird shook its wings hard as it bounced to a landing a few feet beside her.

They both transformed quickly into their human forms.

Straightening her pink top, Livvy gazed at Ross Starr. The moonlight gave his short, blond hair a glow. He wore straight-legged jeans and a sleeveless T-shirt that showed off his muscular arms. He flashed her his Hollywood smile—the smile that had convinced her she needed Ross, needed to bring him with her to the other side.

"Hey, Ross," she murmured. "What's up? That was nice, wasn't it."

He stepped forward and kissed her. "You and me. Flying together. Yeah. That's what it's about, right?"

He tried to hug her, but Livvy pulled away. "I'm hungry. I mean, I'm starving." She held her stomach. "I . . . can't even think straight."

He smiled again. "Oh, yeah. Fresh nectar. I want mine super-sized!"

She kissed him on the cheek. "Get lost, okay?"

He grabbed her around the waist and pulled her to him. "Come on, Liv. I need more than a kiss. You look so hot tonight."

"Ross, please—" She squeezed his hands, then pushed them off her. "I told you I need to feed."

He shrugged. "Okay. I'll come with you."

"Oh, sure. That'll be helpful. You're gonna help me pick up a guy?"

He frowned at her. "I don't like you with other guys."

"What's your problem? He's not a guy. He's a meal."

She didn't hear what he said next. She transformed quickly, stretching her wings, ruffling the stiff tail feathers, a blackbird again.

She bent her thin bird legs, pushed up from the dew-wet grass, letting her wings lift her . . . lift her . . . over the treetops. She saw Ross swoop ahead of her, then fall back, teasing her, following her despite her pleas.

He bumped her playfully, swiped his beak against her side, lowered his head and bumped her again.

They flew side by side, gliding over Millerton Woods, light and shadows over the thick tangle of trees, shivering under the golden moonlight.

Livvy made a wide turn, wings straight out at her sides, and realized she was flying over Collins Drive now. Her father's office came into view. The light glowed from the front window. Was he still at work this late at night?

She swooped higher, away from the little, brick building. I don't want to see him. He's not part of my life anymore.

Flying low, the two blackbirds turned onto Main Street. Livvy landed behind a maple tree and gazed at the people in line at the movie theater. Ross dropped beside her.

They transformed into their human shapes, hidden by the thick tree trunk.

"You know, graduation was this morning," Ross said.

"Shut up," Livvy replied sharply.

"How are we going to get jobs?" Ross said. "We're not high school graduates."

"You're so funny," Livvy replied. "Not."

Ross turned to the movie theater. "What's playing? A vampire movie?"

Livvy's stomach growled. She ignored Ross and his jokes. I've never fed in a movie theater, she thought. It's dark enough—and the sound is loud enough to muffle the scream.

Livvy's victims only screamed once. They always screamed at the first bite, then gave in to the pleasure.

"Oh, no. Oh, wow." A moan escaped Ross's throat.

Livvy turned from the faces in the movie line. "What's wrong?"

He leaned forward, peering around the tree trunk. "My family is there. See them? Mom and Dad and Emily."

Livvy saw Ross's sister first, then his parents. "Don't worry. They can't see us."

"I . . . I want to see them," Ross said. "Livvy, I'd just like to talk to them for a little while. You know. See how Emily is doing and everything. They think I ran away with you. I want to tell them I'm okay."

"Ross, you can't," Livvy said. "You know you can't do that. You'll only upset them. You'll mess them up even worse."

"But—I just want to say hi," Ross said. "I guess I'm homesick."

"It won't work. Trust me." Livvy stared hard at him. She could see how excited and upset he was.

"Maybe I feel homesick too. But listen to me. I made a vow," Livvy told him. "I vowed I'd never go back home. You need to make the same vow. It's not our world anymore. We've chosen a different world. You know. A more exciting life. I . . . I'm not going to torture myself by trying to drop in on Destiny and Dad and . . . and . . ."

She couldn't say Mikey's name. Thinking about Mikey always made her cry.

"I guess you're right," Ross said. "But look.

My family—they're going inside the theater. I could just walk over, say hi, and leave."

"No. Go away, Ross. Fly away—now. You know I'm right."

Sighing, he watched until his family disappeared inside. Then he kissed Livvy on the cheek. "Later."

He changed quickly. Raised his wings and fluttered off the ground. She watched him hover over the sidewalk. Then she changed into a blackbird too, turned and flew away.

I don't want to hear about how homesick Ross is, she thought. A shudder ran down her body. The air suddenly felt cold. The moonlight sent down no warmth.

I shouldn't have brought Ross to this new life. I care about him. I still do. Maybe not like before. But I care about him.

But he's too sentimental. He's too soft.

I thought he was strong, but he isn't. He always seemed so confident. I can still see him with that strutting walk of his, moving down the halls at school, flashing that great smile. I used to wait for him to come by. I had such a major crush on him.

But now . . . he's weak. His attitude is

wrong. He's not thinking right.

He'll get himself killed. I know he will.

Hunger gnawed at her, interrupting her thoughts. She glanced down and saw flashing lights on a big, square building.

Where am I?

Sliding on a wind current, she let herself down and recognized the dance club: Rip.

Oh, yes. Lots of fresh talent here. Kids hanging out in the dimly lit parking lot. Lined up at the entrance. Lots of dark corners, and the woods close behind the parking lot.

Lots of older guys getting trashed at the bar and looking to hook up.

How perfect is that for a hungry vampire?

And there below her she saw Suzie and Monica at the entrance, chatting with two guys, about to go in.

Excellent.

Livvy dropped to the gravel path at the side of the building. She could hear the throbbing beats from inside, hear laughing voices, the roar of a crowd.

Yes, yes, yes. I'm so hungry.

I'm sure some lucky guy will be happy to come to the woods with me.

She transformed into her human body, brushed a few feathers off the front of her jeans, tugged down the top of her top to look sexier— and hurried to meet her friends.

Part Three

Earlier That Day

Chapter Seven

The Evil at Home

"As you leave this high school where you have spent four wonderful years of growth and learning . . . As you go forth into the world—no longer students—you must realize that the world belongs to you now. Your generation will decide where we all go next. You will be the ones to shape the future. You will be the ones . . ."

Destiny tuned out as the graduation speaker droned on. She wiped her sweaty hands in the folds of her blue robe.

"It's so hot in here," she whispered to the girl next to her. "When can we take these things off?"

The flat blue cap, tilted over her head, felt as if it weighed a hundred pounds. Destiny knew it was going to leave a permanent dent in her hair. Sweat streamed down her forehead. Would the cap leave a blue stain on her skin?

She glanced at the rows of robed kids on the stage. As they all gathered in the auditorium this morning, her friends had been bursting with excitement about graduation. Ana-Li May was practically *flying*, swirling around in circles, making her graduation robe whirl around her.

Fletch Green, Ross's best friend, gave Destiny such a big hug, he accidentally knocked her cap off her head. "Do you believe I graduated in only four years?" he exclaimed. "My parents predicted six!"

Ari Stark seemed excited too. He greeted her with a kiss. "Freedom!" he shouted. "A few more hours, and we're *outta* here! Freedom! Freedom!" He started a chant, and a few other kids joined in.

A sad smile crossed Destiny's face. She knew why her friends were so happy and excited. They really were getting out of here, out of Dark Springs. They were going away to college. In a few months Ari would be at Princeton in New Jersey. And Ana-Li would be off at Yale being brilliant the way she always was.

And I'll be here, Destiny thought, unable to fight away her sadness. I was accepted at four schools, including Dartmouth, where I really wanted to go. But no. I'll be here, living at home, going to the dinky Community College.

But what choice did I have? How could I leave Mikey, my poor, troubled little brother? How could I leave Dad? They both need me so much now . . . now that Livvy . . .

She wanted to be excited and happy. Graduating from high school was a major thing in your life. It was supposed to be a day you'd never forget.

And it *was* kind of thrilling to march slowly down the auditorium aisle in time to "Pomp and Circumstance," the music played at every graduation. And to hear your name called, and walk up to receive your diploma.

Destiny smiled and waved the diploma at her dad. She could see him wave back to her from the fourth row.

Kind of exciting.

But then the kids in her class settled into their folding chairs, sweating under their robes, shifting the caps on their heads. And the balding, scratchy-voiced speaker in his tight-fitting gray suit—an assistant mayor, she thought—began to speak.

". . . The future isn't only a promise, it's a responsibility. How will you find your role in the future? By looking to the past. Because the past is where our future springs from . . ."

Yawn.

As he rambled on, his voice faded from Destiny's ears. And she felt the sadness rise over her, like a powerful ocean wave.

There should be an empty seat next to me, she thought. A chair for Livvy. Livvy would have been here with me this morning, and we would have been so happy.

Destiny gazed down the rows of blue-robed kids. And there should be a chair for Ross. Destiny felt a flash of anger. Yes, I had a crush on Ross—and Livvy knew it. And she took him away . . . where no one will ever see him again. So selfish . . . so stupid and selfish . . .

There should be a chair here for Ross. He should be graduating today. And there should be two more empty chairs, Destiny thought. Chairs for our friends, Courtney and Bree, both murdered by vampires.

Four empty chairs. Four kids who will not graduate this morning.

The sadness was overwhelming. Destiny felt hot tears streaming down her cheeks. She turned her head away. She didn't want her father to see.

Poor Dad. He must be thinking the same things, she told herself. Somehow he's managing to keep it together. I have to try hard to keep it together too. She glanced down at the red leather cover on her diploma and saw that it was stained by her tears.

Loud cheers startled Destiny from her thoughts. All around her, kids leaped up and tossed their caps in the air. Blinking away her sadness, Destiny climbed to her feet and tossed her cap too.

The ceremony had ended. I'm a high school graduate, she thought. I've spent twelve years with most of these kids. And now we're all going to scatter and start new lives.

New lives . . .

She couldn't stop thinking about Livvy. No way to shut her out of her mind, even for a few minutes.

"Return your robes to the gym, people," Mr. Farrow, the principal, boomed over the loudspeaker. "Don't forget to return your robes to the gym."

All around her, kids were hugging, laughing, talking excitedly. Some jumped off the stage and ran up the auditorium aisles to meet their parents.

She waved to Ari, hurried to return her robe, then found her dad outside in front of the school talking to some other parents.

It was a warm June morning, the sun already high in a clear blue sky. Yellow lilies circling the flagpole waved gently in a warm breeze. Families filled the front lawn of the school, snapping photos, chatting, and laughing.

Dr. Weller turned when he saw Destiny and wrapped her in a big hug. "Congratulations," he said. She saw the tears in his eyes. She hugged him again.

"We have to make this a happy day," he said. "We really have to try, don't we?"

Destiny nodded. Her chin trembled. She fought off the urge to cry.

"I have to get to my office," Dr. Weller said. "But I'll take you and Mikey out for dinner tonight—our own private celebration. Good?"

"Good," she replied. She saw Ari and Ana-Li come out of the building.

"If Ari would like to come with us tonight . . ." her dad started. He had grown used to seeing Ari around the house at all hours. The two of them got along pretty well.

"I think he's going out with his family," Destiny said.

Dr. Weller nodded. "The three of us. We'll have a nice dinner." She walked him to his SUV. It took him four tries to start it up.

"Dad, you've really got to get this car serviced," Destiny said.

He smiled at her. "It's on my list."

"Dad, you know you don't *have* a list."

"It's on my list to make a list." Tires squealing, he pulled away.

Destiny felt a tap on her shoulder. She turned and Ari kissed her. "Hey, we're graduates. I'm totally psyched. Do you believe it? No more gym class. No more Coach Green telling me what a loser I am."

Ana-Li laughed. "Just because you have a diploma doesn't mean you're not a loser."

Ari pretended to be hurt. "What's up with that? You're dissing me on graduation day?"

Ana-Li opened her diploma and held it up. "Check it out. They misspelled my name. Two n's."

"That's terrible," Destiny said, studying the diploma. "How could they do that?"

"It means you didn't really graduate," Ari told Ana-Li. "No one will believe that's your diploma. Your whole life is going to be messed up now."

Ana-Li shook her tiny fist at Ari. "I'm going to mess *you* up!"

Laughing, Ari raised both fists and began dancing from side to side. "You want a piece of me? Huh? You want a piece of me?"

Ana-Li ignored him. She turned to Destiny. "How you doing?"

"Tough morning," Destiny replied. "You know."

Ari lowered his fists. His smile faded.

"What are you two doing now?" Destiny asked. "Want to come back with me? We can sit around and reminisce or something."

"Is lunch included in this invitation?" Ari asked.

Destiny nodded.

"Count me in."

"Just let me say good-bye to my parents, and I'll meet you at your house," Ana-Li said. She trotted back toward the school.

Ari slid an arm over Destiny's shoulders, and they walked the few blocks to her house.

Cars filled with their friends rolled by, horns honking, music blaring from open windows.

"Did you hear about Fletch's party last night?" Ari asked. "His parents were in L.A. So Fletch had two kegs. Everyone got trashed. And his brother's garage band played all night."

Destiny sighed. "I'm sorry. I know you wanted to go. But I just didn't feel like partying."

They stepped onto her front stoop. Destiny fumbled in her bag for her key. She found it, turned the key in the lock, pushed open the front door—and screamed.

"OH, NO!"

Ari grabbed her and they both stared in disbelief at the living room walls.

Fanged creatures with curled horns on their heads . . . A winged, two-headed demon, both heads spewing black blood . . . A grinning devil . . .

Ugly, black demons painted all over the walls.

Chapter Eight

"The Monster Did It"

"Oh, no! oh, no!" Destiny held onto Ari and pressed her head against his shoulder. Staring at the crude, childish paintings, she led the way into the house.

"This is too weird," Ari muttered.

Destiny opened her mouth to speak. But a shrill cry interrupted her—and Mikey came leaping off the stairs onto Ari's shoulders. He curled his hands around Ari's throat and screamed, "I'm a MONSTER! I'll kill you! I'll KILL you!"

Ari dropped to the floor under the eight-year-old boy's weight. He sprawled on his back and pried Mikey's fingers from around his neck. "Whoa. Easy, man. Mikey, you're choking me."

"I'm not Mikey. I'm a *monster*!"

Destiny reached down to help pull Mikey off.

"Hey, what's up?" Ana-Li burst into the

room. She let out a cry when she saw the crude creatures smeared over the walls. "Ohmigod."

Destiny pulled Mikey to his feet, then tugged him away from Ari. "Calm down. Don't move. Just take a deep breath, okay?"

Mikey tossed back his head and let out a hoarse, demonic laugh.

Destiny kept a hand on his thick, coppery hair, holding him in place. Mikey was slender and light, small for eight, with arms and legs like sticks. He had dark, serious eyes that looked as if they belonged on an adult. His front teeth were crooked because he refused to wear his retainer.

Groaning, Ari climbed to his feet. Ana-Li couldn't take her eyes off the walls.

"I can't believe you did this," Destiny said, shaking her head.

"I *told* you I didn't do it. The monster did it," Mikey insisted, finally back in his normal, high-pitched voice.

Destiny and Ana-Li exchanged glances. Ana-Li knew the problems they'd been having with Mikey. The poor kid had been acting out, severely troubled by the loss of his sister.

He had nightmares that made him scream.

He was afraid to stand near an open window. He'd been getting into fights at school. Sometimes he was afraid of the dark. But he kept his room dark as a cave and spent hour after hour in there with the door locked.

Destiny never knew what to expect. Sometimes Mikey acted like a terrified victim, trembling, crying. And other times, he acted like a monster, striking out, screaming in a rage.

She felt so bad for the little guy . . . and so totally helpless.

Ari stepped up to the wall and examined the paintings. "I think the monster is in trouble big-time," he said to Mikey. "How do you think the monster should be punished?"

"His head should be cut off with a machete," Mikey answered. "And then they should turn him upside down and let all his blood drain out on the floor."

Ari turned to Destiny. "Big trouble," he whispered.

"Wasn't anyone here watching Mikey?" Ana-Li asked.

Destiny sighed. She turned to Mikey. "Where is Mrs. Miller? She was supposed to watch you."

"She had to go home to check something," Mikey said. "She didn't come back. I guess she got busy."

"Mikey's the one who got busy," Ari said, gesturing to the wall.

Mikey let out a roar. His eyes grew wide. *"The monster is coming back,"* he whispered.

"We should get him out in the sunshine for a while," Ana-Li whispered to Destiny. "You know. Take his mind off this stuff."

Destiny nodded. "Hey, how about a soccer game?" she asked Mikey. "You and me against Ari and Ana-Li."

Mikey reluctantly agreed. Destiny grabbed a soccer ball in the garage and led the way to the backyard, and the four of them started a game.

The Wellers' backyard was deep and wide, covered by a carpet of low grass and interrupted by only a few sycamore and birch trees. Almost perfect for soccer.

The wind had picked up, but the sun blazed high in the sky, making the air warm as summer. Destiny passed the ball to Mikey, and they drove down the field toward Ana-Li and Ari. Mikey brought the ball close to the two slender saplings that formed the goal. Ari made an attempt to block his shot. But Mikey sent the ball flying through the trees. *Goal!*

It was obvious to Destiny that her two friends were letting Mikey be a star. But Mikey didn't notice. He jumped up and down cheering for himself.

This was a good idea, Destiny thought. His mood has changed completely. A little sunshine and some physical exercise, and he's acting like a normal kid again.

The game went well for another ten minutes. Destiny loved the intense expression on her brother's face as he moved the ball forward, dodged Ana-Li and Ari and their feeble attempts to block him, and kicked two more goals.

Destiny began to feel hungry. Maybe it was time to stop the game and make lunch. She looked up in time to see Ari give the ball a hard kick that sent it flying toward the trees at the edge of the yard.

Mikey and Ari both took off after the ball. It hit the trunk of an old sycamore tree hard and bounced off. Mikey slid under the tree, chasing the ball.

Destiny heard a cracking sound. She raised her eyes in time to see a high branch of the tree come crashing down.

"Mikey—look out!" she screamed.

Chapter Nine

The Vampire in the Tree

Mikey's eyes went wide.

Destiny heard the crack of branches as the falling limb smashed through them.

Mikey let out a scream, dropped to the ground, and rolled away.

The limb hit the ground a foot or so from Mikey, bounced once, and came to a rest on the grass.

Destiny had her hands pressed to the sides of her face. "Are you okay?" she screamed.

Mikey didn't answer. He jumped to his feet and pointed up to the tree. "Vampire!" he cried. "It's a vampire! In the tree!"

"No, wait—" Ari shouted. He made a grab for Mikey. But Mikey took off, running to the house.

"Mikey, it was just a tree branch," Destiny called. She chased after her brother and caught him at the kitchen door.

"Let go!" he screamed. "It's a vampire. In the tree! Didn't you see it? Didn't you?"

"No. There's nothing up there," Destiny insisted, holding him by the arm. "Listen to me—"

But he jerked his arm free and dove into the house. She heard him sobbing loudly as he scrambled up the stairs to his room.

"Mikey, wait. Please—" Destiny darted up the stairs after him.

He slammed the door in her face. She heard the lock click. She could hear him still sobbing on the other side of the door.

Destiny turned and saw Ari and Ana-Li at the bottom of the stairs. They gazed up at her, their faces tight with concern.

She made her way down the stairs slowly, feeling shaky and upset. "I'd better call Dr. Fishman," she said. "He's Mikey's shrink. He keeps telling us it will just take time. But I've never seen Mikey this bad."

"The poor guy is scared to death," Ari said, shaking his head.

"He sees vampires everywhere," Destiny whispered. "And then sometimes he pretends *he*'s a vampire." She led them into the living room. She motioned to the couches, but no one sat down. They stood tensely near the wall.

"I know the only thing that will help him," Destiny said. "Bring Livvy back. He knows the truth about her. Maybe it was a mistake to tell him. He's so scared now. If I could just bring her back here—"

"Hey, I'm scared too," Ana-Li said, hugging herself tightly. She shuddered. "I mean, Livvy and Ross are out there somewhere, right?"

Destiny nodded.

"And they're full vampires now. I mean, real ones. Needy . . . thirsty." She shuddered again.

Ari raised his eyes toward the ceiling. "Shhh. Not so loud. We don't need to be talking about this in front of Mikey."

"But what if they come back here?" Ana-Li whispered. "What if they're out flying around one night, and they're real thirsty? I mean, so thirsty they can't control themselves. And they fly back here and find us? I mean, they could attack us, right? Aren't we obvious victims here?"

"No way," Destiny replied, shaking her head. "She's still my sister. No way she'd come back here and attack my friends." She frowned at Ana-Li. "Do you honestly think Livvy would come back here and drink your blood?"

"I . . . don't know," Ana-Li replied, her voice cracking. "I really don't."

Destiny opened her mouth to reply, but a sudden noise above her head made her stop.

A flapping sound. Like a window shade flapping in a strong wind.

Destiny raised her eyes to the sound and saw a darting, black shadow.

"Hey—!" Ari let out a cry, his mouth open in surprise.

The shadow swooped low.

Destiny felt a cold whoosh of air sweep past the back of her neck.

It took her a while to recognize the sound— the flapping of wings.

And then she saw the bat. Eyes glowing, it soared beneath the dark wood ceiling beams. Then low over their heads, flapping up to the mirror, turning and shooting over them to the other wall. Then flying over them again, lower each time, raising its talons as if preparing to attack.

Ana-Li covered her head. Ari ducked. Destiny opened her mouth in a scream of horror.

Chapter Ten

Is Livvy in the House?

*T*he bat let out a screech and soared up to the ceiling. Destiny watched it cling to a beam, wings flapping hard. Its glowing eyes locked on Destiny.

"How did it get in?" Ana-Li cried, clinging to Ari's arm. "What's it doing in here?"

Trembling, Destiny stared up at it. "Livvy? Is that you?" she called, but she could only manage a whisper. "Livvy—?"

And then without warning, the creature let go of the wooden beam and came swooping down.

Destiny saw the eyes glow brighter. Saw the creature raise its talons and arch its wings high behind its ratlike head.

She tried to duck away, bumping hard into Ari and Ana-Li, sending them tumbling against the couch.

Then with another whistling shriek, the bat

latched onto Destiny. Wings flapping loudly, it dug its talons into her hair. She heard its ugly cry as she struggled to slap it off.

"*Eeeeee eeeeeeee!*" Like a car alarm going off in her head.

"No! Get off! Get OFF me!"

The talons dug into her scalp. Sharp, stabbing pain swept through her head.

"NO!"

Her heart pounding, Destiny ducked low again, swung her hand, hit the creature hard. She felt its furry warmth. Felt the breeze from its flapping wings, felt the bat's hot breath prickle the back of her neck.

"Get OFF!"

Another hard slap sent the creature sailing to the floor.

Ari raised his foot to stomp on it.

"No—don't!" Destiny screamed, shoving him back.

The bat recovered quickly. It let out a low buzz, then shot back up into the air. Destiny covered her hair with both arms as it swooped low over her again. Then the creature made a sharp turn and flew into the back hallway.

Holding her head, Destiny lurched after it.

"Livvy—?" she called. "Is that you?"

The bat darted out the open kitchen window, leaving the yellow window curtains fluttering behind it.

"Oh, wow." Destiny sank onto a white bench at the kitchen table. She brushed back her hair, waiting for her heartbeats to slow.

"Are you okay?" Ari put a hand on her shoulder. "Dee, you're shaking."

"It . . . attacked me," she stammered. "Why did it attack me?"

Ana-Li opened the refrigerator and pulled out a bottle of water. She spun off the top and handed it to Destiny. "Here. Drink something. Try to calm down. You're okay, right?"

Destiny nodded. She took a long drink of the cold water.

Then she turned back to her friends. "Why would a bat fly into the house in the middle of the day? And why did it attack me?"

Ari shrugged. Ana-Li stared back at Destiny without an answer.

Destiny took another drink. "How can we live our whole lives scared to death?" she asked. She pounded a fist on the table, making the ceramic fruit bowl shake. An apple rolled onto the floor. "I have to do something. I have to find Livvy. I have to talk to her . . . convince her to come back."

"Maybe she *was* back," Ana-Li said softly. "Maybe she was that bat. Maybe she came back to warn you."

"To warn me of what?"

"To stay away from her. To leave her alone."

Destiny grabbed her friend's arm. "That's crazy, Ana-Li. She's my sister. My twin sister. We belong together. She must know that. Even the way she is now . . . she must know that I'll do anything to bring her back to us."

"I have to go," Ana-Li said, moving quickly to the front door. "I have to get out of here. I mean, out of Dark Springs. It's too terrifying here. Bats and vampires and people dying. I'm so glad I'm going to New Haven in a few weeks."

She turned at the door. Destiny could see tears in her eyes. "I'm sorry, Dee," she said in a voice trembling with emotion. "I didn't mean to sound so cold. I know you've lost your sister. I didn't mean to sound selfish. I just . . . I . . ."

She spun away and disappeared out the door.

Ari stepped over to Destiny and wrapped her in a hug. "That was so horrible," he said softly. "That bat . . . when it attacked you, I—"

She silenced him with a kiss. The kiss lasted a long time. She wrapped her hands around his neck and held onto him, and they pressed together tightly as they kissed.

"You . . . you're going away, too," she whispered, finally pulling her lips away. She pressed her cheek against his. "You're going away too."

"Not until August. We have five weeks," he said.

She sighed. They kissed again. She shut her eyes and tried not to think about Ari leaving.

"About tonight," he said, holding her in his arms. "I know we have dinners with our parents tonight. But we can go out later. It's graduation, Dee. Let's go to that dance club that just opened. You know, Rip. Let's go there tonight, and pretend everything is okay . . . just for one night."

His eyes burned into hers. "Okay? Please say yes."

"Yes," Destiny agreed in a whisper.

"Hey, all right!" Ari pumped his fists in the air in victory.

Destiny started to kiss him again, but they were interrupted by a shout from upstairs.

Mikey, at the top of the stairs.

"Dee—hurry! Livvy's back! She's back! Hurry!"

Chapter Eleven
Rip

Destiny ran up the stairs, pulling herself up two steps at a time. At the top, Mikey grabbed her hand and pulled her to his room.

Destiny blinked in the darkness. Mikey kept the blinds closed, curtains pulled, and the lights off. "Where is she?" Destiny cried. "I can't see anything."

She fumbled for the light switch and clicked on the ceiling light.

"No—don't!" Mikey grabbed her hand and pulled it away from the light switch. "Turn it off. Turn it off."

Destiny obediently shut off the light.

"I was only pretending," Mikey said.

"You mean—?"

"I was pretending Livvy was back. That's all."

Destiny let out a long sigh. "Not again, Mikey." She hugged him tightly. "Not again. You have to stop this. Do you understand?"

Mikey didn't reply.

Rip was a tall, barnlike building on the edge of North Town, the old section of Dark Springs. The club had previously been called Trixx, and before that Wild Weasel. Every year a new owner painted the outside a different color and put up new signs. But the inside was always pretty much the same.

As Destiny followed Ari inside, she saw a tall DJ wearing a white cowboy hat hunched over two turntables on a small stage in the center of the room. Red and blue neon lightning bolts flashed over the high ceiling, the light flickered off the dancers, dozens of them jammed together on the dance floor, moving to the throbbing rhythm, the music so loud the concrete floor vibrated.

A long, mirrored bar curved the length of the back wall. Low couches and fat armchairs formed a lounge on one side. Destiny looked up and saw people gazing down onto the dance floor from the narrow balcony that circled the room.

"I'll get us some beers," Ari said, leading her

through the crowd. He opened his wallet and flashed a driver's license. "I have great fake I.D. A guy sold me this for fifty dollars, and it always works."

Eyes on the dancers, she followed him to the bar. Half the graduating class from Dark Springs High is here tonight, Destiny realized. She waved to some girls she knew. She spotted Ana-Li sitting in a big armchair in the lounge, leaning forward to talk to two guys Destiny had never seen before.

In a corner by the lounge, a girl in a sparkly red mini-dress was lip-locked with a guy in black jeans and a muscle shirt. He had a tattoo of a motorcycle on his bicep. As they kissed, he ran his big hands through her blond hair.

Blond hair . . .

No, Destiny thought. Not tonight. I'm not going to think about Livvy tonight.

But she stared at the girl kissing the big, tattooed guy so passionately, and she couldn't help but picture her sister there.

"Here you go." Ari bumped her shoulder. She turned and reached for the beer bottle in his hand. "The guy carded me," Ari said, grinning. "The Delaware driver's license always works.

Want me to get you one?"

She frowned at him. "Ari, you don't even *like* beer that much. What's the big deal?"

He shrugged. "Come on. We're at a club, right? We gotta drink beer. Besides, I've got a lot of time to make up for. All those years, sitting in my room at the computer, going to dorky UFO websites or watching *Star Trek* reruns. I didn't know what I was missing!"

Ari has changed a lot, Destiny thought. I guess all the terrible things that have happened snapped him out of his fantasy world.

Ari started to raise the beer bottle to his mouth—and Fletch Green grabbed it out of his hand. "Thanks, dawg." Fletch emptied the bottle in less than five seconds and handed it back to Ari, a big smile on his face.

Ari stared at the empty beer bottle.

"Sorry you guys missed my party last night," Fletch said, sliding an arm around Destiny. "Hey, Dee, you look hot tonight."

Destiny wore a short, pleated black skirt, a tight, white midriff top, and her favorite red strappy sandals.

"So do you, Fletch," Destiny shot back. He was wearing baggy cargo pants and a black T-shirt with a martini glass on the front.

"It was a great party," Fletch said. "The cops came out three times. We have totally obnoxious neighbors. They call the cops if I sneeze too loud. But it was awesome. Gil Marx threw up in the fishpond. That was kinda gross. But no one else got too sick."

He took Destiny's beer from her hand and finished that one too. He handed the bottle to Ari. "Thanks again, dawg. You know, you're too young to drink." He gave the back of Destiny's hair a playful tug. Then he spun away and shambled off.

"Is he here with someone?" Ari asked, watching Fletch push his way through the dance floor.

Destiny shrugged. "Beats me. I heard he's been drinking a lot. I mean, a *lot*." She sighed. "The poor guy. He and Ross were like this." She held two fingers together. "I think he's a little lost without him."

"Hey, I thought we weren't going to talk about that tonight," Ari snapped. He clinked the empty bottles together. "I'll get another round."

"Not now." Destiny grabbed his arm. "Let's dance, okay?"

But he was already pushing his way to the bar.

What's he trying to prove? Destiny wondered. I thought we came here to dance.

Ari returned a few minutes later with two more beers. He downed his quickly and went back for another.

Destiny sipped hers slowly. She talked with three girls from her class, shouting over the throbbing dance music. They talked about how boring the graduation speaker was, their summer jobs, and what they planned to do in the fall.

Destiny could see the girls were a little uncomfortable. They were trying hard not to mention Livvy. Finally, one of them said, "Have you heard from your sister?"

"No," Destiny replied. "We don't know where she and Ross went."

She saw Ari at the bar, talking to a short, red-haired girl, tossing back another beer. Was he flirting with her?

Destiny made her way through the crowd and grabbed him by the elbow. "Are we going to dance or what?" She pulled him onto the dance floor.

They danced for a while under the flashing lightning bolts. Destiny shut her eyes and tried to lose herself to the music, the soaring voices, the insistent beat.

When she opened her eyes she saw Ana-Li nearby, dancing with one of the guys from the lounge. Ana-Li looked great in low-riding, black denims and a green tube top that showed a lot of skin. They waved to each other. Ana-Li pointed to Ari. They both laughed.

Yes, he was a terrible dancer. He had no sense of rhythm at all. Thrashing his arms around, bending his knees, Destiny thought he looked like a puppet that had lost his strings.

Destiny put her hands on Ari's shoulders and tried to guide him. He gave her a lopsided smile. His eyes were cloudy. How many beers had he drunk?

They danced for a long while. Destiny loved the feel of the floor vibrating beneath her, the lights pulsing, the constant beat of the dance music shutting out all other sound.

Ari had a good idea, she decided. I'm actually enjoying myself.

Then she saw the blond again, the one who reminded her so much of Livvy. She was dancing with her back to Destiny, swaying to the music with her arms above her head, her blond hair swinging from side to side.

With a sigh, Destiny stopped dancing. She stumbled into Ari. Her eyes were locked on the blond in the red mini-dress.

The kind of sexy outfit Livvy would wear. Her hair swinging like Livvy's.

"I . . . can't do this," she told Ari, holding onto him with both hands.

She pulled him off the dance floor. They found a small, round table near the bar and sat down. "What happened?" Ari asked, holding her hand.

"I can't do this," Destiny repeated. "I can't be here dancing and pretending."

"Hey, we came here to have fun, right?" Ari said, rolling his eyes. "Just for once, can't we forget about what's happening?"

"I tried," Destiny said. She found a tissue in her bag and wiped the sweat off her forehead. "But Livvy is out there somewhere." She pointed to the door. "Out in the night. My sister alone in the night. How can I—"

"It's not your fault," Ari shouted. "She made a stupid choice. She made a totally *selfish* choice. She didn't think about you, Dee. Or your father. Or your brother. She only thought about herself. So why are you thinking about *her* all the time? Why can't you lighten up for just one night?"

"You don't understand—" Destiny started. "Knowing that she's out there somewhere, prowling around, searching for God-knows-what, it's . . . it's worse than if she were dead."

Ari jumped up, a scowl on his face. "Give me a break," he muttered. "Enough already." He turned and stormed away, disappearing into the crowd on the dance floor.

"Ari, no—wait!" Destiny jumped to her feet and started after him. She bumped into a guy on the dance floor, then pushed past another couple. The flashing lights started to hurt her eyes, made her blink. The steady, pulsating beats began to pound in her ears.

"Ari—?"

Where was he?

I tried. I really tried, Destiny thought. I understand why he lost it. He's been so patient. He wants to have a little fun before he goes off to college. And I haven't been able to shake off this sadness.

She edged her way to the other side of the dance floor. No sign of Ari. Ana-Li stood with a Coke in one hand, talking to Fletch Green and two other guys from their class.

Destiny rushed up to her. "Have you seen Ari?"

Ana-Li laughed. "You lost him?"

"Kinda." Destiny didn't feel like telling her what happened.

"Lookin' hot, Dee," Jerry Freed, one of the three guys, said, grinning at her. He flashed her a thumbs-up.

Ana-Li pointed to the dance floor with her Coke can. "Isn't that Ari over there? Who's he dancing with?"

Destiny spun around. Squinting into the blinking lights, she saw Ari dancing with his hands on the bare waist of another girl . . . the red-haired girl he'd been flirting with at the bar. He pulled her close, and they danced cheek-to-cheek even though the music pounded even faster.

"I don't believe it," Destiny groaned.

"Did you two break up or something?" Ana-Li asked.

"Looks like it," Destiny said. She started

toward Ari and his new dancing partner.

What is his problem? Is he just trying to hurt me?

He's been totally understanding the whole time, Destiny thought. *Was it all an act?*

She grabbed his arm. "Ari?"

He took his hands off the girl's waist, blinking at Destiny. "Oh. Hi." As if he didn't recognize her.

The red-haired girl frowned at Destiny and continued to move to the music.

"Ari, what's up with this?" Destiny couldn't keep her voice from trembling. "I mean—"

Ari shrugged.

"I mean, what's going on?"

"Just dancing."

She realized her hands were balled into tight fists. Working the turntables, the DJ went into a scratching fit, then changed the rhythm, drum machine pounding in her ears.

"Ari, I thought you and I—"

"Give me a break," Ari said.

The second time he said that tonight, Destiny told herself.

Well, okay. I'm not the kind of person who makes a big scene or screams or carries on in front of people. I can't do that.

So . . . I'll give him a break.

"Good night, Ari," she said through gritted teeth.

She spun away and ran along the side of the dance floor, ran without looking back, out the front door, bursting through a couple just arriving. Out into the cool night air, to the edge of the gravel parking lot, where she grabbed onto a wooden fence pole, held onto it, taking breath after breath.

Okay, okay. I'll give him a break, she thought.

Was she angry or hurt, or both?

Have fun, Ari. Have fun without me.

See if I care.

Destiny had no way of knowing that she would never see Ari again.

Part Four

Chapter Twelve
Livvy's New Love

Livvy stood at the end of the bar, tilting a bottle of Rolling Rock to her mouth. The bartender was a fat, old guy; not interesting. Despite the cold beer, Livvy's stomach growled, and the hunger gnawed at her.

She turned and gazed around the dance floor, searching for Monica and Suzie. Squinting into the darting red and blue lights, she spotted them both. Whoa. Who was Suzie dancing with? Ari Stark?

Uh-oh. Looks like Destiny left her boyfriend behind.

Bad mistake, Dee. Look at the stupid grin on Ari's face. He thinks he's gotten lucky tonight.

Monica stood at the edge of the dance floor, her pale arms around a big guy who looked like he could play middle linebacker. She nestled her head against his shoulder and led him toward the lounge.

Way to go, Monica.

Feeling the powerful hunger again, Livvy brushed back her blond hair, straightened her tube top, and gazed down the bar. A dark-haired guy a few stools down seemed to be staring at her.

Livvy flashed him a smile. He had a beer glass in one hand. He raised it as if toasting her.

Livvy didn't hesitate. She strode over to him, a smile on her face. "I'm Livvy," she said. "How ya doin'?"

"Patrick," he replied. He had dimples in his cheeks when he smiled. He was probably a college guy—in his early twenties—cute.

Livvy clicked her bottle against his glass. "What's up, Patrick?"

He shrugged. "Just chillin'. You know."

He had short, wavy brown hair, dark, serious eyes with heavy, brown eyebrows, and a penetrating stare. Livvy felt that he was staring right through her.

Did he like what he saw?

Livvy did. If the good-looking guys have the tastiest blood, I'm in heaven tonight.

Patrick was tall and athletic-looking. He wore black cargo pants and a dark brown leather vest over a soft gray long-sleeved shirt. An interesting look.

He had a silver ring in one ear. And Livvy glimpsed a tattoo of a spider on the back of his hand when he raised his beer glass.

"Like this club?" Livvy asked, squeezing beside him.

Wouldn't you rather go out for a drink, Patrick?

Out to the woods maybe?

"Yeah, it's okay," he said. "I don't like the five-dollar beers. But it's a pretty nice place to hang."

Livvy flashed him her sexiest smile. "I think it just got nicer," she said. Not too subtle, but she felt too hungry to be subtle.

He has a nice long neck, she thought. *Easy to get to the vein.*

Was she staring at his throat? She quickly raised her eyes to his. "I wouldn't mind dancing," she said. "If someone wanted to ask me."

He was a good dancer, she discovered. He moved easily, gracefully, and never took his eyes off her. When he smiled, those dimples came out, and despite her hunger, Livvy could feel herself melting.

Is this my night or what?

Suzie came into view across the crowded dance floor. Over Ari's shoulder, she flashed Livvy a thumbs-up.

After a while, Patrick took Livvy's hand and led her off the dance floor. She squeezed his hand and leaned against him. Even though they'd been dancing hard, he wasn't sweating. He bought two more Rolling Rocks at the bar and handed one to her.

"I haven't seen you here before," he said.

Livvy grinned. "You're seeing me now." She took a sip of beer. "What do you do, Patrick?"

He snickered. "As little as possible. How about you?"

"I'm in school," she lied. She put a hand on his shoulder. "It's kinda hot in here. And noisy. Want to take a walk or something?"

Say yes, Patrick—or I might attack you right here.

"Yeah, sure," he said, finishing his beer. "But I've gotta tell some guys I came with, okay?"

Livvy nodded. *Tell them you're going out for a quick bite, Patrick.* She felt her heart start to race. Her skin tingled.

I'm finally going to feed.

"Meet you outside," she said. "I'm going to smoke."

She watched him make his way through the dance floor. He had a quick, confident stride. He's hot, she thought. Too hot to die. Maybe I'll bring him along slowly. Then give him a chance to join me, to become an immortal. To live forever with me.

She started toward the exit.

Then what do I do with Ross?

Good question.

I still care for Ross. He was so brave to come with me to the other side. He'd be lost without me . . .

Ross is so sweet. But maybe sweet isn't what I need right now. I need thrills. I need action. I need to live this new life to the fullest.

I need . . . Patrick.

As Livvy passed the lounge, she glimpsed Monica in a dark corner, on a low couch, lip-locked with the guy she'd been dancing with. Monica was pressed against him, holding his head as she kissed him, moving her hands through the guy's hair.

He's toast, Livvy thought.

She stepped out into the night. The air felt cool on her hot skin. Clouds covered the moon. A car squealed out of the parking lot, music blaring.

Livvy stepped to the side of the club, leaned against the stucco wall, and pulled a pack of Camel Reds from her bag. She slid a cigarette between her lips. And felt a soft tap on her shoulder.

Patrick?

She spun around—and let out a startled gasp. "*You*? What are *you* doing here? *Get away*!"

Chapter Thirteen
A Surprise Reunion

The cigarette fell from her mouth. Livvy stared at her sister, at her black skirt and white top, her blond hair pulled straight back so neatly, her plastic bracelets on one wrist, everything so neat and perfect.

Except what was that expression on Destiny's face? Eyes so wide and chin quivering. Destiny stared at Livvy as if she'd never seen her before.

And was that fear in her eyes?

"Destiny, go away," Livvy repeated. "I don't want to see you."

"I'm your sister." Destiny's voice trembled. "Why are you saying that?"

Livvy stared at her. "I'm busy right now. I'm waiting for someone. Take a walk, Dee. I mean it."

Destiny swallowed. She didn't move. "You look so different. You cut your hair. You've lost weight, haven't you? And those dark rings around your eyes—"

"Hey, no beauty tips, okay," Livvy snarled. "I don't read *Cosmo Girl* anymore."

"You're so pale, Livvy," Destiny continued. "You look as if you haven't slept in weeks. Listen to me—"

"No, you listen to me, Dee," Livvy said through clenched teeth. "Read my lips: *Go away.*" She glanced over Destiny's shoulder. Where was Patrick?

"Was that you this afternoon?" Destiny asked, crossing her arms in front of her. "The bat?"

"Excuse me?" Livvy pulled another cigarette from the pack. Her hand shook as she slid it between her lips. "What bat? I don't know what the hell you're talking about."

"It wasn't you?"

"No way. Were you dreaming or something?"

I don't know why I did that, Livvy thought, remembering the afternoon. I'll never do it again.

"I thought I saw you in the club," Destiny said, motioning to the entrance with her head.

"You didn't see me, did you? I was with Ari. But I think he left. We had a fight. I feel terrible. He's so sweet."

"Tell someone who cares," Livvy said. She yawned.

Destiny startled her by grabbing her arm. "Come home, Liv. Come home with me right now."

Livvy rolled her eyes. "Yeah, sure. Good idea." She tugged her arm free.

"No, really," Destiny insisted. "Dad will find a cure. I know he will. He's working so hard, Liv. He'll find a cure for you, and you can be normal again. You know. Back home."

Livvy let out an angry cry. "You never could stand to see me have fun!" she shouted. "Get a clue, Dee. I don't want to go back to that boring life."

"Yes, you do," Destiny replied, tears in her eyes. "You don't mean what you're saying. You can't like what you're doing. The way you're living. You *can't*." A sob escaped her throat.

Livvy took a deep breath. Her hands were clenched into tight fists at her sides. "Don't you see? I've made my choice. I'm going to live forever. That's my choice. You want to stay home and see your boring friends and that boring geek Ari, and go to school like a nice girl and be a nice, boring person for the rest of your life. And I've made a different choice. That's all. No big deal, right?"

"But, Liv—"

"I'm going to live forever. That's my choice. So get out of my face, Dee. Go away and don't come back."

"I . . . don't believe you." Destiny let the tears roll down her cheeks. "You're my sister. My *twin* sister. And the two of us belong together. We—"

"We belong together? Okay!" Livvy cried. She let her fangs slide down over her lips. "You want to stay together forever? Fine. You stay with *me*."

She grabbed Destiny around the waist and started to drag her across the parking lot toward the woods.

"Hey—let go!" Destiny screamed, unable to hide her panic. "What are you doing?"

"We'll be together," Livvy growled, saliva running down her fangs. "You and me. Together."

Destiny grabbed Livvy's arms and tried to

pull them off her. But Livvy held onto her tightly and dragged her over the gravel toward the tall trees.

"You and me," Livvy rasped. "Just the way you want it, Dee."

"Let go! Let go!" Destiny pleaded.

Livvy pressed her mouth against the back of Destiny's neck. "You and me—forever," she whispered.

Chapter Fourteen
The Taste of Night

Livvy held on tight as Destiny squirmed and struggled to free herself. Finally, she gave Dee's hair a hard tug—and let her go.

Destiny staggered forward several steps. Then she spun around to face her sister. "Were you . . . were you . . ." She struggled to catch her breath. "What were you doing? Were you just trying to scare me?"

Livvy grinned at her. She made loud sucking noises with her fangs. "Want to stay and find out?"

Trembling, Destiny studied her for a long moment. Then she turned and ran across the parking lot.

Livvy watched her sister run away. Her heart was pounding in her chest. She suddenly felt dizzy.

I'm so confused. My feelings are all mixed up.

I always loved Destiny. Do I really hate her now?

Is it because she's trying to ruin my new life?

I made my choice. Why can't she leave me alone?

Livvy turned and saw Patrick watching her from the club exit. She slid her fangs back into her gums. Then she straightened her hair and forced a sexy smile to her face.

"There you are," he called, taking those long strides toward her. "I thought maybe you split or something."

"No way." She took his arm. "It's nice out, huh?"

He nodded. She liked his serious, dark eyes, the way they seemed to lock on her as if holding her captive.

The clouds floated away from the moon, and pale light washed over them. "I like the moonlight," he said, glancing up at the sky.

"How old are you?" she asked, leaning against him, guiding him to the trees.

"Old enough," he said. "How old did you think I was?"

"I don't know. Inside the club, you looked

sixteen. But now you look older." She let her hand slide down his arm and gripped his hand. "I'm going to be eighteen soon."

"Are you in college?" he asked. Their shoes crunched over the gravel. He didn't wait for her to answer. He turned and kissed her. He held her chin in his hand and kissed her long and deep.

Yes, she thought. And as she kissed him, a strange phrase played through her mind . . .

The taste of night.

The taste of night.

Where did it come from? She didn't know. But she knew she was enjoying it tonight—the taste of night. The taste of the cool, fresh air and the moonlight, the taste of his lips, the taste of an exciting, new adventure. And in a few moments . . . the taste of blood.

It was all part of the taste of night.

I'm totally into him, she thought. I mean I'm really attracted to him. He's so good looking and mysterious and sexy.

We just met, but I already have strong feelings for him, she realized.

Almost as strong as my thirst . . .

He pulled his face away. They were both

breathing hard. He still had his hand on her chin. "Where are you leading me?" he asked.

She grinned. "Astray?"

He laughed. A big laugh that seemed to come from deep inside him.

"I thought we'd take a walk in the woods," Livvy said. "Such a nice night. We can talk. It's so peaceful out here."

"You're an outdoors-type person? You like to camp?"

"Not really," she replied. "But I like to do *other* things in the woods." She pulled him into the trees. The moonlight seemed to follow them. She pulled him farther. She needed darkness.

"Hey, where are we going? I can't see a thing," he said, tugging her to a stop.

"That's the idea," she whispered. She grabbed the sides of his head and pulled his face to hers. They kissed again, moving their tongues together.

I'm so hungry, she thought.

I can't wait another second.

I need to drink. He's driving me crazy.

She pulled her lips from his and nuzzled his ear with her mouth. "Now, Patrick, I'm going to give you a kiss to remember," she whispered.

"But here's the sad part. After I give it to you, I'm going to cloud your mind so you won't remember it."

"Huh? I don't understand." He held her by the waist and stared into her eyes. "What are you saying?"

So hungry . . . so hungry . . . Oh, damn—I'm so hungry . . .

Livvy lowered her fangs and dug them into his throat. Deep, deep into the soft flesh.

And then she pulled away—and opened her mouth in a scream of horror.

Chapter Fifteen

"I'm Not Just a Vampire"

Livvy staggered back, stumbling over an upraised tree root and landing hard against the fat trunk of a maple tree. Patrick didn't move. He stood still as a statue, a shadow against shadows.

"You . . . you're a vampire too," she whispered finally. She struggled to catch her breath. Her body still tingled from the excitement of nearly finding blood.

But Patrick's blood wouldn't nourish her.

He stepped closer, and she could see the smile on his face. "I'm sorry," he said. "I wanted to see how far you'd go."

Her surprise quickly turned to anger. "You were just playing a game? Having a little joke at my expense?"

He took her hand. "No. It wasn't just a joke. I really like you."

"What were you doing in the club?" Livvy asked.

"Same as you. Looking to hook up."

"But I wasn't looking to hook up with a vampire. I'm so hungry," Livvy moaned. "You've wasted my time."

He laughed. "Hey, don't hurt my feelings. I said I really like you."

"But I don't need a vampire. I need—" Livvy started.

He put a finger over her lips. "I'm not just a vampire, Livvy. Things are going to change now that I'm here."

"Excuse me?" She let go of his hand. "What are you talking about?"

"I'm going to take care of everyone. Make it a lot more exciting for all of us."

Moonlight filtered through the trees, and Livvy could see his smile and his eyes, crazy eyes, intense and unblinking. He seemed to be aiming all his power at her.

She turned away.

"Where do you live?" she asked.

"Same building as you," he replied.

She kept her eyes away from his. "How do you know where I live? You've seen me before?"

"Truth? I've had my eye on you."

"You've been watching me? Why?" she asked.

He didn't answer. He pulled her close, low-ered his face to hers, and kissed her. Kissed her hard, so hard she could feel his teeth pressing against her lips . . . so hard it hurt.

When the kiss ended, her lips throbbed with pain. Heart pounding, she pressed her forehead against the front of his shirt.

Livvy realized she was trembling. I'm hot for him—and I'm afraid of him—at the same time.

Patrick took her by the shoulders and moved her away. "It's getting late. I'm thirsty too."

"But I want to know more about you," Livvy said. She flashed him a grin. "You can't just take a girl into the woods and leave her there."

Once again, he brought his face to hers. And he whispered in her ear. "Later."

He whirled away from her—and trans-formed quickly into a slender red fox. Squinting into the patch of silvery moonlight, Livvy watched the fox scamper away through the thick underbrush.

Yes, later, she thought.

Catch you later, Patrick. I think you and I are going to be seeing a lot of each other.

Chapter Sixteen
Destiny Flies

Destiny searched for Ari in the club but couldn't find him. She wanted to apologize. He was only dancing with that red-haired girl, after all. She shouldn't have embarrassed him by acting so jealous.

This night is a disaster, she thought. No way is it a celebration.

She ended up walking home by herself. The night air felt cool against her hot skin. Crickets chirped. Fireflies danced in front of her, seeming to light her path. The moon appeared and disappeared behind high, gray clouds.

She walked through tall grass along the side of the road. Her shoes became wet from the dew. Cars rolled past without slowing.

She found herself thinking about Ross. She wondered how he was. She couldn't picture Ross as a vampire. He was so good looking and athletic and . . . healthy.

Destiny had a crush on Ross for years, and Livvy knew it. But Livvy went after Ross anyway. And she took him away.

Forever.

The tiny lights of fireflies sparkled in Destiny's eyes, making the world appear unreal. The lights darted and danced around her.

Before she knew it, she arrived at Drake Park, three blocks from her house. As she crossed the street and stepped into the park, she could hear the trickle of water from the narrow creek and the rustle of the trees shaking in the warm breeze.

She followed the dirt path that curved toward her house. A creature scampered over her feet, startling her. A field mouse? A chipmunk?

She thought about Mikey. What did he do tonight? The poor kid. I hope he didn't spend the whole night shut up in his dark cave of a room.

Destiny told herself she should spend more time with Mikey. But it wasn't easy. Tomorrow morning she was starting her summer job at the Four Corners Diner. A waitress behind the lunch counter. Not a very challenging job. But at least the restaurant was across from the Community College campus. Maybe she'd meet some new people . . .

The moon disappeared behind a blanket of clouds. The fireflies had vanished. Destiny felt a chill as the darkness washed over her.

She kicked a stone in the path. The creek trickled behind her now. She knew she was almost home.

And then a figure stepped out from a thick clump of pine trees. A girl. She seemed to float silently onto the path.

"Hello—?" Destiny called in a whisper.

The girl didn't answer. She moved toward Destiny quickly. Startled, Destiny began to move out of the way, but she wasn't quick enough.

"Hey—" Destiny let out a cry—and then recognized her sister. "Livvy? What are you doing here?"

Livvy stared at her for a long moment, her expression intense, eyes locked on Destiny's.

Why did Livvy follow me? To apologize?

Did she change her mind about coming home?

And then to Destiny's shock, Livvy raised

both arms and wrapped her in a tight hug.

The two sisters stood there on the dark path, hugging each other, faces pressed together, tears rolling down their cheeks, tears running together as they sobbed and held each other.

Finally, they backed away from each other. They both wiped away tears with their hands.

"Livvy, I'm so happy," Destiny said in a trembling whisper. "Why did you follow me? Did you change your mind?"

"Yes," Livvy replied. "Yes, I changed my mind. I . . . I'm so lonely, Dee. I need to come home. I need to be with my family again."

"Dad and Mikey . . . they'll be so glad to see you," Destiny said.

And then the two sisters were hugging again, hugging and crying.

Destiny finally released her sister. "Let's go home," she whispered. "It's late, but Dad will still be awake. He doesn't sleep much—ever since . . ." Her voice trailed off.

Livvy clung to her sister. She didn't reply.

"I'm so glad," Destiny said. "I mean, I'm so happy, Liv. I mean . . . I can't really say what I mean."

Livvy's arms remained clamped tightly

around Destiny. Her head was turned so that Destiny couldn't see her face.

"Please let go," Destiny whispered. "I . . . can't breathe."

Livvy didn't move.

"Let go," Destiny repeated. "Come on. Let's go home, okay?"

Livvy didn't reply. Her arms remained clamped around Destiny's waist.

"Livvy—let go!" Destiny cried. "What's wrong? What are you doing? Let go of me. Let go!"

Destiny tried to pull free. And as she squirmed and twisted, she saw Livvy's body begin to transform.

"Livvy—stop! What are you doing? Let go of me—please!"

And now, scratchy brown feathers scraped Destiny's face. She heard a warble from deep inside Livvy's body. And she realized that powerful claws, hard as bone, had replaced her sister's arms.

Livvy had transformed into an enormous, throbbing bird, at least seven feet tall. A giant hawk! And Destiny was pressed tightly against the prickly feathers around its belly, held by the huge, powerful claws clamped around her waist.

"Livvy—NO!"

The bird raised its head, flapped its massive wings, sending a burst of air over Destiny. It dragged Destiny along the grass for a while before it lifted high enough into the air. And then, flapping its wings so slowly, so easily, it floated up into the dark sky, carrying Destiny in its claws like a prize . . . like dinner.

Destiny let out scream after scream as she floated over the treetops of the park, then the houses of her neighborhood.

Is she planning to drop me?

The houses looked like dollhouses now. The car headlights down below looked as tiny as the firefly light that had followed her as she walked.

"Livvy—please!"

She could feel the pattering heartbeat of the huge bird. The oily feathers grazed her cheeks.

And then they were soaring down, swooping with the wind. The onrushing wind blowing so hard in her face, Destiny struggled to breathe.

A hard bounce. The claws let go. Destiny landed on her back. Felt the air knocked out of her. Lay there on hard ground, gasping.

Where are we?

Livvy loomed over her, human once again.

Livvy's hair fell over her face, but Destiny could see her eyes. Wild eyes, bulging with anger . . . with hate?

"Where are we? Where have you taken me?" Destiny cried. She raised herself on two arms and gazed around, blinking in the darkness.

Nothing to see. No trees here. No houses. Flat ground, a black strip against the blacker sky, stretching on forever.

"Where are we?"

"It doesn't matter, Dee." Livvy spoke in a cold whisper. "It really doesn't matter."

"Why? What do you mean?"

Livvy narrowed her eyes at Destiny, and her face hardened to stone. "Because you're never leaving."

"I don't understand, Livvy. What—?"

Livvy's fangs slid quickly from her gums, making a loud *pok* sound. She opened her mouth wide, tongue playing over her teeth, drool running over her chin. Then she sank her fangs deep into Destiny's throat.

Chapter Seventeen
Trouble at Ari's House

Destiny felt sweat run down her forehead. Her nightshirt clung wetly to her back.

She blinked, reached a hand to her throat, and smoothed two fingers across it.

No wound.

She blinked some more, realizing she was gazing into bright sunlight. From the bedroom window.

She jerked herself upright, breathing hard. A dream? Yes.

It had been a dream—all of it. *I didn't walk home last night*, she remembered. *Fletch Green gave me a ride.*

But the feeling of walking home through the park . . . the sparkling fireflies . . . her sister stepping out of the darkness . . . transforming into the gigantic hawk . . . All so real.

So real she thought she could still feel those bonelike claws wrapped tightly around her waist. She could still feel the suffocating rush of wind as the giant bird carried her into the sky.

Could still feel Livvy's fangs . . .

Does my twin sister really have fangs?

A soft cry escaped Destiny's throat. Yes, it was a dream. But the rest of my life is real . . .

. . . and it's a nightmare.

"Dee! Dee!" She heard Mikey calling from downstairs. She jumped out of bed, gazing at the clock radio on her bedtable.

Oh, no. Late. I have to give Mikey breakfast and get him off to day camp. She brushed her teeth, pushed back her hair with her hands, and went running down to the kitchen in her night-shirt.

"Where's Dad?" she asked Mikey.

He was dressed in denim shorts that came down past his knees and a blue-and-red Camp Redhawk T-shirt about five sizes too big for him. He gripped a stuffed lion in one hand. He'd had it since he was a baby. These days it looked more like a washcloth than a lion.

He shrugged. "Work. He woke me up. Then he left. I'm hungry. And so is Lester." He waved Lester the Lion in Destiny's face.

She popped two frozen waffles into the

toaster. "We're a little late. You'll have to eat your waffles fast."

"Take the crust off," he said, sitting down at the table, plopping Lester in front of him.

Destiny turned to him. "Crust on waffles?"

"Yeah. Take off the crust."

He had become the fussiest eater. He suddenly had rules for everything. And he found something wrong with everything put in front of him. A few nights ago, he had even refused to eat the french fries at Burger King because they were "too curled up."

She poured him a glass of orange juice and handed it to him. "No pulp," she said before he could ask.

He tasted it gingerly, a tiny sip. "Too cold."

"What are you doing at day camp today?" she asked, brushing back his thick mop of hair with one hand.

"I'm not going to day camp," Mikey replied. He pounded Lester on the tabletop for emphasis.

"You have to go," Destiny said, lifting the waffles from the toaster. "Ow. Hot. There's no one here to take care of you."

"You can take care of me," he said.

"No, I can't, Mikey. You know that I'm

starting my summer job today, remember?"

"Well, I can't go to camp. Hey—you forgot to cut off the crusts. And I don't want butter. I want syrup."

Destiny took the plate back and carefully pulled the edges off the waffles. "And why can't you go to camp?"

"Because they're showing a movie at the theater." He took another swallow of orange juice.

"You like movies," Destiny said, handing the plate back to him. "So what's the problem?"

"It . . . it's cold and creepy in the theater," he replied. "There might be vampires in there."

Destiny stopped in front of the diner and checked her hair and lipstick in her reflection in the front window. The name FOUR CORNERS DINER was painted in fancy gold script across the wide window.

Destiny chuckled. It seemed an odd name for the little restaurant since it was located in the middle of the block. Surrounding it on both sides were small, two-story brick and shingle buildings that contained clothing stores, a bank, a CD store—shops that catered to

Community College students.

She turned and glanced at the campus. Four square, granite buildings around a narrow rectangle of patchy grass and trees. Not the most beautiful campus in the world.

Destiny let out a sigh. I made the right decision, she told herself. I couldn't go away to college and leave Dad and Mikey now. I'll go to the Community College for a year or two. When things are more in control at home, I can transfer to a better school.

When things are more in control . . .

She turned and hurried into the diner. The smell of fried grease greeted her. Bright lights made the long lunch counter glow. A ceiling fan squeaked as it slowly turned.

Destiny counted three people seated at one end of the counter. Two guys about her age and an older woman. The four booths in back were empty. Mr. Georgio, the owner, stood behind the counter, setting down plates of hamburgers and french fries for the three customers.

"Mr. Georgio, sorry I'm a little late," Destiny said, glancing up at the round Coca-Cola clock above the coat rack in the corner. "I had trouble getting my brother off to day camp."

"Call me Mr. G., remember?" he said, setting plastic ketchup and mustard dispensers in front of the customers. He walked over to her, wiping sweat off his bald head with a paper napkin.

He was a thin, little man of forty or forty-five. The white apron he wore over black slacks and a white sport shirt hung nearly to the floor. He had big, brown eyes, a thick, brown mustache under his bulby nose, and a split between his front teeth that showed when he smiled.

"Late? No problem," he said. "We're not exactly packing them in today." He motioned with his head to the three customers.

"Summer is slow," he said, wiping a grease spot on the yellow counter. "Most of the students aren't here. There are only a few classes. My business is students. Breakfast and lunch. You'll have a nice, quiet time, Ms. Weller. You can read a book or something."

"Please, call me Dee. Remember?" Destiny said.

He smiled. "Okay, you're Dee and I'm G."

"Could we have more Cokes?" a guy at the end of the counter called, holding up his glass.

"Take care of them," Mr. G. told her, pulling

off his apron. "And clean things up a bit, okay? I've got to go out." He pointed to the kitchen window behind the counter. "You remember Nate? The fry cook? He's back there some- where. Probably sneaking a smoke. He's a lazy goof-off. But if you have any questions, he'll help you out."

Destiny had worked some weekends at the diner, so she already knew her way around. She waved to Nate through the window, carried three glasses to the soda dispenser, and filled them with Coke.

The bell over the door clanged as two more customers came in. Destiny didn't recognize them at first because of the white sunlight pour- ing in through the front window. But as they settled into the first booth behind the counter, she saw that she knew them. Rachel Seeger and Bonnie Franz, two girls from her class.

Destiny picked up two menus and carried them over to the booth. Her two friends were talking heatedly, giggling and gesturing with their hands. But they stopped their conversation when they recognized Destiny.

Rachel's cheeks blushed bright pink. She had light blond hair and really fair skin and was an easy blusher, Destiny remembered. "Hey, Dee. What's up?" she asked.

"You waitressing here?" Bonnie asked.

Destiny laughed. "No. Just holding menus. It's like a hobby of mine."

The girls laughed.

"I have a summer job too," Bonnie said. "At the campus. I'm filing stuff in the administration office. Yawn yawn."

"Are you making any money?" Destiny asked.

Bonnie shook her head. "Eight dollars an hour. And my dad said he had to pull strings to get me the job. I mean, like hel-lo. I could make that at McDonald's, right?"

Destiny handed them the menus. "Know what you want?"

"Not really," Bonnie said.

"Are you working this summer?" Destiny asked Rachel.

She made a disgusted face. "I couldn't find anything. So I'm just hanging out this summer. You know. Partying. Getting ready for college. You're going away, right, Dee?"

"Uh . . . no." Destiny hesitated. She didn't want sympathy from her friends. "I decided to stay close to home and go here." She motioned out the window to the campus. "You know. It's kinda tough times at home . . ."

"Have you heard from your sister?" Rachel asked, blushing again. "I mean, she and Ross have been gone so long."

Destiny lowered her eyes to the yellow tabletop. "No. Haven't heard anything yet."

Rachel gripped the big, red menu with both hands. "Do the police still think they ran away together?"

Destiny saw Bonnie motioning for Rachel to shut up.

"The police . . . they don't know *what* to think," Destiny said honestly.

"Sorry," Bonnie muttered.

The two girls stared down at their menus. An awkward silence. The conversation had ended.

Destiny raised her pad to take their orders. Everyone treats me so differently now, she thought. I used to hang with Bonnie and Rachel and goof with them all the time. Once, a sales clerk at the Gap made us leave because we were laughing too loud in the dressing room.

But now, people feel sorry for me. They feel

awkward. They don't know what to say.

"Could we have a check?" a woman called from the counter.

"I'll be right back," Destiny told the two girls. She hurried along the counter to take care of the woman's check.

As soon as she left, her two friends started chattering away again.

After work, Destiny decided to drive over to Ari's house. She'd been thinking about him all afternoon.

I'm going to apologize for last night, she decided. What happened at the club . . . it really was my fault.

Ari wanted to celebrate, to have some fun. And I was a total drag. I should have tried harder to forget my problems, to just go with the flow . . .

She pictured him dancing with that red-haired girl. Thinking about it gave her a heavy feeling in her stomach.

Ari is going off to school soon. And I'm going to miss him terribly. I have to be nicer to him.

Yes, I'm definitely going to apologize.

Thinking about last night, there was no way

to shut out the memory of her meeting with Livvy. Turning onto Ari's block, sunlight burst over the windshield. And through the blinding white light, Destiny saw two blond girls standing on the front stoop of the corner house.

"Oh—!" she let out a cry.

The car moved under the shadow of trees. The two girls disappeared into the house.

Destiny frowned. *Every time I see a girl with blond hair, I think it's my sister.*

Livvy was so mean to me last night. Has she completely forgotten that we're sisters? It's only been a few weeks, and she has changed so much. She looked so pale and thin and . . . and worn out.

Livvy acted so cold and angry. I hardly recognized her.

Destiny saw the tall hedge in front of Ari's yard, the white-shingled house rising up behind it. She turned and pulled into the drive—and stopped.

"Hey—"

Two police squad cars blocked her way, red lights spinning on their roofs.

"Oh, no." Destiny's heart started to pound. She felt her throat tighten.

Ari's dad had a heart attack last summer. Has he had another one?

Hands trembling, she pulled the car to the curb in front of the neighbors' house. Then she went running up the driveway.

The front door was open. She burst inside. She heard voices in the front room. Someone crying.

"What's wrong?" she shouted breathlessly. "What's happened?"

Chapter Eighteen
Who Is the Next Victim?

Destiny ran into the living room. She saw Ari's mother hunched in the tall, green armchair by the fireplace. Her head was buried in a white handkerchief, and she was sobbing loudly, her shoulders heaving up and down.

Mr. Stark stood beside the chair, one hand on his wife's shoulder. He was very pale and, even from a distance, Destiny could see the tear tracks on his cheeks.

Two grim-faced, young police officers stood with their hands in their pockets, shaking their heads, speaking softly to Ari's parents. They spun around when Destiny entered the room.

"What is it? Where's Ari?" Destiny cried.

But even before anyone answered, she knew. She knew why they were crying. They had bad news about Ari. Maybe the *worst* news . . .

"No—!" Destiny screamed, pressing her hands against her face. "No. Please—"

No one had spoken. But she knew.

Mr. Stark came across the room to greet her, walking stiffly, as if it took all his effort. He was a tall, heavyset man, and now he was walking as if he weighed a thousand pounds.

He put his hands on Destiny's shoulders. "It's Ari," he whispered. "It's horrible, Dee. Ari . . . Ari . . ." He turned away from her.

"What . . . what happened to him?" Destiny stammered.

Mrs. Stark uttered a loud sob across the room.

One of the police officers studied Destiny.

"I'm Lieutenant Macy," he said, keeping his voice low. "Are you Destiny Weller?"

Destiny nodded. Her throat felt so tight, it was hard to breathe. "Yes. How did you know?"

"We've been trying to reach you all day," he said. "The phone at your house . . . it rang and rang."

"I started a new job today," Destiny said. "Is Ari—?"

Macy had bright blue eyes and he kept them trained on Destiny. "I'm sorry. He's . . . dead."

A cry escaped Destiny's throat. Her knees folded. She started to collapse to the floor, but

Macy grabbed her gently by the arm and held her up.

She struggled to catch her breath. It felt as if her chest might burst open.

"Come sit down," Macy said softly. He led her to the green leather couch in front of the window.

Tears flowed down her cheeks. She fumbled in her bag for some tissues. "What happened?" she asked Macy. She gritted her teeth. She didn't really want to hear.

"We were hoping you could help us out with that," Macy said, leaning forward, bringing his face close to hers. "You were with Ari last night, right? You were at the dance club?"

Destiny nodded, dabbing at her tears. She glanced up to see Mr. Stark staring down at her, hunched behind Macy. She glimpsed the pain in his eyes and turned away.

"Well, a young couple found Ari at the edge of the parking lot there," Macy said. "It was about two A.M. Were you still with him then?"

Destiny stared at the officer. His voice sounded muffled, as if he were speaking underwater. Ari dead in the parking lot? Two in the morning? She struggled to make sense of it.

"No. I . . . left early," Destiny said finally.

Macy stared at her, waiting for more of an explanation.

"We had a fight," Destiny said. "Well, no. Not really a fight. An argument, I guess. And I . . . I left early."

"How early?" Macy asked.

"I left around midnight, I think. I got a ride home with a friend. I remember it was a little after twelve-thirty when I got home."

"And was Ari still at the club when you left?"

Destiny nodded. "I . . . think so. Yes. Yes, he was."

"You saw him there before you left?" Macy demanded.

Destiny nodded again, wiping at her tears. "He was dancing. I saw him dancing . . . with another girl."

Across the room, Mrs. Stark uttered a loud sob. Mr. Stark hurried over to comfort her.

Destiny raised her eyes to Macy. "How . . . did Ari die?" she whispered.

Macy's blue eyes burned into hers. "Strangest thing. He had two puncture wounds in his neck. His blood was completely drained."

* * *

"Do you really think Livvy did it?" Ana-Li asked.

Destiny shook her head. "I don't know what to think."

They were sitting on the couch in Destiny's room above the garage, the room she had shared with her twin. The couch divided the long, low room in two. Destiny hadn't touched anything on Livvy's side. She'd left it exactly as Livvy had it.

When Livvy comes back, it will be ready for her.

That's what Destiny had thought. Until now.

"Livvy and I talked outside the club," Destiny told Ana-Li, folding her arms tightly in front of her. "We didn't really talk. We just screamed. I mean, Livvy did the screaming. She was awful to me. She . . . she's changed so much."

Ana-Li took a long sip from her Diet Coke can, her dark eyes on Destiny. "What did you fight about?"

"Nothing, really. I begged her to come home. She told me to leave her alone, to stay out of her life. That's all. But it was the way she said it. So cruel. As if she *hates* me."

Ana-Li squeezed Destiny's hand. Her hand was cold from the soda can. "Livvy wasn't angry enough to murder Ari—was she? I mean, she's known Ari as long as you have. No way she'd murder him out of spite or something."

Destiny sighed. "I don't know. I don't know what to think anymore. I thought I knew her. I mean, she's my *twin* sister. But now . . . I don't know her at all."

"You can't believe she'd murder your boyfriend," Ana-Li said. "It had to be someone else, Dee. It's just too sick."

"Yeah. Sick," Destiny repeated. "That's the word. This whole thing is sick."

"What do the cops say?" Ana-Li asked.

"They've been back to question me three times. They interviewed the red-haired girl. She said she danced with Ari a couple of times, and then she didn't see him again. She thinks he went off with another girl, but she doesn't really know."

"That's a really busy parking lot," Ana-Li said. "Didn't anyone see anything strange going on?"

"So far, no one has called the police," Destiny replied.

"The police know there are vampires in Dark Springs," Ana-Li said, tapping a long, red nail fingernail on the Diet Coke can. "They help your father and his vampire hunters, right? So they must know—"

"They're trying to keep it quiet," Destiny interrupted. "The cops didn't reveal what really happened to Ari to the news people. They don't want to start a panic."

She let out a cry. "I just can't believe my own sister could do something so horrible. But she was there. And she told me how thirsty she was."

Ana-Li shuddered. She set down the soda can. "Dee, there's something I have to tell you."

Destiny blinked at her. "What?"

"I'm leaving for school early," Ana-Li said. "I can't stand it here anymore. I'm leaving on Saturday. It's just too frightening here. I have to get away."

Ana-Li didn't give Destiny time to reply. She hugged her, then turned and, with a sad wave, made her way down the stairs.

Destiny remained on the couch, feeling numb. Unable to stop the upsetting whirl of thoughts that troubled her mind.

Ari is dead.
Ana-Li is leaving.
My friends are all gone.
Will I be next?
Will I be the next victim?

Part Five

Two Weeks Later

Chapter Nineteen
"Maybe He's Just What I Need"

"Two over easy, side of toast," Destiny said, poking her head through the window to the kitchen. Then she let out a startled gasp. "You're not Nate!"

The guy at the stove waved his metal spatula at her. "Hey, you're real sharp."

"Where's Nate?" Destiny asked, glancing around the tiny diner kitchen.

"Fired. Didn't Mr. G. tell you?"

"Guess he forgot. Who are you?" she blurted out.

He grinned at her and adjusted his apron. "You can call me Not Nate. Or maybe the Anti-Nate."

"No. Really," Destiny insisted.

"Harrison," he said, his dark eyes flashing. "Harrison Palmer." He saluted her with the spatula. "And you are . . . wait . . . don't tell me." He studied her, rubbing his chin. "Naomi

135

Watts? I loved you in *The Ring*."

Destiny rolled her eyes. "Ha ha."

"You look a lot like her," Harrison said.

"Yeah. We're both blond and we both have two eyes, a nose, and a mouth," Destiny said. "You'd better start that egg order." She narrowed her eyes at him. "Have you ever done this before?"

He grinned. "Yeah, sure. No problem. Uh . . . just one thing." He held up an egg. "How do you get the yellow part out of this shell thing?"

Destiny laughed. He's funny, she thought. I haven't really laughed in a long time.

She watched him break the eggs on the grill and move them around with the spatula. He's cute too. Tall and broad-shouldered. A great smile. Those big, dark eyes that crinkle up at the sides. Short, brown hair spiked up in the front.

I can't believe Mr. G. forgot to tell me he was starting today.

After the lunch crowd left, she and Harrison had time to chat. She mopped the counter clean while he came out front to help collect plates.

"Good work," she said. "You've done this before."

He shook his head. "No. I bought that book last night. You know, *Fry Cooking for Dummies.*"

"No. Really—" she said.

"You have to know where to put that sprig of parsley," he said, dropping a stack of dishes into the dirty dish basket. "Parsley placement. I flunked it twice at cook school."

Destiny laughed. "Aren't you ever serious?"

He didn't answer.

Destiny moved to the back booth and started collecting dirty plates.

"You go to school here?" he asked, motioning out the front window to the campus.

"I'm starting in the fall," Destiny told him. "You?"

He nodded. "Yeah. I finished my first year. Now I'm taking some summer courses. Language stuff. I'm studying Russian."

Destiny turned to look at him. "How come?"

"Beats me." He snickered. "It impresses girls. Are you impressed?"

"Totally," Destiny said. Her face suddenly felt hot.

He's really cute.

"Do you live near here?" she asked.

He nodded. "Yeah, I have an apartment near

137

the campus with a couple of guys. That's why I'm working here, trying to pay the rent. Mr. G. is my stepfather's brother. So he helped me out. Gave me this job."

"Oh. Nepotism," Destiny teased.

"Ooh—big word. You going to be an English major?"

"Probably. Maybe. I don't know."

He laughed. "Luckily, you don't have to decide right away."

"I'm only staying here a year," Destiny told him. "Then I'm transferring out."

"Why didn't you go away to school? Because of the tuition?"

She shrugged. "It's a long story."

You see, my sister became a vampire.

That's a real conversation ender—isn't it?

Harrison picked up the basket of dirty dishes and began lugging it to the kitchen. "Hey, you busy Friday night? My friends and me . . . we're just hanging out at my apartment. Kind of a party. It's my roommate Alby's birthday."

Is he asking me out?

Harrison disappeared into the kitchen. She could hear the dirty plates clattering into the sink.

He's waiting for an answer. Say something, Dee.

I have to get on with my life. Maybe he's just what I need. Someone new. Someone funny and new who doesn't know a thing about me.

She poked her head into the kitchen. "Yeah, sure. Sounds great."

Friday night. As Destiny climbed the narrow staircase to Harrison's apartment, she could hear the party three floors up. Rap music pounded through the stairwell, and she heard laughter and loud voices over the music.

The door to the apartment stood open, and Destiny could see a crowd of young people inside. Two girls sat in the hall with their backs against the wall, smoking and talking. In the corner next to a metal trash can, a tall, blond-haired boy had a girl pressed against the wall, and they were kissing passionately, eyes closed.

Destiny stepped around them and lurched into the doorway. Harrison stood in the middle of the room, talking with a group of guys. He swung around as Destiny entered, and his eyes grew wide, as if he were surprised to see her. He had a Radiohead T-shirt pulled down over faded and torn jeans, a can of Coors in one hand.

"Hey—" he called, pushing his way through the crowd to get to her. "Hi. You made it."

Destiny nodded. "Yeah. Hi. Nice apartment."

Harrison laughed. "You're kidding, right?"

Destiny gazed around the long, L-shaped room. The walls were painted a hideous shade of chartreuse. But a nice, brown leather couch and two La-Z-Boy armchairs were arranged around a big TV screen. A bunch of shouting, cheering guys had jammed onto the couch and chairs and were into an intense PlayStation hockey game.

Two Jimi Hendrix posters were tacked to the wall across from the wide, double windows. Destiny counted five large stereo speakers scattered around the room, all of them booming the new Outkast CD. The speaker tops were cluttered with beer and soda cans and ash trays. A long, aluminum table stood in the alcove of the room. It held two large tubs filled with ice and drinks and open bags of chips.

I've never been in a campus apartment before, Destiny thought. This is totally cool.

Harrison handed her a can of beer. "Hey,

want to meet my roomies?"

"Well, yes. You said it's a birthday celebration, right?"

"Yeah. Alby's birthday. You'll like him. He's kinda serious. Like you."

Harrison's words gave Destiny a start. Is that how he sees me? Kinda serious? Does he think I'm *too* serious?

"That's Mark over there," Harrison said. He pointed to a very tall, black guy with a shaved head. Dressed in gray sweat pants and a sleeveless, blue T-shirt that showed off his big biceps. He had his arm around a girl at least a foot shorter than he was, and they were laughing hard about something.

Harrison called Mark over and introduced him to Destiny. Mark studied Destiny for a long moment. "Where'd you meet her?" he asked Harrison.

"At the diner."

Mark squeezed Harrison's shoulder and grinned at Destiny. "When you get tired of this loser, come see me—okay?"

Destiny laughed. "For sure."

"Hey, who wants to be in the game?" A short, stocky guy wearing a vintage Bob's Big

Boy bowling shirt held up a board game. "We're gonna play Strip Trivial Pursuit. Who wants to play?"

He got a lot of hoots and laughs in reply, but no takers.

Destiny saw some guys watching her from the window. She was wearing a blue-and-white striped top that stopped a couple of inches short of the waist of her jeans. Guess I look okay tonight, she thought.

Harrison placed his hand on her back and guided her through the room, introducing her to people. The touch of his hand gave her a shiver.

"Hey, Alby? Where's Alby?" Harrison called.

A tall, lanky guy in black Buddy Holly glasses stepped out of the kitchen, carrying more bags of chips. He had spiky black hair, a silver ring in one ear, and a short, fuzzy beard.

The bags of chips were grabbed away before Alby could set them down on the table. He came up to Destiny and Harrison. "Maybe we should order some pizzas."

"You're the birthday boy," Harrison said. "Order anything you want."

"Hey, thanks."

"As long as *you* pay."

"Hey—nice guy." Alby turned to Destiny and his eyes went wide behind the big, black-framed glasses.

"This is Destiny," Harrison said. "Destiny, Alby."

"Nice to meet you," Destiny said.

Alby stared at her. "We met last night, remember?"

Destiny squinted at him. "I don't think so."

"Yeah. Sure, we did," Alby insisted. "At Club Sixty-One. Remember?"

"Club Sixty-One?" Destiny's mind spun. "No way. I stayed home with my little brother last night."

Alby turned to Harrison. "She has short-term memory loss," he said. "We studied it in Psych last term."

"I was home—" Destiny started.

"We danced. You and me," Alby said. "We had some Jell-O shooters. Remember? You used that fake I.D.? We laughed about that couple that got totally trashed and had to be kicked out? You wore those low-riding jeans."

"Oh, wow." Destiny began to realize what was going on.

And then Alby raised his head, and she saw the spot on his throat. The two pinprick red wounds on his neck.

"Oh, no. Oh, no."

She stared at the cut on Alby's throat—and ran from the room.

Chapter Twenty

"Now You Think I'm a Psycho Nut"

"I'm sorry. I can't really explain it," Destiny said, shaking her head.

Harrison had followed her out into the hall. A couple was still making out by the garbage cans. Through the open doorway, Destiny glimpsed Alby watching her from the middle of the living room, a puzzled expression on his face.

"You . . . don't know why you freaked?" Harrison asked. He squeezed her hand. "Your hand is ice cold. Are you okay? Do you need a doctor or something?"

"No. I'm fine now," Destiny said, heart still pounding like crazy. "I'd better go. I'm really sorry I ran out like that."

He studied her. "You sure you're okay?"

"Yeah. Totally. I just . . . uh . . . I can't explain it."

Actually, I *can* explain it. But you wouldn't

believe me, Harrison. If I told you that Alby ran into my vampire twin sister at the club last night, and she drank his blood, that wouldn't exactly go over, would it?

"You're shaking," Harrison said. "Can I drive you home?"

"No. I . . . brought my car," she replied. "I'll be fine." She forced a smile. "Now you think I'm some kind of psycho nut, don't you?"

He smiled back at her. "Yes, I do. Definitely."

"Great," she muttered, rolling her eyes.

"But I kinda like psycho nuts," Harrison said.

That made her feel a tiny bit better. She leaned forward and gave him a quick peck on the cheek. "See you at work tomorrow." Then she ran down the stairs and out to her car without looking back.

It was a hot, damp night. The steamy air made her cool skin tingle. She fumbled in her bag for her car key. "Where is it? Where is it?"

A wave of panic swept over her.

What did Livvy think she was doing? Except for her family and Ana-Li, everyone thought she had run off to another town with

Ross. But now, here she was parading around in the clubs that everyone went to.

Why was she showing herself like that? What were people supposed to think?

Livvy must not care what people think, Destiny decided. She must be so hungry, so desperate for blood she doesn't care if she comes out in the open.

Ari flashed into Destiny's mind. He had been dead for two weeks now, and Destiny thought about him every minute. Such a good, sweet person. He didn't deserve to die that way. Destiny missed him so much.

Livvy is desperate . . . so desperate, she murdered Ari. She didn't give a damn that I cared about him.

A tap on Destiny's shoulder made her cry out in surprise.

She turned and saw a flash of blond hair.

"Livvy?" she gasped. "Ohmigod! Livvy?"

The girl took a step back, her hand still in the air. "Sorry. Didn't mean to startle you."

Not Livvy. An attractive platinum-blond girl with green eyes, dark eyebrows, and dark purple lipstick on her lips. "Is the party in there?" she asked, pointing to Harrison's building.

Still shaken, Destiny nodded. "Yeah. Third floor. You can't miss it."

"Hey, thanks." The girl turned and strode to the building, blond hair waving behind her.

I can't keep doing that, Destiny told herself. I've got to stop seeing Livvy wherever I go.

She drove home, gripping the wheel with both hands, leaning forward in the seat, forcing herself not to think about anything but the driving.

Her cell rang. Ana-Li, she saw. She didn't pick up. I'll call her later when I've calmed down.

Entering her neighborhood, she braked at a stop sign. She could see Ari's house across the street, windows dark except for his parents' bedroom in the back. A sad house now.

A few minutes later, she pulled the Civic up the drive and stopped a few feet from the garage door. Dad was still not home, she saw. He's worked late every night this week. Mikey and I never see him.

She entered through the front door and saw Mikey jumping up and down on the living room couch. "Hey—what's up?" she called, pushing the door shut behind her. "Where is Mrs. Gilly?

Isn't she watching you tonight?"

"She's upstairs. In the bathroom," Mikey said.

Destiny could barely understand him. He had plastic fangs hanging from his mouth, and he wore a black cape over his slender shoulders.

Destiny rushed over to him and hugged him. He pulled free with a growl, snapping at her with the plastic fangs.

"Don't you know any other games?" she asked. "Do you have to play vampire all the time?"

"I'm not playing!" he insisted.

"Mikey, listen to me—"

"I'm not playing. I'm a *real* vampire," he shouted. And then he added, "Just like Livvy."

"But, Mikey—"

"Look," he said. "I'll prove it." He held out his hand.

Destiny gasped as she saw the deep red bite marks up and down his skinny arm.

Chapter Twenty-one
Dad Might Kill Livvy

"Dad, Mikey is seriously sick," Destiny said, shaking her head. "And I guess I don't have to tell you it's all Livvy's fault."

Dr. Weller had his elbows on his desk, supporting his chin in his hands. The fluorescent ceiling light reflected in his glasses. "His therapist says he's making progress."

Destiny sighed. She crossed her arms in front of her. "I'm not so sure. You saw his arm. Those bite marks . . ."

"Pretty awful," he agreed. He sat up straight, pulled off the glasses, and rubbed the bridge of his nose. "Mikey has suffered a terrible loss, Dee. We all have. But you and I are a little better equipped to deal with it. He's too young to know how to cope."

A dog howled in the holding pen in the back room, and that set off all the other dogs yipping and barking.

"We have to stop him from pretending to be a vampire all the time," Destiny said. She shuddered. "It's not helping him."

"And in a way, it might be," her dad said softly. "By playing the role, maybe it helps him work out his fears. Maybe it helps him deal with the frightening thoughts he's having."

Destiny stared at the floor. She didn't know what to say. And she hated seeing her father so sad and tired-looking. He's aged twenty years this summer, she thought.

When she finally looked up, he was crumpling the papers on his desk.

"Dad—what are you doing?"

He angrily ripped the papers in half.

"Dad—?"

"I want to bring Livvy home. I want to restore her to a normal life. Ross, too. But my work is going nowhere, Dee. I . . . I can't find the formula. I've missed time and time again. I'm a failure. We have to face the fact."

Destiny wanted to say something to comfort him. But what could she say?

"So many pressures," he muttered. "So many pressures . . ."

And that's when he told her about the

abandoned apartment building near campus. Vampires had been tracked there. Vampires were living there.

"My hunters and I . . . we have to clean the building out," he told her. "The pressure is on to take care of the vampire problem in Dark Springs. I'm the leader of the Hunters. I have no choice. My hunters and I have to go in there and kill as many vampires as we can. In two weeks. Sunday at dawn. After the night of the full moon. That's when we'll strike."

All Destiny could think about was Livvy and Ross.

Were they living in that unfinished apartment building too?

Could her father kill his own daughter?

He couldn't—could he?

"I'm sorry to lay this on you," Destiny told Ana-Li. "But I don't have anyone else I can tell."

Ana-Li sighed. "I just came to say good-bye, Dee. I'm leaving tomorrow morning. I . . . I'm so sorry I won't be here to help you."

She wrapped Destiny in a hug.

"I'll e-mail you as soon as I get moved into the dorm. I promise," Ana-Li said, raising one hand as if swearing an oath. "If I can't get my laptop hooked up, I'll call you."

"Thanks," Destiny said, holding onto her friend.

"What about the new boyfriend?" Ana-Li asked. "Can't you confide in him?"

"Harrison? He's been very sweet. And we've been seeing each other just about every night. But . . . I can't tell him about Livvy yet. I just can't. I don't know him well enough."

Ana-Li grinned at her. "But you'd like to know him really well—right?"

"Well . . . yeah. But I can't think about that now." Destiny started to pace back and forth along the room above the garage. She kept staring at Livvy's bed. Livvy's *empty* bed.

"I have to find a way to warn Livvy. Livvy and Ross."

"Even after she was so horrible to you?" Ana-Li asked. "Even after she dragged you off in that parking lot and threatened to drink your blood?"

Destiny stopped pacing. She gripped the back of her desk chair as if holding herself up. "She's my sister," she said through gritted teeth. A tear slid down one cheek. "She's my sister, and I want her back. For her sake. For Mikey's sake. For all of us."

She took a breath and let it out slowly. "But if Dad finds her in that apartment building near campus . . . if Dad finds her . . ." The words caught in her throat.

"He wouldn't drive a stake through Livvy's heart," Ana-Li insisted.

A chill ran down Destiny's back. "He might."

Destiny couldn't sleep that night. Her thoughts swirled round and round until the room spun and her head pounded.

"Dad might kill Livvy."

She pictured her mother, tall and blond and pretty, like her twin daughters. And so young. Destiny only remembered her mother young.

Her mother was bitten by a vampire, a vampire who wanted to take her away, to make her his. She killed herself instead. She killed herself to escape the vampire's clutches.

That's why Dad became leader of the Hunters. That's why he is determined to wipe them out. They took away the love of his life.

And that's why he has been searching for a

cure, a formula to restore vampires to a normal life. But he has failed. His daughter is a vampire, and he has failed to find a cure.

And now he will hunt her down. And his hatred for vampires will force him to kill her. If he doesn't do it, one of his hunters will.

Unless I get there first, Destiny thought, rolling onto her side, scrunching the sheet to her chin.

Unless I can warn Livvy.

But how?

After that fight in the club parking lot, I don't think she'll talk to me. If she sees me coming, she'll change into a creature and fly away. If I tell her what Dad and his hunters are planning, she won't believe me. She'll think it's a trick to get her to come home.

So . . . what can I do?

The ceiling spun above Destiny's head. Light and shadows danced crazily, like wild creatures let loose in the room. Somewhere in the distance, a siren wailed.

What can I do?

And then she had an idea.

Chapter Twenty-two
One Evil Dawn

Destiny sat straight up and kicked the covers away.

Yes. Yes.

Ross.

Ross will talk to me. Ross always liked me. And he was always easy to talk to.

I'll find Ross. I'll tell him what's going to happen. Then Ross can talk to Livvy. And maybe . . . maybe they'll both be saved.

I'll go at dawn, Destiny decided. When the vampires have been out all night and are falling asleep.

At least I have a plan. I'll go into that building. I'll find Ross. I'll tell him . . . I'll tell him . . .

She settled back down and shut her eyes. But she knew she'd never fall asleep this night.

At a few minutes before six, she crept silently down the stairs, into the dark kitchen, dishwasher light blinking, and out the back door. Her old

Civic refused to start until the third try. She looked to the house to make sure the grinding sounds hadn't awakened her father.

Then she slid the gearshift into drive and headed off, into a gray world, high clouds blocking the rising sun, bare black trees shivering in the cool, morning breeze.

Not many cars on the road. A few sleepy-eyed people on their way to early morning jobs.

Destiny realized she was gritting her teeth so hard, her jaw ached. This is the best time to look for Ross, she assured herself for the hundredth time. The vampires will all be heading in to sleep, weary after a night of prowling.

Will I be able to wake him? Will he recognize me?

Of course he will. He's still Ross.

She drove her car around the campus square. Squirrels scampered over the lawn. The sun still hadn't burned through the clouds.

A few moments later, Destiny pulled the car up to the side of the unfinished apartment building. She climbed out, legs rubbery, heart suddenly pounding. And gazed up the side of the redbrick wall at the rows of open, unglassed windows.

Two large crows stared back at her from a

third-floor window ledge. She heard a fluttering sound and saw a bat shoot into a window near the top.

"Oh, wow."

So many apartments, she thought. How will I ever find Ross?

I'll just have to be lucky, she decided. I have to save him and my sister.

Taking a deep breath, she made her way through the front entrance, into the dark lobby. She stepped past rolls of wire and cable and a stack of Sheetrock squares, past the open elevator shaft, and started up the concrete stairs.

Her shoes echoed hollowly in the stairwell. The only sound until she reached the first floor—and heard the moans and sighs and groans of the sleeping vampires. Squinting into the gray light, she gazed in horror at the row of open apartment doorways.

I'll start here, she decided, gripping the railing. I can't call out his name. It would wake everyone up. I'll have to peek into every apartment until I find him.

Her whole body trembling now, she forced herself to move away from the stairs, into the trash-cluttered hall, up to the first door.

I should have brought a flashlight. I thought there would be some sun. The pale, gray light from the hall windows seemed to lengthen the shadows and make everything appear darker.

Sticking her head through the doorless opening, Destiny peered into the dark apartment. She couldn't see anything, but she heard low, steady breathing. She took a step inside. Then one more step.

And in the soupy gray, she saw two girls asleep on their backs on low cots against the wall, dark hair spread over their pillows, mouths open revealing curled fangs that slid up and down with each breath they took.

Destiny backed into the hall. The next two apartments appeared empty. No furniture. No sounds of sleep.

A long, mournful sigh echoed down the hallway. It sent a shiver down Destiny's back.

She peered into the third apartment. And saw a scrawny, little man asleep on the floor, a pillow under his bald head, his sunken eyes wide open. Destiny gasped and backed away, thinking he could see her. But he was sound asleep.

Moans and harsh snoring followed her to the next apartment. A man and woman, sleeping on a bare mattress, holding hands, their fangs dripping with saliva.

Back into the hall. Nearly at the end now, and no sign of Ross. She stepped around a pile of trash, mostly newspapers and magazines, tossed carelessly against the wall.

The papers rustled. Destiny stopped. What made them move? There was no wind here.

She stared as the papers crinkled. She heard scratching sounds from underneath the pile. "Oh." She uttered a soft cry as two fat rats slithered out.

They turned and gazed up at her, staring for the longest while, as if challenging her.

Her whole body tensed, Destiny backed away. Are these really rats? she wondered. Or are they vampires in rat bodies?

The swooping bat in her living room flashed into her mind. Livvy? Had it been Livvy?

The two rats raised up on their hind legs and took a step toward Destiny. One of them bared its teeth and uttered a shrill hiss.

Destiny wanted to turn and run. But she knew she shouldn't turn her back on the advancing rats.

They stood still now, on their back legs,

long, pink tails whipping back and forth, scraping the concrete floor. Their eyes glowed dully like black pearls. They both opened their mouths and uttered warning screeches, furiously waving their front paws up and down in slashing motions.

I have to get away.

Destiny spun away from them, tried to run—and collided full force with a figure standing behind her.

"Hey—!" She stumbled and fell into him, and they both staggered back. Her cheek brushed the rough fabric of his sweater.

"Ross—?" She grabbed his shoulders to pull herself back on her feet, shoulders hard as bone. Not Ross.

"S—sorry," she choked out. "I didn't see you. I was—"

She stared at him. He was good looking. Young. About Destiny's age. Short, dark hair, dark eyes, a thin, straight nose.

Then he turned—and Destiny opened her mouth in a horrified gasp.

The other half of his face—*missing*! The flesh ended in the middle, a line right down the center of his face, giving way to solid skull.

Destiny stared open-mouthed, too horrified to breathe. No eye in the gaping, empty socket, no flesh over the toothless jaw.

Half a face, Destiny saw. Normal looking on one side, even handsome. An eyeless skull on the other half.

Trembling, Destiny tried to back away.

"What's wrong?" he whispered. His teeth clicked as he talked, and his single eye rolled around in its socket. "Don't be frightened. Don't worry. I'll save my *good* side for you, babe."

He grabbed her. Circled his arms tightly around her. Arms like bones—and powerful, clamping her to him.

"No, please—"

She couldn't breathe.

He held her so tightly, her ribs ached. Her chest felt about to burst.

He lowered his face to her. She could see both sides at once now, the skeleton and the good-looking face. Both grinning at her coldly, half-lips pulled back so she could see his teeth.

He pressed his lips to hers.

Ohh. She felt soft flesh and bone.

Her stomach heaved.

He pulled his mouth away quickly, single eye flashing.

And then she saw the fangs, yellow and curled, slide down from his open mouth.

"So sweet, so sweet," he whispered, sour breath washing over her, making her choke. And then he sank the disgusting fangs into her throat.

Chapter Twenty-three

"I Want to Go Back to my Old Life"

She felt a stab of pain.

Then heard a loud shout.

"GET AWAY FROM HER!"

The vampire seemed to spin to the voice. But then Destiny realized someone had pulled him off her. Another vampire, face hidden in shadow, had grabbed him by the shoulders.

"First come, first served," the half-faceless one said softly, teeth clicking. He tensed his body as if preparing for a fight.

"I don't think so," the other replied.

And then they flung themselves at each other. Growling, cursing, they wrestled from one side of the hall to the other, smashing each other against the concrete walls.

Gasping for breath, Destiny felt the pin-prick wounds in her neck as she tried to back away to safety.

They're fighting over which one gets me,

she realized. Frozen in horror, she watched the battle.

Their cries and shouts had awakened others, who stood in the dark doorways all down the hall, staring in silence as the two vampires slashed at each other, shoving and biting.

I'm pinned here, Destiny thought. I can't run. If I do, the others will get me.

She backed into a corner, hands pressed against the sides of her face, still gasping for breath.

Fighting over me . . .

Fighting to see who gets to drink my blood . . .

With his back to Destiny, the new arrival hoisted up the half-faced vampire by the waist, lifted him high over his head and, with a powerful heave, tossed him out an open window.

Destiny heard the vampire's scream as he fell down the side of the building. Down . . . down . . . And then the scream was replaced by an angry bird cry, which rose up until Destiny could see a hawk, wings spread wide, through the window, sailing up, turning and taking one last glance at her, then floating away.

And now the winner of the battle, panting

noisily, brushing his wet hair off his face, turned to claim his prize. He lurched toward Destiny arms outstretched . . .

. . . And Destiny recognized him. "Ross—!" she screamed. "Ross—it's me!"

His mouth dropped open. He wiped sweat from his eyes—and squinted at her in the inky light. "Destiny—?"

"Yes. Yes, it's me!"

"Whoa." He was still breathing hard, chest heaving up and down. He had deep scratch marks on one side of his neck, and a red welt had formed under one eye.

"I don't believe it," he said, shaking his head hard. Then he lurched forward and wrapped her in a hug. "Dee, I'm so glad to see you."

Destiny let out a sigh of relief. It *is* the same Ross, she thought.

She gazed over his shoulder and saw eyes staring at them in doorways all down the hall, cold faces, angry and frightening.

"Can we . . . go somewhere?" she whispered.

Ross took her by the hand and led her to the stairway. He helped her up the steep, concrete steps to the second floor. Then he led the way to a small apartment halfway down the hall.

The clouds had finally started to burn away, and morning sunlight peeked into the open window. Destiny hugged herself. The room still had the chill of night.

She glanced around quickly. A pile of clothes, mostly jeans and T-shirts, in one corner. A couch with one cushion missing. A metal folding chair. A clock radio on the floor. The only furnishings.

Ross led her over to the couch. "Dee, I can't believe you're here. I'm so happy to see you," he said. He motioned for her to sit down. Then he dropped down beside her, sweeping his hair back with both hands.

He's changed, Destiny thought, studying him. He used to have that spark in his eyes, that flash of fire. But it's gone. He looks so tired . . . exhausted. And not because of the fight with the other vampire.

"How are you?" he asked. "How's Mikey? And your dad?"

"Not great," Destiny replied. "It's been really hard with Livvy gone. I mean, it's hard to explain to yourself why—"

"Livvy," Ross interrupted, shaking his head.

"Livvy. Livvy. She's hard to figure, you know?"

"I . . . saw her the other night," Destiny continued, the words catching in her throat. "She was so horrible to me, Ross. Like she *hated* me. And what did I do to her? Nothing. I only wanted to talk with her."

"She's gotten weird," Ross said, lowering his head. "This was supposed to be so exciting. You know. Livvy and me. Living forever and everything. She promised. She promised me it would be awesome. But now . . ." He glanced to the window. "Now she usually doesn't want to hang with me. She's got new friends that she cares about."

Destiny nodded. She didn't know what to say. "Ross—?"

He kept his eyes down at the floor. "I'm so unhappy," he said finally. "I mean, this life is so hard. I wish . . . I wish I'd never followed Livvy."

"I'm sorry too," Destiny murmured.

"She likes it. I really think she does," he continued, finally turning to face her. "I don't understand it. But I think Livvy enjoys the excitement. You know, the adventure. She likes the . . . *badness* of it. And the idea that she never has to grow old."

Destiny nodded. "When she was little, her favorite cartoon was *Peter Pan*. You know. The Disney one. Now I guess she liked it because Peter and the Lost Boys never grew up, either.

"I don't know why I went with her," Ross said. He climbed to his feet and moved to the window. He leaned on the sill, keeping his back to the rising sunlight as he spoke. "It was crazy. I guess I went a little nuts or something. But now . . ."

He swallowed. "Now I'd give anything to have my old life back. I mean it, Dee. Anything. I'm so unhappy. I just want to see my sister again . . . and Mom and Dad. I just want—"

"Maybe it can happen," Destiny interrupted.

He squinted at her. "Why? Has your dad—?"

"No. He hasn't found anything. Not yet. But he's working on it, Ross. He won't quit till he finds a cure."

"That's great," Ross said. "I don't know how much more I can take. Really."

Destiny climbed to her feet and hugged herself tightly. "Listen, Ross, I came here for a reason. I came to warn you. The Hunters are going to come. They know about this place.

They're going to kill as many vampires as they can."

Ross nodded. He didn't seem surprised. "We knew they'd come after us sooner or later."

"You and Livvy have got to get out," Destiny said. "You've got to talk to her, Ross. She won't talk to me."

He scratched his head. "I . . . I'll try."

Destiny could feel her emotions tightening her throat. "You've got to tell her," she said. "You've got to tell her to get away from here. Maybe you can convince her, Ross. Have you told her you want to give up the vampire life? Maybe you can convince her too."

Ross hesitated. "I don't think so. Whenever I start to talk about it . . ." His voice trailed off in a sigh.

Destiny felt tears rolling down her cheeks. She didn't make any attempt to stop them. "Tell her. Tell her, Ross."

Ross nodded. "I'll see what I can do. Really. I'll try, Dee."

A sob escaped Destiny's throat. Tears blurred her vision. "Tell her I still love her," she choked out. "Tell her I'll do anything to have her back."

And then she ran, out the door of the shabby apartment and down the long hallway . . . ran away from this world of darkness . . . back to her own life.

Chapter Twenty-four
A Death in the Vampire Family

Is that Destiny?

Yes, of course it is.

Livvy hid behind a trash Dumpster and watched her sister run from the apartment building. Destiny dropped her bag, picked it up, then fumbled inside it for her car key.

What is she doing here so early? Livvy wondered. The sun is just coming up. Did she come to see me? Does she still think if she begs hard enough, I'll come home?

She watched Destiny stumble over a pile of broken bricks, then run to the side of the building. Destiny had such a distressed look on her face, Livvy felt a pang of guilt.

I didn't want to cause you so much sadness, Dee. What I did wasn't about you at all. It was about me. But you can't accept that, can you?

Because everything—*everything*—always had to be about you.

Destiny pulled open her car door and plunged inside.

You must have sneaked out of the house before dawn, Livvy thought. Now why would you pay me a visit at this hour? Do you think I know something about Ari? Is that it?

Think I know something about how poor Ari died? Well, Dee, you've got that right.

I do know about Ari. It was my stupid friend Monica. I warned her to be careful, to go slowly, a few sips at a time. But Monica never knows when to stop. She always wants more more more.

Suzie and I both got on her case when she told us she'd killed Ari. "I couldn't help it," Monica said. "I was so hungry, and I lost track. It was an accident. Really."

Accidents happen, right?

No way.

Not when it gets the whole town excited and upset. And the police. Monica should know better. She risked all of us for one night of pleasure. She's my friend, but she's also a stupid cow.

And yes, I felt bad about Ari. I mean, he was a geeky guy, totally clueless. Spending all his time on horror movies and *Star Trek* websites. But he was smart and funny too. And I know you really liked him.

Whatever.

It's done, okay. He's history.

So why did you come to see me this morning? To hear about how Ari died? How would that help you? It won't bring the poor guy back.

Livvy watched Destiny's car pull away, tires squealing. Again, she pictured the distressed look on her sister's face.

Sorry, Dee. I really am. But get over it.

Don't come here begging me to give up my new life.

Livvy licked her lips. Mmmm. A trace of the sweet blood lingered there.

That Alby is a good guy, she thought, shutting her eyes for a moment. Such sweet blood, almost like dessert. I'm going to bring him along slowly, so slowly he won't even notice.

The morning sun spread an orange glow around the apartment building. Livvy squinted at the brightening light.

I'd better get inside. The sun burns my eyes.

I don't have my shades.

She started toward the front door—then stopped.

Whoa. Hold on. Maybe Dee didn't come to see me.

Livvy bit her bottom lip, new thoughts flashing through her mind.

Maybe Dee came to see Ross.

Maybe she came at dawn hoping to find him without me around.

Has she been seeing Ross all along? Destiny always had a thing for him. I think she was really jealous when Ross decided he liked me better.

When Ross decided he loved me . . .

But Ross is so eager to connect to his old life. He begged me to let him see his family in line at the movie theater. Has he also been trying to get together with my sister?

Livvy darted into the darkness of the building. As she climbed the stairs, she could hear the groans and sighs of the sleeping vampires.

But she didn't feel the least bit sleepy. She had to get to the bottom of this.

Her shoes thudded the concrete floor as she ran down the long, narrow hallway toward

Ross's apartment. She edged past a stack of Sheetrock, then a pile of old newspapers.

Ross, please don't tell me you've been seeing Destiny. Please tell me she came to see me.

She stopped at the open doorway to Ross's apartment to catch her breath. Then she burst inside.

"Ross—?"

It took her eyes a few moments to adjust to the bright light that washed into the room from the window. Then Livvy spotted Ross—and she opened her mouth and screamed in horror.

"Ross? Noooooo! Oh, no! Please— NOOOOOOOO!"

Chapter Twenty-five
"It Won't Be Pretty"

Livvy staggered over to Ross's body. sprawled on his back on the floor. Legs spread. Hands raised, still gripping the wooden stake pushed through his chest.

Wooden stake . . .

Livvy gaped at the stake, a plank of light wood. The kind of wood scattered all over this unfinished building.

The stake had been driven through Ross's T-shirt, through the center of his chest. Through his heart.

And now he lay with his eyes wide open, blank, glassy . . . wide open . . . wide open as if still staring up at his attacker.

His head tilted to one side. His mouth hung open in a silent scream. Hands still gripping the stake.

"Ross—" Livvy uttered his name as she dropped down beside his lifeless body. "Oh, no, Ross. Oh, no."

Murdered.

She cradled his head in her arms.

Murdered. His body still warm.

And yes, she knew . . .

Holding onto the boy who had cared enough about her to follow her . . . the boy who had loved her so much, he became a vampire just to be with her. Holding onto Ross's lifeless head, Livvy knew who had murdered him.

Destiny.

She had seen Destiny running from the building. In such a hurry to get away.

Destiny came at dawn, sneaked into the building to kill Ross.

And why?

Cradling Ross's head, Livvy shut her eyes and thought hard.

Why?

To pay me back for deserting the family.

No.

Oh, wait. I get it. I totally get it. That was Destiny's way of paying me back for Ari.

Destiny thinks I killed Ari. So she paid me back by killing Ross.

Poor, sweet, innocent Ross.

Could Destiny really do this? Is she angry

enough? Desperate enough? Crazy enough?

Yes. I saw her face as she ran from the building.

I saw the tears running down her cheeks. Saw the wild look in her eyes. The fear mixed with anger. Mixed with hatred.

She hates me so much, she murdered the boy who loved me.

With a long howl of sorrow, Livvy hugged Ross's lifeless head, pressed it to her, ran her hands through his hair one last time.

"You can't get away with this, Destiny," she said out loud in a cold, hard voice. "I'll find a way to pay you back. Yes, I will. And it won't be pretty."

Chapter Twenty-six

"I'd Like to Tear Destiny to Bits"

Sobbing now, Livvy gently lowered Ross's head to the floor. She climbed unsteadily to her feet, pulled a blanket off his narrow cot, and covered his body with it, tugging the ends of the blanket around the wooden stake.

Livvy's whole body shuddered.

What must that feel like? To have a sharpened wooden stake shoved through your chest into your heart?

She couldn't imagine the agony Ross must have felt. The pain from the puncture. Waves of pain shooting through his body like electric currents . . . as he realized . . . realized he was about to lose his life.

She grabbed her own chest. She suddenly felt as if she couldn't take another breath.

I have to get out of here.

Still holding her chest, she turned away from Ross and stumbled to the door. She started to breathe again out in the hall. And then she climbed the stairs and ran to her room, shoes thudding noisily . . . How wonderful to be able to make a noise, to be alive, to run . . . Ross will never run again . . . never.

Sunshine poured in through the open window. She fumbled on her dresser top until she found her sunglasses. Slipped them on, blinking, heart thudding, two pictures remaining in her mind.

Two pictures refusing to fade . . .

Ross dead on the floor, his hands—his beautiful hands—gripping the wooden stake that killed him.

And Destiny running from the apartment building, tears running down her cheeks, her expression so angry, so upset.

Livvy paced back and forth in the small, nearly bare living room, her hands balled into tight fists. The anger boiled up in her until she felt ready to explode.

I'd like to follow Dee home right now, she thought. Burst in at breakfast and drag her away. Slash her, tear her to bits with my own hands.

Oh, wow. Could I do that? Could I do that to Dad and Mikey?

Maybe. It's not like I was ever appreciated at home. Or like anyone tried to understand me. Destiny was always the princess. And I was always . . . trouble.

Well, I tried to escape all that. I tried to escape my family. I tried to do them a favor. Go away so I wouldn't be trouble anymore.

So why couldn't my sister leave things alone?

Stay home and be the good twin, Dee. Stay with Dad and Mikey and be the princess.

Don't come here and kill someone I really care about.

She could feel the anger rising again, feel all her muscles tensing. And then suddenly, she felt as if she weighed a thousand pounds.

So weary.

Out all night, and then come home to such horror.

She yawned. I need to sleep. Sleep will help me think more clearly. I can make a plan. I can—

She heard a scraping sound from the other room. Footsteps.

"Monica? Suzie? Are you in here?"

No answer.

Livvy stared at the doorway to the bedroom.

She took a few steps. "Who's in there?"

And as she stared, a figure stepped out of the shadows. He smiled at her.

"You?" Livvy cried. "What are *you* doing in here?"

Chapter Twenty-seven
Blood on Her Lips

*P*atrick came toward her slowly, hands in the pockets of his black denim jeans. His dark eyes locked on hers. As his grin widened, she saw the dimples in his cheeks—and remembered the way he smiled at her at the dance club.

"How long have you been here? What are you doing here?" she asked.

He shrugged. "Just waiting for you."

Livvy rushed to him. "Oh, Patrick. I'm so glad to see you. Something . . . something *terrible* has happened."

His smile faded quickly. "What is it? Are you okay?"

"No. No, I'm not. I . . . I . . ." She grabbed his arm and pulled him out of the apartment. "You've got to see. I . . . I'm so upset."

She pulled him through the hall, then down the stairs to Ross's apartment. They stepped through a square of bright sunlight on the floor, to the back of the apartment, to the body covered by a purple blanket, wooden stake poking straight up into the air.

"Here," Livvy said, trembling. She tugged away the blanket.

Patrick gasped and bent to examine Ross's body closer. "Oh, no," he murmured. "I don't believe this."

Angrily, he grabbed the stake in both hands and ripped it from Ross's chest. Then he flung it against the bedroom wall, where it hit and clattered to the bare floor.

He turned to Livvy, his features tight with anger. "Who did this? We can't let them get away with this."

"He . . . was my friend," Livvy said in a whisper. "He was a good guy. He . . ."

Patrick leaned his back against the wall and brushed a hand through his long, brown hair. "Murdered in his own apartment," he murmured. "He was your friend?"

Livvy nodded, tears running down her cheeks.

He raised his eyes to her and studied her. "When did this happen? Do you have any idea who did it?"

Livvy hesitated.

Yes, I have an idea who did it.

But I can't tell him.

I can't turn my sister over to him so easily. I want to handle her myself. I want to make Destiny pay for what she did. I don't want someone else to get the revenge *for* me.

"No. I don't have a clue," Livvy said, lowering her eyes to the floor. "It probably happened this morning. I'm sure Ross was out all night. His body . . . his face . . . it was still warm when I came in here."

Patrick narrowed his eyes at her. "Do you always come in to see him early in the morning?"

"Uh . . . no," Livvy replied. "Not usually."

"Well then, why did you come to his apartment this morning?" Patrick asked.

He sounded suspicious. Livvy didn't like the question.

"I wanted to ask him something. I wanted to ask Ross if he knew a guy I met last night." A total lie. Was Patrick buying it?

He seemed to. He scratched his head. "And you can't think of anyone who had a grudge against Ross? Who might've wanted revenge or something? No enemies? You were his friend, Livvy. No one comes to mind?"

She shook her head. "No. No one." She glanced down at the body and let out a sob. "I . . . I'm really going to miss him."

Patrick crossed the room quickly and wrapped Livvy in a hug. She pressed her hot, damp cheek against his. He tightened his arms around her waist.

It felt good to be held by someone, someone solid and strong.

Livvy raised her face to his and kissed him. She wrapped her hands around the back of his neck and held his head as they kissed.

"Mm." She let out a sound as she felt his teeth bite into her lips. He pressed his mouth against hers, and she felt a shock of pain.

Suddenly, he ended the kiss. He pulled his face away, then lowered it to hers again—and licked the blood off her lips.

Livvy realized she was breathing hard, her heart racing. For the first time in her life, she felt dizzy from a kiss.

Patrick held her tightly, licking the top lip clean, then the bottom. When he backed away, he had her blood on his lips.

"I'll see you later," he said, and vanished from the room.

"Yeah. Later," she repeated. She stood unsteadily, eyes clamped shut, waiting for her heart to stop racing. And then . . . she thought about Destiny.

Destiny, who had murdered Ross.

Chapter Twenty-eight
Livvy's Revenge

A few days later, unable to forgive Destiny, unable to control her rage, Livvy found the Four Corners Diner. Peering through the front window, she saw Destiny behind the counter.

Seeing her sister working so calmly, so normally, as if nothing had happened . . . as if she hadn't murdered someone who'd been close to them both . . . made Livvy boil with anger.

What can I do? How can I pay her back for this?

What could she have been thinking? How could Destiny hate me *so much* that she would murder Ross?

Heart pounding, Livvy made her way to the back of the restaurant. Then she used her powers to transform into a tiny, white mouse.

Down on all fours, she found a crack in the back wall. She squeezed through it, into the kitchen. Creeping along the molding, Livvy moved silently toward the front. The aroma of frying eggs and bacon made her stand up and sniff the air with her pink nose.

As she stood up, the young man behind the fry grill came into view. Very nice looking, Livvy thought. Check out those big, brown eyes. And he looks like he works out.

He turned away from the grill. Livvy ducked under a cabinet.

"Tuna salad on whole wheat," Destiny called from the front. "And Harrison, are you working on that cheeseburger rare?"

So his name is Harrison, Livvy told herself.

She started to feel hungry. Not from the smell of the food frying on the grill—but from the look of Harrison's broad shoulders, those eyes that crinkled at the corners, that long neck, the perfect throat . . .

She let out a soft squeak.

Oh, wow. Control yourself, Livvy. Did he hear you? She pressed tighter under the cabinet.

Why did I come here? She wondered, staring up at Harrison.

To spy on Destiny, of course. To see her face, the face of a murderer. Why? Well . . .

Because . . . Because . . .

I'm not sure.

I'm so confused and upset, I can't think straight.

Destiny appeared in the kitchen, carrying a stack of dirty dishes. She dropped them into a basket on the sink counter.

"Whew." She wiped her forehead with the back of her hand, then washed her hands in the sink. Livvy watched her walk over to Harrison.

"How's it going?" Destiny put a hand on Harrison's shoulder.

"Not bad," he replied, scraping the grill. "Want some eggs or something? A little lunch break?"

"No, thanks. Check this out." She held up a coin. "A quarter. That table of four—they tipped me a quarter."

Harrison stared at it. "You and I split that, right? When do I get my share?"

They both laughed. The quarter fell from Destiny's hand and rolled onto the floor.

Then Livvy watched them kiss, a long, tender kiss.

And she knew what she wanted to do.

Harrison is my guy. This is going to be so *sweet*.

Destiny, dear, let's see how eager you are to kiss your lovely Harrison after I turn him into a vampire!

Part Six

Chapter Twenty-nine

The Party Crasher

"I think you're definitely helping Mikey," Destiny said.

Harrison shrugged. "I didn't do anything."

"He responds to you," she replied. "He likes you. I mean, you got him to come out of the Bat Cave—his room—and actually throw a Frisbee around in the backyard. That was an amazing accomplishment."

"Yeah, true," Harrison agreed. "That poor guy seemed so stressed out when he got outside. Until I made him chase after the Frisbee a few times, he was shaking like a leaf. He kept gazing up at the sky, checking out the tree limbs. I don't know what he expected to find up there."

He expected to find Livvy, Destiny thought.

But Harrison doesn't know that.

She told Harrison that Mikey had a lot of problems because their mother had died so suddenly. She hadn't told Harrison anything about

Livvy. He didn't even know she had a twin sister.

Destiny felt her throat tighten. She had been thinking about Livvy. Did Ross talk to her? Did he pass on my message to her?

It had been three days, and she hadn't heard from Ross or her sister.

Destiny chewed her bottom lip. Should I go back there and talk to Ross again? Was sneaking over there at dawn a waste of time? Is Livvy just going to ignore my visit?

Harrison pulled the car to the curb. Destiny slid down the visor and checked her lipstick in the mirror. She gazed out at the row of townhouses, aging three-story buildings—paint peeling and shingles missing—that had been turned into apartments for community college students.

Lights blazed in the front windows of the house on the right. And Destiny could hear rap music blaring without even opening the car door.

"Do I look okay?" she asked. She wore a light blue tank top, baggy, white shorts, and flip-flops. It was a steamy hot July night and she wanted to be comfortable.

Harrison smiled and nodded. "Awesome."

He started to open his door, then stopped. "Are you getting tired of these crowded, noisy parties?"

"No way," Destiny said without having to think about it. "I'm meeting some nice people. And it kinda makes me feel like I'm already part of the scene. You know. Like I'm already in college."

She climbed out of the car and straightened her shirt. She saw groups of young people on the grass in front of the building. Several sat on the stoop, cans of beer in their hands. Two large golden Labs with red bandannas around their necks chased each other across the street and back.

Harrison took her hand and they walked up the stoop, stepping around two girls on the steps who were smoking—both talking heatedly at once—and into Harrison's friend's apartment.

Destiny stepped into the big, smoky front room, filled with people her age in shorts and jeans, sprawled over the furniture, standing in clumps, shouting over the deafening music. She recognized some girls she met at Alby's birthday party and hurried over to say hi to them.

Livvy was always the party person, she thought. But I'm starting to enjoy them more. Maybe because I'm older now—and being out of high school makes *everyone* more relaxed.

Harrison introduced her to Danny, his best friend from high school. He was a short, stocky guy, kind of funny-looking with tiny, round eyes on top of a bulby nose, and thick, steel wool hair standing up on his head.

He and Harrison walked off talking, and Destiny crossed the room to get a Coke. She ran into Alby at the food table, and they hung out for a while.

Destiny tried not to stare at the bandage on Alby's neck. But it made her very uncomfortable. She made an excuse and hurried away.

People were scattered all over the townhouse, and Destiny gave herself a tour. Wish I could live away from home, she thought. The fun of college is being away from home, living on your own for the first time.

But why even think about it? No way she could leave Dad and Mikey now.

She returned to the front room and talked to some people she'd met at the diner. A couple of guys hit on her, and she brushed them off easily.

After a while, she realized she hadn't seen Harrison for a long time. She glanced at her watch. She hadn't seen him for at least half an hour.

Weird.

Destiny gazed around the room. Harrison, where are you?

She saw Alby in the corner with a skinny, red-haired girl a foot taller than him, and made her way through the crowd to him. "Have you seen Harrison?" She had to shout over the loud voices and the booming rap music.

Alby shook his head. "No. Not for a while. Do you know Lily?"

No. Destiny didn't know Lily. She stayed and talked to her for a while. She kept expecting Harrison to appear at her side, but—no sign of him.

She searched the back rooms and the kitchen, piled high with garbage and empty beer and soda cans. He's got to be here somewhere, she thought.

Doesn't he wonder where I am?

Destiny returned to her spot in front of the fireplace in the living room. A few minutes later, Harrison turned from the drinks table, spotted her, and his eyes went wide, as if he was surprised to see her there.

He carried two cans of Coors and hurried over to her. "Here's the beer you wanted," he said. "How'd you get back here so fast?"

Destiny stared at him. "Excuse me? I didn't ask you for a beer."

He crinkled up his face, confused. "Of course, you did. Outside on the stoop, you—"

"Huh? Outside?"

Destiny's heart leaped up to her throat. She narrowed her eyes at Harrison, her mind spinning.

Outside.

He was talking to me outside on the stoop.

But no. No. It wasn't me.

Livvy!

·

Chapter Thirty
Livvy and Harrison

Destiny handed the beer back to Harrison and took off. She heard him shouting to her, but she didn't turn around.

Livvy is here. On the front stoop.

Did Ross talk to her? Did he convince her to come see me?

She bumped into a couple leaning on the wall by the door who had their arms around each other, cheeks pressed together. They both let out startled cries as Destiny pushed past them.

"Sorry," she called.

She pushed the screen door open and burst out onto the stoop. "Livvy? Are you here?" she called.

A blond girl in a red halter top and jeans spun toward Destiny.

"Livvy—?"

No.

Destiny ran down the steps onto the grass. The sun had gone down. The moon floated low in a clear, purple sky dotted with stars.

The people on the lawn were all shadows. A few couples were lying in the grass, wrapped up in each other. A circle of guys down near the sidewalk were singing a Beatles song at the top of their lungs.

"Livvy? Are you here?"

Destiny cupped her hands around her mouth and shouted. "Livvy? Livvy?"

No. No answer. Gone.

But she had been here. Harrison had talked to her. And thought he was talking to Destiny.

Did she do that deliberately? Did Livvy come here to trick Harrison? Was it some kind of joke she was playing on Destiny?

Destiny gazed around the front lawn. Music boomed from the open windows. "Livvy? Livvy? Please?"

Then Destiny saw the bat. It fluttered off a slender tree near the curb and flapped slowly toward her. Eyes glowing, the bat swooped low over her head, then spun away and floated toward the street.

Heart pounding, Destiny turned and chased after it.

The bat floated slowly, low to the ground, its wings spread wide, gliding easily. Destiny ran under it, reaching for it with both hands, calling her sister's name breathlessly.

"Livvy, stop! Please—!"

The bat swooped away, just out of her reach.

Running hard, Destiny made another grab for the bat—and missed.

"Ohh—!" Destiny let out a cry as she ran full force into the side mirror of a parked car. The mirror hit her chest. Pain shot through her ribs. She staggered back.

She raised her eyes in time to see the bat vanish into the inky night sky.

Livvy, why did you come? she wondered. If you didn't want to talk to me, what were you doing here?

Chapter Thirty-one

"You're Still Connected to Your Sister"

Livvy swooped to the side of the abandoned apartment building, fluttered high against the wall, then dropped gently onto the sill of a glass-less window. The night air felt cool on her wings. For a moment, she thought she might turn around and fly out again, fly away from her troubled thoughts, cover herself in the darkness above the trees.

But no. She changed her mind and scuttled inside, shutting her eyes and willing herself to change back to the body that was familiar to her—and unfamiliar at the same time.

Here I am, Livvy Weller once again. Only I'm not really Livvy Weller. I'm someone else, someone new.

She took a deep breath. It always took a while for her heartbeats to slow from the racing rhythm of a bat's heart. And it took a minute or two for her eyes to adjust to normal, for the night vision to fade, for her hearing to return.

Livvy reached for the floor lamp she had found on the street. Would it work? The electrical generator downstairs was usually broken. She clicked it, and a triangle of pale, yellow light washed over the floor.

"Oh." She blinked as Patrick climbed up from the floor, dusted off the seat of his faded jeans, torn at both knees, and slowly ambled over to her.

She laughed. "Don't you ever knock?"

He grinned, showing those dimples, and pointed behind him. "No door."

She kissed him on the cheek. His skin felt cool and smooth.

"Where've you been?" he asked.

She gave him a sexy smile. "Like it's *your* business?"

"Yes, it is my business," he said, smile fading. He swept a hand back through his dark hair. It had been brushed straight back, but now he'd messed it up. "I . . . I'm interested in you, Liv. I like you, okay? So I want to make sure you don't mess up."

She narrowed her eyes at him. "Mess up? Mess up what?"

He shrugged. "Everything."

Livvy ran her finger down the side of his cheek. "What are you talking about?"

"Where were you tonight?" he asked again.

"Out flying around," she said. "You know. The usual."

He turned those dark, deep eyes on her, and she could feel their power. "You're lying, Liv. Why would you lie to me unless you knew you were out looking for trouble tonight?"

Livvy stared back at him. Was he hypnotizing her or something? Using his powers to invade her mind?

She turned away, but she could still feel the strange power of his stare.

"You went to your sister's party," Patrick said. "You pretended to be your sister, and you fooled her boyfriend, that guy Harrison."

Livvy let out a groan. "I don't believe this. So you're *spying* on me?"

He nodded. "Yes. Why did you do it, Liv? Explain that to me."

Livvy shrugged. "I don't know. I . . . I just don't know. For fun, maybe."

Patrick shook his head. He crossed the room to her. "You didn't do it for fun. You did it because you're still connected to your sister."

"Connected? What the hell is that supposed to mean?" Livvy snapped.

"You've chosen a new life, right?" Patrick asked. "You're one of us now. But you're not really here yet, Liv. You're not whole."

"Not whole?"

"You won't be whole as long as you have a soft spot in your heart."

Livvy stared at him, hands on her waist. "You mean for Destiny? Listen—"

"Your heart still beats for your sister," Patrick said. "You still care about her."

He's wrong, Livvy told herself. I hate Destiny. Hate her! She killed Ross.

"You're crazy," she snapped at Patrick. "I just went to that party to mess with Destiny's mind."

"But, why?" Patrick demanded. "See? You've proven my point, Liv. Why did you go to mess with Destiny's mind? Why did you go to that party? Because you still care about her. You still care what she thinks."

"That is *so* wrong," Livvy insisted.

Patrick softened his tone. "You know I'm right. Admit it. Admit it."

"Stop trying to push me around," Livvy said.

"Listen to me," he said. He wrapped his arms around her. "Listen to me," he repeated, whispering the words now. "You want to be immortal?"

"Of course."

"Then you have to break all ties with the other world."

"I . . . I don't know if I can do that."

"Well then, you have no choice. Don't you see, Livvy? Don't you see the answer? You will never truly be an immortal—*until your sister is one of us!*"

Chapter Thirty-two
A Date with a Vampire

"Destiny a vampire too?" Livvy stared hard at Patrick. "Yes. I like that idea."

The perfect revenge for what Destiny did to Ross, Livvy thought. Why didn't I think of it?

Maybe I do still care too much about her. Maybe that's why I didn't imagine a revenge this good.

"Yes," she told Patrick. "You might be right. Destiny would be much better off as a vampire. And then I wouldn't have to think about her, about my family back home."

"I knew you'd agree," Patrick said, sitting down on the window ledge, gazing up at the nearly full moon. "Most people finally agree with me."

"It's not like you're an egotist or anything," Livvy said.

He laughed. "I like you, Liv. I really do. And I think I'm really going to like your sister too."

Livvy narrowed her eyes at him. "Like Destiny? What do you mean?"

"I'll go after Destiny myself and turn her into an immortal. You take care of the new boyfriend. Harrison Palmer." He grinned. "You'll enjoy that, right?"

Livvy nodded. "It won't be hard work. I already spent time with Harrison at that party tonight. We hit it off really well. And he didn't have a clue I wasn't Destiny."

"Excellent!" Patrick rubbed his hands together. "A little project for the two of us."

He wrapped his arms around her waist in a tight hug. Then he kissed her hard, grinding his teeth against her lips until she cried out in pain—and in pleasure.

Destiny arrived at the diner and found Mr. G. behind the grill. "Where's Harrison?" she asked, sliding behind the counter.

"Some kind of mix-up at school," Mr. G. shouted over the crackling and hissing of the eggs and bacon. "He had to go straighten it all out. Don't look for him today. Once you go in that administration building, they don't let you out."

Destiny went to work, clearing dirty dishes off tables, refilling coffee cups, taking orders. Breakfast was the busiest part of the day. A lot of the professors, instructors, and other college workers stopped here before heading to their offices.

"I asked for rye toast, not white."

"Could you top this cup off for me? No— decaf. Make sure it's decaf."

"I asked for *extra* crisp bacon. Look at these soggy things."

Breakfast was the busiest time—and the most difficult.

Destiny wondered what kind of trouble Harrison was having. He hadn't mentioned anything to her at the party last night.

The party . . .

Luckily, Harrison hadn't seen her chase after the bat. If he had, he'd think she was totally nuts!

And of course she didn't tell him he'd spent half an hour talking with her vampire twin. If Harrison knew the truth, he'd freak.

He's a great guy, Destiny thought. I wish I could confide in him. Tell him everything. But I don't want to lose him . . .

A young man leaned over the counter, staring at her.

She shook her head hard, forcing away her troubled thoughts. "Sorry. I didn't see you there." She wiped her hands off on a towel, picked up a menu, and carried it over to him.

He smiled. He had the cutest dimples in his cheeks. Dark eyes, very round and wide, dark hair brushed straight back over his broad forehead. "You were off on some other planet," he said.

She handed him the menu. "Just daydreaming. How long were you watching me?"

He shrugged. "A little while. You look like someone I know."

She studied him. "Oh, really? Are you from Dark Springs?"

"No. Not really. I mean, I am now. I teach across the street. I'm a teaching assistant. For Professor Clark. Heard of him?"

"No. Sorry. I'm starting there this fall. What do you teach?"

"English. Creative writing, actually." He lowered his eyes to the menu.

"I'm very into creative writing," Destiny said. "Maybe I'll be in your class sometime."

He smiled. Again those dimples. "I'd like that."

How old was he? Maybe twenty? Except his eyes looked older somehow.

He stuck out his hand. "My name is Patrick."

She reached over the counter to shake it. "Destiny Weller. Do you know what you want?"

He eyed her meaningfully. "I'm thinking about it." He held onto her hand for the longest time.

Destiny could feel herself blushing. She wasn't sure why. Something about the way his eyes locked on hers?

"Guess you have a lot of time for daydreaming in this job," Patrick said.

She shrugged. "Once the breakfast crowd leaves, it gets kinda quiet."

His grin grew wider. "And what do you daydream about?"

She grinned back at him. "Things that are none of your business."

"Didn't you daydream this morning that a nice guy was going to come in, order ham and eggs, and ask you out for Friday night?"

"Is that what you want?" Destiny pulled out

her pad. Why was her hand shaking like that? She suddenly felt fluttery. "Ham and eggs?"

She looked up to see his dark eyes trained on hers. "Yes, that's what I want. Ham and eggs. And for you to go out with me Friday night."

"And how do you want the eggs?" Destiny couldn't remove her eyes from his gaze. It was as if he held her there, froze her with those deep, dark-jeweled eyes.

Suddenly, she felt very frightened. *This isn't right. Something very wrong is happening here. I feel like . . . a prisoner.*

"Scrambled, please," he said. "And could I have a toasted bagel with that? And what time should I pick you up Friday night?"

His eyes . . . the stare was so intense, it made Destiny's head hurt.

Then slowly the pain faded. And she felt comfortable again. No. More than comfortable. She felt as if everything was floating. As if she were floating off the floor. And the whole diner became soft, and shimmering, and bright. Not real . . . not real at all.

And she saw things in Patrick's eyes. She saw clouds and blue sky, and a pale, white moon, fluffy like tissue paper, round and full.

A full moon in Patrick's eyes. And he was saying something to her. But she was floating now, and he was so far away, his voice so distant and muffled.

What was he saying?

Something about Harrison.

No. Harrison and I don't have an exclusive arrangement. No, Patrick, I'm free to go out with anyone I want. Yes, I'd love to see you Friday. Can you pick me up at home?

Yes, that would be great.

And what will we do Friday night?

She struggled to hear his voice, muffled by a strong wind, the wind that blew behind the full moon in his eyes. All that blue sky, so clear and bright, and the full moon trembling in the middle of it.

What did you say? You want to take me into Drake Park, sink your fangs into my throat, and feed on my warm blood?

Oh, yes. Excellent. That sounds awesome.

Yes. I'm definitely up for that.

And then Destiny felt as if she were sinking. Suddenly heavy, she dropped from the clouds. The blue sky faded away, taking the full moon with it. And she stood heavily behind the counter, leaning on the yellow Formica, in the darkness of the diner, the smell of grease and bacon invading her nose, and stared at the young man with the dimples, sitting on the stool across from her.

What was his name? Patrick?

Yes. Patrick and I are going out Friday night after work.

I'll have to be careful not to let Harrison know.

"I'll get those eggs," Destiny said, taking the menu from Patrick. "Anything to drink?"

"Just your blood."

He didn't say that. Destiny, why are you making up these things? Why can't you concentrate this morning?

"Coffee," he said. "Black is fine."

"You got it," she said.

"I'm looking forward to Friday," Patrick called after her.

Chapter Thirty-three
Harrison and Livvy

Livvy met Harrison at the Cineplex at the Dark Springs Mall at eight o'clock. A warm night, the air heavy and wet. She wore a white shirt over a sleeveless green tank top and white shorts. Something Destiny would wear.

She had put on clear lip gloss, a dab of peach-colored eye shadow. Totally boring, Livvy thought. But Destiny likes that clean-cut, all-American-girl look.

Can I fool Harrison into thinking I'm my sister? Livvy watched him climb out of his car and come hurrying toward her. Well, Harrison was totally clueless at that party. No reason to think he'll figure it out tonight.

I'll bet Destiny hasn't even told him about me.

Afraid she'll frighten him away by making her family seem too weird.

Well, guess what, Harrison, my boy? You *should* be frightened. Because an evil vampire is out to get you—namely me.

Tonight I'm going to start getting you ready. No big deal, guy. A few sips of blood from your lovely throat. You'll hardly feel it, a big healthy hunk like you.

So sweet . . . I know you're going to taste so sweet.

Once we get started, we won't want to stop, will we? Sunday night is the full moon. That's your big night, Harrison. Sunday night when the moon is at its height, you and I will hook up in the best way.

We will mix our blood. I'll drink yours and you'll drink mine. It's so sexy and so delicious and so . . . *hot*, Harrison. Wait and see.

I'm getting all tingly just thinking about Sunday night.

Oh, wow. I just want a taste. I'm *dying* for a taste, Harrison. Can you see how much I want you?

He's so cute and nice and . . . sincere. That's why you like him, isn't it, Dee? That's why he's your new guy.

Well, how are you going to like him after Sunday night when he's one of us? A vampire, Dee. Your summer hunk is going to be a vampire.

Will you still go to his house parties? Still

hang out with him on campus?

I don't think so.

Hey, don't blame me, sister. It's all *your* fault. I'm just paying you back. You murdered Ross. You came into my building at dawn and murdered my boyfriend.

Did you really think I would just hang back and not do anything at all?

You're going to pay, Dee. Patrick and I will see to that.

Where are you tonight? Probably home thinking you're safe and sound. Well, Patrick will be there soon. Sunday night the two of you will mix *your* blood under the light of the full moon.

Then you can rejoin Harrison—forever. You can have him forever, Dee, because you'll be an immortal too.

The perfect revenge? I think so.

And then Patrick and I . . .

Patrick and I . . .

Livvy pictured Patrick, tall and strong. A leader. Smart and quick.

But with those dimples. Those adorable dimples and the wavy, brown hair. Is he to die for? Yes.

She thought about the way he held her so tightly, as if she were his prisoner. And she thought about his kisses, tender for only a second, and then so hard, so hard and passionate, they hurt.

Blood on my lips. As if he *wanted* to hurt me.

Cruel kisses. Exciting and frightening at the same time.

Like Patrick.

And now Harrison came trotting up to her, jamming his car keys into his jeans. He flashed her a smile. "Hey, Dee. Am I late?"

"No. Right on time."

"You look great."

"Thanks."

He motioned to the movie theater. "So you want to see something tonight?"

Livvy wrapped her arm in his. She licked her lips. "Wouldn't you rather take a walk?"

Chapter Thirty-four
Destiny and Patrick

Destiny balanced the cordless phone on her shoulder as she used her hands to check the oven. "Dad, I thought you were coming home tonight," she said into the phone.

"I can't, Dee." Dr. Weller sounded tired, his voice hoarse. "We're down to the crunch here."

"The crunch? What do you mean?"

"Sunday night is the full moon. My hunters and I are going into that abandoned apartment building at dawn Monday morning. I've got to get everyone prepared. I—"

"Hold on a sec, Dad," Destiny said. "Mikey's pizza is burning."

She pulled on oven mitts and lifted the pizza tray from the oven. Then she carried it over to the white Formica kitchen counter. "Hey, Mikey—it's almost dinnertime!" she shouted. "It just has to cool."

She lifted the phone back to her ear. "Dad?

Are you still there? I'm terrified about this whole thing. Do you really have to go into that building?"

Destiny never told her father that she'd already been inside it. Never told him how strange and frightening it was with vampires—dozens of them—settled in the empty apartments.

She knew he'd be furious that she took such a risk.

But now *he* was determined to take an even bigger risk. To attack the vampires in the building at dawn as they slept, to kill as many as he could.

"Dad, do you really think these vampires will just keep on sleeping as you wipe them out one by one? Don't you think they might fight back?"

A long silence at the other end.

"We've taken all precautions," he replied finally. "We'll be heavily armed against them. We're going to surprise them, Dee. They won't know what hit them."

"But, Dad—"

"I can't talk about it, Dee. When is Mrs. Gilly supposed to come take care of Mikey?"

"At seven. I hope she comes on time. I'm going out tonight."

"With Harrison?"

"No. A new guy. I met him at the diner."

Why am I going out with a new guy? What about Harrison? What if he finds out? Why did I say yes to Patrick?

Destiny couldn't remember.

"Well, make sure Mikey eats his dinner," Dr. Weller said. "And tell him—"

Destiny's phone beeped.

"Dad, I have another call. Can you hold on one sec?"

She pressed the flash button and waited for the second caller to come on. "Hello?"

"It's Mrs. Gilly, Dee. Hi."

"Oh, hi. I have my dad on the other line, so—"

"I'm terribly sorry. I can't come tonight to take care of Mikey. My cousin Jill is sick, and I have to hurry over there."

"Oh." Destiny's brain raced. That means I can't go out. I have to stay and take care of Mikey. "Sorry about your cousin. Thanks for calling."

Mrs. Gilly hung up after a few more apologies.

Mikey entered the room, stood on tiptoes to sniff the pizza on the counter, and went to the fridge. "Sit down," Destiny told him. "I'll slice your pizza for you."

She realized she'd forgotten about her dad. She clicked the phone. "Are you still there? Mrs. Gilly can't come. I'll stay with Mikey."

"What about your date?" Dr. Weller asked. "Can you call him?"

"Uh . . . no." Why didn't she get Patrick's cell number? "Guess I'll just have to tell him when he gets here. Well . . . bye, Dad. I'd better—HEY!"

She let out a shout as she saw the red liquid puddling over the kitchen floor.

"Mikey—stop it! Are you crazy? Dad—he's pouring a big can of tomato juice on the floor. Mikey—stop! Put it down!"

"It isn't juice!" Mikey screamed. "It's BLOOD! It's BLOOD!"

Patrick arrived a little after seven-thirty. Destiny met him at the door. "Ready to rock?" he asked, flashing her his smile. He wore a black T-shirt under an open white sport shirt, straight-legged black denims.

Destiny shook her head. "I'm really sorry, Patrick. I didn't know how to get in touch with you. I have to stay and take care of my little brother."

Patrick's smile faded. "Oh. Wow. I'm sorry." His dark eyes flashed. "Hey, no problem. I'll stay and take care of the little guy with you."

Destiny could hear Mikey up in his room shouting about something. She had to fight him away to clean up the tomato juice. Then he refused to eat his pizza because he said the pepperonis were bugs.

"I don't think so," she told Patrick. "Mikey's being really difficult tonight. I think he needs *all* my attention."

Patrick sighed. Destiny felt the weight of his eyes on her. And once again she began to feel as if she were floating off the ground.

"How about Sunday night, Destiny?" Patrick asked. His voice seemed so muffled and far away. "Sunday is the night of the full moon. We could have fun Sunday night. Are you free?"

Destiny tried to focus, but everything was a blur. Finally, she turned away, lowered her gaze from his, and started to feel normal again.

"Yes. Sunday night," she repeated. "Okay,

Patrick. Sorry about tonight. See you Sunday."

She started to close the door, but Patrick pulled it open again. He brought his face close to hers, and once again she fell under the spell of his eyes.

"I'm going to drink your blood Sunday night," Patrick whispered. "And you will drink mine. We'll have such a nice night, Destiny."

Then he wiped her mind clean and pulled his face from hers.

"Sounds great," Destiny said. "Can't wait, Patrick. See you Sunday."

Chapter Thirty-five

An Evil Creature of the Night

"Whoa! I feel great!"

Harrison came bursting into the diner. He started dancing in front of Destiny, shaking his booty, hands high above his head.

Destiny stood behind the counter, a stack of dirty plates in her hands.

"I feel great! I feel so great!" Harrison exclaimed.

A few customers laughed. Mr. G. stuck his head out through the window from the kitchen. "You're the fry cook, remember?" he called. "Not the entertainment. Get back here before you scare all my customers away."

Grinning, Harrison ducked under the counter. He took the stack of plates from Destiny and kissed her on the cheek.

"Harrison, are you losing it?" she whispered. "What's your problem?"

"I'm in a totally awesome mood," he said.

"Is that a problem?"

He tried to kiss her again. Destiny saw Mr. G. watching them and slid away.

Harrison handed the dirty plates through the window to Mr. G. Destiny picked up her order pad and went to talk to two customers in the booth near the window.

When she returned, Harrison was still grinning at her. He brought his face close to hers. "That was great last night," he whispered.

She stared at him. "Excuse me?"

"Order?" Mr. G. poked his head out the window.

"Oh, yeah." Destiny lowered her eyes to her pad. "Two All-Americans with ham, hold the potatoes, white toast."

She pulled down two white coffee mugs, moved to the coffee-maker, and filled them with the steaming hot coffee. She put the mugs on a tray with a small milk pitcher and carried it to the two men in the booth.

Harrison grinned at her again. "Didn't you hear me? I just said I had a great time last night. That was really so totally excellent. I mean—"

Destiny narrowed her eyes at him. "Have you lost your mind? Last night?"

Oh, no. She had a sudden feeling of dread. It tightened her stomach and made her head spin for a moment.

Last night?

And then she saw the two tiny red points on Harrison's throat.

And she knew.

Livvy. Again.

Livvy was coming after Harrison. First Ari, now Harrison.

But why?

Didn't Ross tell Livvy how much I still care about her? That I'll do anything to help her and bring her back to us? Didn't Ross tell her?

Why is she going after Harrison?

Destiny spun away from him. She couldn't bear to see the two wounds on his neck.

There's only one reason why Livvy is doing this, she decided. She trembled so hard she had to grab the counter to hold herself up. Only one reason . . .

She is beyond saving. She has truly become one of them . . . an evil creature of the night.

Chapter Thirty-six

An Unexpected Murder

"Does my hair look okay?" Livvy asked. "I never realized I'd miss mirrors so much."

"It looks fine," Monica said, brushing the back of Livvy's hair with her hand. "That purple lipstick looks really hot."

Livvy snickered. "It used to drive my family crazy. One night my dad asked me why I wanted to look like a Halloween witch."

Suzie sighed. "You were lucky. My dad never paid that much attention to me. He'd never comment on my lipstick or . . . anything."

"I miss my mom and dad," Monica said, turning to the window. "They didn't deserve me. They deserved someone better."

Livvy gave her a gentle shove. "Hey, don't get down on yourself. You have your good qualities, you know. You're a really good friend. You're kind. You're generous . . ."

"And I'm a vampire," Monica said. She

shrugged. "I made my choice, right? But sometimes I wonder."

"You're just hungry," Suzie said, adjusting the top of her striped tube top. "We're all hungry."

"Party night!" Livvy exclaimed.

"*Every* night is party night, right?" Monica said, but without much enthusiasm.

"Hey, are you still feeding on that guy, Alby?" Livvy asked.

Suzie grinned. "Yeah. Both of us. Monica and I have been sharing him." She giggled. "He doesn't have a clue."

"Tomorrow night is the full moon," Livvy said, carefully applying purple eye shadow over her lids.

"Duh. Tell us about it," Monica said.

Livvy turned to them. "Are you going to make Alby a vampire?"

Suzie shrugged. "Why not? He's so cute."

Monica turned to Livvy. "What about that mystery guy you've been chasing after?"

"He's toast," Livvy replied. "Tomorrow night, he starts to live the good life."

Monica squinted at her. "Is he really hot? Why are you so into him?"

An evil smile spread slowly over Livvy's pale face. "Because he was my sister's boyfriend." She laughed.

Monica shook her head. "Weird. All three of us still have family problems."

Livvy shook her head. "No problem," she said softly. "No problem at all."

As a bat, Livvy swooped low over her old house. Through the front window, she glimpsed Destiny. Destiny on the couch and beside her . . . yes, Harrison.

Lucky guy.

Harrison with his arm around Destiny, the glow of the television washing over them, bathing them in dull reds and blues.

Ah, look. The two of them cuddling together.

What a sweet scene. Enjoy it, Harrison. Tomorrow night you will be mine. And Destiny will be Patrick's. And it will all change.

Your world will end. And a new one will begin.

Livvy raised her wings and swooped higher. One circle of the house, she thought. A house I'll never enter again.

The light was on in Mikey's room but the curtains covered the window. Livvy circled again and perched on the narrow window ledge outside her old room above the garage. The room Destiny and I shared . . . before the murdering . . . before the blood began to flow . . . before the *hunger*.

She saw her bed, carefully made. Her old stuffed leopard standing on the pillowcase as if on guard. The shelves of CDs against the wall beneath her Radiohead poster.

She felt a sudden pang—of what? Sadness? Loneliness? Longing for her old life?

No way.

No way. I don't feel anything. I'm just hungry, that's all.

But she pictured Ross. Sitting on the edge of her bed, the two of them wrapped up in each other. Her hands in his hair. His arms tight around her. Kissing her . . . kissing her for so long, until they were both breathless, until their lips were dry and chapped. Kissing and then . . .

No!

I don't want to remember any of this. I don't feel anything. Not anything.

She kicked off with her spindly bat legs,

flapped her wings hard, feeling the warm air against her skin, and soared away from the house, high into the charcoal night sky.

She flew low over the trees, breathing the warm air, refreshing herself, sending all thoughts away, except for the thought of feeding. And on the edge of town, where the last tiny cottages stood, a few blocks from the rock quarry, she found a guy just waiting to feed her.

He stood beside his Harley motorcycle at the curb, shiny blue helmet in his hand, the light from the streetlamp revealing his shaved head, the bushy, dark mustache spread over his lips. Black vest over a black T-shirt, tight black jeans. Cowboy boots with big heels.

Livvy landed on the sidewalk in the next block and quickly transformed into her own body. She straightened her short skirt over her bare legs, adjusted her halter, and strolled up to the chopper dude.

"Hey, what's up?" she asked, gazing into his narrow, brown eyes.

He shrugged his broad shoulders.

The guy must work out twenty hours a day, Livvy thought. But he won't be strong enough to fight me off.

He grinned at her and patted the seat of the motorcycle. "Lookin' for a ride?"

"Not really."

She lowered her head and bulled into him and knocked him onto his back before he even realized what was happening. The blue helmet bounced down the sidewalk.

He let out a groan and started to lift himself to his feet. But Livvy was on top of him and sank her fangs into the tender skin under his chin. A howl of pain burst from his open mouth. But it faded to a whisper as Livvy began to drink.

A few seconds later, he was sprawled on his back, whimpering like a frightened dog. Livvy had his arms pressed against the pavement. Her hair spread over his face as she drank, making loud sucking, lip-smacking sounds, grunting softly with pleasure as the thick, warm liquid oozed down her throat.

She stopped before she had her fill. She never could drink enough to be satisfied. That was the curse of it all, she knew. Never to be satisfied. Always to need more.

She climbed to her feet and wiped blood off her chin with the back of her hand. The guy lay sprawled on his back, half on the curb, half in the street. His eyes were shut and he was still whimpering.

Humming to herself, Livvy strode down the sidewalk a few yards, picked up his helmet, carried it back, and placed it on the guy's stomach. She licked her lips. She loved the taste of dried blood, so sharp and sweet at the same time.

"Bye, cutie." She transformed to a bat once again and took off without looking back.

She returned to the apartment building early. Dawn was still a few hours away.

I need my beauty sleep, she decided. Tomorrow night is the full moon—and my night to shine. A big night for Harrison, and for my sister. I want to be ready for it.

She stepped into the building in human form and made her way up the dimly lit staircase. On the first floor, rats scampered through piles of garbage. A tall stack of old newspapers teetered in the late-night breezes.

As Livvy walked past open apartment doors, she heard low moans, groans, and whispers. Orange light flickered in the apartment that Suzie and Monica shared.

Were they back? Were they still awake?

Livvy heard a scuffling sound. A hard *thud* from deep in the apartment.

Curious, she stepped into the doorway and squinted into the flickering light.

Oh, no. She pressed both hands over her mouth to stifle her cry.

Monica lay on her back on the floor, fully dressed, one shoe on, one off. Her hands outstretched, legs apart—a wooden stake standing straight up. A wooden stake through her chest. Monica's head tilted at a harsh angle, eyes still open.

No. Oh, no.

Monica murdered in her own apartment.

Hands still pressed to her mouth, Livvy heard noises in the bedroom.

A scraping sound. A groan. A sharp cry.

A shiver of terror rolled down Livvy's body.

The murderer—he was still in the apartment!

Chapter Thirty-seven
The Real Murderer

Her legs rubbery and weak, Livvy staggered forward a few feet. Holding her breath, she stepped over one of Monica's outstretched legs. Fighting off her panic, she moved silently to the bedroom doorway. And peered inside.

Her breath caught in her throat when she saw the struggle in the bedroom. She pressed her back against the wall and watched in silent horror as Patrick and Suzie battled.

"You're weak!" he cried, his face red, eyes bulging with anger. "You're too weak. I can't let the weak ones survive!"

He slammed her into the wall as if she were weightless. Suzie bounced off, let out a painful groan, and fell onto her back on the cot.

Before she could move, Patrick raised a pointed stake high over her body—and with both hands, swung it down hard. Suzie let out a shrill scream as the stake penetrated her chest, drove through her heart, and poked out of her back with a loud sucking sound.

No! Livvy thought, frozen in terror, unable to move, unable to take her eyes away. *She's my friend . . . my friend!*

Suzie writhed and kicked, her hands and feet thrashing the air like a pinned insect. Patrick held the stake, thrust it deeper through her chest, gripping it with both hands, sliding it through her body.

Another cry from Suzie, weaker this time. She grabbed at the stake, tried to shove it away. But her strength was fading. And her body was beginning to disintegrate.

Her skin peeled off quickly. Large chunks fell off her arms, her face. Her eyeballs dropped from their sockets and rolled across the room. The flesh of her cheeks and forehead melted away, revealing bone underneath.

Her skeletal arms still grabbed for the stake, thrashed and swiped at it—until the bone began to disintegrate.

Livvy gaped in horror as Suzie's skull crumbled into powder. Her arms—just gray bone now—fell motionless to the floor and crumbled to chunks, then powder. In a few seconds, her crumpled clothing lay spread on the floor, no body inside, a few ashes blowing in the breeze from the window.

She was older than I thought, Livvy realized. So old she crumbled to ashes. She . . . she didn't deserve to die like this.

"Too weak," Patrick muttered, heaving the stake angrily against the wall. "I can't allow the weak ones to stay. I can't!"

A soft cry escaped Livvy's lips.

Did he hear it?

She didn't wait to see. She spun away and started to run. Stumbling over Monica's body in the living room, she caught her balance, and kept running.

She darted frantically down the long hall, tripping over garbage and piles of newspaper. Breathing hard by the time she reached the stairs, she grabbed the metal rail and pulled herself up, forced her legs to carry her higher.

Gasping for breath, she reached the second floor, and ran blindly to her apartment halfway down the hall. Into the warm darkness, a hot breeze from the open window area.

Into the darkness and safety of the bedroom where she stood shivering, hugging herself tightly. She shut her eyes and gritted her teeth, forcing her body to stop its trembling.

But she couldn't shut out the picture of Patrick, shoving the stake through Suzie's chest, the fury that twisted his face, the sick sound the stake made as it poked through Suzie's body. Her bony hands in the air as if begging . . . begging for mercy.

Livvy's stomach lurched. She felt sick. She stumbled to the glassless window hole, leaned out, and vomited up some of the blood she had drunk—her dinner. It had tasted so sweet going down. Now it sickened her, sour and acid.

Still gagging, she heard a sound behind her. Wiping her mouth with the back of her hand, she turned to the door.

Patrick?

No. The footsteps passed. Some other vampire returning home after a night of feeding.

Livvy kicked off her shoes and climbed into bed. She pulled the blanket over her head and tried to stop shaking. But how could she stop thinking about her two dead friends?

Patrick. Patrick murdered them.

He's weeding out the weak.

And that means . . . *Patrick killed Ross.*

Buried under her blanket as if in a dark, warm cocoon, Livvy's mind whirred. It was becoming clear to her. The horror of her situation. The danger she was in.

It all began to come clear.

Destiny didn't murder Ross. Patrick murdered Ross because he was weak. Because he wanted to see his parents, because he was homesick.

Patrick is the murderer. He is killing his own.

Destiny is innocent. She probably came here to warn me. Or just to plead with me to give up this life and come home so Dad can cure me.

And now I've agreed to let Patrick go after Destiny, to let him turn my sister into a vampire, too. And I agreed to trick her boyfriend into exchanging blood and becoming an immortal.

Livvy gasped. It's all a test. Patrick is testing me.

And do I have a choice? I have to go through with it.

If I try to stop Patrick from attacking Destiny, then he will know that I am weak.

And he will kill me too.

Part Seven

Night of the Full Moon

Chapter Thirty-eight
Harrison's Big Date

*H*arrison gazed up at the full moon as he pulled his car to a stop. The moon floated low in the blue-black evening sky. It had rained earlier in the day. And now the moonlight was reflected in dozens of puddles and tiny pools all along the road, making the whole earth seem to sparkle.

Unreal.

Harrison slapped his hands on the steering wheel in rhythm to the dance music beat on the car stereo. He sang along, waiting for the light to change to green.

He thought about Destiny. Also unreal.

Picturing her made his heartbeats drum, almost as fast as the music. She had been different lately. So much needier. So much sexier.

Harrison flashed back to the other night. Destiny kissing him, kissing him so passionately, pressing herself against him, moving her hands through his hair.

And making those little sighs, the soft moans. Kissing his face . . . his neck. Yes. Kissing his neck.

It was all so unreal.

Harrison touched the little bite marks on his throat. Destiny had really gotten carried away.

Man, she was suddenly so *hot*!

The light changed. Harrison lowered his foot to the gas pedal. He couldn't wait to see her tonight. She had promised him something special.

Something special . . .

He knew what that meant. And now, his heartbeats were drumming *faster* than the music on the radio!

He turned onto Union Street. He could see the entrance to the mall up ahead. They planned to meet where they met last time in front of the Cineplex.

Harrison brought the car around to the front of the movie theater and ducked his head to search for Destiny through the passenger window.

No. Not here. Where was she?

He checked the dashboard clock. Eight-thirty-six.

Destiny said she'd be here at eight-thirty.

Yes. Eight-thirty. She said she had a nice surprise for him. But she wanted to give it to him when the full moon was high in the sky.

Unreal.

What did the full moon have to do with anything? Why was Destiny being so mysterious?

He glanced up at the moon. Higher in the sky now, more golden than orange, with a single wisp of black cloud cutting it off in the middle.

"Dee, where are you?"

He drove past the theater, turned and pulled into a parking place between two SUVs. He drummed his fingers on the wheel. Checked his wallet to make sure he'd remembered to bring some money. Gazed up at the full moon again, hazy behind a thin film of cloud. Then back at the clock—eight-forty-five.

Destiny was always on time. This was not like her.

Leaving the car running, Harrison climbed out and stood in front of it, searching under the bright lights at the front of the Cineplex. He saw a short line of people in front of the box office. Two teenage girls waiting for someone at the side of the theater.

No one else. No Destiny.

I want my special surprise, Destiny. I want you to keep your promise. Where are you? You don't want to keep me here in suspense, do you?

He took a few steps away from the car. "Hey—!" He saw a couple of guys he knew going into the theater. He waved to them and called out, but they didn't see him. They vanished inside.

Harrison strode back to the car and dropped behind the wheel. Almost nine o'clock. Maybe she got hung up. Maybe she couldn't make it for some reason. No. She'd call. Maybe she was in an accident or something.

Harrison sighed. He hated to wait for people. It always made him very tense. Most of his friends showed up half an hour late to everything, and it drove him crazy. He was always on time. That probably drove his friends crazy!

He picked up his cell phone. He stared at it for a few moments. Nine-oh-seven on the clock. He punched in Destiny's cell number. And listened to four rings. Then her voicemail message: "This is Destiny. Leave a message, okay?" The long beep.

He clicked off the phone.

Where is she?

He tried her cell number again. Maybe the phone was buried in her bag, and she didn't hear it. Again, he listened to four rings. When her message came on, he clicked off the phone and tossed it onto the seat.

He climbed out of the car, slamming the door behind him. He paced back and forth in front of the movie theater for a while.

At nine-thirty, he climbed back into the car. He gazed up at the full moon, high in the sky now, a bright, silvery circle. Then he backed out of the parking place.

Where are you, Destiny? Did you stand me up?

That's so not like you.

Harrison felt his muscles tighten, felt a weight in the pit of his stomach. This wasn't like Destiny at all.

Something must be wrong. Something must be terribly wrong.

He sped out of the mall and turned left on Union Street.

He decided to drive to Destiny's house. He had to find out what was going on.

Chapter Thirty-nine
Destiny Surprises Patrick

*P*atrick couldn't take his eyes off Destiny's throat.

The skin pale and smooth, like velvet. Her neck long and straight. He could taste it. He could taste that spot just under her chin, that soft spot without muscle where the veins ran free and close to the skin.

As they danced, he watched the veins throb, a subtle blue against the smooth, soft skin. She said something to him, shouting over the loud music. But he didn't hear her. He was concentrating so hard on the tiny, throbbing veins, on her delicious throat.

Soon, Destiny, you and I will be together forever, he thought, returning her smile.

The beat changed as the DJ worked his mix. Destiny changed her rhythm and Patrick changed with her, moving his body slowly now, bumping against her. Any excuse to touch her. Eyes on her throat. If only he could sink his teeth into that soft skin right this minute and drink . . . drink until she moaned and sighed.

He knew the full moon was high in the sky by now. The dance club had no windows. But Patrick could *feel* the moon above him. His excitement rose with the moon. And so did his hunger.

Destiny's face held its smile as she danced under the flashing lights over the dance floor. She's gentler than her sister, Patrick decided. She has a sweetness about her—an innocence?—that Livvy doesn't have.

He wondered how Livvy was doing with Destiny's boyfriend, Harrison. She seemed so eager to go after him, so eager to take him under the moonlight and turn him into a vampire.

Did she hate her sister *that* much?

Patrick wondered why. He wondered why one twin chose the vampire life—and the other had to be forced into it.

Tonight . . .

I will force her tonight. She won't know what is happening until it is too late.

What drove the sisters apart? Why does

Livvy carry such anger against her twin?

And then as he danced, his thoughts changed, and he thought about the group of vampires he had joined. So many weaklings and fools who were endangering the whole group. Patrick knew the Hunters were organizing. He knew the Hunters would soon find their hiding place and try to drive them out.

He had to weed out the weaklings before the battle began.

He intended to win this battle. For nearly a hundred years, he had been driven from town to town. Forced to flee, to hide.

No more.

He intended to take a stand here. If the Hunters think they can chase us away so easily, bring them on. We'll be ready.

But first, he had to make sure everyone was strong.

Will you come through for me tonight, Livvy? Will you complete the job on Harrison? Or will you let him go, and prove that you are also one of the weaklings?

Patrick knew he didn't want to kill Livvy. He was attracted to her, drawn to her—to her sister too. But if he had to, he would kill Livvy the same way he had killed her friends.

We're going to be strong, strong enough to kill any Hunters that invade our homes.

He turned to Destiny. He realized she was squeezing his arm. "Patrick, what's wrong? You have such an unhappy look on your face."

"I . . . was thinking about something," he said. He took her hand and led her off the dance floor. "Enough dancing? I've worked up a real sweat." He picked up a cocktail napkin from the bar and mopped his forehead.

"That DJ is great," Destiny said. "That's why I like this club."

"Let's get some fresh air," Patrick said. He guided her through the crowd and out the front door. He heard shouts and saw a group of people in the parking lot. "What's going on?"

They followed the path to the parking lot. "An accident," Destiny said. "Someone backed an SUV into that Mini."

"Ooh." Patrick made a face. "The Mini is wrecked. Why didn't the SUV pick on someone his own size?"

A tall man in a wrinkled suit was screaming at the parking valet and shaking his fist in the air. Two women were screaming at him.

"Let's get out of here," Patrick said. He glanced up at the full moon. "It's such a nice night. Would you like to take a walk?"

Destiny smiled and took his arm. "Nice. Do you know Drake Park?"

He shook his head. "Not really."

"There's a path I like to walk. It's real pretty at night, especially under a full moon." Destiny glanced up at the moon too. "It leads to a pretty little creek."

"Let's go," Patrick said. He suddenly felt so hungry, he wiped a gob of drool off his chin and hoped Destiny didn't see.

They drove to Drake Park. Patrick kept a hand gently on her shoulder as they made their way along the twisting, dirt path, through thickets of tangled trees and low shrubs, to the creek.

As they walked, Destiny talked about her job at the diner, about her father, a veterinarian, and about her little brother, Mikey. Patrick didn't listen. His hunger had become a roar in his ears, like a pounding ocean wave crashing again and again.

He couldn't hear her. He could think only of

his thirst, of the gnawing in his stomach, the ache . . . the ache . . .

The moon had risen high in the sky. It filled the creek with silver light that made the narrow, trickling stream shimmer and glow.

Destiny took his hand. She gazed at the sparkling water. "Isn't it beautiful?"

"Yes," he managed. He knew he couldn't hold back much longer. "Yes, it is."

She squeezed his hand. "With the moon lighting the water, it's almost as bright as day."

"Yes," he agreed again. His fangs slid down over his lips.

Destiny was staring at the creek. "I've done all the talking," she said. "You haven't told me a thing about yourself."

"Well . . ." His brain was spinning now. All dazzling bright lights and wild, throbbing music. The hunger so strong he wanted to toss back his head and howl.

Instead, he grabbed Destiny by the shoulders. Lowered his face to her throat. Dug his fangs deep into the soft flesh of her throat.

He dug deeper, making loud sucking sounds, holding her tightly, pressing his forehead into her chin.

And then with a cry of disgust, he staggered back. Dizzy, his stomach heaving. "Noooooo." A sick moan escaped his throat. He lurched away from her, bent over, and started to retch.

Chapter Forty
Livvy Surprises Patrick

"You're . . . not . . . Destiny," he whispered when he could finally talk. He stood up straight and shook himself.

She hadn't moved the whole while. Moonlight washed over her, making her blond hair gleam, making it appear that she was standing in a spotlight.

"You're Livvy, aren't you," he accused.

"Patrick, you're such an ace," she replied. "Really sharp. You just pick up on things so fast, don't you?"

He stared at her in disgust, holding his hands in front of him as if shielding himself from her. "What are you doing here, Livvy?"

"My sister decided she didn't want to go out with you. She said you're just not her type. But I didn't want you to be lonely."

Patrick narrowed his eyes at her. "Are you crazy?" He pointed to the moon. "You know you have an assignment tonight."

Livvy shrugged.

His anger grew quickly. "Don't you realize how dangerous it is to play this trick on me? To disobey me? What about Harrison, Livvy? What about your assignment?"

"Oh, I stood him up. I gave myself a new assignment," she said. Her body tensed. Her smile faded.

Patrick scowled. "What the hell are you talking about?"

"I brought something from home," Livvy said. "I brought it out here to the woods earlier . . . just for you. A surprise."

She bent behind a tree, grabbed something in both hands, and swung to face him.

"It's the stake," Livvy said, her voice trembling now, her face tight with fury. "The stake you used to kill my friends."

Patrick's hands flew up. His eyes bulged in shock.

She raised the stake high—and, with a loud cry, thrust it into his chest.

But he moved quickly, stumbling back. He grabbed the stake before it could penetrate his skin. Grabbed it in both hands and struggled to wrench it away from Livvy.

He caught her off-balance, still moving forward in her attempt to stab him. Now she gripped one end of the stake, and he gripped the other.

Patrick swung the stake hard and sent her spinning against a tree.

Livvy let out a cry as the stake flew out of her hands.

She shoved herself off the tree trunk and spun to face Patrick.

"Nice try," he said breathlessly. "But not nice enough."

He raised the stake in both hands—and cracked it in half over his thigh. Then he kept the pointed end and tossed away the other half.

"I've given *myself* a new assignment," he said, moving in on Livvy. He raised the pointed stake in one fist. "Can you guess what it is?"

Chapter Forty-one
A Vampire Must Die

*H*e brought the stake down hard and fast, aimed at Livvy's heart.

She transformed into a bat, and the point sailed past her, barely grazing a wing. With a loud screech, she brought her wings up and sailed over Patrick's head. Then she stuck out her talons—and swooped down.

Hissing and shrieking, she scratched at his eyes.

He let out a cry of pain and stumbled back.

She scraped his cheeks with her talons. Blood streamed down his face.

With a groan, he swiped her hard with the back of his hand. His hand caught her in the belly, knocking her air out.

Stunned, Livvy toppled to the ground.

She gazed up in time to see Patrick raise a shoe to trample her. She scuttled out just as the heel slammed the ground.

Flapping her wings hard, she shot back into the air. He had dropped the stake and was bent, searching for it.

Livvy swooped to the ground behind him, transformed back into her own body, and grabbed up the stake as Patrick spun around.

"No—" he uttered as she slammed the stake with all her strength into his throat.

A sick cry burst from his open mouth as the stake poked through the skin, deep into his neck. His eyes bulged, and he grabbed for the stake with both hands.

But Livvy was too fast for him this time. She tugged the stake out, staring at the gaping hole in his neck. Then she slammed it into his body again, thrusting the point into his chest, into his heart.

He fell back, cracking his head on a tree trunk.

He didn't utter a sound. He stared up at Livvy as he collapsed onto his back. His legs folded, and his arms dropped limply to his sides, and didn't move.

A shaft of silver moonlight washed over the stake, tilted up in the air now as Patrick lay on his back, not moving. And then his skin started to melt and crumble away. Big chunks dissolving quickly, revealing the bones underneath.

Struggling to catch her breath, her chest heaving up and down, Livvy turned her back on him.

I don't want to see what happens to him.

I killed him.

I killed him because he killed my friends. And I killed him to save my sister.

Livvy felt upset now, confused. She didn't feel as if she'd scored any kind of victory.

What will happen next?

Her thoughts turned to Destiny.

Have I saved you tonight, Dee?

Or have I killed you too?

Chapter Forty-two
"One Last Kiss . . . Before I Kill You"

Dr. Weller stood trembling in the abandoned apartment building, listening to the screams of agony all around him.

Vampires were dying. His hunters were working fast, catching them while they slept in their open apartments, piercing their hearts with wooden stakes, and quickly moving to the next apartment.

Dr. Weller had trouble moving as quickly. He had killed one vampire in his bed, a young man with dried blood caked down his chin. He had thrust his pointed stake between the young man's ribs, watched him come awake, eyes bulging in disbelief. Listened to his scream of pain as he realized what had happened to him. Then watched him die.

He's not really a human, Dr. Weller told himself. He's a creature now, an evil creature in a human body. He preyed on living humans, innocent humans. He ruined lives. He deserves to die.

But now as the sun began to rise in the glassless windows of the unfinished building, Dr. Weller stood trembling in front of a low cot, unable to act, unable to move or think straight.

This is not a human, he told himself, staring at the sleeping girl in the long, black nightshirt. This is an evil creature now.

He gripped the stake tightly in his right hand. His left hand was raised to his feverish forehead.

This is an evil, inhuman creature now.

But she is my daughter.

He gazed down at Livvy, gazed through the tears that blurred his eyes, that ran down his cheeks. This is my daughter, and I have no choice—I have to kill her.

I am the leader of the Hunters, and I have vowed to rid Dark Springs of these blood-sucking killers.

A vampire murdered my wife, their mother.

And now I'm about to lose another precious family member to the evil ones.

Dr. Weller raised his eyes and cursed the sky.

His stomach tightened. For the second time that night he felt he might retch.

How can I kill my own daughter?

Could I ever face Destiny again? Mikey?

Could I ever tell them the truth: *I killed your sister. I killed Livvy with my own hands.*

I . . . I can't, Dr. Weller thought. He staggered back from the cot, his eyes on his sleeping daughter. Her blond hair flowed over the pillow. Her fair skin caught the glow of the red morning sun from the window.

I can't do this. It's asking too much of any man.

I'm not a coward. I'm a brave man. Here I am in this apartment building, risking my life, attacking vampires where they live. No, I'm not a coward.

But . . .

He heard a high, shrill scream from down the hall. A girl's scream. Another vampire murdered by one of his hunters.

A high wail of pain floated down the hall. Another victim of the hunters.

Dr. Weller gripped the walkie-talkie attached to his belt. So far, no calls for help. The operation seemed to be going flawlessly.

He sighed, staring down at his daughter's sleeping face.

I'm the one who should call for help.

I should call for one of my hunters. I should leave the room, whisper good-bye to Livvy, and leave the room. And let my hunter do the job we came here to do.

Can I do that?

Livvy stirred. She let out a soft sigh.

She turned toward him, eyes still closed.

It isn't really Livvy anymore, he decided. His heart began to thud in his chest. It isn't my daughter.

He took a deep breath. Raised the stake high.

Changed his mind.

I just want to kiss her good-bye.

Kiss her good-bye . . . before I kill her.

And as he leaned his tear-stained face down to kiss her cheek, Livvy's hands shot up—and grasped him tightly around the neck.

"LIVVY—NO!" he shouted. "LET GO!"

She opened her eyes. "Don't do anything, Dad!" she cried, holding onto his neck, wrapping her arms around his neck. "Don't, Dad! It isn't Livvy. It's me."

He blinked. Stared hard at her. "Destiny—?"

She nodded. She kissed his cheek, then let

go of his neck. "I'm sorry, Dad. I didn't want to scare you. But I had no choice. I—"

"Destiny?" he repeated. "Destiny?"

She nodded. "Yes, it's me. I traded places with Livvy. I had to save her life."

Chapter Forty-three
Thicker Than Blood

Later, Destiny explained to her father. "Livvy and I planned it all last night. She risked her life by taking my place with a vampire named Patrick."

"But why did you take her place in the apartment?" Dr. Weller asked.

"I had to," Destiny replied. "Livvy risked her life for me. I had to risk my life for her. It was the only way to prove to her how much I want to save her."

"You took a terrible risk," Dr. Weller said. He poured milk into his coffee mug, then slid the milk carton across the table to Destiny.

"We couldn't really say it out loud. But we showed how much we cared by risking our lives for each other," Destiny said. "Crazy, huh?" She poured milk into her mug and took a sip of coffee.

Dr. Weller stared at her across the kitchen

table, thinking hard. He raised his hands from around his coffee mug. "Look at me. I'm still shaking. We've been home for half an hour, and I can't stop shaking."

Destiny lowered her head. "I'm sorry, Dad."

He grabbed her hand. "No. Don't say that. You did a very brave thing tonight."

"So did Livvy," Destiny replied.

Dr. Weller nodded. Behind his glasses, his eyes teared over. "Twins," he murmured. "Twins stick together, right?"

Destiny took a long sip of coffee. "Yes. Being sisters meant a lot more to both of us than . . . than anything else."

"And you hatched this plan last night?" he asked.

"Last night," Destiny said. "Livvy flew into my window. She explained that she was furious at me. She told me about Ross. She—"

Destiny stopped. Her voice broke. She raised her eyes to her father. "Ross is dead, Dad. Killed by another vampire."

"Oh, no," Dr. Weller whispered. "No . . ."

Destiny nodded. "Yes, he's dead. I suppose we have to tell his family. Livvy thought I murdered him. That's why she was so angry."

Dr. Weller shook his head. "Ross dead," he murmured. "He was a good guy. And Livvy could be dead too. If only—"

"She may be okay, Dad. I'm sure I'll hear from her again."

"Tell her to come home," Dr. Weller said. "Tell her if she comes home, I'll work even harder on finding a cure. I'll do everything I can."

"I'll try, Dad. I'll try." She squeezed his hand. "But don't get your hopes up."

Destiny left out one part of the story. She didn't tell her father that she and Livvy planned to meet the next night in their room above the garage.

"Don't tell him," Livvy had insisted. "I'll come see you, but I just can't see Dad. Not yet."

Destiny had agreed. And now it was the next night. The night after the full moon and all the horror it brought.

Destiny paced back and forth in her room, clasping and unclasping her hands, feeling so tense she could barely think straight.

Did Livvy survive last night? Did she kill Patrick? Is she okay? Will she come? Will she keep her promise?

Dr. Weller was working late at his lab. Mikey was closed up in his room watching Nickelodeon.

A warm breeze ruffled the curtains in the open window. Destiny heard a car horn honking far down the block. White moonlight washed into the room and slanted across the carpet.

Hugging herself, Destiny stepped into the square of moonlight. Cold moonlight, she thought. Moonlight is always so silvery hard and cold.

The curtains fluttered again. A blackbird landed gently on the sill. It shook itself, raising its wings, then hopped onto the bedroom floor.

Destiny jumped back. The bird tilted its head, gazing up at her with its shiny black bead of an eye.

"Livvy—?" Destiny whispered.

The blackbird transformed quickly, its body rising, arms poking out where the wings had been . . . a head . . . blond hair. All so quick and silent.

In seconds, Livvy stood across from Destiny. She brushed back her hair and glanced around the long, narrow room they had shared. "You . . . haven't changed a thing," Livvy said. She picked up her stuffed leopard and pressed it against her cheek. "Everything is the same."

Destiny stared at her sister. Livvy wore a tight white midriff blouse over a black miniskirt. Long, red plastic earrings dangled from her ears. She had a tiny rhinestone stud in the side of her nose.

A laugh escaped Destiny's throat. "You haven't changed, either," she said. "I mean, you look exactly the same."

Livvy frowned. "I've changed a lot, Dee. Don't think I'm the same old Livvy." She tossed the leopard onto the bed.

"You . . . you're okay?" Destiny asked. "I mean, last night—"

"I killed him. I killed Patrick," Livvy said. "See? I'm not the same. I've *killed*, Dee. Do you believe it? I've killed."

Destiny let out a sob. "I'm just so glad you're okay." She rushed to her sister. They hugged, hugged each other tightly, pressing their cheeks against each other. Destiny's cheek was damp from her tears. Livvy didn't cry.

A voice from downstairs made them jump apart.

"Hey, who you talking to?" Mikey called up.

Livvy's eyes grew wide. She took a step toward the window. Destiny could see she was thinking of escape.

"No," she whispered to Livvy. "Let Mikey see you. He needs to see you and talk to you. You can help him, Liv."

Livvy looked doubtful, but she stayed.

"Come here, Mikey." Destiny went down and guided Mikey up the steps. "Livvy is here. She came back because she wants to see you."

As she and Mikey walked up the stairs, a feeling of panic swept over Destiny. Maybe this isn't such a good idea. Maybe Mikey will totally freak.

He stepped into the room. His eyes went from Destiny to Livvy. He froze.

"Mikey—" Destiny started.

Mikey took a few steps toward the two girls. He stared suspiciously at Livvy. He stopped a few feet away and studied her.

"Are you real?" he asked finally.

Livvy laughed. "Huh? Am I *what*?"

Mikey narrowed his eyes at her. "Are you real?" he repeated.

Livvy's expression softened. "Yes, Mikey, it's really me."

She hurried to him and wrapped him in a hug. Mikey burst into tears and began to sob at the top of his lungs.

"It's okay. It's okay," Livvy whispered, holding him. "It's okay, Mikey. Really. I love you. I still love you."

Destiny bit her bottom lip to keep from crying too. Would this help the poor little guy? Would it help him to know that Livvy was still around, still his sister, still loved him? Or would it make him even more sad and crazy?

Livvy held him until he stopped crying. Then he backed away from her, rubbing his eyes.

He studied her again. "Can you really fly?"

"No," she lied. "I'm just me. Really."

"But don't you fly and bite people in the neck?"

"No. I don't do that. That's *sick*," Livvy told him. "I . . . I just had to move out for a while. That's all."

He thought about what she said. Destiny couldn't tell if he believed Livvy or not.

"Are you coming back? Will you take me swimming?" he asked.

"Someday soon maybe. Not today," Livvy said.

They talked a while longer, with Livvy reassuring Mikey that she was normal and that someday she'd return. Livvy hugged Mikey again. Then Destiny took him to his room and put him to bed.

When she returned, Livvy stood staring out the window. "I have to go," she said. She shuddered. "Seeing Mikey . . . that was really hard."

"He seemed very happy," Destiny said. "I think maybe you helped him." She grabbed her sister's hand. "Don't go, Liv. I won't let you go again."

"Don't be stupid, Dee. I can't come back here. I've gone too far into the dark world. I can't return—even if I wanted to."

"Yes, you can," Destiny insisted. "Dad will find a cure. You *can* come back."

Livvy pushed Destiny's hand away. "Bye, Dee."

Her body began to shrink, so fast Destiny could hardly see the transformation. The wings sprouted . . . the black feathers . . . the spindly legs hopping on the carpet.

Livvy, a blackbird once again, jumped into the pool of silvery moonlight on the windowsill.

"Don't go! Please don't go!" Destiny shouted. She made a grab for the bird.

But Livvy took off, raised her wings high, and soared into the moonlight. Then she swerved sharply, and vanished into the darkness of the night.

"Don't go. Don't go. Don't go," Destiny whispered.

So close. I was so close to reaching Livvy, to convincing her to stay. So close . . .

She spun away from the window when she heard the doorbell downstairs.

She's back. She changed her mind. I *did* reach her!

Destiny raced down the stairs, taking them two at a time. She bolted through the kitchen, into the front hall.

The doorbell rang again.

"I'm coming. I'm coming, Liv."

Breathlessly, she pulled open the front door.

And stared at Harrison.

"Dee? Are you okay?"

She nodded. Struggled to catch her breath. "I ran the whole way from upstairs," she explained.

He squinted at her. "Where were you last

night? You were supposed to meet me, remember? How come you didn't show?"

"Last night?" Destiny sighed. She pulled him into the house. "Harrison, that's a very long story . . ."

"You know, Craig, I won't break if you kiss me."

Craig had to fight every impulse and muscle in his legs to keep from stepping back well out of kissing range. Not that Caroline was actively trying to plant her lips on his, but she was blinking those intoxicating eyes at him, the invitation clearly extended.

"I just think that maybe we should wait for..." For what? Why would an engaged couple wait to kiss each other? The problem was that they weren't the average engaged couple. Or even a couple at all. He seized on that logic. "I was just waiting until you regained your memory. I don't want it to feel like you're kissing a stranger."

As impossible as it was, the small living room got even smaller, and it felt as though a cinch belt was squeezing across Craig's chest because there was no way Caroline was buying any of this.

"I know I don't remember you, but how could I ever think of you as a stranger? Even if I'd never laid eyes on you before I'd hit my head," she continued, and he froze, wondering if she was aware of how close she was to the truth.

* * *

**MONTANA MAVERICKS:
The Lonelyhearts Ranch—**

**You come there alone,
but you sure don't leave that way!**

Dear Reader,

The Maverick's Christmas to Remember is my first book set during the holidays, which for me is one of the busiest times of the year. It feels as though I never have enough hours to get everything done. One of my closest friends is the kind of woman who has it all together—she easily plans events, remembers everyone's favorite gifts and never forgets to send a thank-you note.

In fact, the first time I ever met Katie, a mutual friend brought her over to my house for dinner and she showed up at my door with a fancy bottle of wine. Considering the fact that we were in our early twenties and my roommate had stumbled upon a box of Rice-A-Roni in the pantry while I heated up some frozen chicken from Costco at the last minute, nobody was expecting a hostess gift. But Katie is one of those people who is laid-back and can engage in an easygoing conversation with anyone—including strangers in the checkout line.

Caroline Ruth, the heroine in *The Maverick's Christmas to Remember*, reminded me so much of Katie because she has flawless manners and always knows what to do in any situation—even when that situation involves amnesia and a make-believe fiancé. When Caroline catches her first glimpse of Craig Clifton, she knows he's the cowboy for her. However, the more experienced and cynical Craig remains determined to prevent the young, lively wedding planner from wrangling his heart.

For more information on my other Special Edition books, visit my website at christyjeffries.com, or chat with me on Twitter, @ChristyJeffries. You can also find me on Facebook, Facebook.com/authorchristyjeffries, and Instagram, Instagram.com/christy_jeffries. I'd love to hear from you.

Enjoy,

Christy Jeffries

The Maverick's Christmas to Remember

Christy Jeffries

HARLEQUIN® SPECIAL EDITION

Special thanks and acknowledgment are given to Christy Jeffries for her contribution to the Montana Mavericks: The Lonelyhearts Ranch continuity.

Recycling programs
for this product may
not exist in your area.

ISBN-13: 978-1-335-46608-2

The Maverick's Christmas to Remember

Copyright © 2018 by Harlequin Books S.A.

Printed in U.S.A.

Christy Jeffries graduated from the University of California, Irvine, with a degree in criminology, and received her Juris Doctor from California Western School of Law. But drafting court documents and working in law enforcement was merely an apprenticeship for her current career in the dynamic field of mommyhood and romance writing. She lives in Southern California with her patient husband, two energetic sons and one sassy grandmother. Follow her online at christyjeffries.com.

Books by Christy Jeffries

Harlequin Special Edition

American Heroes

A Proposal for the Officer

Sugar Falls, Idaho

A Family Under the Stars
The Makeover Prescription
The Matchmaking Twins
From Dare to Due Date
Waking Up Wed
A Marine for His Mom

Montana Mavericks

The Maverick's Bridal Bargain

Visit the Author Profile page at Harlequin.com.

To Kate Gove Campbell,
one of my favorite people on earth and a member of my Golden Girls. You are always the first to order my books, the first to respond to my texts and posts and the first to laugh at my dumb jokes. Even from across the country, your support is always constant. Not only do you give the best and tightest hugs, you have taught me how to be a better friend and you make the world a warmer and happier place. You are the Rose to my Dorothy, and I can't wait to share a lanai with you...

Chapter One

Caroline Ruth loved romance and happily-ever-after stories and all sorts of things that her academic-minded mother considered nonsense. That was how she knew with absolute conviction that this career as an assistant wedding planner in Rust Creek Falls, Montana, was tailor-made for her. And so did her boss, who was currently on her honeymoon and had left their newest client in Caroline's more-than-capable hands.

Josselyn Weaver sat across the desk from her, poring over bridal gown catalogs as they both waited for the groom to arrive to the couple's initial consultation. Picking a gown always seemed to hold the most excitement for the brides, but Caroline knew that booking a venue was the foundation of building a successful event.

After all, the guest list and decorations and theme usually depended on the location.

Caroline's stomach growled and she wished she had stopped for a breakfast croissant at Daisy's Donuts on her way to work this morning. But she'd been so eager to get to the office and prepare for this meeting that she'd barely allowed herself time for a couple of bites of a disgusting protein bar she'd found smashed in the bottom of her giant tote bag.

"So when we met a couple of months ago, you were pretty adamant that you wouldn't be getting married anytime soon," she finally said when Josselyn looked up from a glossy magazine spread. Not that she wanted to rush the bride, but Caroline had too much energy for long periods of silence, no matter how comfortable they were. Besides, the more she could learn about the couple she was working with the better. "I'm glad to see you changed your mind."

"I know. I remember you telling me that you'd be planning my wedding soon and I thought it was the craziest thing I'd ever heard." Josselyn's eyes were bright with humor, and Caroline smiled since she was well accustomed to people not really taking her instincts seriously. The bride continued, "I'd just moved to Rust Creek Falls to take the school librarian job and wasn't even looking for a date, let alone a relationship. I know people say that love finds you when you're not looking for it, but if someone had told me that I'd be engaged by Christmas, I never would have believed it."

Caroline gulped as a shiver made its way down her back.

Engaged by Christmas.

The words brought back the memory of Winona Cobbs's prediction that Caroline would be engaged before she turned twenty-four. That was a bit more than a month away, which meant that if the old psychic was correct, the right man would need to come along soon.

Shaking off the tingling vibration along her skin, Caroline glanced down at the wastebasket by her feet and wondered if she'd been a little too quick to throw out the half-eaten protein bar. She was suddenly feeling a bit light-headed and needed to keep this meeting moving along.

"So tell me about your fiancé," she suggested. She was almost as new to the small town as Josselyn was, and despite the fact that she'd already assisted with a few weddings out at Sunshine Farm, Caroline hadn't met the groom yet.

"Drew is an obstetrician at the Rust Creek Falls Clinic. His first wife died in a car accident several years ago, and since this is his second wedding, I want to make sure that I'm being respectful to her memory."

"Of course." Caroline nodded sympathetically. "And if I remember correctly, he also has an adorable son that introduced you two, right? I'm guessing you'd like him to be involved in the wedding somehow."

"That would be wonderful," Josselyn replied as her cell phone vibrated. She looked at her screen. "Drew just texted. Apparently, he ran into his brother at Daisy's, but the good news is that he's bringing donuts to apologize for running late."

"No problem." Caroline waved a hand in dismissal as

her stomach clenched in anticipation of a sugary treat. Josselyn picked up another bridal gown magazine, and Caroline decided to steer her toward the more important decisions. "Have you guys talked about the size of the wedding or whether you want it to be indoors or outdoors?"

"Well, he's originally from Thunder Canyon, so we were kind of thinking something in Kalispell might be a bit more accommodating for everyone traveling. I'm not really sure how many people we're inviting, but his family is huge. And I was hoping we could set the date within the next couple of months, so we would probably need an indoor venue since Montana winters can be pretty unpredictable."

"I know the perfect place!" Caroline jumped up so quickly she hit her knee on the corner of the desk drawer. "Hold on, I have more information on it in one of these binders."

Their current office building used to be an old train depot at Sawmill Station, and when her boss, Vivienne, converted it for her wedding planning business, her husband had built her a wall of bookshelves. Cole had promised to install a rolling ladder when they returned from their honeymoon, but until then, Caroline had to drag a piece of furniture over and climb up on it every time she needed to reach something on the top shelf.

To take her mind off the fact that she was balancing on an antique wooden chair in a pair of high heels, Caroline kept talking, hoping her enthusiasm disguised her nervous energy. "There's a historical brick building in Kalispell that is currently an art museum, but the back opens up into this huge open space. And get this. It used to be a Carnegie library before the city relocated the library to their current location. But the historical society rents it out for events and, well, if I wasn't so short I could reach the brochure and just show you."

"Can I help?" Josselyn asked, coming to stand nearby.

"Nope, I almost have it." It wasn't very ladylike—especially in an above-the-knee ruffled skirt—but Caroline put one foot onto a shelf to shimmy up just a little higher and stretched her arm as far as it would go until her fingers could grasp the bottom of the binder. As luck would have it, that was the exact moment when the front door opened.

"Drew…!" Josselyn said, her voice trailing off as she obviously walked away from the bookshelves and toward the entrance. Caroline would've stayed focused on what she was doing, but then the bride added, "I didn't know you were bringing Ben and Craig with you."

Caroline turned in surprise at the mention of unexpected people and brought her foot off the shelf a little too quickly. There were three men standing in the entryway. However, she only had eyes for the one carrying the pink bakery box. He was wearing a tan Stetson with a red plaid shirt, but that kind of standard cowboy attire was a dime a dozen around this town. What made her dizzy with excitement was the hook-shaped scar on the right side of his neck…just like the man Winona Cobbs had predicted.

Biting her lip, Caroline blinked in wonder at the new arrival. This was it. He was here. She just knew it.

Overwhelmed, underfed and perhaps a bit too eager, Caroline rocked the chair as she tried to climb down. Unfortunately, her high heel hooked onto one of the narrow armrests and she went down fast. The last thought to go through her mind was *Engaged by Christmas.*

Craig Clifton saw the woman fall as if it was happening in slow motion. Dropping the box of donuts, he sprinted toward her just as he heard the deafening *thunk* of her forehead bouncing off one of the wooden shelves. Still a couple of feet away, Craig dived at her in a last-ditch effort to brace her landing. But the odd angle and the impact of her deadweight knocked them both to the ground.

Luckily, he was able to pivot his torso at the last minute, and the back of the lady's head, as well as her shoulders, landed on his abdomen instead of the hardwood floor. Craig had absorbed most of the impact, but they were now sprawled out in the shape of a T and his childhood friend was yelling at them to stay still.

"Don't move her," Drew ordered as he knelt by Craig's hip. Catching his breath, which had been knocked out of him when they'd collided, Craig sucked in a gulp of air and saw the woman's long brown hair rise and fall with his chest.

"I can barely move myself," Craig replied, lifting a hand to the bump rising along the back of his scalp, not surprised to find his Stetson missing. His brothers referred to it as his "going to town hat" since he tended to wear it whenever he left the ranch. Craig wiggled his toes inside his boots and relaxed when he was confident that all his appendages were in working order.

"She's unconscious," Drew continued as he touched the lady's neck, probably checking for a pulse or a broken bone or whatever else it was that doctors checked for. Then Drew looked over to his brother, who was also a physician and currently crouched down with his hands on his knees, staring at the unresponsive woman instead of asking how his best friend's spine was. "Ben, I left my bag in my car back at Daisy's. Do you have yours in the truck?"

"I'm on my way," Ben replied.

"Should we call an ambulance for her?" Josselyn asked as she stood over all of them, concern etched on her forehead.

"It would probably take too long for one to drive here from Kalispell," Drew replied. "Her heartbeat and breathing seem to be stable and I'm not feeling anything broken. But judging by how hard she hit that shelf on the way down, I wouldn't be surprised if she has a concussion."

"That was my first thought," Ben said as he returned with his doctor bag. "We could take her to the clinic in town, but she's going to need a CT scan and would have to go to the hospital in Kalispell for that anyway. If we're going to drive her anywhere, it should be there."

"Wouldn't it be dangerous to move her?" Josselyn asked her fiancé, and Craig found himself thinking the same thing.

"Well, we can't leave her on top of Craig forever, as much as he might enjoy that." Ben smirked, then must've noticed the concern on his soon-to-be sister-in-law's face. "I promise she'll be fine."

Craig had grown up with the Stricklands and knew that if Ben could make jokes during a time like this, the situation couldn't be entirely dire. He forced his muscles to relax and wondered how he'd gotten roped into accompanying two of his best friends over here for a wedding planning appointment of all things.

One minute he'd been in line at Daisy's Donuts with Ben, discussing leasing fees for bulls, and the next, Drew was taking them both over to the new ranch at Sawmill Station to get a look at the latest herd of longhorns the Daltons were selling. Apparently, it just so happened that the wedding planner's office was located on the same property.

"I'm fine, by the way," Craig said, since nobody seemed to be concerned about his health after he'd taken a dive like that. He looked across the floor to where the pink bakery box had opened and spilled out its contents all over the wooden planks. "But since I'm stuck down here, can someone hand me a donut?"

"If you're healthy enough to complain, you're healthy enough to wait your turn." Drew's eyes flickered briefly over Craig before he slipped a Velcro cuff onto the arm of the unconscious woman, whose head was still propped up just below Craig's chest. "Besides, I've seen you take worse falls off a bucking horse back in the day. Now, hold still while I get her blood pressure."

"But he's not a young buck anymore," Ben said, wiggling his eyebrows with humor and making Craig feel every one of his thirty-five years. The hard floor underneath him and the odd angle of his body weren't helping the uncomfortable stiffness settling over him.

"I could still outride you," Craig challenged. "Unless you're getting in a lot of saddle time in between shifts at that fancy hospital of yours in Billings."

"Possibly," Ben said, passing him a glazed twist that had landed halfway on top of a piece of wax paper. "I haven't seen you move that fast since Brown Fury slammed you up against the pen in the midstate finals."

"That bull was one mean son of a—"

"Should I call someone?" Josselyn asked, interrupting Craig's reminiscing about his rodeo days. But it was either talk about something else to get his mind off the injured woman currently on top of him or lie here thinking about the last time he'd been powerless to help a different injured woman.

"She's stable," Drew responded. "But we should get her to the hospital in Kalispell to have some tests run."

Having grown up on his family's ranch in Thunder Canyon, Craig was no stranger to small towns and medical emergencies. The people there were used to taking care of their own. Not that this particular lady was his own. Hell, he didn't even know this woman resting so peacefully against him, the porcelain-white skin of her cheek relaxed against the red plaid checks in his shirt. But if the doctors said they could drive her from Rust Creek Falls into Kalispell, then that was what they would do.

As Drew and Ben gently lifted her off him, Craig left his uneaten donut on the floor and rose to his feet, tamping down his impulse to scoop the woman into his arms and carry her himself. After all, he was the one who'd saved her from a second blow to her head when he'd landed underneath her. That kind of bond made a man feel a certain responsibility. But Ben already had her off the ground, with Drew stabilizing her head as they walked toward the door. Which was probably for the best considering they were both trained in moving patients, whereas Craig was better trained to haul her around like a bale of hay.

"I'll grab her purse," Josselyn said as everyone seemed to spring into action.

Craig had barely enough time to scoop up his fallen hat and make it outside to open the back door of his crew cab truck. He quickly hopped up and slid across the seat to help gently maneuver the unconscious woman inside. He found himself with her head resting on him again, but at least this time it was on his lap as he sat upright on the bench seat. If he'd wanted to badly enough, he probably could've switched spots and let Drew sit back here with her. However, Craig had already taken on the rescue role inside the office and he didn't feel right about abandoning the poor lady now.

He had to shift his hips carefully in order to fish the truck keys out of his front pocket and pass them to Josselyn, who volunteered to drive so that Drew could be available to check the woman's vitals during the twenty-five-minute drive. Ben, realizing that there wasn't enough room in the truck, decided to drive Josselyn's car back to Sunshine Farm.

"Who should I notify?" Ben asked, and all eyes turned to Josselyn.

"Um, she works for Vivienne Shuster, but Viv and Cole Dalton are in Fiji on their honeymoon. Like me, she's new to Rust Creek Falls, so I'm not really sure who she'd want me to call locally. I think her parents are college professors or something but I don't know where they live."

It seemed so intimate to be talking about the personal details of a woman he'd never met. A woman whose brown hair fell in soft waves against the denim of his jeans. Craig cleared his throat. "What's her name?"

"Caroline Ruth," Josselyn said, then put the truck into gear.

Caroline.

Her body was slender and petite, but she had curves in all the right places. A rush of shame filled him as he realized he was blatantly staring at an unconscious lady. An unconscious and vulnerable lady with a body encased in delicate, clingy feminine fabric that would never suit life on a ranch. Not that Caroline looked like the type to spend much time working in the outdoors. He narrowed his gaze toward her high-heeled sandals and the bright pink polish on her toes. She never would've fallen off that chair if she'd been wearing sturdy boots and functional jeans. But she was a wedding planner, so what did she know about physical labor?

Josselyn took a bend in the two-lane highway a bit too sharply and Craig instinctively wrapped his hand around Caroline's waist to make sure she didn't accidentally tumble off the seat. The touch sent an electric vibration up his arm, making him feel like even more of a creep, so he yanked his hand away quickly, but didn't know where to put it. Lifting his elbow to the top of the backrest, Craig studied her face for signs of pain or discomfort. Fortunately, she appeared to be completely relaxed in her unconscious state, almost as though she were blissfully at peace.

Caroline Ruth was definitely an attractive woman, he'd give her that. Still. He was in no position to be noticing such things, and she was clearly in no position to be receiving his unwanted attention. Craig shifted guiltily in his seat and Caroline's eyes suddenly shot open.

"Hey there," Craig offered weakly. What else was he supposed to say to a complete stranger with her head in his lap? Caroline smiled dreamily at him before her lids fluttered closed and she was out cold again.

Chapter Two

Caroline heard steady beeping before feeling something squeeze around her upper arm. It took considerable effort to raise her eyelids, and when she finally got them to stay open, there were a few seconds of blurriness.

Where was she?

What had happened?

"She's awake," a woman said, and Caroline blinked several times until the light fixture in the middle of the white ceiling came into focus. She wiggled her toes as her hands flexed against something that felt like a starched sheet. Was she in a bed? She was definitely lying down.

"Caroline?" someone else asked and she turned toward the voice, her eyes narrowing on the person standing beside her. A woman with steel-gray curls and smooth skin the color of dark copper placed a calming hand on Caroline's shoulder. "Can you hear me?"

"Where am I?" Caroline asked.

"You're in the emergency room at Kalispell Regional. I'm Dr. Robinson. Do you remember what happened?"

Caroline shook her head and then flinched at the stabbing pain that shot through her forehead.

"Careful, now," the doctor continued. "From what I understand, you hit your head pretty hard. Your friends brought you in and we did an MRI while you were still unconscious. We think you have a concussion, but we'd like to get a CT scan of your brain to rule out anything more serious."

"My friends?" Caroline asked, then turned toward the other woman in the room. She sighed when she saw Josselyn Weaver on the other side of her bed.

"Hey, Caroline." Josselyn squeezed Caroline's hand, accidentally dislodging some little white wires and causing a shrill beep.

"Don't worry. It's just the oxygen reader," the doctor offered, putting the plastic device back over Caroline's pointer finger. "You up for answering some questions?"

"Sure," Caroline said as she tried to sit up. She was relieved that the rest of her body cooperated and that her head was the only thing hurting.

"Do you know your name?" Dr. Robinson asked.

"Caroline Ruth."

"And what day is it?"

She blinked a couple of times until it came back to her. "November 21."

"Good." The doctor's bright white smile was reassuring. "And what did you have for breakfast today?"

Caroline's stomach rumbled at the reminder. "Only a couple of bites of a protein bar. I should've gotten a breakfast sandwich at Daisy's this morning but I didn't want to be late for my appointment."

"Oh? What kind of appointment?"

"I'm a wedding planner."

The physician looked over to Josselyn, who nodded in agreement. The questions must be part of some kind of test and Caroline hoped she was passing.

Dr. Robinson lifted a finger in front of Caroline's nose. "Do you know where you live?"

Caroline's eyes followed the finger as she rattled off the address for the tiny guest house she'd rented in the heart of Rust Creek Falls several months ago. The sooner she answered everything and proved she was perfectly fine, the sooner she could get something to eat.

"What's the last thing you remember before coming to the hospital?"

"I was talking to Josselyn about her wedding and I climbed up on a chair to get the binder with a brochure for a venue when…" Caroline trailed off as she couldn't recall what had occurred after that. Lifting her fingers to stroke her forehead, she asked, "Is that how I fell?"

"Yes," Josselyn said, sighing as though she'd been holding her breath up until this point. "You went face-first into one of the shelves on your way down and were out cold. We didn't want to wait for an ambulance, so we brought you straight to the ER."

"We?" Caroline asked and looked around the room.

There was another man near the partitioned curtain of the exam room, but he'd been talking to a nurse outside and she'd assumed he was another doctor.

"That's—" Josselyn started, but Dr. Robinson cut her off.

"Do you know the name of this man?"

"No idea," Caroline replied, hoping her honesty wouldn't mean that she couldn't get a snack soon. When she'd been ten years old, her dad had to be rushed to the hospital near the faculty housing at Berkeley. He'd insisted that it was only heartburn and asked Caroline to go to the cafeteria and get him some vanilla soft serve to soothe the acid. Turned out it was a perforated gallbladder and because he'd eaten the ice cream, the anesthesiologist delayed the surgery until his stomach was empty. It had been a long ten hours of her dad doing his awful Oliver Twist impression by begging for more food and insisting he was starving.

"Technically, she hadn't met me prior to her fall." The man the doctor had just asked about stepped forward and placed an arm around Josselyn's waist. "I'm Drew Strickland, by the way. You're planning our wedding. We had just walked in the door and you'd turned to look at us. That's when you got your foot twisted in the chair and fell."

"We?" Caroline asked again, feeling like a parrot. Her eyelids were getting heavy again and all she wanted was a hot breakfast sandwich and a nap. "Who's we?"

"Me and—" Drew was cut off by Dr. Robinson holding up a hand like a stop sign.

"Do you remember them walking in the door before you fell?" the emergency room physician asked.

Caroline focused on a bright red electric outlet on the wall in an effort to concentrate, trying to form an image in her mind. But nothing was coming to her. She replayed the events of the morning over and over again, and the weight of the silence in the room suggested that everyone else knew what two plus two equaled and were desperately waiting for her to shout out, "Four!"

However, she was drawing a complete blank. In fact, she was positive that there wasn't anything else that happened after that. She was getting tired again, probably from concentrating so hard, and just wanted to fall asleep. Couldn't they simply tell her what had happened and let her take a nap?

"Sorry, I don't." Caroline shrugged, then yawned. "The last thing I remember was reaching for that binder on the top shelf."

It was then that a second man walked into the room and Caroline's breath caught as he took off his cowboy hat and ran a golden hand through his black, close-cropped hair.

Her entire body eased back onto the bed and she smiled in relief, everything finally making sense. "Oh, there you are."

"So you know him?" the doctor asked, jerking a thumb to the newcomer.

"Of course," Caroline said, then blinked slowly as the pillow cradled her head. "That's my fiancé."

Her fiancé?

Craig's head whipped around to the hallway behind him. But nobody else was there. He opened his mouth to tell the doctor that he'd never even met this woman, but nothing came out. The air had been sucked out of his lungs, and probably out of the entire room, judging by the equally confused expressions on everyone else's faces.

Caroline's head injury must be more serious than they'd originally thought if she was babbling incoherent randomness. Scratch that. Her statement had been clear and articulate, but it made absolutely no sense. Nor did the way she was looking at him, her doe-shaped brown eyes all dreamy and her wide lips parted in a hazy smile as though he was the only one in the room, or at least the only person who mattered. It was the same look Tina had given him before she'd died, and the comparison made his blood go cold.

Caroline looked nothing like his high school sweetheart, but Craig's memory had already been triggered, and that rush of helplessness filled his veins the same way it had all those years ago when they'd been trapped on the highway, waiting for the rescue workers to pry them out of the wreckage. He would've looked to Drew or Josselyn for an answer, but he couldn't tear his gaze away from Caroline.

Logically, he knew he wasn't reliving that awful night nearly fifteen years ago, but when Caroline's eyes finally drifted closed, Craig raced to her bedside and grabbed her hand as though he alone could will her back to consciousness.

"She'll be fine," the ER doctor told him with a gentle pat on the shoulder, a move likely designed to reassure loved ones. No doubt, it had worked for the doc countless times in the past. The only difference in this situation was that Craig didn't know the current patient, let alone love her.

"But I'm not—" Craig started and Dr. Robinson interrupted him.

"Let's step into the hallway where we can talk." The physician's reassuring pat turned into a firm nudge as she steered him toward the nurses' station.

Craig turned back toward his friends, who were slowly following them. Josselyn's mouth was slightly open and there were a few squiggly creases between her eyebrows while Drew simply stared in concern as though Craig had been the one to hit his head and get the sense knocked out of him.

Not that Craig could blame the guy. There might be plenty of reasons why Caroline accidentally called him her fiancé, but there was absolutely no explanation for his intense emotional reaction to someone who was a total stranger.

While it was already embarrassing that the others saw him respond like that, it would be even more confusing and downright mortifying to explain what prompted him to run to her side and clutch her hand as though she was dying.

Despite the couple approaching, Dr. Robinson faced Craig and directed most of the information his way. Something about a concussion and needing consent for a CT scan to rule out any long-term damage. "My recommendation is to run a few more tests and then have her stay overnight for observation. Does your fiancée have any other family members we should notify or can you authorize consent?"

"She's not my fiancée." The words finally tumbled out of Craig's mouth in a rush as he tugged on the collar of his work shirt. "In fact, I've never met her before."

"Well, she certainly lit up when you came in the room," Dr. Robinson replied, one hand on her hip as though she wasn't buying Craig's version of the situation. "I didn't even need to shine my light in her eyes when I was examining her because her pupils contracted and focused on you like you were the be-all and end-all."

"I promise I've never seen her before today. Right?" Craig shot a pleading look toward Drew for confirmation. "I have no idea why she would think we knew each other, let alone that we're engaged. Maybe I resemble her real fiancé and the concussion just has her brain rattled?"

"I'm pretty sure she's single." Josselyn finally spoke up and Craig felt the oxygen slowly return to his lungs. "We've only talked a handful of times, but she's never mentioned a significant other. Plus, she doesn't have an engagement ring."

At first Craig was filled with a sort of vindication from the proof that he wasn't her fiancé. However, that was soon replaced by utter bafflement. "Then why would she imagine herself being in a serious relationship at all?"

"Maybe she has amnesia?" Josselyn suggested.

"I suppose that's possible." Drew turned down one corner of his mouth, his expression suggesting that it wasn't possible at all. "However, she had full recollection of all the events leading up to her fall."

"It could be confabulation." Dr. Robinson now spoke to Drew, her voice lowered as she threw out phrases such as *memory production* and *cognitive distortion* and something else Craig couldn't quite make out.

"Hmm." Drew nodded. "I've read case studies, but have never seen it manifested in a patient."

Craig rolled his eyes. "Do you think you guys could use some layman terms for us nondoctors?"

"Confabulation is similar to amnesia in that it's a memory disturbance. It can happen when there is some type of damage to the brain. Caroline seems to remember almost everything leading up to her injury, but to fill in the gaps on what she doesn't know, her mind has invented a story to explain it."

Oh, boy. He should've stayed in Thunder Canyon this week. Pinching the bridge of his nose, Craig asked, "But why would she need to make up a lie about being engaged?"

"It's not a lie." Dr. Robinson shook her head. "To her, it's very real."

"Okay, so then we just tell her that she doesn't know me and that she doesn't have a fiancé and she's good to go." He slapped his palms together as though it were that simple. And it would've been if Craig had been speaking to the vet out on the ranch. Cows and horses never had issues like this.

Dr. Robinson shared another look with Drew before answering. "In theory, we would always recommend telling a patient the truth. But in this case, she hit her forehead, where the frontal lobe is encased, and that makes it hard for her to retrieve and evaluate memories. So in instances of confabulation, it doesn't matter what you say. Her brain is in a fragile state right now and will only be able to understand what her frontal lobe is telling her."

"How long does this last?" Craig folded his arms across his chest and looked longingly toward the ER exit doors. "I mean, do I actually have to pretend to be her fiancé?"

"I'm sure Dr. Robinson doesn't want you to pretend to be anything," Drew offered, looking at his watch.

"No, of course not. I'm simply recommending that we don't upset the patient until all the tests come back and we know more about what's going on."

"So when will that happen?"

"As soon as her fiancé gives us consent?"

"But I'm not—"

Dr. Robinson held up her palm. "I was kidding. When she wakes up again, we can get her verbal consent. But is there anybody else we should notify in the meantime? Anyone else who can give us a better medical history?"

All eyes turned toward Josselyn again. "I looked through her purse, but I couldn't find her cell phone. I heard back from Vivienne earlier, and she confirmed that Caroline's parents are out of the country right now on some sort of teaching sabbatical and she doesn't remember her mentioning any friends or family nearby. I would hate to leave her here all alone. What if she wakes up and is confused again?"

"Obviously, we can't leave her here alone," Craig said.

Drew looked at his watch a second time. "I have to get back to Rust Creek Falls before my son gets out of school."

"I'd stay, but I have to speak at the city council meeting this evening to ask for extra funding for the elementary school library. If I miss it, I'll have to wait another month to get my proposal approved."

"Maybe I'll call Ben and ask…" Drew started.

"No way," Craig said, shaking his head before his friend could even finish the thought. "I can stick around."

Chapter Three

The words had flown out of Craig's mouth before they'd had a chance to logically form in his brain. Not because his skin itched with jealousy at the mention of another man staying with Caroline when she was this vulnerable, but because Craig hadn't been able to shake this sense of responsibility for her since he'd seen her slipping off that chair. If he tried to explain this impulse, it wouldn't make sense to his friends. Hell, it didn't even make sense to him.

"I mean, if I'm her... I...uh...mean...if Caroline thinks I'm her fiancé, then obviously she'll be expecting me to be here when she wakes up. I wouldn't want to make things worse. And it's not like it's a big deal," Craig added, more for his own benefit than to convince his friends. "I'm not really doing anything else today."

It was true. The late fall season was the slowest time on his family's ranch because they'd already sent their latest herds to market and didn't plan to start breeding the new calves until after the new year. He was in Rust Creek Falls to visit two of his brothers and to check in with some of the other local ranchers for what his dad referred to as "old-fashioned market research."

Josselyn frowned. "I'm not sure if it would be in Caroline's best interest to let her continue thinking that you two are really engaged. After all, she'll get her memory back eventually, won't she?"

Dr. Robinson lifted her shoulders in a shrug. "Like I said, we'll know more after her tests. I'd feel better holding off on any treatment plan or official diagnosis just yet, but if it *is* confabulation strictly caused by a brain injury and not caused by a mental health issue or dementia, then this memory setback likely won't last too long. With all that being said, while I wouldn't advocate lying to a patient, I don't necessarily see any harm in letting them believe in whatever is going to give them a sense of peace for the time being. Our biggest goal right now is to keep Caroline as calm and relaxed as possible."

Drew looked at his watch again. "Are you sure you want to stay, Craig?"

"I don't *want* to," Craig clarified, more for himself than for anyone else listening. "But if it's the easiest solution and it will keep Caroline calm so that she can heal, then I'll do it."

There, that sounded plausible enough, even to his own ears. After several more rounds of "Are you sure?"

followed by Craig's growing insistence, he eventually found himself sitting on the miserable plastic chair beside her bed in the exam room, drinking cold coffee and scrolling on his smartphone for the latest feed and grain reports. It wasn't the same as getting out to the other ranches and talking directly to his fellow cattlemen, but he couldn't just blow off all his work duties to sit around playing nurse.

Normally, he rarely used the device except for making calls and often told his brothers that any cattleman worth his salt didn't rely on fancy gadgets that could easily get busted working on the ranch. If Craig was in the field and needed information off the internet, he usually just asked his brother Rob or waited until he could use the computer at the house. However, now that their father had been bitten with the technology bug and insisted on sending group texts with links to online articles, Craig found himself a reluctant user.

"Do you think I could have one of your Life Savers?" Caroline's soft voice was so unexpected that Craig dropped his phone, its reinforced hard-shell case preventing the screen from cracking on the tile floor.

"Huh?" Craig asked, then wanted to kick himself for sounding like such a dope.

"One of your Life Savers." Caroline pointed to the front pocket of his shirt, where he always stashed a roll of his favorite cherry-flavored candy.

His chin dropped toward the empty pocket. Okay, now that was weird. He'd had less than half a roll when he'd left his brother's house this morning and then had nervously plowed through the rest of them by the time

Caroline had undergone her MRI. Since she'd never been conscious during any of the times he'd popped one into his mouth, there was no way for her to be aware of his little sugar habit.

"How do you know about my Life Savers?" he asked, trying his best not to completely disregard the doctor's instructions about keeping Caroline calm.

"You always have them," she replied, her smile all dreamy again and his insides responding the same way they had the last time she'd woken up and grinned at him. "Plus, you smell like cherries."

Craig let out the breath he'd been holding, mildly relieved with the second part of her explanation. "Do you know who I am?"

Caroline's smooth forehead pinched into several lines as she studied him. Thinking that maybe she'd lost a pair of glasses in the fall and couldn't see his face clearly, Craig leaned closer as intense concentration took over her expression. She opened her pouty bow-shaped lips several times before defeat filled her eyes. "I don't know why I can't think of your name."

"It's Craig," he replied, wanting to pump his fist in celebration. Not that he should be basking in her confusion, but if she didn't know his name, then she'd finally realized that he was actually a complete stranger. That meant that her amnesia spell or confabulation—or whatever it was—had finally passed and she no longer needed him to take care of her. He extended his hand as he introduced himself. "I'm Craig Clifton."

Caroline inhaled deeply through her nose as she nodded. But instead of taking his proffered handshake, she laced her fingers through his. "Of course you are. I must've hit my head pretty hard to forget my own fiancé's name."

Poor Craig looked about as confused as Caroline felt. It must be difficult for him to see the woman he loved like this. But then again, at least he wasn't the one who'd completely forgotten most of the specifics about the person he was supposed to be marrying. Hopefully, it wasn't a bad omen for their relationship if she could perfectly recall every other detail of her life except for the one that was arguably the most important.

She squeezed her eyes closed as though it might help paint a more accurate picture of the man in her mind. Caroline remembered the hook-shaped scar on his neck, she remembered he liked cherry-flavored candy and… And that was where all the details stopped.

"Are you in pain?" Craig asked. "Should I call for a nurse?"

"Oh, no." Caroline's lids popped open. "I was just trying really hard to recall something more concrete about us, like how long we've been together or where we first met or where you live and work. But I'm drawing a complete blank, and to be honest, it's making me a little nervous."

"Don't be nervous," he said quickly, then rolled his lips inward, causing him look like a child who was trying to bite back a secret. The expression didn't exactly alleviate her fears. Her growing anxiety must have been obvious because he added, "The doctor said that when you hit your head, it might have caused a few problems with your memory."

Panic clawed at her throat, and she could feel the cold, dry air hitting her eyes as they grew wider than normal. "Like amnesia?"

"Not exactly." Craig rubbed the scarred area of his neck. "The doctor called it something else, but it's similar. She can probably explain it to you way better than I can."

Craig stood up, and his cowboy boots clicked against the floor as he strode over to the open curtain and waved down a hospital employee in surgical scrubs. Caroline couldn't hear what he was saying, but his thumb gestured her way and her gaze traveled from his hand down his tan, muscular forearms to where his red plaid work shirt was rolled to the elbows. Because of the way he was standing, Caroline could only study him from a side angle, but as she took in his well-rounded shoulders and flat abs and long, strong legs encased in faded denim, she couldn't help but wonder how in the world she could possibly have forgotten a perfect form like his.

When he pivoted to walk back toward Caroline, her tummy dropped and she got light-headed again. The view from the front was just as good as the one from the side. Heat flooded her cheeks and she asked, "Do you think I could possibly have a drink of water?"

"I asked the doctor about you being able to eat or drink when you woke up and she said only a sip of water until after your CT scan. She doesn't anticipate you needing any sort of surgery, but they haven't ruled it out yet."

The mention of surgery should've had her concerned. Instead, a sense of relief blossomed inside her chest. It was reassuring that her fiancé knew her well enough to understand that she'd be worried about eating and drinking and obviously had taken steps to provide answers for her. Maybe she'd even told him the story about her dad's gallbladder surgery and the soft-serve ice cream. It was crazy to think that this man beside her was probably privy to all of her secrets and all of her needs. Now if only she could recall some of *his* preferences—besides candy, obviously—then they'd be on equal footing.

Craig picked up a water bottle from the bedside tray table and unscrewed the plastic cap before gently holding it to her lips. "Not too much, now."

As she drank, she made the mistake of lifting her eyes to his face and was hit with such an intense attraction that she swallowed way too quickly and began coughing. Craig used the back of his hand to wipe the water that had dribbled down her chin. It was such an intimate gesture, not necessarily in a sexual way but in the way someone would take care of a loved one.

Something warm spread through Caroline's body. She was loved. By this man. While the feeling wasn't entirely familiar to her, it was certainly exciting. And very welcome. After all, Caroline had known that she wanted to be a wife and a mother since kindergarten, when she and five-year-old Scott Sullivan had staged a mock wedding during recess. Unfortunately, they'd barely gotten through the first-grade minister's line of "You may kiss the bride," before the teacher had put a stop to things and called Caroline's and Scott's parents to inform them that students needed to keep their hands—and their lips—to themselves at school. When her mother asked why she'd wanted to marry Scott Sullivan, Caroline had told her that he was the only boy who wasn't playing handball that day. After that, Rita Rodriguez, department chair for Women and Gender Studies at Wellesley College, had made her daughter promise that she would never settle for a man.

And Caroline never did again. In fact, she hadn't so much as had a boyfriend because every guy she'd ever gone out with hadn't felt like "the one."

So, while she couldn't remember a thing about the handsomely rugged cowboy before her, Caroline had every confidence that she belonged with him. Unlike her recess-length courtship with the first available kindergartner, there was a powerful emotional connection between Caroline and Craig. Because of her absent memory, she didn't understand it right that second but she felt it deep in her core. In twenty-three years, her instincts had never led her astray, and even her normally evidence-based mother had to admit that when Caroline felt something, she really felt it. In fact, after her college graduation, Caroline's father had given her a framed quote by Charles Dickens that read "A loving heart is the truest wisdom."

Her mother hated that quote.

Luckily, her parents were currently in India, her mom conducting research on the history and success of matriarchal tribes as her father compiled literary works by the lesser-known authors of the British colonies. Which meant they were too far away to question her every decision.

"How's everyone feeling in here?" Dr. Robinson asked, sliding back the partition.

Craig immediately stood up, because, of course, he would. As if Caroline would ever pick a guy who wasn't a complete gentleman at all times. However, his current white-knuckle grip on the bedside rail suggested his good manners were also helping to mask his discomfort and the nervous way his eyes were looking everywhere but at her.

"I'm still a little fuzzy on some things," Caroline replied before reaching out the hand not connected to the oxygen wires and placing it over Craig's. His fingers were warm, his skin slightly rough and very bronzed— probably from working outside or wherever it was that he worked. Caroline would worry about remembering those kinds of details later. She didn't want to make her fiancé feel awkward or unimportant. That was why her smile wasn't forced when she added, "But I'm content and comfortable for now."

Dr. Robinson nodded before looking away, lines scrunching across her otherwise smooth brow. Caroline followed the woman's gaze in time to see Craig give a brief shake of his head.

They were obviously referring to the fact that she hadn't fully regained her memory and Caroline wanted to kick her feet in frustration like a petulant child. But her legs were tucked in under a weight of blankets, reminding her of the utter lack of power she had over both her mind and body. "So when can I go home?"

"Well, the radiology tech is on his way now. After the CT scan, we'd like you to stay the night so we can keep an eye on your concussion. As long as all the tests come back negative, I don't see any reason why you couldn't go home tomorrow."

Caroline didn't even realize she was now clutching Craig's hand until his fingers slid through hers and squeezed with reassurance. "I've never stayed the night in a hospital before."

"Nothing to worry about." Dr. Robinson tsk-tsked, reminding Caroline of her Nan, who made that sound anytime she thought her granddaughter was too skinny and not eating enough. The physician nodded toward Craig. "And your man here said he plans to stay the night with you. So between him and all our nurses, you'll never be alone."

"You're going to stay?" Caroline smiled at Craig and his eyes seemed to turn a darker shade of blue.

He cleared his throat and focused on the blood pressure machine beeping behind her. "Um, if that would make you feel more comfortable. Sure."

If she had the full use of her faculties, Caroline would probably be able to better guess at what the man was thinking. However, she had absolutely no clue what her fiancé's normal response would be in a situation like this. Did he really want to stay? Or was he just being polite? Judging by the forced expression on his face, Caroline would assume the latter. But before she could let him off the hook, the tech showed up to take her for the CT scan.

As the hospital employee maneuvered her hospital

bed through the corridors, Craig walked beside Caroline, her bright pink tote bag looped over one of his broad shoulders. She recognized the purse as the one she'd picked out this morning to go with her new heels and had to swallow a giggle at how much it clashed with his red plaid shirt.

But when it got caught in the elevator door behind him, Caroline could no longer hold in her laughter. "Do you always carry my purse for me?"

He gave a slight grunt, then hefted it higher onto his shoulder. "It was either this or leave it behind in the exam room where anyone could walk by and steal it."

After the radiology tech helped her transfer off the bed and onto the cold platform for her scan, he asked her a series of questions, like whether she was wearing any jewelry or had any metal implants anywhere in her body. Then the tech asked the one question that really threw her. "Any possibility that you're pregnant?"

Caroline's lungs seized and her mouth froze into a circle, unsure of what the answer was. Surely she would remember something like that, wouldn't she? She was only twenty-three years old and had been waiting to have sex until she'd found "the one," which she'd obviously found. She turned pleading eyes to Craig, hating that she couldn't even recall if they'd had intercourse before, let alone whether they'd used any form of birth control. "Have we... I mean is there...?"

She couldn't finish the embarrassing question with the radiology guy looking on, his clipboard not even raised high enough to cover his curious smirk.

A rosy shade of pink stole along Craig's hardened

jawline and his eyes went wide, probably as he realized that he was the only person in the room who could possibly answer such an intimate thing.

"Uh…" His mouth opened and closed several times before he finally cleared his throat. "I think they did a blood test in the ER before the MRI. Maybe it says in her chart or something?"

"Let me take a look," the tech said before flipping a few pages. Caroline wanted to yell at the man for not bothering to check her file first. But she was too busy forcing her muscles to relax against the narrow sheet-covered table underneath her. "Nope, no baby on board. We're good to go."

Caroline almost sighed out loud as the air finally left her chest in a whoosh. Not because she didn't want to have a baby—she most definitely wanted to be a mother someday. She just wanted to fully remember the man who could possibly be the father of her child. Unfortunately, the more she tried to drag the information from her brain, the more her head pounded.

The tech raised and lowered the table and gave her some final instructions about remaining still. At some point, the room went darker, but Caroline's breathing remained ragged and her thoughts kept spinning.

While knowing that she wasn't pregnant gave her one less thing to worry about in the overall scheme of things, it didn't stop her from craving more details about the man she was planning to marry. And what their current physical relationship was like.

Watching Craig's retreating form as he exited the

room, she came to the pulse-elevating realization that just because she couldn't remember having sex with him didn't mean she couldn't vividly imagine it.

Chapter Four

Man, Craig had dodged a serious bullet back there in the radiology room when Caroline looked at him with those doe-shaped brown eyes and wanted to know if they'd ever had sex. How in the hell was he supposed to know the answer to that? Okay, so obviously he knew the actual answer, but he'd been clueless on how to phrase it out loud.

She'd fallen asleep again during the procedure, but Dr. Robinson assured him that it was pretty normal for a concussed patient to doze off occasionally and that resting could actually help her brain heal. As long as Caroline's pupils weren't dilated and she could hold a conversation when she was awake, she was supposedly fine.

By the time they finally got her admitted and assigned to a room, it was getting close to dinnertime and Craig was starving. When she'd confessed that she'd never stayed overnight in a hospital, she'd looked so scared, so frail.

The main goal was to keep her from getting stressed or putting any more strain on her traumatized brain. However, in order to keep his wits about him and do that, he also needed to eat something. Although, what kind of fake fiancé would he be if he sneaked off while she was sleeping to go down to the cafeteria to get some dinner?

Looking around for a pad of paper so he could leave a note, his eyes landed on her ridiculously huge purse sitting in the corner of the room. He had saddlebags smaller than that thing and never understood why some women insisted on hauling everything they owned all around town with them. If he were a betting man, he'd place odds that she had plenty of paper and at least several pens in the thing. The problem was, there was no way to look inside without feeling like he was invading her privacy.

Rubbing a hand through his close-cropped hair, he asked himself for the thousandth time today, "How in the hell did you get yourself into this situation?"

"What was that?" Caroline's sleepy voice was deep and husky, a stark contrast to her delicate and feminine looks. It was also as arousing as anything he'd ever heard before.

"I was just wondering where I could find a pen and paper."

Her sigh came from the back of her throat. "I always carry some in my purse."

"Yeah, I assumed as much but it didn't seem right snooping through your things when you're sound asleep."

"It wouldn't be considered snooping since I don't have any secrets from you." Clearly, her mind was way too fragile to grasp the magnitude of just how many secrets they actually had since they didn't know the first thing about each other. When he didn't respond, she continued, "Are you always this proper around me?"

"I…uh…I guess I'm just a proper type of guy." Or a guy who was simply way out of his element.

She studied him in the dim glow of the room, the sun fading outside the window. He rocked back on his boot heels and looked over his shoulder at the door. They should probably keep that open so nobody got the wrong idea about what was going on in this private room. And since when did hospitals have private rooms?

When Craig had surgery after his second clavicle fracture, he'd been stuck in traction next to an old man who used to confuse the emergency call button for the television remote. The volume on the evening news would go up every time the man didn't get his bedpan in time. If Caroline had a roommate like that, Craig wouldn't have to worry about that electric current charging through his body every time she turned those pretty eyes his way.

"Why did you need paper and a pen?" Caroline asked, and Craig turned back to her.

"Oh. I thought about grabbing a bite to eat downstairs and wanted to leave you a note in case you woke up and I wasn't here."

"So, you're both proper *and* thoughtful." Her full lips turned up at the corners, but her questioning gaze remained steadily fixed on him, as though she were awaiting more discoveries about him. "I'm starving."

"The doctor cleared you to eat after she got the radiology report and there was nothing to indicate you needed immediate surgery. They delivered a tray for you earlier," he said, wheeling the small table over to her bed. "I think it's meat loaf."

She lifted a plastic cover off the plate and crinkled her pert little nose at the cold gray lump underneath. "I'm missing part of my memory, not my taste buds. Since you're going to the cafeteria, would you mind bringing me something from there instead?"

"Sure." He replaced the lid and moved the offending plate out of the way. "What do you want?"

"Anything. Surprise me."

Crap. He'd walked right into that trap. Craig eyed her small frame and couldn't even begin to guess what kind of food she ate. Obviously, it wasn't his preferred meal of steak and potatoes because she looked like a strong wind would blow her away before the next winter storm. For all he knew, she was one of those women who constantly monitored every calorie in order to keep her waist so tiny.

"Maybe a salad?" he suggested because he got the impression that she didn't maintain her lithe shape by being a hearty eater.

"Ugh, no." Caroline stuck out her tongue and made

a gagging sound. "I hate vegetables. Except for french fries."

"I don't think french fries count as a vegetable."

"They're from potatoes, right?" Caroline's voice held a trace of laughter.

"Fine. I'll get you some french fries. How about a double bacon cheeseburger to go with that?" he offered, trying to match her playful tone but sounding more facetious.

"Mmm. That sounds perfect," she replied, and he did a double take at her flat stomach under the hospital gown. Where was she going to put all that food? "Oh, and if they have onion rings, I'll take a side of those, too. See, there's another vegetable I eat."

Apparently, her food preferences aligned more with a growing teenage boy than a consummate dieter. "Something to drink?"

"Strawberry milkshake, if they have it. If not, I'll just take a large orange soda. Oh, and a tapioca pudding. When I was ten, my dad had gallbladder surgery and I remember his hospital had the absolute best tapioca pudding in the world."

He tilted his head and wondered how she could remember a thing like the tapioca pudding she'd eaten when she was a kid, but not be able to remember that she'd never laid eyes on him before today.

When he didn't respond right away, her face turned a charming shade of pink and she pointed toward her purse. "Um, I have money in my wallet. I know it's kind of a big order and I'm not sure how we usually split costs—"

"I'm not taking your money," he interrupted loudly before she insulted him by implying that he'd let the woman he was marrying reimburse him for a meal. Not that he was actually marrying her. He ran a hand through his hair and lowered his voice. "I was just trying to figure out how to carry it all back to the room. Never mind. Don't worry about it. I'll hijack one of these tray tables or a wheelchair or something to push it on."

"Okay, then," she replied, not seeming to pick up on his sarcasm, or at least choosing to ignore it. "Can you hand me my cell phone before you leave? I should probably let my parents know what happened."

"Josselyn said she looked for your phone back at the office but only saw your purse."

"I don't suppose you have my parents' numbers in your contact list." She gnawed her lower lip, but Craig was saved from responding—as well as from staring at her sexy mouth—when she added, "Actually, they're probably out of cell range if my mom is still with the Khasi tribe. I'll just send them an email tomorrow."

"The Khasi tribe?"

"Yes. I'm sure she told you all about her latest research trip. Wait. You've met my parents, haven't you?"

"Uh, not in person. At least, not yet." There, that should be ambiguous enough. After all, Josselyn mentioned her folks were out of the country so it was plausible that he might've talked to them on the phone or via a video chat. Not that Craig knew the first thing about video chatting.

Caroline tilted her head at him. "What about you?"

"What about me?"

"I'm sure you probably need to call someone to let them know you're staying here overnight?"

He lifted a brow. "Like who?"

She shrugged, a deep V forming above her nose. "Do you live with anyone? Like roommates or your family or, um…me?"

His ribs squeezed with pity. It was bad enough that she couldn't remember the fact that they hadn't had sex. The poor thing really must be confused if she couldn't even recall whether they lived together.

It was on the tip of Craig's tongue to tell her that if they were sharing the same bed, he would've left a more lasting impression on her. Instead, he replied, "I live at my family's ranch in Thunder Canyon."

"Oh, good." She relaxed onto her pillows. "I was worried about who would take care of your cat while you're gone."

Craig took a couple steps forward and lowered his chin. "My cat?"

"Yeah, the one with only three legs!" Caroline exclaimed, her face brightening as though she'd just had a miraculous breakthrough in modern science. "I can't think of his name, but I'm sure it will come to me."

Disbelief and a slow-growing sense of alarm kept him from celebrating her achievement. How in the hell did this woman know about his pet? Not that it was completely inconceivable given the fact that most ranches had barns filled with various animals, but the three-legged part confounded him.

"Do you work there, too?" Caroline asked, seemingly

ignoring the fact that Craig was staring at her with his mouth hanging open in shock.

"Where?" Craig gave his head a slight shake to clear his thoughts.

"At your family's ranch," she said slowly, as though it was *his* brain that had been concussed recently.

"Uh, yeah. We raise cattle."

Caroline got that satisfied, faraway look in her eyes again. Every time she made that face, Craig's collar seemed to shrink around his neck and his skin got all tight. Her next question made his toes twitch inside his boots. "So I really am going to marry a cowboy?"

Craig didn't know about that. She certainly wasn't going to marry *this* particular cowboy. No woman was. But he kept his jaw clenched as his feet fought the urge to run right past the sign for the cafeteria and straight toward the exit.

After several more tests, including an EEG before bed, Caroline was surprised by how soundly she slept through the night. Of course, anytime a nurse came to check on her or take her vital signs, all Caroline had to do was look over to where Craig was partially reclined in a too-small chair, his cowboy hat pulled low over his eyes. Then a bubble of security would surround her, making her happily drift back to sleep.

She felt rested when her first visitor arrived.

"Is our patient allowed to have chocolate croissants this morning?" Josselyn asked as she carried in a cardboard tray of coffee drinks in one hand and a white bag in the other.

"She most definitely is," Caroline said, sitting up straighter and resisting the urge to clap excitedly by adjusting the blanket across her lap.

Craig just grunted, before standing up to stretch. Judging by the frown on his face, he either wasn't a morning person or he didn't particularly care for flaky breakfast treats. Caroline hoped it was just the croissants because she couldn't imagine a cowboy not being an early riser. Actually, she couldn't imagine someone not liking fresh-baked pastries, either.

A cracking sound echoed through the room as he twisted at the waist. "I'm getting too old not to sleep in a bed anymore."

Caroline took a quick gulp of coffee to keep from asking the question on the tip of her tongue. How old was he? It was another thing she should know about her fiancé, but couldn't remember. He certainly didn't look old, but there were a few more creases around his eyes than most men her age might have.

"Thanks for bringing breakfast," Caroline said to Josselyn.

"I also brought you a pair of comfy pajamas and some toiletries, not knowing how long you'd be here." Josselyn patted the small tote bag resting against her hip. "Since I didn't have a key to your apartment, you'll have to make do with things from the superstore in Kalispell."

"Anything is better than this hospital gown," Caroline replied, suddenly curious about where her own clothes were. The ones she'd been wearing right before she'd hit her head. She was about to ask, but Dr. Robinson entered the room.

As the physician examined her, Caroline saw Craig slip into the hallway and pull out his cell phone. It was difficult following the doctor's penlight with her eyes when her gaze kept returning to Craig and the way his jeans cupped his rear end as he casually leaned against the nurses' station and spoke into his phone.

"So all the tests suggest that there isn't any long-term damage," Dr. Robinson said just as Craig returned to the room. "Any changes with your memory?"

As much as Caroline sensed the connection with Craig, there was also an underlying nagging sensation in the pit of her stomach every time she smiled at him and he looked away. Had they had a fight recently? Or maybe it was just the fact that she couldn't remember any clear details about the guy and she was projecting her own sense of guilt onto him.

"I feel like things are slowly starting to come back to me." Caroline was trying to remain positive but it was impossible not to notice the way Craig, Josselyn and the physician all looked at each other.

Dr. Robinson finally nodded. "Good. Everything should resolve itself eventually as long as you give your brain time to heal and don't add any additional stress."

The older woman gave a pointed look toward Craig, who scrubbed at the lower half of his face, where dark stubble had blossomed overnight.

"So then I can go home this morning?" Caroline couldn't keep the hopefulness from her voice.

"As long as you're not left alone. With the concussion, I want to be sure someone is keeping an eye on you."

"I have to be at the school library during the day." Josselyn spoke up. "But you can come stay with me out at Sunshine Farm until you're feeling more like your old self."

"I *do* feel like my old self," Caroline insisted, hating the sympathetic looks directed her way. "The only thing that's off is my memory about Craig, which means I should probably stay with him to help jog my brain."

Josselyn sucked in her cheeks before looking at Craig, whose eyes had gone dark again. However, the man kept his lips pressed firmly together. In fact, nobody said anything and it made Caroline wonder what was really going on. What weren't they all telling her?

Finally, Josselyn spoke up. "Craig, you're staying at your brother's ranch while you're in town, right?"

"Right," Craig agreed a little too quickly for someone who'd just been so hesitant to say a word. "I'm bunking with Will and his wife, Jordyn."

"That might be a little cramped, huh?" Josselyn nodded the answer at them as though she were talking to her kindergarten reading circle. "But there's plenty of room out at Sunshine Farm."

"There's also plenty of room at my own house," Caroline said as her gaze narrowed at them in suspicion. "Unless you guys aren't telling me why my fiancé shouldn't be staying with me there..."

Like perhaps Craig was planning to call off the engagement. Caroline's throat constricted.

Josselyn looked up to the ceiling, then said, "Well, here's the thing—"

"It's okay, Josselyn," Craig interrupted. "Of course I don't mind taking care of Caroline."

Chapter Five

Craig felt the heat of Josselyn's eyes on his back as they followed the discharge nurse who was pushing Caroline's wheelchair toward the parking lot. He knew his friend's wife-to-be was staring at him like he was nuts, but all he could do was shrug.

"What about your own ranch, Craig?" A muscle ticked in Josselyn's jaw as she kept her voice too low for Caroline to hear. "Shouldn't you be getting back to Thunder Canyon soon?"

"We just sold the bulk of our herd in Helena and breeding season won't start until after Christmas." Craig fished in his pocket for his truck keys. "My dad and Rob can handle things during the slow season. Besides, the doctor said this was only temporary. I'll be back home before next week."

"You know that you can't stay with Caroline at her place, right? She lives in the center of town and Rust Creek Falls is a small place. People will talk."

"I'll mention that to her when we get in the truck and head in that direction. I'm sure I can convince her during the drive that staying at my brother and sister-in-law's house is for the best."

Unfortunately, when they got to Will and Jordyn's ranch house, Craig realized his sweet and agreeable fiancée wasn't as easy to convince. And if he kept insisting, she was likely to counter his argument and then they'd both be stressed out.

Caroline stood in the middle of the small living room, one arm wrapped across her waist as she stared in confusion at her surroundings. "None of this looks familiar. Have I been here before?"

"Um, I don't think so." Craig regretted not putting a little more confidence into his voice. He'd won the Professional Bull Riders World Championship two years in a row. When had he ever lacked confidence?

"Have I even met Will and Jordyn?" Caroline asked.

"I'm sure you have. Rust Creek Falls is a small town and chances are you've run into them before."

"You mean, you've never introduced us?" Caroline moved her hands to her hips and Craig suddenly wondered how he ever could've thought this petite woman was delicate or fragile. "Have you been keeping our engagement a secret from your family?"

When she turned her full glare at him, she looked eight inches taller than the five-foot-four height listed on her hospital admission paperwork. And a heck of a lot more intimidating than any bull he'd drawn during his time on the rodeo circuit. Craig knew this whole idea was crazy, and right now, he'd gladly welcome Josselyn's presence and her pointed looks of disbelief because that would at least take some of the attention off him. Or she'd at least help dig him out of this mess.

"It's not a secret. It just hasn't been that long since we became engaged." He flicked his eyes toward the clock on the wall. About twenty-four hours to be exact. Instead of keeping things closer to the truth, though, Craig added, "We were just waiting until the next family dinner to make our big announcement."

"And when exactly is the next family dinner?" One of Caroline's eyebrows shot up.

"Thanksgiving," he answered, then gave a silent prayer that Caroline would regain her memory by then.

Her lips parted as she blew out a puff of air, making her entire face soften. A shot of electricity zipped along his nerve endings. She really was a beautiful woman.

"Fine." She exhaled again. "I guess I can wait until next week to meet them all."

Wait. Next week? Damn, he hadn't realized how close the holiday was. That didn't give him much time to prove to Caroline that they really weren't engaged. Or for Caroline to regain her memory and figure it out for herself. For now, all Craig could do was offer a stiff smile and pray that he could untie himself from this lasso of deception that was twisting around him.

"Sorry for getting so snappy like that." She lowered her arms and clasped her hands behind her back and he tried not to notice the way her dainty sweater looked much snugger on her when her proud shoulders were thrown back like that.

"No problem," he said because he couldn't very well just stand here letting her get worked up thinking they had an actual problem. Other than the problem that there was no possible way he was going to take some stranger to Thanksgiving dinner and have his entire family think they'd *both* lost their minds. Not that it was Caroline's fault she'd lost hers temporarily. But Craig didn't have the excuse of a concussion to explain his recent bout with irrational decisions.

"You have been so patient with me through all of this and don't deserve to have me doubting our entire relationship like this." She held out a palm when he opened his mouth to protest that he wasn't the saint she was making him out to be. "I mean, obviously I'm experiencing this connection between us, but it's just so frustrating not being able to remember all the details of our life together."

Imagine how he felt. He was standing in his brother's living room with a woman he didn't know, trying to keep her calm and relaxed as he pretended like he was her soon-to-be husband.

Hold on. He pushed the brim of his hat back on his forehead. "You're experiencing a *connection*?"

"Of course I am. I didn't hit my head that hard." Caroline rolled her eyes, then winced as she brought her fingers to her temples.

Craig was by her side in an instant. "Does it hurt?"

"Just when I move too quickly."

He put his hand on the small of her back and tried

to direct her toward the sofa. But her pointy high heels didn't budge. Maybe a strong wind wouldn't blow her over after all. "Why don't you lie down and rest?"

"Actually, Craig, I would really feel more comfortable if we just went back to my place."

"Honey, I can't very well stay the night at your place with you. You know how people love to gossip around small towns."

"Honey," she repeated before smiling wide. She took a step toward him and his knees went all rubbery, probably because he'd hardly slept a wink in that hospital chair. "That's what we call each other? I like it."

He rolled his lips inward to keep from admitting that it was the same term of endearment he used on all the young calves at the ranch when he was trying to herd them into a corral or lead them somewhere they didn't want to go. But she'd given him a lead and he didn't waste it. "Speaking of names people call each other, I would hate for anyone to say something unflattering about you if I were to spend the night at your house."

"Surely you know me well enough by now to realize that I don't care what people think about me." She waved a dismissive hand before resting her palm against his chest. A blast of heat lit underneath her fingertips and he stood there absolutely still, hoping the unfamiliar sensation passed. However, when she took another step closer to him and her eyelids lowered, the flame spread. "Plus, I'm sure it's not the first time we'll be staying the night together."

He gulped. "How do you figure?"

"How else would I know that you use two pillows?"

A jolt traveled down the back of Craig's neck as he wondered how she'd found out about his sleeping habits. Maybe that was just another good guess on her part. Plenty of people used more than one pillow.

"Anyway," she continued as her fingers made slow circles along the third button on his shirt, "I really think we would both be more comfortable at my place. Not to mention the fact that things are more likely to come back to me if I'm in my normal environment."

Craig searched her face, trying to control his breathing. The first problem was that if she continued touching him like this, there was no way he could remain in the same room with the woman, let alone the same house. At least, not unless he wanted to take their fake, temporary relationship to a real, permanent level. The second problem was that he had absolutely no idea where her house was, and he couldn't very well admit as much without further raising her suspicions.

While he may be willing to go along with this little delusion of hers to an extent, he wasn't about to have anyone believing that he didn't normally pick up his dates at their front doors like a gentleman.

When she was this close to him, it was impossible to concentrate on forming an acceptable excuse as to why he shouldn't stay with her. Only a weak-willed jerk would take advantage of a woman in this situation. And Craig had never been accused of being weak-willed.

"Please?" Her hands slipped up to his shoulders.

"Fine," Craig bit out, saying the only thing that would allow him to politely step out of her embrace and buy himself some more time. "Let me go get my gear and we'll head over to your place."

When he was in the spare bedroom packing up the duffel bag he'd brought to visit his brother, he shot off a text to Josselyn asking for Caroline's address. He shoved his toiletries in next, hoping that Joss wouldn't respond with a lecture on how he was making a massive mistake by taking Caroline home. Instead, the only thing she sent was an address to a smaller rental unit behind one of the historical houses in the heart of Rust Creek Falls.

"Ready to go?" he asked Caroline when he returned to the living room.

"Yes," she replied, setting down the picture frame she'd been studying. "Your family is huge."

He glanced at the photo of all his brothers and sisters and their spouses at his parents' anniversary party last year. "There used to be just eight of us kids, but our numbers keep growing."

"And you're the oldest in the family?" she asked.

"Yep," he replied as he walked toward the front door, hoping she'd follow. Something prickled at him. Why would she automatically assume he was the oldest? Did he look elderly next to his siblings? Because he was beginning to feel that way when he was with her. According to the hospital bracelet still on her wrist, Caroline was only twenty-three, and suddenly he wondered if she was aware of the twelve-year age difference between them.

She picked up another frame, this time a picture of all his brothers at Jonathan and Dawn's wedding, then set it down before walking past him to get to the front porch. "Do you always look so solemn in your pictures?"

First she'd accused him of being proper, and now she was calling him solemn. Perhaps her "oldest in the family" comment was simply an accurate observation. After his rodeo career ended, everyone had begun referring to him as the stuffy, serious big brother. "Well, someone has to be in charge and take care of the others. Besides, the photographer was taking forever to get the perfect groomsmen shot and all I wanted to do was get inside the reception and grab a beer."

"Speaking of photographers and receptions," Caroline said when Craig opened the truck door for her. "Have we started planning our wedding?"

He rubbed a hand on the side of his neck as he looked anywhere but at her face. Of course, she would've already been planning her wedding. It was what she did for a living. "I think you wanted to wait until after we told my family before we set a date."

"That makes sense." She nodded, and the ball of guilt that had slowly been building in Craig's gut got a little bigger.

He wanted to yell that none of it made any sense whatsoever. Instead, he climbed into the cab of his truck and steered toward Cedar Street, driving himself deeper into the next round of make-believe.

By the time he turned off Main Street, Craig had convinced himself that Caroline most likely had an actual fiancé or even a serious boyfriend who looked just like him. He was no brain surgeon, but it was truly the only way any of this could possibly make any sense. Josselyn had pointed out that Caroline wasn't wearing a ring, but that didn't mean anything nowadays.

When they got to her house, he was bound to see signs of whoever this mystery guy was. Of course, if there was in fact another man, Craig would need to figure out a way to explain why he'd gone along with the whole ruse.

He pulled into a long driveway of one of the large historical homes on Cedar Street and Caroline pointed toward the smaller cottage in the rear corner of the lot. "You can park in my space back here."

Her unit was a miniature version of the Craftsman-style house in front. There were well-tended flower bushes surrounding the green clapboard shingles, and a small cornucopia filled with mini pumpkins and colorful gourds sat on a table next to a white wooden rocking chair that was way too big for the dinky porch.

As Caroline unlocked the dark walnut door, Craig realized that this might be his last chance to make a run for it. There were no other vehicles parked near the property, but what if her real fiancé was sitting inside? Even a framed picture of another man with Caroline could be waiting in there, on full display to counter every falsehood he'd allowed the poor woman to believe about him.

Another unfamiliar pang of envy shot through him at the thought that this beautiful and optimistic woman might belong to someone else. Not that he should be jealous, he reminded himself as he cautiously followed her inside. If he didn't already know that Caroline was most definitely not his type, he would've been able to figure it out just by looking at her interior decorating choices.

There was an overstuffed white sofa in the middle of the living room and all Craig could think was how impractical the color was—it would be impossible to keep clean. Then there were the twenty or so throw pillows in varying floral and swirly prints piled on it, as well as the dollhouse-size chairs on either side of the full bookshelves that lined one entire wall. Okay, so maybe the chairs were a tad bigger than a doll, but he doubted they could hold all 190 pounds of him. Frilly yellow checkered curtains framed the windows, and expensive-looking paintings hung on the pale blue walls.

Craig had definitely been right about Caroline the first time he'd gotten a look at her silly high heels. A girlie girl like her would never last on the family ranch.

"I'm going to hop in the shower and wash the hospital smell off me," she said, setting her large tote bag down on the white kitchen table. "I think I have some deli meat in the fridge and I picked up a couple of bags of chips at the market a few days ago if you want to help yourself to a snack."

"I'm good," Craig said, trying not to think of what Caroline would look like naked, with the water sluicing off her.

Since the kitchen looked out into the living room, he guessed that the doorway she walked toward led to the bedroom. The only bedroom, judging by the look of things. That meant Craig would be bunking on the sofa tonight because there was no way he was going to sleep in a bed next to her, no matter how many pillows she thought he used.

He dropped his duffel bag near the sofa, and when he heard the water pipes hum to life, he began carefully examining the contents of the bookshelves. There were paperback novels shoved next to old-fashioned leather-bound volumes of those boring stories his high school English teacher referred to as "classics." There were ancient-looking artifacts and modern-looking sculptures. He recalled Josselyn mentioning something about Caroline's parents traveling quite a bit. She obviously had quite the collection of random souvenirs.

There were also plenty of framed photos of Caroline in all stages of her young life—from a pigtailed toddler to a college graduate—standing in between a proud man and woman who Craig assumed were her parents. He saw a handful of pictures of Caroline with other women her age, but there was nothing suggesting another man in her life.

His shoulders sagged in relief. Unfortunately, he didn't know if that relief was a good thing or a bad thing.

Chapter Six

Caroline wrapped her wet hair in a bun on top of her head and slipped on her favorite pair of cropped pink pajama pants. She debated putting on a bra, but her breasts were small enough that she could get away with a camisole-style tank. In the interest of modesty, she threw on her faded gray University of Montana sweat-shirt, the one with the women's tennis team logo on the front.

While it was still the middle of the afternoon and she should want to impress Craig with her more fashionable wardrobe, she was pretty exhausted and just wanted to be comfortable. As a wedding planner, she always felt the need to be well put-together with a professional hairstyle and a businesslike appearance that conveyed to her clients that she could handle any situation. But she wasn't going into the office today.

Before she walked out of the only bathroom in her one-bedroom house, she swiped on a layer of mascara and applied some strawberry-flavored lip balm so she would at least look somewhat healthy.

She wasn't sure if her fiancé had seen her in her most natural state before, but if they were going to eventually be living together, he might as well get used to it. As she walked out of the bedroom, she found him staring at one of the oil paintings on her living room wall.

"My dad painted that when we lived in Nice," she said, going for her most casual voice since there was a chance she'd already told him the story about the café near the Sophia Antipolis. It was one thing to allow the guy to see her in comfy clothes; it was quite another to bore him to death with repeated anecdotes from her family's travels.

"You know what," Craig said suddenly, taking a step back. "I'm going to go to the pharmacy and pick up your prescription."

"But I'm not having any pain right now. And I have some Tylenol in my medicine cabinet if I need it."

He couldn't seem to stop glancing toward the front door, and she wondered just how badly he was yearning to get away from her. Was it because of the plain way she looked? Or was something else going on with him? Not willing to be the source of his discomfort, she gave him an out. "Seriously, though, you really don't have to sit around here with me. I'm sure you have plenty of other things you could be doing on a Friday afternoon."

She couldn't tell if that was relief flashing across his face, but the short-lived expression was soon replaced with steely determination. "The doctor didn't want you to be left alone."

Caroline flicked her wrist. "But she didn't mean every single second. I'm sure you could leave and come back."

Despite the fact that *he'd* been the one who'd just suggested going to the pharmacy, he didn't appear convinced. So Caroline continued, "Actually, my phone and laptop are still at my office and if you could go and get those for me, I'd be able to get a little work done before tomorrow."

"What's tomorrow?"

"I'm meeting the organizers of the Presents for Patriots event. They're having a formal fund-raiser at Sawmill Station, and my company volunteered to host the event and coordinate the party planning."

Craig lowered his chin as he studied her. "I don't think you're supposed to be working yet."

"Well, my boss is out of town, so I'm the only one who can attend the meeting. Besides, most of the actual work is already done, but all the notes are on my laptop and I'd like to refresh myself with the details beforehand."

"Maybe I should call Josselyn and see if she can come over and watch you while I'm gone."

"Watch me? Like I need a babysitter?"

"Here we go again." Craig nodded at Caroline's arms, which were now crossed in front of her.

"What does that mean?" She narrowed her eyes at

him. "Has my work schedule been a problem for you in the past?"

"In the past?" He mumbled something else under his breath but she didn't quite catch it.

"Or currently?" Her bare toes dug into the plush rug under her feet as she prepared to stay rooted to the spot until she got some answers.

"Um…" Craig took a step back.

"Please tell me you're not one of those old-fashioned macho types who think their women need to be taking care of the farm and raising their babies?"

"I don't even have a farm." Craig was now backed up against the arm of the sofa. "It's a ranch. And no, I don't have a problem with what you do for a living. You can work wherever and whenever you want. I was just concerned about your injury."

"Then what did you mean by 'here we go again'?"

"I meant that when you get determined to do something, you go from a sweet, docile little thing to some sort of broncing—I mean, fierce warrior like that." He snapped his fingers.

Broncing? Caroline really hoped that the man hadn't been about to compare her to an angry rodeo animal. They were both pretty worn-out, though, so she decided to give Craig the benefit of the doubt.

"Well, if it's any consolation, I rarely bring out this so-called 'fierce warrior' unless absolutely necessary. At least not with most people." She tugged her lower lip between her teeth as she studied him. Then she asked, "Do we usually argue a lot?"

"What? No." One side of his mouth curled downward. "What would we have to argue about?"

"Sorry. Again." She felt her chest ease back, realizing she hadn't been aware she'd puffed it out in the first place. "I guess I'm just on edge because I'm pretty exhausted, even though it feels like I've been in a deep sleep for the majority of our engagement. Anyway, I was focusing on all the things I can't remember instead of being grateful for all the stuff that's clearly in front of me."

"In front of you?" Craig's skin seemed to lose some of its tan color.

"You." She rubbed his biceps in an effort to reassure him, but the physical contact only reminded her of how hard and well-shaped his muscles were under his shirt. She yanked her hand back a bit too quickly. "*You're* here in front of me. A wonderful man who was willing to spend the entire night in a miserable chair beside my hospital bed. A man who is willing to risk his proper reputation to spend the night with me at my house in order to nurse me back to health, even though I'm totally healthy, by the way."

He coughed. "Risking *my* reputation?"

Really, Craig was quite adorable when his eyebrow dipped into a squiggly line like that. Caroline had to wonder how often she confused the poor guy. Probably all the time if that was the cute face he made whenever she did.

"Thank you for being so good to me." She rose on her toes and kissed him on his cheek.

Craig didn't jump away from her in a desperate

panic, but he also didn't return her kiss. He just stood there, stiff as a granite statue, his eyes dark and full of caution.

So far, she got the impression that he was definitely the type of guy who would be overprotective. She hoped his lack of response was because he didn't want to unleash his passion and accidentally injure her. The alternative would be that he didn't feel any passion for her at all, and Caroline didn't want to think about that dismal possibility.

"I'm going to go take a nap," she finally said, because one of them needed to say or do something. His only reaction was a brief nod.

As she walked to her bedroom, she was too nervous to turn around to look at him. But she listened to him unzip his duffel bag as her head hit the pillow. She fell asleep before she could hear anything else. When she woke up an hour later, she found a note by her bed.

Went to pick up your stuff from your office. Craig.

There was nothing about when he'd be back. Or if he'd even be back at all.

Craig was trying another key off the same ring Caroline had used to open her front door when his cell phone rang. Still standing in front of her office, he scrambled to pull the vibrating thing out of his back pocket, thinking Caroline had woken up and needed him. But she didn't have her cell phone, and he hadn't seen a landline at her house. In fact, she didn't even have his number. Which might present quite a problem once she realized the man she thought she was going to marry wasn't listed in any of her contacts.

Looking at the name on the display, Craig sighed before sliding his finger across the screen and answering. "Hey, Rob."

"Oh, good, you finally found time to answer your phone, big brother." Rob's voice always had a teasing edge, but today it was downright buoyant, as though nothing was going to sink his good humor. "Mom wants to know if you'll be bringing your new lady friend home for Thanksgiving."

Craig squeezed his eyes shut and counted to three. "What new lady friend?"

"The one our baby sister, Celeste, heard you had in the front seat of your truck about an hour or ago."

"How could C.C. hear about that already?" Craig asked, using the youngest Clifton's nickname. "She's not even home from college yet."

"Some kid from her vet science class used to baby-sit for Will's neighbor, who saw you with the pretty gal that works for that wedding planning outfit over at Sawmill Station. Said you both went into Will and Jordyn's house and then little bit later, you left together. With your duffel bag."

That was how things went in a small town. A neighbor told a friend, who told a cousin, who told their former fourth-grade teacher, and before a person could blink, it was on the front page of the *Rust Creek Falls Gazette*. He knew it was bound to happen. He just hadn't expected word to get all the way to Thunder Canyon that fast.

Stupid him.

"It's a long story, but there is absolutely nothing going on between me and Caroline Ruth." Craig immediately looked around the wooden platform in front of the old-fashioned train depot, hoping none of the Daltons, who owned the land, overheard the blatant lie. Clearly, there was *something* going on between him and the beautiful woman who, brain injury aside, should've known better than to kiss him. Even if it was only on his cheek.

Those sweet lips of hers held a promise of something more. What that was, Craig didn't want to know. Finding out wouldn't be fair to either of them, but especially not to Caroline, who looked incredibly innocent and fresh standing in front of him in those pajama pants that were so thin they showed the outline of her rear end. He didn't even want to start thinking about that sweatshirt that fell off her shoulder, displaying a slinky spaghetti strap against her smooth, creamy skin.

"Caroline Ruth," Rob repeated, his smug tone latching onto the slightest revelation of new information. "Good thing our grandfather is coming for dinner this year. He eats so slow, you'll have plenty of time to tell your family all about this so-called 'long story.'"

"Nothing to tell."

"Want to know what I think?" Rob asked.

"Actually, no. I don't really care what you th—"

"I think that there's *plenty* to tell about this Caroline Ruth and that's why you're trying to keep everything under wraps."

"Speaking of wraps, have those new posts come in

yet for the southeast fence line?" Craig knew the best way to deal with his family was to redirect.

"Dad and I already took care of the fence," Rob replied, making Craig think that he'd successfully changed the subject. But his brother was like a mangy dog with a bone. "You know we're all going to find out about her anyway. Might as well come clean."

"Nothing much to tell." Craig scratched the scar tissue along his neck, thinking of ways to downplay the recent events that had completely bucked him like a greenhorn with his hand stuck in the bronc rein as he got dragged along for the ride. "Caroline is planning Drew and Josselyn's wedding. She took a pretty big fall in her office and smacked her head. When she came to, she thought she knew me, and the doctor said it was best not to correct her until she regained her memory."

"No way!" Rob whooped and Craig had to pull the phone away from his head before he ruptured an eardrum. "Like she's got amnesia? I didn't think that kind of thing happened in real life."

"It's not exactly amnesia," Craig started, before deciding it was probably best not to overexplain and get caught up in the details. "Anyway, that's why I said it was a long story. And I would appreciate it if you didn't tell anyone else what's going on. Caroline might not want strangers knowing her personal business."

"Right. So then how exactly did *you* get involved in her business?"

Craig sighed, but it came out as more of a growl. "Because her boss is out of town and her family's in another country and, with the concussion, the doctor didn't want her to be alone. So I gave her a ride home and I'm keeping an eye on things."

"Keeping an eye on things, huh?" Rob didn't bother to cover the mouthpiece on his end as he snorted.

"What's that supposed to mean?"

"You're my big brother. I know how you keep an eye on things. Growing up, you watched all of us like a hawk."

"I'm protective. So what?"

"*Protective* is an understatement, Craig. Remember the time we went to the county fair and Dad told you to watch us at the mutton busting competition? I was in third grade, but you told the judges I was only six because they made all the kids in that age bracket wear helmets."

"I'd like to point out that you were small for your age and the following year, they made everyone wear helmets. I was simply ahead of the times."

"Then," his brother continued, refusing to cede Craig's point, "you followed me into the pen and slipped the sheep I was riding a huge chunk of caramel apple. When the announcer blew the horn, instead of sprinting around the arena, the animal just stood there chewing its sticky cud."

"That sheep was nicknamed Wooly Widowmaker and I probably saved you from a broken arm and a lifetime of embarrassment. So, as much as I'd like to sit around and listen to you grovel out your eternal thanks, Rob, I actually need to get going."

"Anyway, back to the reason why I called. Are you

bringing your new lady friend for Thanksgiving or not?" his brother asked.

"It depends."

"On what?"

Craig looked at Caroline's key ring hanging limply in the office door. "On whether she remembers who the hell I am before then."

Chapter Seven

Caroline drenched the chicken pieces in flour as the oil sizzled in her cast-iron skillet. How could she remember the exact temperature for getting a perfect scorch on her fried chicken, yet not remember whether or not her fiancé even liked her cooking?

Glancing at the digital clock on the stove, Caroline realized that she was stressing about what to feed Craig when she should be worried about the fact that he might not be coming back at all.

No. Of course he would come back. Her gut knew it, even if her head was slow to see all the other signs. He'd sat with her in the hospital all night. If he was going to bail out on her, he would've done it long before now.

She'd spent the past hour walking around her house, looking in drawers and pulling out old family photo albums, gaining more comfort and confidence each time she'd come across another detail in her life that she recalled clear as day. If she had her laptop, she would get online and do some research on amnesia and concussions and anything else that could be wrong with her brain.

Not that anything else seemed to be wrong. As far as she could tell, Craig was the only person in her world that she didn't remember. Sure, it was disconcerting, but it would've been downright eerie if she didn't have that steady sensation that there was definitely something about the man that felt right.

Turning up the volume on the music channel on her television, Caroline sang along with the classic country station, taking further solace in the fact that she still knew all the words to every George Jones, Dolly Parton and Conway Twitty song by heart.

When Tammy Wynette came on and encouraged her to stand by her man, Caroline hiccuped a little giggle. Her mother had once caught her only child listening to that particular song and immediately put on her Helen Reddy CD and had her daughter memorize the lyrics to "I Am Woman" instead.

Caroline really needed to email her parents. She'd video chatted with them on Monday, but they never went more than four or five days without at least a text conversation. They were bound to get worried if they didn't hear from her soon. Not that Caroline would tell them about being in the hospital. Her dad had a writer's imagination and she didn't need him thinking the worst and flying back to the States early just to check on her.

A light knock sounded at the door and she padded out of the kitchen in her pink fuzzy slippers. Looking through the peephole, she felt a charge of excitement surge through her when she saw Craig standing on her porch.

"You didn't have to knock," she told him as she yanked the door open so quickly, it bumped against her shoulder. "I left it unlocked for you."

"I didn't want to just barge in and scare you, especially if you were still asleep."

"I'm awake." She smiled, then felt her lips falter as she realized she was standing there like an eager cocker spaniel, stating the obvious. Caroline stepped aside to let him into the house.

Craig handed her the laptop case and her smartphone with twenty-four missed calls and twice as many text alerts. He sniffed and asked, "Are you cooking something?"

Caroline was still leaning against the open door frame and the chilly air reminded her that she'd taken off her sweatshirt when she'd started working in the kitchen. Craig's eyes dropped to where her hardened nipples pressed against the soft cotton fabric of her tank top. However, instead of shivering from the cold, Caroline was filled with a rush of warmth from his intense stare.

If it had been any other person standing there, she would've clutched the laptop to her chest and blocked his view. But there was something slightly empowering about having this type of effect on her man. Overcome with a boldness she couldn't explain, Caroline pushed her shoulders back, making her small breasts thrust further out. She saw the muscles in his throat swallow and then she actually did shiver.

"Yes," she finally said, then spoke louder. "I'm making fried chicken and mashed potatoes. I wasn't sure what you liked to eat so I hope that's okay?"

Walking toward the kitchen, she set her laptop down on the dining table along the way. She heard Craig closing the front door and wondered if she should've also grabbed her sweatshirt off the back of the sofa and covered up. Even though they were engaged, she was completely alone in her house with the man. A man who looked at her as though she was the most attractive woman in the world and he was just now seeing her for the first time.

Of course that was silly on both accounts—she was by no means beautiful and, obviously, Craig had seen her before. But why did it suddenly feel as though she was now playing with fire?

Trying to ignore all these unfamiliar emotions battling inside her, Caroline flipped the chicken over in her trusty skillet, needing to ground herself in something she understood. Food.

A tingling crept up the back of her neck and she glanced over her shoulder, spotting Craig leaning one of his jean-clad hips against the counter.

"That's my favorite," he said, still staring at her, his nostrils slightly flared.

Caroline's mouth went dry. "What is?"

"Fried chicken." But his dark blue eyes weren't focused on the food in the pan. They were studying her and all that lovely heat was spreading through her body again. "You asked if it was okay."

"Oh." Caroline forced her own attention back to the stove.

"Do you need any help in here?" he asked.

She allowed her head to turn only slightly in his direction. "You know how to cook?"

"Of course. I'm the oldest of eight kids and I grew up on a ranch. My parents made all of us learn how to do every job around the place from wrestling steers to feeding baby calves to churning homemade butter."

"When I was a kid, I didn't even have baby dolls to take care of. I wish I had grown up with siblings. What was that like?"

"Trust me, my brothers and sisters were way more needy and annoying than baby dolls. But once in a while, they would come in handy when we had a lot of chores to do."

"Are ranches a lot of work?" she asked, wanting to keep the conversation off anything that would make her think about how close he was to her in this tiny kitchen.

"You have no idea." Craig made a weird huffy sound that came out as a chuckle. It was the same noise her college roommate had made when Caroline enrolled in the same linear algebra class as the serious math major. By the end of the semester, the roommate was coming to Caroline for tutoring.

There were few things in this world that Caroline actually found to be all that challenging once she set her mind to it. So when someone implied that she couldn't handle something, it only made her want to master that very thing. It didn't matter if it was ranching, advanced mathematics or mashing some potatoes while a sexy cowboy stood so close, her tummy felt like it was doing flips.

Oh, and she could also do flips, thanks to her years on two different junior high gymnastics teams.

She was tempted to say as much to Craig, but it was always easier to just show people what she could do. Although she had to admit that she'd been the first one to question *his* abilities when he'd offered to help her cook.

Instead, Caroline forced a smile and told her fiancé, "I've got things under control in here."

"Oh. Okay." He put his hands in his back pockets and she turned to the fridge to pull out more ingredients for the potatoes. She was reaching for a pint of half-and-half when he added, "Then would you mind if I used your shower?"

She turned around so quickly, the carton of butter she'd been holding slipped out of her grip, and one of the sticks popped out and landed near the toe of his cowboy boot. Before he could bend down to pick it up, she was already forming an image of a very naked Craig in her small, steamy bathroom.

"Unless you'd rather I stay here to help," he said, holding out the butter that was still wrapped in its wax paper, one corner completely dented. It was then that she noticed he was wearing the same clothes he'd had on at the hospital yesterday. No wonder he wanted to take them off. She stared at the buttons on his shirt, thinking how easy it would be to slip them through their little holes and... *Stop*, she commanded herself, then drew in a deep gulp of air and found her voice.

"No, I'm fine. I'll get you a towel as soon as I turn the heat down in here," she offered, then caught her breath at the double meaning. "The heat on the stove, I mean. Unless you already know where the towels are. Assuming you've taken a shower here before. Not that you would have, unless there was a time when you needed to. Although how would I know either way? It's not like I've been giving a lot of thought to you being in my shower. And now I'm just babbling and not making sense at all. I better just show you where the linen cabinet is."

Except he didn't seem the least bit confused by her rambling, awkward speech. In fact, his normally questioning eyebrow remained firmly in place as he lifted one side of his mouth and replied, "I think I can figure it out."

Caroline Ruth had almost as many bottles lined up on her tiled shower wall as she did on the narrow shelf above her pedestal sink. Although he'd never shared a bathroom with his sisters, Craig knew perfectly well that women tended to like a variety of beauty products, especially ones that smelled good. However, the amount of choices on display before him had to be some sort of record.

Craig sniffed at the open lid of the fancy shampoo. At least, he assumed it was fancy judging by the French label. He also assumed it was shampoo since he didn't speak French. But it wasn't like he was some young, inexperienced buck. He was thirty-five years old and had stayed the night at ladies' places before. But that was mostly when he'd been traveling on the pro circuit, and he usually did so only after a night out celebrating a good ride. Then he'd be back on the road, heading for the next city. He'd never really been all that invested in a relationship enough to pay much attention to what the women he dated stocked in their bathrooms.

Well, except for Tina. She'd been his neighbor and they'd practically grown up at each other's houses. Tina had been the type to use whatever soap was on sale at the local market. It was why she'd been the perfect partner for Craig. She didn't care about all these frilly, girlie things like—he squinted his eyes at the label across the white bottle he'd just knocked over—Paraben-Free Volumizing Conditioner with Added Boost. She cared about horses and working hard and merging her family's ranch with his. Unfortunately, Craig's dream of the perfect partnership and the perfect relationship had died along with Tina many years ago.

Pretending otherwise with Caroline wasn't fair to either of them.

Foregoing the shampoo bottle's posted recommendation of a five-minute wait time, Craig stuck his head under the nozzle to rinse off. Then he turned the water as hot as he could stand it, hoping the steam would drive away all the cravings the pretty wedding planner had recently brought back into his world.

His skin was red and stinging when he finally shut off the water. Maybe he should've taken a cold shower instead. He grabbed a fluffy lavender towel—because apparently there was nothing masculine in this house—and wrapped it around his waist. Wiping his hand across the fogged-up mirror above the sink, Craig stared at his reflection.

What was he doing here?

He needed to go out there and tell Caroline the truth. He needed to call Josselyn or Drew or Dr. Robinson and inform them that he couldn't do this. He couldn't keep lying to that poor, sweet girl.

No. She wasn't a girl, he reminded himself as he saw an edge of lace peeking out from behind the damp towel hanging off a hook on the back of the door. She was a woman. A woman who clearly wasn't wearing a bra right this second. And he'd boldly stared at her small, firm breasts as though he'd had a right to look. He'd stood there in her open doorway wondering what shade of pink her nipples would be as his palms had itched to slide up underneath her skimpy tank top.

Now that his body recalled the image, he had to refasten his towel over his growing arousal. Cursing, he dug into his duffel bag to pull out his shaving kit and ended up knocking the whole thing off the toilet. This bathroom was so tiny.

Hell, the whole house was tiny. It felt as if everything was shrinking in on him. How was he going to last the entire night with Caroline and not accidentally touch her? There had to be someone else who could stay here with her.

As though reading his exact thoughts, Craig's phone lit up with an incoming text from Drew. How's our patient?

She seems to be completely fine, Craig's big fingers tapped out awkwardly on the minuscule keyboard.

It was the truth. Caroline looked totally healthy. Almost too healthy, if one asked Craig's growing libido. He stared at his screen, hoping that his buddy would give him permission to abandon his caregiver duties.

Head injuries are like that. They can seem fine one minute, and the next minute… Drew didn't finish his sentence, letting three little dots at the end of his sentence imply all the potential risks to Caroline.

Those three dots were the reason Craig was here. Nobody knew what to expect.

When Craig didn't reply, another text bubble appeared from Drew. *Has she regained her memory yet?*

As far as I can tell, she knows everything else about her past except who I am. It's weird.

The brain is a weird and complex thing.

Thanks for the anatomy lesson, Dr. Drew. But what do I do in the meantime? I can't keep pretending that we're engaged.

What else do you have going on right now?

Craig pushed a lock of wet hair off his forehead before typing, *It's not a matter of my time.*

You want me to see if Ben can come stay with her?

Even with all the hot air surrounding him, Craig went cold at the thought. No, he typed and hit the send button.

It's me she wants, not Ben, he began typing, then immediately deleted the words. That would make him sound jealous when he clearly had nothing to be jealous of because none of this was real. Caroline didn't truly want him. She didn't even know him.

It's that none of this feels right. She's going to be so pissed when she finds out we have been tricking her, Craig wrote instead, purposely using the word *we* to remind Drew that he was in on this asinine plan.

There was no response for a while, so Craig set his phone down and lathered his face. He was halfway done shaving when Drew's next text came through. Just try to be as honest as possible without stressing her out. And remember, it's not YOU tricking her. It's her brain.

But why did her brain pick me? he replied. Not that he would've preferred it picking Ben.

This time, he didn't have to wait long for Drew's response. Buddy, I may be a doctor, but even someone as smart as me doesn't know why ANY woman's brain would pick you.

Haha, Craig texted, then added an emoji of a hand making a crude gesture. That was pretty much the extent of his technology skills.

He finished shaving and found a clean pair of jeans in his duffel bag. However, all the steam in the enclosed space made his skin damp and he had to wrestle the jeans over his legs. After he finally buttoned his fly, he decided he needed to let in some cool air before pulling on one of his T-shirts.

When he opened the bathroom door, Caroline stood on the other side, one arm raised as though she'd been about to knock. At first, her eyes were round with surprise, but then her lids lowered toward his bare chest. He resisted the urge to flex his pectoral muscles, but he also couldn't bring himself to break her concentration as she studied him, a slight hitch in her breathing. After all, it had been a while since his body was whole. Since a woman had been so obviously and physically responsive in her assessment of him.

They stared at each other for what felt like minutes before she finally squeaked, "Dinner's ready."

Caroline pivoted quickly and her slim legs practically ran toward the living room. When she was finally a safe distance away, Craig's only thought was that if they both kept looking at each other like that, they would never get through the night.

Chapter Eight

After accidentally confirming that every ounce of his upper torso was indeed made out of rippling muscle, Caroline decided that she couldn't face Craig across the dining table and carry on a conversation without thinking of his steamy tan skin underneath his T-shirt.

"Why don't we put something on TV while we eat?" she suggested, carrying their plates to the coffee table she'd found at a local antiques store and painted a soft shade of butter yellow.

"Wow, this looks great," he said when he sat next to her on the sofa, which was really more of a love seat. It was too late when she realized that being this close to him, sitting side by side, was almost as bad as making eye contact with him.

"What do you want to watch?" she asked when he had

a forkful of mashed potatoes and gravy in his mouth, then had to wait for him to finish chewing before he could answer.

"I don't care. What do you normally watch?"

"Whatever I programmed on the DVR the week before." She picked up the remote control and turned on the television and a list of her new recordings popped up on the screen.

He let out a little chuckle. "Looks like my choices are either all of last Saturday's college football games or else an assortment of movies from the Hallmark Channel."

"That'd be pretty much it," she said, scrolling down. "I'm guessing you don't want to watch this one about a big shot fashion designer returning to the small town where she grew up to attend her former prom date's wedding to another woman?"

"Pretty sure I already read the book," Craig said before biting into a crispy chicken thigh. His thick lashes actually fluttered closed as he moaned.

"So football, then?" Caroline said brightly, turning up the volume so the sportscasters drowned out Craig's sighs of satisfaction.

"Sure," Craig said as he wiped his hands on a napkin. "But I already watched the University of Montana game last Saturday."

"I know they lost, but they're still the top seed in the Big Sky Conference, and if they beat Portland State next week, they'll go to the FCS playoffs."

"Wait. You actually watch college football?" The squiggly eyebrow was back, but instead of looking surprised, his accompanying smirk made him appear doubtful.

"Craig, my parents have been guest lecturers at most of the top universities in the United States. So I've been to a football game at every Division 1 stadium and most of the Division 2 schools."

"Wow. I guess I didn't see that coming."

"Seems as if we're both still learning things about each other." She smiled as she picked up a piece of chicken.

"Why don't we see what's on live TV?" he suggested and then shoveled another forkful of potatoes into his mouth. "This gravy is almost as good as my grandma's."

"Almost?"

"Well, it's better, but don't tell my Meemaw."

"Will I be meeting your Meemaw at Thanksgiving?" Caroline tried to get her voice as neutral as possible. Now that the subject of his family had come up again, she didn't want to seem too eager or even pushy. But she was dying to know more about the rest of the Cliftons. It would give her more clues about the man she was planning to marry.

"Probably. Unless she and my grandpa get into one of their fights beforehand. Even then, she might still show up just to make him mad. If they *are* going at it, though, you have to be very careful not to pick sides."

"Please. I'm a wedding planner. Diplomacy during the heat of family disputes is my specialty." She pushed the live-TV button on the remote control and since it was already set to a sports channel, an announcer welcomed them to the North American Championship Rodeo. "How long have your grandparents been married?"

"Oh, they aren't married to each other. Meemaw is my grandma on my mom's side and Grandpac is my dad's dad."

"His name is Grand Pack? Two words?"

"No." Craig gave a slight grin and Caroline realized it was the first time she'd seen him not looking so blasted serious. Her knees would've gone all wobbly if she hadn't already been sitting down. "Grandpac. One word. When I was a kid in Wrangler Camp, we had to learn how to work with leather, and I decided to hand tool Grandpa Clifton's name onto the back of a belt. Unfortunately, as I started running out of room, my letters got squished closer together and I could only fit *Grandpa C*, which ended up looking more like *Grandpac*. My brother Jonathan had just learned to read, and when he sounded it out as one word, the name just kinda stuck."

"Aw." Caroline's rib cage felt all warm and liquidy, just like her gravy. "I bet your Grandpac was so proud to wear something you made especially for him."

"Oh, no, he couldn't actually wear it. My grandfather is a man of considerable stature." Craig extended his arms into a circle in front of his belly for emphasis. "And I'd used myself as the model and then added two inches because I had absolutely no concept of waist sizing. But he did put it in a display case and still brings it out every time Meemaw wears the feather-and-bead earrings I made her."

"That's sweet that your grandparents love showing off the gifts you made them."

He shook his head, but kept glancing at the television as he spoke. "It's not sweet, it's calculated. They've never gotten along and are always competing with each other to be the favorite grandparent. It usually means lots of great presents at Christmas and birthdays, but the rest of the year we all just try to get out of the room as soon as the bickering starts."

Craig shrugged before directing all of his attention at the bull rider on the screen and effectively ending any further discussion.

She finished eating and soon lost interest in whatever the commentator with the turquoise bolo tie was saying about the combined score in the short go-round. Plus, Caroline still needed to email her parents and look over her notes for tomorrow's meeting at work. Craig didn't seem to notice as she stood up and retrieved her laptop off the dining room table. When she settled back onto the couch, she powered on the computer and got to work.

At some point she'd brought her legs up into a criss-cross position and Craig's elbow ended up resting on her knee. Caroline enjoyed the discovery that they could spend a pleasant, ordinary evening side by side, in companionable silence. At least, they were enjoying it until the announcer said, "Our next rider is on pace to beat the record for consecutive rides, a record that was set six years ago by Craig Clifton before he retired from the pro circuit."

At the mention of her fiancé's name, Caroline lifted

her head in time to see an image of a younger Craig flash on the screen.

"That's you!" she said, pointing to the TV.

"Yep." His hand slipped between their bodies and Caroline held her breath, wondering if he was finally going to make some sort of move. Instead, he found the remote wedged into the cushions and hit the power button. "It's getting pretty late, huh?"

"I didn't know you rode in the rodeo," she said, pivoting her upper body toward him and resting an arm across the back of the sofa.

He wasn't rude enough to point out the obvious—that there were actually a lot of things she didn't know about him. But he also didn't seem particularly inclined to provide her with the details, either.

"Is that how you got your scar?" She had barely traced the hook shape when he pulled away.

"I'm going to do the dishes," he said, his hip knocking into her knee as he stood up quickly. Carrying their plates into the kitchen, he glanced back at her with a pointed look and added, "You should probably get to bed."

The guy had barely said two words for the past hour and now he only spoke when he wanted to boss her around. Caroline stood up and followed him, remaining on the opposite side of the kitchen counter that separated the sink from the rest of the living area. "What about you?"

"What about me?" he asked, not bothering to look up as he rinsed off their silverware.

"Are you coming to bed?"

"I'll go to sleep after I clean up the kitchen." Craig was proving to have quite the habit of carefully phrasing his answers.

Caroline angled her head, trying not to let the frustration settle onto her expression. "But where will you be sleeping?"

"I can bunk on the couch." He might have shrugged, but it was too difficult to tell since he was leaning sideways to load the dishwasher.

"It's more of a love seat," she replied, estimating that he had to be at least six feet tall. "I mean, it can fold out into a bed but the mattress is thin and the frame is kind of wonky with the support bar going right across the middle."

"I've slept on worse," he replied, his knuckles turning white as he tightly gripped the cast-iron skillet.

"Yeah, but don't you think you'd be more comfortable in my bed?" The words were out of her mouth before she could stop them. It wasn't exactly like she was eager to hop into bed with the man she was still trying to remember. But she also recalled his comment this morning about his back and she didn't want him spending another night in agony.

Besides, she was learning that she never got any answers out of Craig unless she pushed him.

"Here's the thing, Caroline." Craig glanced toward the bedroom, but when he faced her, he wouldn't meet her eyes. A pit settled into her stomach as she realized the answer before he said it. "We haven't slept together yet."

* * *

Craig hated the fact that he'd obviously brought that shocking pink color to her cheeks last night, but there had been absolutely no way he could've lain next to her in a bed all night and maintained his distance.

Hell, he was having a hard time maintaining his distance this morning as the scent of sizzling bacon woke him from his crooked sleep on the uncomfortable sofa bed. Caroline stood in front of the stove, stirring scrambled eggs in her cast-iron skillet, looking like one of those old-fashioned housewives from the *Leave It to Beaver* era.

A silky, flowery dress hugged her backside before flaring out above her knees, and she had another pair of high heels on her feet. Who dressed like that to cook breakfast?

When she turned around to pass him a mug of hot coffee, he noticed that a white apron with a cherry print covered the front of her dress. Her brown hair was clipped away from her face and fell in soft waves down her back. Craig didn't know what looked more appealing—her or the plate of perfectly crisped bacon she handed him next.

If he hadn't already seen how much food she could put away in her petite frame, he would've assumed that she was trying to impress him with her cooking skills. But since she divided the eggs into equal portions on their plates, it was obvious that she enjoyed food as much as he did.

"What time do you need to be at your office this morning?" he asked.

"I was hoping to go in around eight and get things set up for the meeting."

He glanced at the digital clock on the stove. "That was thirty minutes ago."

"I know, but I don't have my car and you were out cold on the sofa bed, so I didn't have the heart to wake you."

Craig rubbed his neck and tried not to think of the stiffness in his back that had kept him awake the first half of the night. Well, it was his aching muscles along with a side of guilt and a constant awareness of Caroline's physical proximity that had kept him from getting to sleep before two in the morning.

"Let me just grab a quick shower and I'll take you," he offered before carrying his coffee into the bathroom with him.

Fifteen minutes later, he was backing his truck out of the long driveway and she was handing him an English muffin filled with the eggs and bacon he hadn't wanted to take the time to eat.

When he pulled into the gravel parking lot at Sawmill Station, her little blue MINI Cooper was the only vehicle there. Just as it had been yesterday afternoon. Grabbing her laptop case out of his crew cab, Craig followed her inside the former one-room train depot that served as her office. The Daltons had bought the surrounding land last year for their ranching operation, but because the train depot and the larger freight house next door were historical landmarks, they couldn't tear them down. From what Craig understood, Vivienne, Cole Dalton's wife, had moved her wedding planning business to Rust Creek Falls and they now used the space to hold big parties.

Perfectly good waste of grazing land, if you asked Craig.

"You don't need to hang around," she said, flipping on the lights and setting a bright yellow tote bag—similar to the one she'd had yesterday—on an antique desk with fancy scrollwork.

"But there's no one else here," he said, dropping to his knees beside a modern wood-burning stove in the corner. It was freezing in this place.

"I know, but Brendan and Fiona will be here soon. Plus, it's not like I'm at risk of falling asleep or knocking myself out. Again."

"But the doctor said we shouldn't leave you alone," he reminded her.

"Did she say for how long?"

"Not exactly. Though I was under the impression that you needed someone with you until you got your memory back."

"But, Craig," she said as she smiled, "I *do* have my memory back. Or at least most of it."

So then why did she still think they were engaged? He wanted to ask her as much, but he didn't know how to without it sounding like some sort of test. Plus, he heard a car pull into the lot outside.

He got the fire going and rose up just as Brendan Tanner and his girlfriend, Fiona O'Reilly, walked inside. They greeted Caroline first, and when Fiona turned Craig's way, she did a double take.

"Hey there, Craig. I wasn't expecting to see you

here." Fiona's family owned a local ranch, and when Craig had been stuck in the hospital with Caroline and bored out of his mind, he'd read one of her online articles about the free-range grazing habits of Herefords. "Are you volunteering for the Presents for Patriots fundraiser, too?"

"Nope," Craig answered a bit too quickly and his single syllable response did nothing to wipe the curious expression from Fiona's face.

"My car got left here in the parking lot, so Craig had to give me a ride to work this morning." Caroline's explanation wasn't helping the matter, either. He held his breath as his supposed fiancée turned toward him. "You're more than welcome to stay, honey, but I'm sure you have other things you need to do today."

There was a slight gasp at her use of the endearment and he realized that it had come from his own mouth.

That settled it. There was no way Craig was sticking around and waiting for Brendan and Fiona's questions that would be sure to follow. He squared his shoulders and took Caroline up on her suggestion that he leave.

"Okay, then I'm going to head over to the Daltons' stable and talk to them about their new longhorn." It was his way of letting her know that he'd still be nearby if she needed him.

"We're supposed to be meeting Bailey Stockton here," Brendan called out to Craig, who paused as he made his way toward the exit. "So if you see a guy in the parking lot who looks like he's got a chip on his shoulder and would prefer to be out riding horses instead of inside talking to actual humans, go ahead and point him in this direction."

Craig knew some of the Stocktons from his past visits to Rust Creek Falls, but not Bailey. He was the most recent one to move to town, and Craig didn't blame the guy for wanting to get as far away from the wedding planner's office as possible. In fact, if Craig *did* run across the man, he'd probably invite him to hop in the truck with him so they could both get the hell out of Dodge.

Chapter Nine

No sooner had Caroline heard Brendan and Fiona pull away in their car than Craig swung the office door wide-open, bringing in the crisp late-afternoon autumn breeze. In fact, if she didn't know any better, she'd think he'd been purposely waiting for the others to leave before rushing back to her rescue.

It was on the tip of her tongue to remind him that she was more than capable of being by herself for a few minutes, but when she saw him standing before her in his dusty jeans and sweat-soaked T-shirt, her heart sent a little flutter along her nerves.

"Why are you all dirty?"

"The Daltons got a young bull this morning and he was pretty testy about there being a buffer field between the steer pasture and the heifers in the grazing pasture. Young buck busted through the first fence and was scratching his head against the second when I got there, totally oblivious to the thousands of jolts zapping him. I had to help get him back in the pen while they re-trenched the ground posts and ran the galvanized wires deeper underground to conduct a stronger current."

"I literally have no idea what you just said," Caroline said.

"Basically, one of their new bulls got loose and was trying to get to the female herd to get a jump start on the breeding season. We had to calm him down and then fix the electric fencing so that he wouldn't try it again."

"And here, I didn't need an electric fence at all," Caroline mumbled under her breath. Last night, Craig had made it clear that he didn't require any sort of buffer zone to stay well clear of her bedroom.

"What was that?" he asked, stepping inside and closing the door behind him.

She couldn't very well admit that she'd actually been comparing him to an overexcited farm animal. Or feeling jealous of whichever lucky cow had been on the receiving end of that bull's pent-up desire. "I just need to power off my computer and grab a couple of files and then I'll be ready to go," she said instead.

"No problem," he said. His boots paced over the wood floorboards as he walked toward the bookshelf. "I hope you didn't stand on any chairs today."

"Nope. Everything was on the lower shelves."

"Did you eat lunch?" he asked.

"Actually, we had a menu tasting with the caterer who is doing the fund-raiser. I saved you a portion of beef Wellington, but when you didn't come back by two o'clock, I assumed you were eating with the Daltons. Plus, Bailey Stockton was getting pretty antsy, so I gave him your food. But if you're hungry, we can stop at Buffalo Bart's on the way home and get some wings. Or if you're sick of chicken, I can whip up a lasagna for dinner."

"You say 'whip up a lasagna' like it's the easiest thing in the world to make."

Caroline shrugged as she took a step closer to him, wondering if he normally kissed her hello at the end of a workday. "I like cooking. It gives my hands something to focus on so that my brain can work on all the bigger things."

"Speaking of your brain, how's your head been feeling today?" He reached out to trace a finger across her forehead and she all but sighed and leaned into his hand. "Any headaches?"

"Nope," she replied, using his favorite word. She must've fallen in love with his protective and caring nature, because she certainly hadn't fallen in love with his quiet and aloof conversation style. Actually, he was not always reserved when he was speaking. If the topic involved ranches and cattle, he could go on for days.

But when he touched her tenderly like this, or studied her with those blue eyes dark with concern, he didn't need to use any sort of conversation. Her thighs trembled and she felt as if she could actually pass out. Again.

"You okay?" he asked, cupping her elbow. "I should've known putting in a full day at the office would be too much for you."

No, it was being too close to him—breathing in his musky fragrance of hard work and the outdoors—that was making Caroline suddenly grow weak. "Craig, I promise I'm perfectly healthy."

He took a step back, yet watched her carefully as she gathered her things—as though he wasn't the least bit convinced that she wasn't going to collapse at his feet at any minute.

Then, later that evening, when they were again sitting side by side watching television while they ate dinner, Craig kept his body practically glued to the opposite end of the sofa. It was almost as though he was worried that if he touched her, she would completely go to pieces.

Steeling her spine, she turned toward him to tell him as much. "I've been noticing that you've been keeping your distance from me lately."

"Lately?" he asked, but his tone wasn't incredulous as much as it was sarcastic, suggesting that the word was some sort of understatement.

"Ever since my accident, you back up every time I move closer to you," she said, then scooted across the cushion to prove her point. Since the armrest prevented him from moving any more to the left, he shot forward, knocking his knee into the coffee table. "See? Every time. That's exactly what you do."

"What am I doing?" he asked, standing up with their plates.

"You're trying to get as far away from me as you can."

He opened his mouth as though to deny it, but nothing came out. She also stood and took the plates from him and set them back onto the table. Then she swallowed the last bit of orange soda in her glass, wishing it was merlot for an extra boost of courage, before turning back to him and placing her palms on the fresh shirt he'd put on after his shower.

"You know, Craig, I won't break if you kiss me."

Craig had to fight every impulse and muscle in his legs to keep from stepping back and well out of kissing range. Not that Caroline was actively trying to plant her lips on his, but she was blinking those intoxicating eyes at him and pouting her pretty little mouth, the invitation clearly extended.

"I just think that maybe we should wait for…" For what? Why would an engaged couple wait to kiss each other? The problem was that they weren't the average engaged couple. Or even a couple at all. He seized on that logic. "I was just waiting until you regained your memory. I don't want it to feel like you're kissing a stranger."

As impossible as it was, the small living room got even smaller, and it felt as though a cinch belt was squeezing across Craig's chest, tethering him in place. There was no way Caroline was buying any of this.

"I know I don't remember you, but how could I ever think of you as a stranger? Even if I'd never laid eyes on you before I'd hit my head," she continued and he froze, wondering if she was aware of how close she was to the truth. But instead of going with that more accurate description of the relationship, she slid her palms up to his shoulders and countered, "We've spent the past forty-eight hours together."

He looked at the digital readout on the cable box. "More like sixty hours."

"My point is that a loving heart is the truest wisdom."

Huh? Were they talking about hearts or wisdom here? Because in Craig's mind, the two never seemed to work well together. "I'm not following you."

"It's a quote by Charles Dickens. He's my dad's favorite author and I was named after one of his books."

"Still doesn't make any of this clearer," Craig replied.

"What I'm trying to say is that your actions these past two days speak louder than anything else, and my heart already knows everything it needs to know about you based on how well you've cared for me." Her thumbs traced circles above his shoulder blades and she asked, "Why are your muscles so tight?"

"Because I'm trying really hard not to move right now." There was absolutely nothing stopping him from walking straight out her door, yet he'd never felt more trapped.

As much as he'd fought it, his attraction to Caroline was like that headstrong young bull trying to bust out of its corral today. Obviously, Craig didn't believe in any of that nonsense about her having a wise heart or his actions speaking loudly or whatever else it was she was suggesting. But there was some sort of unexplainable connection between them. Some sort of magical fencing that zapped at his senses if he so much as moved, so much as acted upon this attraction.

"Here," she said, sliding her hands down his arms

and pulling his wrists around her waist. "Let me help you."

Craig gulped. He certainly didn't need her help moving closer. Yet, she felt so damn good, her tiny waist warm under his loose grip. At this point, he might need a jolt of ten thousand electric volts just to keep him away.

When her fingers returned to his shoulders and traced underneath the opening of his collar, he offered one last warning. "What happens if you end up regretting this?"

"How will we know unless you kiss me?" she asked, her breath whispering against his lips.

Oh, hell. One little kiss wasn't going to hurt.

When he dipped his head to hers, pain was the last thing on his mind. In fact, finally kissing her felt like pulling into his driveway after months of being on the road. She opened her lips and her tongue tentatively reached out to his. Heat and urgency filled him and he drew her in closer and responded with his own tongue, more forceful and more exploratory.

Caroline pressed her small, lithe body against his and every alarm inside him went off. This was too much. She was too much. Craig couldn't let things go any further. Breaking his lips away from hers was the easy part. Maintaining the distance and getting his breathing under control was way more difficult.

Well, that and trying to ignore the way Caroline's chest pressed against his as her lungs expanded with each of her little breaths. Her fingers were twisted into his collar and his hands were still cupped under her backside and he slowly dragged them back up to her waist.

Her cheeks were flushed and her lids appeared to be heavy since they were halfway closed as she studied his mouth.

"Are you okay?" he asked, more for himself than for her. He'd kissed plenty of women before, but none as responsive as her. Craig didn't know if he would ever be okay again.

"I think I felt something," she whispered and he tried not to take the words personally. He'd just felt his entire world burst out of the chute and she thought that perhaps she might've felt *something*? "But just to be sure, maybe you should kiss me again."

Compelled to make her feel more than just something, Craig lowered his head to hers again, then pulled back right before their lips met.

"Just one more," he murmured, needing all of his energy to fight this inner battle of self-control. The inner battle he was clearly already in danger of losing. "We can't go any further."

When he kissed her the second time, it was even better than the first. Their lips already knew how to move over each other's. Her mouth already knew how wide it needed to open to accept his probing tongue, and her hips knew just where to press against his, cradling his stiff arousal.

Caroline's fingers slipped into the open neck of his shirt, working the buttons loose as she slid her palms down his chest. His own hands were busy squeezing and massaging her rounded rear end, the silk fabric of her dress gathering together and lifting higher with each caress. The hem rose enough that the material no longer served as a thin barricade to the heat of her warm skin underneath. His thumbs traced the lacy edge of her panties and Caroline threw back her head and moaned.

His lips followed along her exposed neck down to her collarbone and her breath came in soft little pants. It took every ounce of strength Craig possessed to drag his mouth away from her a second time. Again, he moved his hands back up to her waist, but only because he was worried that if he completely let go of her, she would melt against him. Or he would melt against her. At this point it, his blood was pumping too fast to figure out where her body started and where his ended.

Also, by holding her this close, he didn't have to look at her eyes, didn't have to face the damage he might've inflicted. He drew in a ragged breath, resting his chin on top of her head. "We really should stop, honey."

Again, he hadn't meant to use the endearment, but he wasn't sorry for acknowledging the tender and protective feelings she evoked in him. Not that there weren't plenty of other things he could be sorry for.

She nodded, and when she lowered her arms, Craig stepped back to allow his body the opportunity to cool down, but then he was forced to observe her upturned face.

Instead of that dreamy expression she often got when she was comfortable with him, the one where her eyes fluttered closed and her smile lit up the room, Caroline was staring at him like he'd just poisoned the herd's drinking water. Her eyes were huge and round and her mouth was frozen into a little O, as though she were in shock.

Oh, no. Had they gone too far? Had he pushed her too much? Was she completely disgusted by him? He hoped he wouldn't regret the answer, but he had to ask, "Caroline? Is everything okay?"

"Never better," she squeaked out in a hoarse voice before running to her bedroom and slamming the door closed.

Chapter Ten

Caroline had absolutely no idea who that man was out in her living room, but he most definitely was *not* her fiancé.

Lying on her bed and staring blankly at her ceiling, Caroline touched her swollen lips. There was no way she could ever have forgotten what *that* felt like. After their first kiss, she was sure that she'd never kissed Craig Clifton before in her life. But she'd begged him to continue the make-out session just to confirm it, and it was during their second kiss that all of it came back to her. When he'd pulled his lips from hers, everything flooded into her mind at once.

Yet, instead of confronting him about any of it, she'd run straight to her bedroom and slammed the door closed. Twenty minutes later, she was still struggling to get her breathing under control.

They weren't engaged. Craig wasn't even her boyfriend. She'd been thinking about the words of Winona Cobbs when she first laid eyes on him two days ago. The images from that morning came back with the kind of clarity that can only be seen by events being replayed in slow motion. All the pieces finally clicked into place—the way she'd been balancing on that stupid chair, seeing him come into her office wearing that sexy tan cowboy hat, spotting the hook-shaped scar on his neck and, finally, the way the pink donut box went flying in the air as he ran toward her.

Engaged by Christmas. That was what she'd been thinking before knocking herself out. Had the doctor specifically said Caroline had suffered from amnesia, or was there another word she'd used? Reaching for the smartphone on her nightstand, she did some research online and read about an amnesia-like condition called confabulation.

So I made it all up? Caroline thought, staring at her screen. She heard the television in the living room go off and the sound of something bumping into a piece of wood furniture, followed by Craig's muffled curse. No, the man was completely real and currently getting ready to fall asleep on the other side of the wall, oblivious to the fact that Caroline had just remembered the truth.

Which brought everything back full circle. Obviously, she hadn't imagined Craig, but for some reason, she'd imagined that they were engaged. Yet why *him*? Why not Drew Strickland or his brother, Ben, both of whom were strangers and also in the office when she'd injured her head? Because neither one of them was Craig. It was as simple and as complicated as that.

Before Caroline had moved to Rust Creek Falls, she and some of her friends from the dorms had driven to town on a lark. Their favorite reality show, *The Great Roundup*, was being filmed nearby and the other girls wanted to be close to the action. Caroline had been coming out of the Ace in the Hole bar for a breath of fresh air when an older woman passed along the sidewalk. There'd been something familiar about her and it wasn't until the woman got to the corner of Buckskin Road that Caroline realized she was Winona Cobbs, the psychic from that nationally syndicated show Rita Rodriguez didn't approve of her daughter watching.

Caroline had caught up to Winona, not because she wanted to ask for a free reading or an autograph, but because the woman was walking with a slow limp and approaching a dark intersection. Caroline had asked the little old lady if she needed help crossing the road and when Winona took the offered arm, a strange expression had crossed her weathered face. Her eyes had grown bright and stared right through Caroline, like Dr. Robinson's penlight, trying to search for answers.

Winona's voice was lower in person than it had been on her shows, but it was just as authoritative when, without warning, she'd predicted, "You'll find what your heart is looking for here."

"Here?" Caroline had asked. "In Rust Creek Falls?" The old psychic had nodded, but didn't explain what it was Caroline was looking for or how she would find it. "When?"

"Be patient, child," Winona had replied, patting her gnarled, freckled hand against Caroline's. "It'll happen before you turn twenty-four."

"What will happen?"

"Your engagement."

The pronouncement had taken Caroline aback, but she'd always wanted to get married and knew with absolute certainty that a wedding was the thing her heart was looking for. She hadn't been able to keep the eagerness out of her voice when she asked, "To whom?"

"To the one with the pocket full of Life Savers and the three-legged cat that sleeps on both his pillows. Just remember, your cowboy is scarred for a reason, so be careful not to let him go."

But before Caroline could ask for more details, the other patrons had spilled out of the bar and Winona Cobbs was caught up in the crowd, leaving Caroline standing on the street corner, full of hope and unanswered questions.

Until Craig had walked into her office over two years later.

Actually, seeing him hadn't really answered anything. But, according to one of the brain injury articles Caroline had just read online, her concussion had forced her mind to fill in the blanks with what she'd wanted to see—that Craig was the scarred cowboy from Winona's prediction. Everyone in that hospital room when she'd finally awakened must have thought that she was completely nuts. Even Caroline could see how absolutely crazy it sounded for her to think she was engaged to a total stranger. It certainly explained why Josselyn and Drew and Craig had all stared at her that day as though she'd lost her mind.

However, the only thing Caroline couldn't explain was why any of them would go along with the whole charade in the first place. Especially Craig.

Throwing off the comforter, Caroline stood and walked to her bedroom door, determined to wake him up and ask him exactly that. Her hand gripped the knob and it took two tries to twist it open because her palms were so damp. She'd barely opened the door a crack when she saw the mound under the blankets on her sofa bed move. Then she heard his soft sigh as he nestled deeper into the thin mattress and something pulled at her heart.

Standing there frozen, Caroline was flooded with another realization. If she went out there and admitted that she remembered they weren't truly engaged, there would no longer be a reason for Craig to stay and take care of her. Not that she really needed anyone looking out for her anymore, but if he left she would probably never see him again.

Not only had she made a complete fool of herself insisting that they were engaged, but then she'd doubled down on her belief by spouting all that stuff about a loving heart and the truest wisdom and trusting her instincts about a man who, in reality, was a total stranger.

In Caroline's defense, though, she'd suffered a head injury and had been relying on the very random mutters of an old psychic walking down the road late one night.

Not that believing in fortune-tellers made her appear to be any more rational, but when Winona Cobbs had spoken those words, Caroline had felt the premonition all the way down to her bones.

She'd believed it way before she'd met Craig, and now that she'd kissed him, she knew it with even more certainty. It wasn't scientific, but being with him just felt right. Besides, how else would she have known all those details about him? The pocket full of Life Savers, the three-legged cat, the sleeping with two pillows?

The scar?

The only part of Winona Cobbs's prediction that hadn't actually come true yet was Caroline being engaged by her twenty-fourth birthday—which was this Christmas.

Bracing her body between the small opening of the bedroom door and the frame, Caroline took several deep breaths as she contemplated her best course of action.

As much as she should admit the truth to Craig, she only had one more month to make him fall in love with her. Would it really be all that wrong to let him go on believing that they were engaged? Or that Caroline *thought* they were engaged?

She pressed her fingers to her pounding temples as she mentally sorted through all the confusion and her conflicting emotions. Caroline walked back to her bed, wishing she had someone to talk it over with. Someone who could make sense of it all.

Someone who could tell her how to keep the man she'd been destined to find.

* * *

The following morning, Craig was coming out of the shower when he heard Caroline talking in the kitchen.

"Oh, good, you're safe." Another female's voice echoed inside the small rental house and Craig froze in the doorway. He'd left his duffel bag in the living room and, having just slept in his boxers, the closest item of clothing he could shimmy into when Caroline came out of her room was a nearby pair of jeans, which was all he'd worn when he'd made a beeline for the bathroom earlier. If they had company, it would look pretty odd for Craig to walk out there bare-chested.

"It was just a concussion, Mom," Caroline replied and Craig eased away from his hiding spot behind the bathroom door. Her parents were out of the country, which meant they couldn't possibly be here at her house.

"We got your email, angel," a male baritone added to the conversation. "Who is this Craig fellow?"

She must have the speaker feature turned all the way up on her phone. His own father had once tried to show Craig how to do that so he wouldn't have to stop working anytime one of his brothers or sisters called, but he always hit the wrong button and ended up disconnecting the call.

"Oh. I forgot I mentioned him in the email," Caroline said as she walked to the edge of the kitchen, a mixing bowl cradled in one arm as she whisked some batter. She caught sight of Craig and gave him a tense smile before putting her forefinger to her lips in the universal sign to mean "Please keep quiet."

She didn't have to ask twice. The last headache Craig

needed was for her parents to find out some stranger was lying to their daughter and shacking up with her. Luckily, they weren't there in person. Craig's nose twitched at the scent of freshly brewed coffee and the promise of the maple-pecan waffles Caroline had said she was making when she'd woken him up this morning.

"Are you really engaged?" her mom asked as Craig practically tiptoed toward his duffel bag, unsure of how much sound her cell phone could pick up.

"We don't even know him," her dad added.

"You're not cooking for him, are you?" her mom asked. "Did you know that in the Aka society in Africa, the men do all the cooking? Many of the males even breastfeed the babies. Although, I suppose technically it would be suckling since they can't produce—"

"I like to cook, Mom," Caroline interrupted, thank goodness. Craig got to his duffel, only to discover that most of his clothes were missing.

Mrs. Ruth, or perhaps Dr. Ruth since she was a college professor, continued on about some pygmy tribe halfway across the globe and Craig tried to wave at Caroline to get her attention and ask where his shirts were. But her back was to him as she faced the stove.

Craig walked into the kitchen to whisper in her ear, and that was when he realized Caroline wasn't on speakerphone. Her laptop was propped on the counter and two very surprised people appeared on the screen facing him.

Oh, crap.

"He's real." Her dad was the first to speak.

"He's really *naked*," her mother replied, moving her reader glasses down her nose.

Craig looked behind him to judge the distance to the front door and tried to determine how cold it would be outside if he made a run for it. But Caroline shoved a cup of coffee into his hands before he could take off.

"Mom, you spent eight months in the Polynesian islands studying the history of ancient hula performances. You even made Dad dress in a loincloth."

"It wasn't a loincloth," her mother replied and Craig suddenly wished he would never have to hear the word *loincloth* again. "It was a ceremonial *malo* and it was a gift to your father from Professor Ka'ukai."

Caroline poured batter into the waffle iron on the opposite side of the stove as though making breakfast and video chatting with her parents about her half-naked fiancé was part of her normal Sunday morning routine. "My point is that you're well accustomed to seeing men without their shirts."

Too much information, Craig thought, resisting the urge to pull the cherry-printed apron off the sink and cover up.

"It's a pleasure to meet you, Dr. and Dr. Ruth," Craig offered weakly. Hopefully, nobody was appraising his chest for either breastfeeding suitability or hula-dancing capabilities.

"It's actually Dr. Ruth and Dr. Rodriguez," Caroline's father corrected with a wink. "We're not married."

Dr. Rodriguez then began a long lecture using phrases such as *female servitude* and *matrimonial bondage*, and

Craig whispered out one side of his mouth to Caroline, "Where are my clothes?"

"I needed to run a load of laundry," she said, her lips equally tight.

"Did you say *laundry*, Caroline?" Her mom's face moved closer to the screen, as though the woman could hear better by looking more closely into the little web-cam. "Please tell me that you're not already falling into the stereotypical gender roles that Western civilization has forced upon females as a means to exert the imbalance of power of a male-dominated society."

"I didn't ask her to do my laundry," Craig defended, one palm up as though he was being asked to swear on a stack of Bibles. "I normally do it myself."

"And he knows how to churn butter, too," Caroline added, making Craig glance at her sideways.

"Let them work out the distribution of domestic chores for themselves, Rita. It's still early in their engagement." Then the older man turned back to the screen. "And speaking of engagements, when our angel sent us an email mentioning some fiancé from out of the blue, we were a little worried, thinking we had our own Miss Havisham on our hands."

"Who's Miss Havisham?" Craig asked. There were a million ways this conversation should be steered, but he had no idea who was holding the reins. So he just tried to follow along.

"From *Great Expectations*?" her father said. "She's this old spinster woman who was jilted at the altar and goes around in her wedding gown—"

"Okay, Dad, I have to get to the office," Caroline interrupted quickly. But her father continued his dissertation as Craig's phone suddenly rang. Relieved for the excuse to get out of the kitchen, Craig quickly walked toward the coffee table.

Trying to mute his phone, he accidently swiped on the wrong button and his own mother's voice echoed on the speaker. "Craig? Are you there?"

"Hey, Mom," he said, looking for the button to switch off the speaker, but the entire display had gone black. Really? The one time he didn't want the feature to work was the one time he couldn't shut it down.

"I hear you're bringing a woman for Thanksgiving," Carol Clifton said, drawing Caroline's attention from her own parental inquisition.

"Word travels fast," Craig muttered. He was trying to push the circular home button on his phone, but it wasn't recognizing his thumbprint. Probably because his hands were so damn sweaty.

He heard more talking from the kitchen, where Dr. Ruth and Dr. Rodriguez were still visible on the laptop. Unfortunately, his mom heard the same thing.

"Oh, my gosh," his mother practically squealed. "Is that your new fiancée?"

Fiancée? That was more serious than the "lady friend" gossip Rob had mentioned. Craig glanced over his shoulder to make sure Caroline hadn't heard and then lowered his voice. "You know about that?"

"Oh, yeah. Ben Strickland told your brother Jonathan about it," his mom replied as though it was every day that one of her sons managed to find himself in the middle of a pretend engagement. "Put her on the phone."

"She's talking to her own parents right now," Craig replied, running his fingers over his scalp and wondering if it would be worth catching pneumonia to go outside with wet hair.

"You guys aren't going to her folks' for Thanksgiving, are you? It's the first year in a long time that I'm gonna have all my kids at the house together."

"No, we can come there, Mrs. Clifton," Caroline said from behind him, apparently disconnected now from her own conversation.

"Fantastic," his mom replied. "Dear, I can't wait to meet you. Craig, make sure you stop by Daisy's on your way out of town and bring a pie."

His free hand dropped from his damp head to his neck as he tried to massage some of the tension away. "But I thought Meemaw was baking the pies."

"She is. However, Grandpac is also coming now and unless you want your new girlfriend to see a repeat of the Pecan Pie Controversy of 2011, you'll bring an extra one."

"I'd be happy to make a pie, Mrs. Clifton," Caroline volunteered. Craig pivoted to face his pretend fiancée and shook his head at her before it was too late.

"That might work as long as Meemaw doesn't know you made it yourself, dear. And please call me Carol. Or even Mom?"

Okay, his mother's tone was a bit too hopeful and Caroline's smile was a bit too pleased. Taking her to his family's ranch for Thanksgiving would all but seal their fate. It was entirely too risky.

Luckily, Craig still had a couple of days to get out

of this mess. "Let's not finalize anything until later in the week, okay, Mom?"

"Sounds like a plan," his mom said and Craig wanted to reply that there was absolutely no plan. But the woman, who had raised eight children—and knew her way around the very best stall tactics—continued, "I'm guessing you two will be coming out on Wednesday? Everyone else is coming out on Wednesday."

"Probably Thursday morning, Mom," Craig sighed and Caroline smiled even wider.

"It's a long drive to Thunder Canyon from Rust Creek Falls, though. So don't be late."

Chapter Eleven

"Why couldn't I make the pie myself?" Caroline asked Thursday morning as she climbed into the passenger side of Craig's vehicle.

For the past three days, he'd insisted on driving her to and from work and he'd always held open the door.

"Remember I told you about making sure you don't take sides between Meemaw and Grandpac?" he asked, reaching across her legs to place the pink bakery box he'd picked up from Daisy's yesterday on the floorboard between them. It was the closest he'd gotten to her since the night they'd kissed.

Thousands of times this week, she'd been prepared to tell him that she'd regained her memory. But then he'd call her "honey," and her breath would bottle up in her lungs and all she could do was smile at him. Or he'd show up at her office, his boots and jeans all dusty from whichever local ranch he'd visited that day, and his concerned blue eyes and his sexy cowboy hat were a welcome sight after a long afternoon dealing with pushy vendors or mind-changing brides.

Then there was the morning when his brother had called him while they were in the truck. Craig's Bluetooth had automatically switched on and she heard Will ask if he and Caroline wanted to carpool to Thunder Canyon for Thanksgiving.

At that point, her curiosity became stronger than her guilt and she thought that meeting his family might give her some sort of insight about the man who'd established himself as her protector, while simultaneously keeping his distance from her. Maybe he wasn't as physically attracted to her as she was to him. This trip would give her the opportunity to find out.

Caroline reached for her seat belt. "And remember I told *you* that I can handle squabbling family members in my sleep? I do it at work all the time."

"That's the other reason I didn't want you to make the pie. You've been so busy at work and every night you come home and make me these fabulous home-cooked meals when you should be resting and taking it easy. Did you know that it can take weeks for a person to recover from a concussion?"

"I know." Caroline rolled her eyes and then sing-songed the same thing he'd been saying to her at least twice a day. "'Just because I can't see my injury doesn't mean it doesn't exist.'"

Normally, she would think it was sweet that he tried

so hard to take care of her, but she was running on limited time here. She needed to impress him with her domestic abilities and get him to fall in love with her so that he'd propose before Christmas. But Craig seemed to be thwarting her attempts at every turn.

While she'd been working at Mikayla Brown's post-birth baby shower at Sunshine Farm on Sunday afternoon, he'd finished the laundry and ironed every single article of her clothing, including her sports bras, her hand towels and her Egyptian cotton bedsheets. On Monday, he'd done the grocery shopping at Crawford's General Store while she'd been at the office, and on Tuesday, she'd come home to a spotlessly scrubbed bathroom.

Last night, he'd tried to grill rib eyes for her on her landlord's outdoor grill, but they'd run out of propane. And by the time he got back from the hardware store with a new tank, it was pouring rain and the wind was howling like crazy. She'd saved the meal by broiling the steaks and then wowing him with au gratin potatoes and her knowledge of useless college football stats.

If Craig needed a party thrown, Caroline had quite the résumé to show him. But Craig didn't seem to need anything. Or anyone. He certainly didn't need to kiss her again, she thought as he closed her door and climbed into the driver's side.

The sun was barely rising as they began the three-hundred-mile drive to Thunder Canyon. Since Craig didn't seem inclined to keep up any sort of conversation, Caroline turned on the radio. A blast of screaming electric guitar shot through the speakers, and her first instinct was to cover her ears.

But Craig raised the volume and then began singing along with the heavy metal song. When he noticed her staring at him in shock, his voice trailed off. "What?"

"You mean, you purposely have this station programmed on your radio?"

"What else would I listen to?" he asked.

"Um, maybe country music? You're a cowboy."

"Oh, really?" He winked at her and a shiver ran down her spine. "I didn't get the memo."

They ended up compromising on a classic rock station and Caroline closed her eyes to prevent herself from chattering on senselessly. The past few nights that he'd stayed at her house, they'd settled into a routine of comfortable silence when the television was on or there was music playing, and she didn't want to do anything now that might rock the boat.

Or to remind her that she really had no business tagging along for a family holiday when they weren't really engaged. Yet.

That "yet" part was what gave Caroline an unprecedented bout of nausea. She would've liked to blame it on motion sickness but she'd never been carsick before in her life. It had to be her nerves telling her that this was a bad idea. Sure, his mom had invited her, but did his family really know the truth? That she and Craig had really only known each other a few days? On the other hand, if she didn't call him her fiancé or perpetuate this myth that they were in a legitimate relationship, then she wasn't technically deceiving anyone.

Plus, if she was being truly honest with herself, she really didn't want to spend Thanksgiving alone.

Halfway there, they pulled into a truck stop restaurant and gas station. Caroline used the restroom while Craig ordered them some breakfast sandwiches and coffee to go. The closer they got to Thunder Canyon, the more nervous Caroline's tummy became. Maybe meeting his parents and the rest of his family was a bad idea. After all, they'd been practically living together the last few days and not once had they socialized with any of his married siblings who lived nearby. Craig saw them while she was at work, but when he was with her, they didn't so much as go to the Gold Rush Diner to share a meal, let alone be seen anywhere out in public together.

Not that most of the people in Rust Creek Falls didn't already know there was something going on with them. But nobody seemed to know what that "something" was. In fact, a small group of ladies at the baby shower on Sunday had brought up his name with questions in their eyes, but Caroline had been in work mode and didn't think it would be professional to talk about her dating life. Or the fact that she and Craig had never truly gone on an actual date.

The irony was, the more nervous Caroline grew with each passing mile that brought her closer to lying directly to his family, the more relaxed Craig became. Okay, so maybe she wasn't exactly lying to his parents. Initially, she'd really thought she and Craig were engaged, and since he still hadn't corrected her, their engagement could be construed as a form of implied consent on his part. Perhaps he really *did* want to marry her.

Still, the fact remained that Craig had been quiet and tense during the first half of the drive. Yet now he began to speak more, pointing out landmarks and telling her a story about the creek where Grandpac had taken him and his brothers fishing when Craig had been in the sixth grade.

"Rob, my youngest brother, had been eager to catch the biggest trout and didn't bother looking behind him before casting his line. We hear this shout, followed by a slew of four-letter words, but it was too late. Rob had got his hook caught in Grandpac's ear, then felt so bad about it he yanked the pole to try and pull it out. He ended up ripping right through the cartilage."

"Your poor grandfather!" Caroline shuddered.

"More like poor Jonathan. He's the second oldest and was closest to the first-aid kit when it happened. Grandpac cussed up a blue streak when Jonathan tried to disinfect the wound and bandage it up. Between you and me, I think that's why my brother became a pediatrician instead of going into geriatric medicine."

"So one of your brothers is a doctor?" Caroline turned in her seat. She recalled that day coming home from the hospital, when Craig had admitted that she hadn't met any of his family yet. So it wasn't like she had to pretend that she didn't know anything about his siblings. "Tell me about the others."

"Jonathan is married to Dawn, who is a nurse. Next is Will. We went to his and Jordyn's house that day..." Craig didn't have to say which day that was. She remembered. It was the same day she'd insisted that he come stay with her at her house.

"Got it." She tried to sound casual. "Who's next?"

"My sister Catherine and her husband, Cody, then Rob, who is single and still lives on the ranch. Cecelia is after him—she's married to Nick—then Calista and her husband, Jake. My sister Celeste, everyone calls her C.C., is the baby. Maybe I should've written it all down for you ahead of time."

"Craig, it's my job to remember who's who. We once planned a wedding for a bride with thirteen bridesmaids. To this day, I can tell you their dress sizes and whether their dates requested the prime rib or the salmon." Then Caroline proceeded to list the names of his siblings in order, along with their spouses. "I got this."

When he smiled at her across the cab of his truck, her throat constricted. It occurred to Caroline that she had never seen Craig smile so broadly. She'd seen looks of concern, looks of curiosity, even looks of desire. She'd even seen several grins. But she had never seen him as truly happy as he looked at that exact moment.

Apparently, his family was everything to him. Caroline really hoped she didn't blow this.

When they'd passed the turnoff to Interstate 90, Craig's blood had run cold at the sight of the wooden white cross on the side of the road.

It was why he hadn't said much to Caroline during the first half of the road trip. No matter how many times he'd driven the stretch of highway from Rust Creek Falls to Thunder Canyon, seeing that small handcrafted monument to one of his biggest failures always haunted him.

He hadn't brought a woman home to meet his family

since Tina, and even then, he technically hadn't brought her home since she'd practically been there the whole time. In fact, it had been the opposite when she died. They'd been at a bar with some of her cousins outside Kalispell and returning to Thunder Canyon late at night. Craig had been sound asleep in the passenger side and Tina behind the wheel of her daddy's old Jeep, probably too exhausted to have even seen the stalled logging truck before it was too late.

After the crash, he'd been lost and hurt, his relationships with women more about filling a temporary physical need. But he could only ride bulls for so long before his body began reminding him that he was no longer in his prime. Eventually, Craig had been forced to go home to confront his past as well as the rest of life. The life he was now meant to have without Tina.

Craig liked to think that he'd made his peace with all of it. After all, he'd driven this exact same route hundreds of times before. But he'd never driven it with another woman. Fortunately, with each mile that separated him and that white cross, his guilt was slowly replaced with an eagerness to be home. To see his ranch and his family and his future.

By the time he and Caroline stopped for breakfast, Craig's muscles had lost most of their tension. And by the time they passed the sign welcoming them to Thunder Canyon, he was downright chatty. In fact, he felt like he'd been talking nonstop for the past twenty minutes while Caroline seemed to shrink against the passenger seat. His family was huge and overwhelming, and, of course, a city girl and an only child like Caroline—even if she could easily memorize and recite everyone's name—might be feeling out of her element.

He'd called his dad yesterday and spoken with all of his brothers, explaining Caroline's condition and urging them to just go along with the fake engagement. Craig knew better than to appeal directly to his mom and sisters. All of his female relatives would tell him that this was a horrible idea.

As if Craig wasn't already perfectly aware of that, thank you very much.

Still, what if someone in his family slipped and said something? Chances were that there was going to be a slew of people huddled on the front porch when they arrived, eager to meet her and bombard them both with questions. Perhaps he should gently prepare her for the fact that one of his relatives was likely to say something that might trigger her memory.

"So," he started, tapping his fingers against the steering wheel. "Your parents seemed a bit surprised that you were engaged."

Okay, so that wasn't exactly what he'd wanted to bring up. He was still trying to be cautious about not adding any undue stress on her, but he wanted her to understand that his family, too, might have a similar response. They might exhibit the same kind of curiosity to this unexpected engagement of theirs.

"They *did* seem surprised," Caroline replied, but didn't add any theories on why that might be.

"Are you feeling sick?" he asked and she followed his eyes to where her palms rested against her stomach.

She yanked her hands away quickly, then fiddled

with the strap on her seat belt. "I guess I'm just a little nervous."

"It's not too late to turn back," he offered even as he made a right onto the long driveway that would lead to his family's ranch house.

"No," she said, turning in her seat toward him, her brown eyes full of determination. "Don't turn back. I really do want to be here."

She also thought she wanted to marry him. And the longer he let her go on believing that, the more attached she would get. Even *he* was getting a little too comfortable in this alternate universe they'd inadvertently created. The problem was that when she finally remembered that he wasn't the man she thought he was, this carefully constructed bubble of theirs would burst. It was like chewing gum. The bigger the bubble got, the bigger the mess it would make when it finally exploded in his face.

But that didn't stop him from continuing down the gravel road toward his home.

Despite all the vehicles parked in the circular drive, Craig had been wrong about his prediction of everyone waiting on the front porch to greet them. In fact, when they got out of his truck, the only member of their welcoming committee was an old tomcat sunning himself on the front steps and watching their approach with equal parts mild interest and total disdain.

"You really do have a three-legged cat." Caroline shifted the pie box into the crook of her left arm and slowly approached the porch, holding out an open palm to the normally cantankerous feline. He was surprised the old grouch was allowing a stranger to pet him.

Craig reached out to scratch the tabby between the ears but was suitably rejected in favor of Caroline's ministrations. He stood back up, knowing the cat could only ignore him for so long.

"Yep, and he always punishes me like this whenever I've been away from the ranch. Don't you, Tiny Tim?"

The box wobbled against Caroline's hip and she set it down on the wooden step. "Wait, your cat's name is Tiny Tim?"

"Yeah, but he's obviously not very tiny, are you, boy?" The tabby finally purred at Craig before nudging its chin against his leg. "He also doesn't have the same sunny disposition as his namesake."

"His namesake?" she asked and Craig bent down to rub Tim's back when he realized Caroline's hand wasn't moving.

"I know what you're thinking, that it's not very politically correct to name a three-legged cat after the kid from that Scrooge movie. But my sister C.C. was the one who came up with it and since she was only seven at the time and already spoiled rotten, we never really corrected her."

"It's called *A Christmas Carol*," she offered, her eyes wide with disbelief.

"What is?"

"That Scrooge movie you're talking about. It's actually a book by Charles Dickens. I'm named after that story."

The hairs along the nape of his neck stood up and Craig's hand paused in midair above Tim's pointy ears.

Not wanting to acknowledge the coincidence, he replied casually, "That's right. I remember that night. You told me you were named after a Dickens book. But later on, your dad mentioned something about a Miss Havisham."

"No, that was just my dad's way of making a joke about my love for wedding dresses. Wait." She stood up straighter on the step above him. "Of all the things you remember from *that* night, me babbling on about my name is what stands out the most?"

"Not the most." He rose to his full height, unable to resist coming face-to-face with her and meeting her challenge. There was something about being on his own property, in his own element, that made Craig finally feel as if he was on solid footing. "I also remember every single sigh you made as you kissed me to within an inch of my control."

Color flooded Caroline's cheeks, but she didn't back away. Instead, she lifted her hands to the back of his neck and pulled him closer. "Maybe this time I can make you lose all your control."

Her lips had just met his when the unmistakable sound of his grandfather's truck horn blared through the yard.

Chapter Twelve

"You must be the little filly Craig plans on marrying," an older, heavyset gentleman said as he lumbered up the porch steps. Caroline's response was immediately muffled against the shoulder of the newcomer's tobacco-scented sheepskin coat as he swept her into a bear hug.

"Grandpac, you're gonna suffocate my fiancée before anyone else gets to meet her," Craig said from behind her.

"So you're sayin' I'm the first to welcome her to the family?" the man asked as he pumped a triumphant fist in the air, thereby loosening his grip while keeping one beefy arm planted around her shoulders. "So, when's the wedding?"

Caroline opened her mouth to explain they still had time to figure all of that out, but then she flashed back to her earlier vow to not say anything that might mislead his family. She aimed her tight-lipped smile at Craig so he could field this particular question.

"We haven't set a date yet," Craig replied vaguely, just as he'd done that day she'd been released from the hospital. And just like then, he looked at something off in the distance, probably so he wouldn't have to make eye contact with anyone. While Caroline was relieved to see that he seemed uncomfortable with playing fast and loose with the truth, her muscles also relaxed at his nonanswer. She didn't want to be complicit in any blatant lies.

"Well, as soon as it happens, I want to be the first to know." The older Clifton released his hold on Caroline so he could pull his grandson into an equally enthusiastic bear hug.

"The first to know what?" The front screen door slammed behind a woman with silver hair cut into a sleek bob. She was shorter than Caroline and wore a two-piece velvet tracksuit in a bright purple color that clashed with the turkey-printed dish towel cinched around her still-trim waist. There also appeared to be rhinestone letters spelling out something across the seat of her pants, but Caroline couldn't see the word from this angle.

"Happy Thanksgiving, Meemaw." Craig had to push against his grandfather's elbow to slip out of what looked to be a hearty and somewhat territorial embrace. He then gave his grandmother a hug and the smaller—and possibly stronger—woman didn't allow him to pull away either until he gasped, "I want to introduce you to Caroline."

"I already met her." Grandpac's barrel chest puffed out as Meemaw passed by him. "Before anyone else."

"You don't count, you ol' grizzly bear." The woman flicked her wrist at the older man before also pulling Caroline into a tight hug. Caroline's ribs threatened to snap in half. Yep, Meemaw was definitely the stronger of the two grandparents. Craig's grandmother whispered in Caroline's ear, "Just ignore him. I always do."

At least, she'd tried to whisper. Unfortunately, she didn't seem to realize how loud her voice was.

"I heard that," Grandpac called out. "Instead of wasting all that money on a new hearing aid that doesn't work, you should've invested in another one of your fancy cruises for single seniors. In fact, I'll pay for it myself if it means I can send you halfway around the world and get you outta my hair once and for all."

"What hair?" Meemaw rose onto her tiptoes as she knocked the sweat-stained cowboy hat off his forehead, exposing a shiny bald head. Then the older woman winked at Caroline as she sauntered toward the door. "Come on inside, you two. I'm gonna cut into my famous pecan pie so we can have a little dessert before dinner."

"The only thing that pie is famous for is a bad case of constipation," Grandpac muttered before bending down to retrieve his Stetson. But Caroline noticed the way the older man's sparkling blue eyes—the same color as Craig's—remained riveted on Meemaw's backside. When he rose, Grandpac slapped his hat against his thigh and stomped past them in full pursuit. He was barely stepping inside the house when he shouted, "And why in the hell does it say 'DIVA' across your rear end, woman?"

"So those are my grandparents," Craig said, hands planted on his hips as he rocked back on his boot heels.

"I think they're adorable." Caroline smiled.

"Well, everyone else thinks they're insufferable."

"Insufferable relatives are my specialty, remember?" She looped her arm through his and patted his muscular forearm, trying not to think of the way it had felt wrapped around her waist a few moments ago. "Don't worry. This isn't my first rodeo."

When it came time to eat the Thanksgiving meal, there was a brief skirmish between the grandparents as they fought over who got to sit next to Caroline. In the end, Craig's sister Catherine had to ask her husband, Cody, to scoot down a spot to accommodate Meemaw, and Caroline found herself sandwiched right in between the two bickering seniors.

Calista and Jake sat across from them, and poor Dawn, Jonathan's wife and a registered nurse, got stuck on the other side of Grandpac and was forced to endure endless questions about his new blood pressure medication, his elevated cholesterol levels and whether Meemaw's store-bought biscuits contained more saturated fat than Cecelia's crescent rolls.

"Whose biscuits are you calling store-bought, you ol' sourpuss?" Meemaw leaned forward, glaring over her crystal goblet.

"Is that your fifth or your sixth glass of wine, Doris?" he replied.

"You two need to knock it off," Carol Clifton called out from the head of the table. Caroline was relieved someone was trying to smooth the waters between the two feisty elders, because Craig was at the opposite end with Rob and C.C. and Will, pretending to be in a deep discussion about the vaccination schedules for calves. Fakers.

"Not that I would know where she gets her biscuits," Grandpac said under his breath to Caroline. "I wouldn't eat anything that woman put before me."

"Looks to me like you don't really discriminate about where your food comes from." Meemaw reached around Caroline and poked a finger right into Grandpac's generous belly.

"I know you normally have a hard time keeping your paws off me, lady, but you really need to control yourself in front of the kids." Grandpac swatted his napkin at the older woman's hand.

Meemaw's reflexes were too quick, though, and she snatched a corner of the orange linen cloth. Caroline plastered a smile on her face and stood up, using her body to break up their impromptu game of tug-of-war.

"Mr. Clifton, your sweet potato casserole is looking a bit cold. Why don't I go pop that in the microwave for you?"

Jordyn, Will's wife, had already reheated the man's plate when he'd complained that the gravy Meemaw made was coagulating. But when Caroline made the offer, several gasps sounded throughout the dining room and everyone's attention shifted to the chair Caroline had just vacated.

Nick, Cecelia's husband, appeared at her side and whispered, "Go. Save yourself. I'll slip into your seat and try to keep them separated for as long I can. The new in-law always gets Wall Duty at their first family dinner, and so far, you've lasted longer than any of us did our first go-rounds."

Luckily, Craig grabbed the empty bowl of mashed potatoes and followed her into the kitchen. It gave Caroline the opportunity to ask, "What is Wall Duty?"

"It's the person who ends up with the unfortunate task of being a literal barrier between my grandparents so they don't physically attack each other. They've never actually come to blows, so no need to look concerned. Although, it got real close that year when Grandpac allegedly fed Meemaw's secret recipe stuffing to her Yorkshire terrier."

"Allegedly?" Caroline asked, punching in the numbers on the microwave.

"Nobody actually saw him do it, but when Scruffins puked all over my dad's favorite recliner, Grandpac suggested it was proof that Meemaw's cooking wasn't fit for dogs, let alone human consumption." Craig used a wooden spoon to heap more potatoes into the serving dish. "Anyway, sorry you got put in the middle of the two of them. My family does it to all the new members as a sort of initiation, but let me know if it gets to be too much for you."

Something burst inside Caroline's chest as she followed Craig out of the kitchen, feeling about as warm and gooey as the yams and melted marshmallows on the plate she carried back to his grandfather.

She'd gotten Wall Duty. That meant his family had accepted her as one of its newest members.

"So tell me more about this amnesia of yours," Rob said to Caroline when Craig finally sneaked the remote control away from a sleeping Grandpac.

"Rob." Craig's voice issued a warning to his little brother. It was after dinner and several of his siblings had already left to return to Rust Creek Falls, but those were the ones who'd arrived the day before and hadn't already made a five-hour drive this morning. The thought of climbing back into his truck so soon for the return trip brought a throbbing ache to Craig's upper spine.

So far, most of his family had been pretty good about just going along with the flow and not asking Caroline any personal questions. Granted, it had helped to have his grandparents' constant quarreling as a diversion most of the day. But now that it was late in the afternoon and things were quieting down, some of his more daring siblings were getting a bit bolder in their curiosity.

"What do you want to know?" Caroline's smile was pleasant, but they were sitting so close to each other on the sofa, Craig could feel her muscles tense.

"Why don't I put on the football game?" he said, trying to distract everyone from the direction of the conversation. But his fingers were a bit too overeager and he pressed the wrong channel.

Goldie Hawn's face popped up on the screen instead.

"Oh, hey," his sister C.C. said, coming into the living room. "I love this movie."

"I don't think I've ever seen it," Caroline replied, leaning forward to hear whatever the actress was saying to Kurt Russell.

"It's about this rich lady that hires a guy to do some work on her yacht, but doesn't pay him. Then the woman falls overboard, knocking herself out and waking up in the local hospital with amnesia. The worker guy needs someone to watch his kids and clean his house and figures since she still owes him money, he should pretend to be her husband and…" C.C.'s eyes widened as she trailed off, then wrestled the remote out of Craig's grip. "Actually, isn't there a college bowl game on right now?"

But C.C.'s words hung in the air and Caroline apparently was no longer interested in football because Craig could feel her narrowed gaze studying him. Of all the movies that had to be playing, it had to be one about tricking someone who was suffering from amnesia.

Luckily, Meemaw chose that exact moment to walk into the room. "Who wants to play gin rummy?"

"Deal me in," Grandpac said, slapping his hands together. He'd been snoring, but at the sound of his nemesis's challenge to a card game, he suddenly rose from the recliner like a bifocal-wearing phoenix rising from the ashes to reclaim his glory.

"Okay." Meemaw scanned her remaining grandchildren as though she were a general choosing which soldiers to lead into battle. "Craig, you and Rob can be on the old fart's team. I'll take C.C. and Caroline."

"All right." Caroline began to stand up, but both

Craig and Rob grabbed onto an elbow and pulled her back down between them.

"Actually, I was going to take Caroline outside and show her around the ranch." Craig congratulated himself on the quick thinking even though he doubted someone like Caroline, with her impractical heels and her wispy dress, would want to go traipsing around the stables.

"At this hour?" Grandpac argued. "It's too dad-gum dark to see anything out there right now. You can show her around tomorrow."

"But we're going back to Rust Creek Falls tonight," Craig said.

"No, you're not," C.C. replied. For being the youngest of eight kids, his baby sister had no problem bossing everyone else around. "You're too tired and you've been rubbing your neck for the past hour."

"My neck's fine," Craig insisted, trying not to rotate it to stretch out the muscles.

"There's no way you're leaving me and C.C. alone to play cards with the grandparents." Rob leaned behind Caroline to whisper to Craig. Then his brother winked before raising his voice for everyone to hear. "I know senior citizens like you need their sleep, but stop being such an old fuddy-duddy, Craig."

"Fuddy-duddy?" Craig lifted an eyebrow.

"How old are you, Caroline?" Rob asked.

"Robert Clifton, you know better than to ask a lady her age." Meemaw flicked her dish towel against the back of his brother's head and Craig felt a brief moment of satisfaction.

Yet Rob pressed on. "All I'm saying is that if Craig is gonna go around robbing the cradle with a much younger—and much prettier—fiancée, then he should act like he isn't too old and broken down to actually fill a cradle when it comes time."

Meemaw smacked at Rob's head again and C.C. asked, "What do you mean 'fill a cradle'?"

"I believe they're talkin' about baby making," Grandpac volunteered, making the situation worse.

Caroline's cheeks blazed pink, and C.C., who was only a year younger than Craig's supposed fiancée, made gagging sounds. "Ew, gross."

"Making babies is a normal part of life," Meemaw told her youngest granddaughter. "Maybe if you went on one of those singles cruises with me you could find a nice gentleman to make babies with."

"Pish," Grandpac said with a shudder. "C.C., don't you dare go on a cruise with this man-hunting, she-devil grandmother of yours. She'll set you up with one of her wrinkly geriatric boyfriends. The kinda guy who'll buy you a cemetery plot right next to theirs for your wedding gift. Better to be a cradle robber like Craig than a grave robber like your Meemaw."

Craig wanted to draw Caroline to him and tuck her head against his shoulder so he could shield her from this humiliating conversation. And prevent her from hearing the repeated reminder of their age difference. But when he stretched his arm behind her, he realized she was shaking with silent laughter. Craig groaned. "Can everyone just stop talking about cradles and filling them?"

Meemaw pulled a deck of cards out of her purple velvet pocket. "I can as soon as you guys get your butts to the table and we start playing."

Chapter Thirteen

Carol's and Rudy Clifton's faces both jerked up from their newspapers when Caroline and the other five entered the recently cleared dining room.

"Oh, no," Carol muttered, her eyes darting to the playing cards in her mother's hand.

Laughter bubbled inside Caroline's chest as she realized why Craig and Rob had been so quick in their efforts to stop her from agreeing to this game. Apparently, everyone else in the house felt the same way. However, she'd never been a part of a big family game night and surely all the Cliftons were overreacting about the ferociousness of Meemaw and Grandpac's constant competiveness.

"Guess those Black Friday deals aren't gonna shop themselves." Craig's dad stood up so quickly, his chair fell over backward. "Better head out to the stores now."

"Whoa." C.C. put out both of her palms. "You two have never been Black Friday shopping a day in your lives."

"So then we'll get a jump start on our Cyber Monday deals," Mr. Clifton replied.

Rob rolled his eyes. "It's still Thursday, Dad."

"Back in your seats," Craig commanded his mom and dad before using his thumb to gesture toward Meemaw and Grandpac. "They're *your* parents. If we have to play cards with them, then so do you."

When everyone moved to the opposite side of the table, Caroline decided to take matters into her own hands and suggested that they play with four teams and then orchestrated it so that the grandparents were paired together. Craig gaped at her like she was absolutely insane.

"Trust me," she whispered to him as his dad shuffled the cards. And when Meemaw and Grandpac won the first hand, everyone else relaxed and they were able to sit back and enjoy the game.

At least, it was relaxing until Rob had to leave to go check on the timer for the sprinklers in the south pasture and C.C. had to write a term paper and Mrs. Clifton told Craig that there was no way he was going to be driving back to Rust Creek Falls this late at night.

"I'll be fine." Craig stood, then held out his hand toward Caroline as though she needed his help to rise. Or maybe it was just his way of signaling to her that it was time to go.

"You of all people should know better than to risk it when you're this worn-out." His mom gave him a pointed look and even the grandparents disappeared. Quietly.

A pained expression crossed Craig's face and his jaw hardened to a rigidity Caroline had never seen on him before. Not that she knew him well enough to be an expert on his moods.

What she *did* know, though, was that even with his grandparents' perpetual squabbling—which she was pretty sure was mostly a ruse to gain attention from their grandchildren—she'd never had a better Thanksgiving. His huge family was loyal and hardworking and loving and everything she'd ever wanted to be a part of. However, if Craig was determined to leave, then she would stand by him.

"I can drive if you really want to go home tonight." Caroline placed her arm on his biceps, which was even more rigid than his jaw.

"Out of the question," Craig gritted out.

Caroline got the feeling that his determination didn't have anything to do with her head injury, yet, as an outsider, she wasn't sure what it was. Something wasn't right and she couldn't fix the problem unless she understood the source. And she wouldn't understand the source unless she got Craig to relax and tell her what was wrong.

All that muscle clenching was apparently taking its toll because Craig reached behind his neck and pressed three fingers to the base of his scalp. Since they were standing side by side, he must not have seen Caroline's hand lift up, causing him to give a slight jolt when she began to massage his neck. But at least he didn't move away. Taking that as a good sign, she stepped in front of him, forcing him to look at her.

"Honey," she started, smiling encouragingly at him until she had his undivided attention. "I'm fine with staying the night here."

"Don't you need to work tomorrow?" he asked, a muscle ticking along his upper jaw.

"I have the day off."

"But you didn't pack an overnight bag."

"She can borrow something from C.C.," his mom said from behind Caroline. "I'll go get some stuff now."

"See, I can borrow something from your sister," Caroline repeated, wanting Craig to understand that she was truly fine with staying the night. Rudy followed his wife out of the dining room, leaving Caroline and Craig alone.

Some of the tension eased from Craig's face and he lowered his voice to a whisper to ask Caroline, "But where will you sleep?"

Caroline thought she'd been in control until that point. Heat flooded her body and she licked her lips.

"She can sleep in your room," Meemaw said, coming out of the kitchen with the pink bakery box from Daisy's. "Anyone want more pie?"

Even though they were "engaged" and it was no secret that Craig had been shacking up with Caroline at her tiny rental house, Craig's mom knew the truth and insisted on her oldest son giving Caroline his room and sleeping in Jonathan and Will's old bedroom.

It was really for the best, Craig thought, staring

blankly at the shelf containing Will's 4-H trophies and Jonathan's science fair award. Caroline fitted in so perfectly with his family and it had been all he could do to keep his hands off her since that interrupted kiss on the front porch this morning. But then Rob had gone and made that joke about robbing the cradle and Craig's pride—as well as his prior aches and pains—had flared up, and suddenly, he'd never felt more like an old man. An old man who was taking advantage of a much younger, much more naive woman. A woman who was under the mistaken belief that he planned to marry her.

The truth was, Craig didn't plan to marry anyone. He'd had his shot at the perfect partner with Tina, but all of that had crashed around him. Literally.

Seeing Caroline at his family's ranch only served to remind him that she was too young, too feminine, too citified to ever suit this life. Working on a ranch required commitment and strength and hard work and... and...proper footwear. Did the woman even own a pair of boots?

Granted, she didn't buckle under the pressure of his grandparents. However, Caroline was a tiny, dainty thing with a closet full of high heels and a bathroom full of beauty products. She had to be miserable being stuck out on a ranch in the middle of nowhere. Not to mention meeting his entire family must've been a total overload for her recovering memory. He was supposed to be keeping things calm for her so her head injury could heal, not bringing more chaos into her life.

If she'd had her tiny little European car here, she

probably would've been gunning its four-cylinder engine down the driveway the second Rob had called him a fuddy-duddy. Actually, probably well before then—like when his elderly grandparents practically knocked each other over in their race to get the seat next to Caroline at the dinner table.

Craig scratched his head, wondering if he could actually use his boisterous and pushy family to his advantage. Perhaps the more time she spent here, the sooner Caroline would come to the conclusion that they were worlds apart. That they were never meant to be together.

Although, she *had* been so diplomatic and understanding with his ornery grandparents when she didn't have to be. Then she'd been helpful to his parents in the kitchen when she could've just sat back and been a guest. Caroline had also demonstrated complete ease with his siblings and their spouses, asking them questions about their jobs and their hobbies.

Another thought took root. As an experienced party planner, perhaps Caroline had simply switched into professional mode and spent the day dealing with his family as though it was some sort of pro bono requirement. It was hard to read someone else's thoughts when they didn't even know their own mind. Maybe she'd been miserable the entire time.

Regardless of whether it was all a performance on her part, the fact remained that Craig had invited her here. He was supposed to be acting as her host and he couldn't fall asleep if he kept pacing around his brothers' room all night, worried about her discomfort. Opening the door, he peeked out to see if everyone else had already gone to bed. Pulling off his boots, he hoped his socks muted his footsteps on the old squeaky floorboards as he sneaked down the hallway.

Craig lightly tapped on the door to his own bedroom and when Caroline opened it, he sucked in his breath. Not that she looked breathtakingly sexy with her hair pulled into a high ponytail and dressed in a borrowed pair of pajamas covered with dancing pugs in Santa hats. No, his lungs refused to work because she was giving him that wistful smile again, the one that looked so happy. So comfortable. So confident that he couldn't possibly stay away from her.

Instead of asking her how she was, he stepped over the threshold and placed his hands on either side of her face, leaning down to claim the kiss that had been interrupted this morning when they'd first arrived.

As his lips melded to hers, he felt her arm against his waist before hearing the lock behind him click into place. Craig had been so absorbed in the taste of her, he'd lost all foresight to keep this late-night meeting private. That was the thing about Caroline—she knew things about him and she knew what he wanted, without even asking him.

He finally pulled away, studying her face for any signs of discomfort. Her eyelids were heavy and her lips were full and swollen, a hint of a smile still playing at their corners. His pulse picked up tempo and he had to command his hands to keep her at an arm's distance until he could get his breathing under control.

"Before I went to bed," he started, then made the mistake of glancing over her shoulder and toward the foot of his own queen-size mattress. The hammering in his heart spread to his lower extremities, and he had to shake his head and clear his mind before he could continue what he was saying. "I just wanted to check and make sure you were comfortable in here. Is there anything you need?"

With her face turned up to his and her eyes focused on his mouth, she tugged her lower lip between her teeth, then released it. "Only you."

Craig groaned and pulled her against him. The next kiss was deeper than the first and in that loose pajama shirt, it was easy for his hands to slip underneath the hem.

Just for a second. He would only let his work-calloused palms stroke the intoxicating silkiness of her skin for a second. But it wasn't enough time.

Just another inch. He would only move his thumbs up another inch. But then the rest of his fingers followed suit and he was splaying his hands on either side of her rib cage.

Just hold still. He wouldn't go any further. In fact, now was the time he should stop this maddening kiss, as well. But Caroline dragged her head away first, breaking her lips apart from his long enough to pull the pajama top over her head.

Just make her yours already. It was his last thought before he totally consumed her. His mouth slanted over hers, coaxing her tongue deeper inside so that he could suckle it.

She wasn't wearing a bra and, while he hadn't been able to get a good view of her chest before she'd immediately plastered her body against his, her rounded breasts easily filled his hands and her nipples tightened into tiny buds against his palms.

Caroline's soft little moans increased and he felt her pulling against his belt buckle. Anticipation raced through him as she got the first button of his fly undone. When the backs of her warm fingers dusted the tip of his erection, an electric current shot through him.

Craig was trying to shrug out of his own shirt when a deep, scratchy meow sound stopped him cold. His head whipped up and he saw Tiny Tim using his sole front paw to claw, press and reshape the stacked pillows on his bed. "What's my cat doing in here?"

"Well, this is *his* room, isn't it?" Caroline looked over her shoulder at the overweight tabby, who was now pacing in circles around the comforter and scowling at them. "He looks pretty mad at us for waking him."

"Actually, he looks like that when he's happy, too. But I think you're right about his level of annoyance at this moment. He's not used to having a lot of late-night activity going on in his bedroom." Then Craig winced at his own implication. Only an old fuddy-duddy would admit to going to bed alone every night with his cat.

"Maybe we should move to your brothers' room and let Tiny Tim get his sleep." Caroline's thumbs were still hooked above the fly of his jeans, her breathing still shallow.

It took every last drop of strength he possessed to encircle her wrists and drag her hands away. "Honey, we can't."

"Do you not want to?" she asked, staring at him with

such a deep longing, Craig felt completely exposed. "Or is it that you don't want to right now?"

"I think you just felt how much I want to," he replied before buttoning his jeans back up so that the evidence of his desire wasn't further tempted. "But when I make love to you, I want you to know who I am."

"So you're saying that as soon as I remember, you'll finally make love to me?"

If you still want me to, he thought. But all he said was "Yes."

She sighed and backed away, but there was a promise glinting in her eyes. As he walked back to his brothers' room, he wondered if he'd just made a deal with the devil.

Because if Caroline Ruth finally learned the truth and she still wanted him, Craig would do much more than make love to her.

Chapter Fourteen

"I think I may be in way over my head," Caroline confided to the palomino in the stall before her. She'd already admitted as much a few hours ago to Tiny Tim—who'd ignored Craig's commands to follow him down the hall to a different room last night. The cat clearly regretted his choice in bedmates because after hours of Caroline's tossing and turning and talking out loud about what she should say to her pretend fiancé, Tim began scratching at the door, demanding to be let outside well before dawn.

But at least the cranky tabby had led her to the stables, where there were more pairs of triangle-shaped ears to listen to Caroline's venting. Obviously, she knew the animals couldn't really understand her, but growing up, she'd moved too often to keep a pet and she'd never had a sibling to use as a sounding board. She'd always been able to talk out her problems with her parents, then with her sorority sisters and, more recently, with her boss, Vivienne. But none of them were currently around, so these new four-legged friends—or three-legged in Tiny Tim's case—would have to do.

Caroline stroked the horse's silky blond muzzle as she went on. "I mean, how embarrassing and frustrating that he got me all worked up like that last night. And then he simply walked away, leaving me breathing all funny and wanting more."

The horse snorted in response.

"I know," Caroline continued. "You get it. You've probably had a stallion or two come sniffing around your stall. Maybe nipping you in the neck to get your attention. What I wouldn't have given for a good neck nip last night. Anyway, this might sound totally human of me, but this attraction I'm feeling for him? It's more than just the physical. I'm worried that if I lose him, I'll also lose all of this."

The mare's soulful brown eyes followed Caroline's arm as she gestured toward the rest of the ranch outside. She wanted Craig, but she also wanted the holiday dinners with all of the Cliftons and her own children carrying on their family's legacy. She didn't know it twenty-four hours ago, but his perfectly happy home out in Thunder Canyon, Montana, contained the entire life she'd always envisioned for herself and didn't know existed.

"I was trying to seduce him last night, I'll willingly admit that." At least, Caroline would admit that to a stable full of animals who couldn't reveal her secret.

"But only because I was hoping to make him want me as much as I want him. Instead, all of his damn restraint and chivalry are now only making me fall harder for him."

The horse gave a little whinny, throwing back her nearly white mane and stomping her forelegs, probably in a show of sisterly solidarity.

"You're wearing jeans." Craig's voice surprised her and she caught her toe on the lower rung as she hopped down from the stall. The sun was starting to rise outside and his gaze traveled over her in the dim light, making her shudder in excitement. "And boots."

"Thanks for the warning," she whispered into her new friend's fury neck before turning toward Craig. "C.C. loaned everything to me."

"Everything except for the jacket," he replied, using his chin to gesture at the coat made of faux red leather with faux fur lining.

Caroline pulled it closer around her torso, feeling like a complete faux herself. She wished she had brought suitable attire with her to the ranch so it didn't appear as though she was overplaying the roles of both fiancée *and* cowgirl.

"I saw it on the hook by the back door and assumed it was your sister's, as well."

"Nah, Meemaw just thinks she's of a similar age as you and C.C. and shops accordingly."

Caroline's steps faltered as she thought about the way Craig's body had stiffened beside her last night when his brother Rob had made the joke about him robbing the cradle. She'd never really given his age any thought, but it was interesting that she and his so-called "baby sister" were only a year apart.

Yet, as she approached him, Craig stared at her legs encased in the tight denim as though he wasn't thinking of either his sister or grandmother at that exact second. A jolt of hope surged in Caroline's veins and she asked, "Why are you looking at me like that?"

"I guess I'm not used to seeing you in anything but skirts and dresses and high heels," he replied, rubbing the scar along his neck. "You almost look like you could fit in here."

"Almost?" Seeing the dark circles under his eyes put a little more swagger into her walk. Not that she wanted to see him exhausted, but it was somewhat of a relief to know they were both on a level playing field as far as lust-filled sleep deprivation went.

"I mean, we'd have to get you on a horse to really be sure." He smiled and she wondered if he was hoping to avoid any conversations about how hot and heavy things had gotten between them last night.

Recklessness coursed through her and she rested a hand on a jutted-out hip. "Is that an invitation to ride?"

"You actually want to go for a ride? On a horse?"

"Show me where you keep the saddles."

Caroline followed Craig to the tack room and looked at the rows of reins and bits hanging from the walls. This ranch operation of theirs was definitely bigger than she'd first thought. If she wanted to get to know the man, then she really needed to get to know all aspects of him, including his land. A little thrill of excitement shot through her.

But it sputtered to a halt when he patted a leather horn. "This one should fit you okay."

"It's a Western saddle, though." She pulled her bottom lip between her teeth as she studied her choices. Sure, the one Craig had picked out was smaller than most of the others, but it was still huge. Maybe she'd gotten a little too cocky when she'd suggested going for a ride. "Do you have an English one by any chance?"

"Wait." Craig did a double take in her direction. "You know the difference?"

"My parents were at Oxford when I was eight and then again when I was fourteen. I took equestrian lessons both times."

Craig studied her before finally hefting the smaller saddle onto his shoulder. "Trust me. Since we're not doing any show vaults or playing polo today, you're gonna want the bigger one to distribute your weight."

"And do you have a horse in mind for me to ride?" Caroline asked as she picked up a plaid-patterned saddle blanket and followed him out of the tack room.

"I figured you'd want to take Marley out this morning. Looked like you two were pretty deep in conversation when I walked in."

Despite the low temperatures outside, heat filled Caroline's cheeks. *Lord, please tell me Craig was too far away to hear what I was saying to the mare.*

But the only answer was his boots crunching along the straw-covered concrete. With his arm lifted high to balance his load, the hem of his work jacket rose above the waistband of his worn jeans, exposing his well-muscled rear end.

That's it, she thought, racing across the stable floor to catch up with him. From now on, Caroline would have to always stay one step ahead of him. She was supposed to be the seducer, not the seducee. There was no way she was going to let this man and his perfectly shaped cowboy butt ride in front of her.

Craig tried not to watch the way Caroline's hips rocked in the saddle as she cantered along the trail in front of him. However, after a sleepless night with nothing but some unfulfilled fantasies to keep him company, he couldn't think of anything but his attraction to her.

Well, his attraction to her *and* her age. Rob's cradle-robbing comment from yesterday had been fleeting and made in jest, but Craig's doubt about their age difference still lingered.

Caroline was young and adventurous and had her whole life in front of her. And she was full of surprises. Every time Craig found out something new about her, he was taken aback. He shouldn't have been shocked since she'd grown up traveling all over the world and had experienced things most people could only dream about.

He was beginning to think that there was nothing she couldn't do. Last night, he'd learned that she could easily count cards and would hold on to a winning hand before folding so that his competitive grandparents didn't get so huffy at losing. And now, this morning, he was still in a state of wonder at how well she rode a horse.

But looking the part was easy. Real ranch work was tough, and if Craig were to ever change his mind and get married, it would have to be to someone mature, someone who could step up to that kind of responsibility.

"I don't think I've ever seen a more perfect sunrise," Caroline called over her shoulder as they approached the trailhead. A pinkish glow outlined the mountains off in the distance and when he turned to look in that direction, he was immediately reminded of the exact shade of her dusky nipples last night as he'd cupped her breasts in his hands.

Groaning, Craig shoved his Stetson lower on his forehead and asked, "Are you ready to head back now?"

"Back to the ranch? Sure." Caroline clicked her tongue at the mare, then pulled the reins around until Marley was nose to nose with his own mount. "Back to Rust Creek Falls? Not quite yet."

"You mean you want to stay here?" Craig felt the creases on his forehead push against his hat brim.

"I would love that." Her smile was bold and confident. "If I didn't have Josselyn and Drew's wedding to plan or that Presents for Patriots party we're hosting next week, I'd be all for staying right here with you."

"That's because it's the slow season now." Craig squeezed his knees against his stallion's sides to get moving. "Give it a day or two during calving season when we're busy from sunup to sundown rotating the herds, reseeding our grazing pastures, maintaining the equipment and then spending the entire night on birthing watch. You'll think the chores will never end."

"I don't mind hard work." Caroline shrugged.

"Well, working hard at planning parties and working hard at wrangling cattle during a muddy spring are two different things."

"Says who?" she asked, and he recognized that squared-off shape to her shoulders. "I've never worked on a ranch and I'm guessing that you've never pulled off a successful outdoor wedding for four hundred guests in the middle of a thunderstorm. Therefore, neither one of us would be qualified to make those kinds of comparisons about whose job is more difficult. But if you know someone who has done both, then I'd be glad to hear the results of their findings."

"Fair enough," Craig replied. "There's no way I could do what you do for a living."

"Is that why you were so quick to beat a hasty retreat every time you dropped me off at my office this week?"

"Pretty much." He nodded. "Discussing flower arrangements and table seatings and poofy white dresses surely has to be one of the most headache-inducing tasks on this earth. Just thinking about dealing with all those brides and their talk of having a perfect day makes me squirm."

"Says the man who works with bulls and artificial insemination," she replied.

"Exactly. I *still* wouldn't trade any of my duties on the ranch for any of the mind-boggling demands and events you have to wrestle with every day. Except for maybe cake tasting. I could probably handle that responsibility."

Caroline laughed. "I bet you could handle any responsibility where you're in charge."

"Are you calling me bossy?"

"I'm just saying that you really like to look out for other people."

Craig grunted, unsure whether that was supposed to be a compliment or not, then clicked his tongue at his stallion to move along. "Come on, Jake."

"Jake?" Caroline said, drawing on her own reins to slow down. "You've got to be kidding me."

"What's wrong?" he asked, appraising her startled expression for any sign of injury.

"Let me get this straight. Are we currently riding horses named after Ebenezer Scrooge's business partner—Jacob Marley?"

"Technically my horse's name is Jake, not Jacob. And C.C. named your horse after that book about the dog." Still, Craig couldn't deny the coincidences of so many references to *A Christmas Carol*. But he merely faked a casual shrug and urged his horse forward.

They trotted along silently for a few minutes and then she eased her mount closer to his as the trail narrowed. She really was accommodating nicely to this different style of saddle and it made Craig wonder if she could actually accommodate other parts of his life.

No. He shouldn't even be letting his mind wander in that direction.

"Did you always want to be a wedding planner?" he asked. Not that he would ever want a woman to give up her career to better facilitate his own. But it wouldn't hurt to confirm that there was no chance she was actually willing to relocate to Thunder Canyon and become a cattle hand. The confirmation would be another red flag to add to his list of warnings on why he shouldn't let their relationship go any further.

"No way." Caroline chuckled. "I didn't know a thing about the industry until Vivienne Shuster hired me."

"So then how did you end up in Rust Creek Falls?"

"I'll tell you if you promise not to laugh at me." Her face was solemn as she held up her palm, as if she was expecting him to repeat an oath. Craig humored her by crossing his finger over his heart. "It's a long story, so I won't go into the boring details, but when I was fifteen, my mom was doing a lecture series at the University of Montana about the history of overlooked female buffalo hunters. Anyway, I fell in love with the area and the campus, breaking my parents' hearts because they'd hoped I'd choose to attend an Ivy League school."

"Why would I laugh at that?" Craig sat up a little straighter as he surveyed the land. "I definitely can't blame you for loving Montana."

"That's not the odd part. So I visited Rust Creek Falls a couple of years ago before I graduated college. And I... Well, let's just say I had a premonition."

"A premonition?"

"You promised. No laughing." She narrowed her gaze at him until he forced the smirk from his face. Then she continued, "I have a degree in biology. Trust me, I understand science and reason and, therefore, realize exactly how crazy this must all sound. But the truth is, I've always known I had a destiny."

"And planning weddings in Rust Creek Falls is your destiny?" Craig was trying to make sense of it without appearing to sound doubtful.

"Ever since I was a little girl, I've dreamt of getting married. Not like in a creepy Miss-Havisham-pining-for-a-bridegroom sort of way, but just in an excited, purpose-driven way."

"A purpose-driven way?" he repeated. Like she'd been so determined to get married, her brain seized on the first potential groom it could find and then completely fabricated him as the lucky guy? But before he could go down that road, she continued on.

"When I was debating where to move after graduation, I saw an online ad for an assistant wedding planner and it just seemed logical that if I wanted to eventually get married, I should work around like-minded people."

"Like-minded people?"

"Why do you keep repeating everything I say?" she asked and he shrugged. He had no idea why he was having such difficulty wrapping his brain around her words. "Anyway, I saw the job opening as a way to reach my destiny."

"So your destiny is to get married? That's it?"

"Well, to get married to the right man, obviously."

"And how are you supposed to know if you find the right man?"

"I already have." Caroline smiled and Craig's stomach dropped.

"But *how*?"

"Like I said, I can't really explain it. I've always been of the mind-set that I'll know when I know. And finally, I know."

Craig hadn't noticed that his horse was completely standing still as he stared at Caroline. Surely she wasn't saying that she thought *he* was her destiny or that they were meant to be together in some mystical way. He'd promised not to laugh, but he couldn't prevent the sarcasm lacing his voice. "Sounds very scientific."

"Science can explain a lot of things, but it can't always explain emotions. Some intuitions are so powerful, they just feel right. Okay, let me try and break it down another way. Have you ever felt so connected to someone or something that you just knew it was part of your future?"

"This ranch," Craig admitted. "I always knew I was going to work the land and carry on my family's legacy."

He didn't admit that he'd originally planned to do so with Tina.

"So just out of curiosity," she asked as she tilted her head, "if ranching is such grueling work, why do you do it?"

"Because I couldn't imagine doing anything else."

"What about the rodeo?" she asked.

"Life is full of detours, I guess."

"Exactly. Some people might refer to those detours as fate. As though there's a driving force that brings you right to where you belong."

"If by *driving force* you mean a busted collarbone, then yeah, that's what brought me home."

"So that's how you got your scar?" She reached out toward him, but the horses kept them too far apart.

He touched the warm, jagged line along his neck. "Not exactly."

The silence hung between them, but as the wooden outbuildings appeared in the distance she asked, "Then was it another detour?"

Chapter Fifteen

"When I was twenty-one, I was coming home from my engagement party of sorts in Kalispell," Craig began. He continued talking but he'd used his boot heels to urge Jake forward, so he was no longer making eye contact with her as he spoke, and all Caroline could focus on were the three words he'd said. *My engagement party.*

He'd been engaged before. She gave her reins more slack and Marley took the few steps to catch up when she heard him say something about a crash.

"What kind of crash?" she asked, her pulse pounding. "What happened?"

"Tina didn't get to see her cousins very often, so she wanted to go out to a bar with them after the party. I was exhausted and needed to be back in Thunder

Canyon early the next morning to meet with the veterinarian about one of our prize heifers. Tina wasn't a drinker and told me that she was fine to drive home while I slept in the passenger seat."

Tina.

Caroline's heart was clawing for more information, needing to know more about the woman Craig had been in love with, but she pressed her lips into a tight line, letting him tell his story uninterrupted.

"The highway patrol officer who did the investigation said she probably didn't even see the stalled logging trailer when she took the turnoff too quickly."

Caroline's hand flew to her mouth. Oh, no. Craig's strange reaction to his parents' not wanting him to drive last night when he was tired suddenly made more sense. It was then that she recalled his tension during the first half of the drive here yesterday and she blurted out, "The cross!"

"What?" Craig's head pivoted toward her as though he'd just remembered she was still beside him, still listening.

"We passed a white wooden cross when we were on Highway 90," Caroline offered.

"That's where her Jeep went off the embankment. She'd swerved, but the left fender still swiped the back of the trailer. The initial collision woke me up, but by then we were already skidding off the road. It was her daddy's old ranch vehicle and the windshield was one of those fold-down types. The hinges had gotten rusty, so when we rolled, the impact caused the whole thing to go in the opposite direction toward us. I don't remember landing, but when I came to, the top corner of the windshield frame had me pinned against the roll bar."

By this time, the horses were standing still again, as though Jake and Marley were in equal stages of grief and couldn't move. Anguish covered Craig's face and Caroline wanted to climb down off the mare and drag him into her embrace. She wanted to hold him, to comfort him. "How long were you stuck like that?"

"The responding officer said it was only five minutes. The driver of the stalled rig had seen us go off the road and called 9-1-1."

"And Tina?" Caroline asked, already knowing the answer.

"We should've driven a safer vehicle, but I'd just sold my truck because we were saving money to build our own house on the property line between our parents' places. The Jeep was built well before anyone had even heard of airbags. Hell, it was so old, we only had lap belts. So there was no way to prevent the steering wheel from breaking her ribs and puncturing her lung."

Caroline bit down hard to force back the gasp rising in her throat, then looked up toward the sky to keep the tears from trickling out of the corners of her eyes.

"I couldn't get to her." Craig's voice was flat when he spoke again. Flat and so defeated. It made the tears Caroline had been holding back spill over. "I fought against the broken windshield but the struggle drove it in deeper. The only part of her I could reach was her hand. I was holding it when she took her last breath and all I could think was that it should have been me driving. I was supposed to protect her. She was looking at me, smiling at me, before she died. But I couldn't save her."

"I can't imagine how painful that must have been for you, Craig. I'm so sorry."

His only acknowledgment of her condolences was a brief nod. "We'd grown up together and had always planned to eventually join our families' cattle operations. But being here at the ranch was a constant reminder of that dream dying alongside her on the highway. I stayed long enough for her funeral, but left for Billings the next day. I had a friend doing the PBR circuit and, at the time, it seemed like traveling from town to town while simultaneously punishing my body in the arena would be the easiest escape."

"But then you came back." Caroline understood why he'd left, yet she also understood why he couldn't stay away. Not only was this land beautiful, but it also filled a person with a sense of peace. A sense of belonging.

"Yep. A few broken bones and one career-ending surgery later, I came home. I had nowhere else. She was gone, but I could still make the ranch live on."

"You must have really loved her," Caroline whispered. He possibly loved her still.

Craig was gazing at something in the horizon, seemingly lost in his own world, when he said, "Tina was the perfect woman for me."

"I think Tina would've loved her," Will said as he drove the all-terrain vehicle along the perimeter of his property the following day.

Craig kept his hat low and his face averted, studying his brother's fence line for any loose posts or fallen wires. "Loved who?"

"Caroline. You know? The woman you're engaged to?"

Clenching his back molars together as Will swerved to avoid a rut in the narrow dirt trail, Craig tried to remember why he'd agreed to come to Will's ranch today and help him do some minor repairs before the breeding season started. Oh, because he'd poured his heart out to Caroline yesterday morning in Thunder Canyon and then she'd barely said a word to him the entire drive home last night.

Her home, that was. Not *his* home. Craig didn't really know what to call the little rental house here in Rust Creek Falls. Although, he'd packed a second duffel bag and brought it with him as if he'd planned to move into the place with her.

It had been late when they'd finally pulled into her driveway, and while he'd been relieved that she didn't invite him to sleep in her bed with her again, Craig had spent the remainder of the night on the sofa wondering if he'd done something to hurt her feelings.

When an emergency call came in this morning from a bride demanding Caroline drive to some dress shop in Kalispell, Craig grabbed his keys off the hook by the kitchen. But Caroline insisted that she could drive herself and then proceeded to tell him in painful detail what it would be like when an elderly, no-nonsense seamstress told a very vain and very stubborn bride that she would need to lay off all the bridal shower cake and mimosas if she wanted to fit into her dress on her wedding day.

So instead of subjecting himself to that particular brand of misery—which was only slightly worse than worrying about Caroline driving herself—Craig had accepted Will's request for help on his ranch. Too bad they couldn't have taken a good old-fashioned work truck out to the fields instead of this four-wheel-drive Raptor.

"We're not engaged," Craig ground out as his stiff neck rocked side to side against the five-point harness. "Remember, I already told all of you about her head injury and the confabulation and how she thinks I'm her fiancé."

"So then why don't you just explain it to her like you did to all of us? She seems like a smart woman to me." Will looked in his review mirror, probably to make sure one of the shovels hadn't bounced out after that last bump.

"She's incredibly smart. But it doesn't have anything to do with intelligence. Drew said that it's her *brain* tricking her, not me. So no matter what I tell her, she's going to listen to her brain."

"Then what happens when her brain stops tricking her?"

"What do you mean?" Craig snatched his hat off his head because he was tired of adjusting it every time his skull banged into the headrest.

"Well, eventually, she's going to get her memory back. What are you going to do then?"

"I've been trying to figure that out. Jeez, Will, have you ever thought of getting a bulldozer out here and doing a little grading? Perhaps smoothing out a real road?"

"What's there to figure out?" Will asked. "From what I can tell, she's perfect for you. That's why I said that Tina would've loved her."

"Caroline? But she and Tina are nothing alike."

"Apparently, both of them wanted to marry you, which means they were born with the same misguided taste in guys." Before Craig could bark out a retort, Will purposely swerved the ATV to hit a bump in the road, making Craig's butt completely lift off the seat.

"If you keep driving like a maniac, I'm gonna walk back to the stable."

"Speaking of stables, I heard you took Caroline for a ride when you were at Thunder Canyon. Rob said she looked pretty good in the saddle."

"Rob needs to find a woman with her own saddle," Craig muttered.

"Jealous much?" his brother asked, then chuckled.

Craig only growled.

"My point," Will continued and Craig pinched the bridge of his nose since there was apparently no end to this conversation in sight, "is that Caroline seemed pretty comfortable on a horse. Hell, she seemed pretty comfortable in general out there on the ranch. I know that's what you're looking for in a wife."

"I'm not looking for a wife."

"She's also diplomatic and intuitive and has a good head on her shoulders," Will went on as though he hadn't heard Craig's objection. "Plus, I heard you've been eating all of your meals at her house, so I assume she's a decent cook."

"The best." Craig groaned, thinking of the Nutella-filled crepes she'd whipped up that morning. "But don't tell Meemaw."

"Pish," Will scoffed, then took his foot off the accelerator as they came to the end of the fence line. "As if I want her to think I'm taking Grandpac's side about anything right before she goes Christmas shopping."

A series of beeps chimed and Craig immediately reached for his cell phone, his chest filling with worry that something had happened to Caroline. But it wasn't his phone that had rung.

"That's probably Jordyn," Will said, idling the engine and pulling out his cell phone to read his wife's text. "Like everyone else in town, she's curious about what I've found out about you and Caroline."

Craig rolled his eyes.

"Nooooot muuuuuch." Will sounded out the words as he typed a response.

The phone pinged again.

"Jordyn thinks we might have better luck getting you to talk if you have a couple of beers in you."

"Well, you two would have firsthand experience at how alcohol can lower a person's inhibitions," Craig pointed out.

"I'm going to tell Jordyn that you're teasing us about the night we met." Will began typing and Craig tried to grab the phone from his brother when it vibrated again. "She's suggesting we go out tonight and celebrate your engagement."

"You mean my fake engagement?" Craig asked.

"Who cares if it's real or fake? At least you *got* an engagement, unlike me and Jordyn, who accidentally drank some of Homer Gilmore's spiked punch one night and woke up married."

Craig snorted. At least he hadn't gotten himself into a similar predicament. Although, things seemed to have worked out pretty well for Will and Jordyn.

"I'll tell her we should be done with the south pasture around four," his brother said. "We can hit the Ace in the Hole after that."

"Sorry, man," Craig said, not the least bit sorry. "Caroline has a meeting with the food and beverage director over at the Maverick Manor late this afternoon. So we'll have to take a pass on the celebration that's really an inquisition."

"No problem." Will tapped at his screen for several seconds, then looked up and smiled. "The Maverick Manor has that fancy bar inside the massive lobby. I just told Jordyn we can all head over there after Caroline's meeting."

Craig had texted her about the last-minute get-together with Will and Jordyn. However, Caroline certainly hadn't been expecting an impromptu engagement party of sorts until Jonathan and Dawn showed up, followed by two of the Clifton sisters with their spouses, along with several of the Stricklands.

When she finally realized what was going on, Caroline wanted to come clean then and there about her restored memory. It was one thing to let people be under a mistaken impression. It was quite another to celebrate it.

Unfortunately, before she could say anything, Ben Strickland raised his glass in a toast. Craig shot death looks at his childhood friend, but didn't correct the well-wishers or turn down any of their hearty congratulations.

Her original question, the one she'd pondered the night of that first intense kiss, returned with a cold force.

Why was Craig going along with this?

Now that she knew about Tina and how he'd tried to save her, Caroline could somewhat understand his desire to redeem himself by taking care of Caroline after her concussion. She could even understand how he might indulge an injured woman by allowing her to go on believing whatever she wanted. However, the thing she absolutely couldn't figure out was why Craig wasn't telling his closest friends and family the truth.

Why was he silently drinking to their toasts instead?

There must be a reason why he hadn't already put a stop to all of this—especially if Craig was still in love with another woman.

The only person who could help solve that riddle was Josselyn Weaver. She'd been there when Caroline had hit her head and then again when Caroline had woken up and thought Craig was her fiancé. But Josselyn wasn't here now, and Drew, who'd also been at the hospital part of the time, was never alone long enough for her to ask any meaningful questions.

Questions such as *What's in it for Craig?* and *How far is he willing to go to keep up this pretense?*

The champagne bubbled inside Caroline's tummy and it felt as if corks were popping inside her head. She needed to go somewhere quiet and think this through before people actually began expecting invitations to their wedding.

"Excuse me," she whispered to Craig, who had just clinked beer bottles with his brother Jonathan. "I need to use the ladies' room."

The tight line of his mouth softened with concern and he put the backs of his fingers to her forehead. "Are you feeling okay? Maybe you shouldn't be drinking so soon after your concussion. I told them you probably weren't up for a big night out like this."

"Did you know that everyone was going to be here?" she asked. "That it was going to be like…this?" She'd caught herself from referring to it as an engagement party, because the idea might fill her with too much hope.

"I had a feeling, but I also knew that when my family and friends get an idea in their heads, they're not going to be deterred. It was either this or risk having everyone show up at your office to offer us their congratulations." His arm was draped around her waist as he leaned down to speak in her ear. Suddenly the champagne bubbles weren't the only thing tingling inside her. "But I can take you home if it's too much."

"No, it's fine," she replied, taking another sip before setting down her glass on the polished mahogany bar inside the old log mansion. "I'll be right back."

A few minutes and two enthusiastic congratulatory hugs later, Caroline stared at her reflection in the mirror over the bathroom sink, telling herself it was too risky to keep this pretense up.

She couldn't very well seduce a man who was probably still in love with someone else. Although, during their quiet drive home last night, she'd wondered more than once if he was staying at her house because he genuinely cared for her.

Touching her lips, Caroline remembered the kiss they'd shared in his childhood bedroom. She might be young and inexperienced, but even she knew that wasn't the type of kiss a man gave a woman if he was only feeling protective. The bottom line was that she'd fallen in love with Craig and her underlying instinct that he was the one for her wasn't likely to go away. However, she needed to know that Craig was with her because he actually loved her, not because he was trying to save her.

Unfortunately, she didn't quite know how to do that without telling Craig that her memory had returned. And if she admitted as much, would he consider his hero duties fulfilled and leave her?

A toilet flushed and Caroline quickly turned on the faucet to pretend she was there to wash her hands and not to give herself a strategic pep talk.

"Just the woman I wanted to see," Cecelia Clifton Pritchett said as she came out of a stall. "You're coming to the Presents for Patriots dinner dance next week, right?"

"Oh, um, yes. Our company is actually sponsoring the event and planning it out at Sawmill Station."

"Good. That means Craig will finally be going to a social function. My big brother needs to get out more. I haven't seen him this happy in a long time."

"Really? Because I was just thinking he seemed pretty uncomfortable out there with everyone congratulating us on the *engagement*." Caroline emphasized the last word to gauge Craig's sister's reaction.

With the exception of his grandparents, nobody had mentioned their relationship status at Thanksgiving, let alone questioned it. Surely his family must be wondering what was actually going on.

"Nah." Cecelia dried her hands on a paper towel. "He just hates being the center of attention. And, because he carries the world on his shoulders, he probably thinks he should be feeling guilty."

"Guilty?" Caroline's fingers shot up to the V-shaped collar on her dress and toyed with the ruffled edges. "Why would he feel guilty?"

"For finally moving on and allowing himself to open up to someone a second time."

Cecelia stood beside her, applying lipstick while Caroline sucked in her cheeks, fighting the impulse to ask for some sort of proof that Craig really was in fact ready to fall in love again.

Chapter Sixteen

Yesterday, when Will had railroaded him into the party at the Maverick Manor, Craig had known he should level with all of his family and friends. But then the toasts had started and Caroline, who hadn't spoken to him much during their drive home from Thunder Canyon on Friday, had gotten all flushed and became even more subdued before rushing off to the bathroom. He'd been worried that the impromptu celebration was too much for her—especially on the heels of meeting all of his family at Thanksgiving—and he'd just wanted to get her home and comfortable and away from all the pretending.

Other than the accident investigators, Craig had never really spoken to anyone else about the night Tina had died, and maybe he'd been a little too open with

Caroline during their ride. But she'd been talking about all that destiny stuff and people knowing where they belong and he needed to make her see that his entire life was the ranch.

That was *his* destiny.

Tina had understood more than anyone else what sacrifices it would take for that lifestyle. But she was gone and Craig would be better off alone than forcing a young and vibrant woman like Caroline into a world that wasn't for her.

It would be one thing if she had her memory back and was able to make rational decisions based on full disclosure. However, he worried that she was just acting upon some childish fantasy of getting married and, as much as he desired her physically, there was no way Craig could be with any woman under false pretenses.

"Let's go get a tree today," Caroline had said that morning, taking a tray of homemade cinnamon rolls out of the oven. "It's going to be a crazy week at work for me and I don't know when I'll have another chance since I've got weddings and parties booked every weekend this month. Besides, Christmas is my absolute favorite holiday and I can't wait to decorate."

Apparently, neither could the rest of Rust Creek Falls, Craig thought grudgingly a couple of hours later when they arrived at the tree lot adjacent to the Masonic Lodge downtown. The town was already getting into the Christmas spirit with lights and garlands going up on Main Street and notices announcing collection locations for Presents for Patriots, as well as the upcoming holiday pageants at the local schools.

"Where are we going to put it?" Craig scratched the back of his neck as he studied the eight-foot-tall Douglas fir.

"If we move one of the bookshelves over to the left, we can put it in front of the living room window."

The word *we* was getting passed around in this conversation an awful lot. But Caroline's eyes were bright and the tip of her nose was turning pink as the first flurries of snowfall dusted the green branches around them. Her enthusiasm for the holidays was contagious, and since the moment she'd opened her eyes in that hospital emergency room, Craig really hadn't been able to deny her anything.

The Freemasons had partnered with the varsity football team to sell Christmas trees as a fund-raiser, and Craig tipped the defensive tackle who'd carried the freshly trimmed bundle to his truck for them.

"Thank you, sir," the teenager said before turning to Caroline, who, in her knit beanie and oversize red plaid scarf, appeared young enough to be the kid's homecoming date. "I'm also supposed to tell all the customers that if you're looking for homemade ornaments or decorations, they're having a craft fair right now inside the high school gym."

Caroline slapped her mitten-covered hands together and gave an excited bounce before turning those pleading, doe-shaped eyes at Craig. And that was how he ended up spending the rest of his Sunday afternoon picking out glass balls covered in glitter, rolling his eyes in camaraderie with the other men hiding out at the hot chocolate stand and tipping his hat at the ladies from the quilting club who offered to sell him a hand-sewn tote bag for all the purchases he was carrying as he walked behind his pretend fiancée.

Not wanting to be a complete Scrooge and begrudge her the excitement and wonder of the season, Craig followed along and whipped out his wallet to pay for her decorations. In fact, if was being honest with himself, he was kind of getting a kick out of her enthusiasm as she practically skipped along, gushing at the displays at each booth.

Later that night, as a cinnamon-scented candle filled the air, they were hanging their new ornaments on the tree that barely fitted inside her tiny house. Caroline reached into one of the paper bags and pulled out matching red velvet stockings with each of their names stitched along the tops.

Craig gulped and all the pleasure from his earlier indulgences faded away, leaving nothing but a guilty taste in his mouth. "When did you get those?"

"I saw them when you were at the caramel corn stand, getting us those popcorn balls. The Embroidery Club was selling them and offered free customizing while we shopped."

"Don't you think we're a little too old for stockings?" he asked. And where would she even hang the things? It wasn't like she had an actual fireplace in this doll-house of hers.

"Says the man who ate an entire roll of cherry Life Savers on the drive home." She winked at him. "Didn't you have a stocking growing up?"

"Yeah, but as I got older, my parents put me in charge

of filling them for the younger ones. Same thing with hiding the Easter eggs."

"Well, I figured we could start our own family traditions." Her last two words hit him with a force, and panic clawed at the back of his throat.

Or maybe it was guilt. After all, if it wasn't for him going along with all of this imagined-fiancé business, she wouldn't be under the misguided impression that they had any family traditions to start.

Either way, he could feel a line of perspiration dampen his hairline as he studied their embroidered names. The only thing more permanent would've been a tattoo. Or a scar.

He swiped at the prickling skin along his neck.

How could he convince Caroline that she shouldn't allow herself to get too attached to him? That she shouldn't believe this fanciful notion of hers that he was the man for her. If he had permission from Dr. Robinson, he would gladly steer her in that direction right this second.

But since he couldn't risk stressing her out by saying what he wanted, Craig said the first thing he could think of. "There comes a certain point in everyone's life when they need to grow up and stop believing in Santa Claus."

Last night, Caroline had tried to pretend Craig's words hadn't hurt, pasting on her smile that she used when dealing with an overpriced vendor or a client's negative mother-in-law. They'd gotten the Christmas decorations up—minus the stockings, which she'd discreetly slipped back in the bag—and then she'd made creamy tomato basil soup and grilled cheese sandwiches for dinner because that wasn't quite as juvenile as chicken nuggets and tater tots, which were the only things she had in her freezer.

Despite going to bed early to escape the awkward tension, she'd been awake until midnight, tossing and turning and rethinking what he'd said about her believing in childish things. Thank goodness he didn't know about the psychic or he'd really think Caroline was naive and impressionable.

If she and Craig were meant to be together, then Caroline needed to prove to him once and for all how much of a woman she was.

Sitting at the conference table in her office that morning, Caroline stared absently at her blank notepad, trying to figure out how to do that. Cecelia had implied that Craig was willing to move on, so maybe it wouldn't be such a bad thing for Caroline to seduce him after all.

She tapped her pencil against her chin. The problem with that was she didn't know how to go about it. Especially since her past attempts at physical intimacy with Craig had been rather unsuccessful and only left her wanting more.

"I go away for two weeks and come back to find my favorite employee engaged."

At the sound of the familiar voice, Caroline looked up to see Vivienne entering the office.

Smiling widely and looking sun-kissed and refreshed

from her honeymoon in Fiji, she gushed, "I can't wait to hear all about it."

"Yeah, it kinda happened fast," Caroline said, then let out a deep breath and slouched against the chair's brightly upholstered fabric. "The engagement, that is. It took on a life of its own, if that makes any sense."

"You have no idea how much sense that makes to me." Vivienne gave a little chuckle. "Did I ever tell you how Cole made up an entire fiancée in order to have me plan his pretend wedding?"

"But Cole loves you," Caroline said, referring to Vivienne's new husband.

"He barely knew me when he came up with the plan."

"What plan?" Josselyn Weaver asked as she came into the office for her rescheduled consultation. Ever since their first meeting had ended in a hospital stay, Caroline had the feeling her client had been purposely avoiding her. Fortunately, the woman still had a wedding to plan, which meant Caroline could finally get some answers.

"We were just talking about my engagement." Caroline studied her for any signs of conspiracy. Josselyn gave a discreet cough and looked away, practically inviting the next question. "Did you know I wasn't engaged to Craig when I woke up in that hospital?"

Josselyn gasped before narrowing her eyes. "Wait. Did *you* know you weren't engaged to him?"

"Not at the time I didn't." Caroline sighed in frustration, sinking lower in her seat. "I really believed he was my fiancé when I first saw him."

"But now you know…" Josselyn made a circular

motion with her wrist, encouraging Caroline to fill in the blanks. "What exactly do you know?"

Caroline went on to tell the two women about everything, from Winona Cobbs to her late-night research on confabulation to how her memory had come back as soon as Craig kissed her.

"So you guys kissed?" Josselyn asked, settling down into one of the chairs at the conference table. "How was that?"

"Wonderful and confusing and then wonderful again when I met his family."

"Oh, boy, you already met his family?" Vivienne asked, joining them at the table.

"Yes. I went there for Thanksgiving. And then some of them and his friends had this impromptu engagement party for us at the Maverick Manor the other night and everyone was congratulating us, and I sat there, knowing the truth yet saying nothing."

"Well," Josselyn started, "if it's any consolation, Craig also knew you weren't really engaged."

"Exactly. Craig knew it and, for the life of me, I can't figure out why he would go along with a pretend engagement." Caroline placed her elbow on the table and braced her forehead in her hand. "Who else knows it isn't real?"

"Well, Drew and I knew since we were there at the hospital when you came to and made the surprising announcement. Sorry for not speaking up sooner about that, by the way. The doctor didn't want us saying anything that could give you any more anxiety. Plus, Drew promised me that you were in good hands with Craig."

"But what does his family think of your relation-ship?" Vivienne asked.

"I'm not sure what they think." Caroline looked over to Josselyn, who only smirked.

"So, I wasn't able to attend the party at the Maverick Manor, but I heard that his siblings nominated Cecelia to be the one to tell you that they approved of the engagement."

Her tummy flipped in excitement. Having the rest of the Clifton family's approval boosted her confidence. But just to be sure her feelings weren't completely one-sided, she asked, "You guys don't think all of this is totally nuts?"

"From what I understand, there have been crazier courtships in Rust Creek Falls," Vivienne offered. "If you want him, I say go after him."

"I definitely want him, but only if he wants me in return. What happens, though, when he realizes that I remember everything? Will he be relieved that he can finally walk away?" Caroline rested her head against the back of the chair and studied the ceiling. "How do I come clean and still keep my cowboy?"

"I don't know Craig as well as the rest of the Stricklands do." Josselyn leaned forward and wiggled her eyebrows. "But I've seen the way that man looks at you."

Hope blossomed in Caroline's chest and she sat up straighter. "How does he look at me?"

"Like he's in no hurry to walk away."

She sincerely hoped that Josselyn was right. But just to be sure, Caroline decided to take matters into her own hands.

Chapter Seventeen

"Your drink matches your outfit," Craig said over the strains of the band's rendition of Mariah Carey's "All I Want for Christmas."

"Huh?" Caroline's nerve endings were pulsating along with the tempo of the festive music.

He nodded at her rum-laced eggnog in a miniature Mason jar and repeated himself.

Caroline had carefully chosen an ivory cashmere sweater and paired it with a matching fitted skirt that flared into a short ruffle of chiffon above the knee. Despite the snow outside, she'd kept her legs bare and her feet festive in a pair of glittery gold pumps. "Well, that's a party planner's job. To work from behind the scenes and blend in with the surroundings."

"As if you could ever blend in anywhere," Craig said,

his unconcealed stare turning her pulsing nerves into a throbbing ache under her skin.

It was the night of the Presents for Patriots fundraiser and they hadn't driven to the party together because, technically, Caroline was working. At least she had been the first half of the evening. But the caterers and the band and even the bartenders had worked previous events at Sawmill Station and didn't need much direction. So, after dinner and the silent auction, the only thing left for her to do was dance.

Of course, the sexy cowboy standing in front of her didn't seem all that eager to pull her onto the dance floor despite the fact that his warm hands kept sliding lower along her back each time he'd come over to check on how she was feeling.

In fact, judging by the way his palm was now resting along the upper curve of her bottom and threatening to dip lower, Caroline got the impression that he was much more eager to get her alone.

And truthfully, Caroline didn't want to wait any longer to make Craig hers.

They'd been living together for almost two weeks now and there was no way she was going to let him sleep on her sofa one more night. Maybe it was the intoxicating fragrance of all the swags of pine branches and mistletoe running along the white linen-covered farm tables. Or maybe it was the warm glow from the white twinkling lights hanging from the rustic wooden beams of the old freight house. Perhaps it was the spiced eggnog concoction warming her veins. More than likely, it was a combination of all three making her grow bolder and more confident by the minute.

It was either now or never.

"Are you ready to go home?" she asked, turning toward him and laying her hand on the lapel of his dark sport coat. "I want to give you your Christmas present early."

She saw the muscles of his neck contract as he tipped back his head and swallowed down the rest of his beer. Setting his empty bottle on the nearest table, his voice was low and rushed when he said, "Let's go."

Vivienne—who was standing with her husband beside the vintage red sleigh loaded with gifts donated for the Presents for Patriots charity—gave Caroline a thumbs-up as Craig guided her toward the exit.

The ten-minute ride back to her house was the same one he drove every day. But now it seemed as though it only took seconds before they were pulling into Caroline's driveway.

Maybe he knew what she had planned and he was just as eager for it. Snow was falling as they walked to her front door, yet her skin was on fire and anticipation raced through her. The sight of her spare key attached to his key ring gave her another jolt of confidence that Craig wasn't in a hurry to go anywhere. At least, not yet.

"Wait here," she said, pointing toward the sofa because it would've been too mortifying to suggest he wait on her bed. And trickier to explain without giving the surprise away. And she had a feeling that she was going to need the element of surprise.

Caroline went into her bathroom and carefully removed her sweater and skirt, then reached in the vanity to find the matching lace bra-and-pantie set she'd hidden there for this exact moment.

Her cheeks turned the same crimson shade as the lingerie and Caroline was glad she'd been smart enough not to wear such a sexy thing under her clothes earlier. She would've been entirely distracted throughout the party, constantly aware of what she had on underneath and thinking about who would see it later.

She was dying to splash some cold water on her face, but didn't want to ruin her carefully applied makeup. Instead, she settled for a gulp of water out of the faucet, then stared at her reflection wondering if there was anything she'd forgotten when she'd come up with this plan. *Don't think of it as a plan*, she told herself. *Try to act natural.*

Unfortunately, the longer she stood in this bathroom, the more she would second-guess herself. Steeling herself, she listened to that initial instinct—the one that had never steered her wrong before—and walked out into the living room.

Caroline heard Craig's sharp intake of breath, saw the heat fill his eyes, and it was all she could do not to smile in triumph. She was sure he could see her heart thumping behind her rib cage.

"I have to tell you something," Craig blurted out. His voice held a slight tremble and Caroline guessed that he was just as nervous as she. Another ounce of courage filled her and she straightened her back, causing her breasts to thrust forward.

"Don't you want to unwrap your gift first?" she asked.

His only response was his Adam's apple bobbing up and down. Normally, when he was uncomfortable or trying to avoid a question, he focused on some distant point while he spoke to her. Right now, though, his eyes were drilling into her, and Caroline's confidence soared.

He'd already discarded both his heavier outer coat and his sport coat and was now only wearing a white dress shirt. She walked toward him and slid her hands up his chest until her fingers landed on the first button-hole. "Or can I unwrap mine first?" she asked him as she opened his buttons.

"I'm not who you think I am," he said in a rush, and Caroline didn't quite feel like herself, either. Boldness had overcome her, and right now, if she allowed him to distract her with all his chivalrous excuses of why they couldn't be intimate, she would surely lose more than her memory. She might lose her mind.

Putting a finger up to his mouth to gently shush him, Caroline ended up tracing his lower lip. "But you're ex-actly who I want."

"How do you *know*, though? Your head—"

She cut off his words with a kiss. Caroline was tired of explaining that her concussion was perfectly healed. Her only option now was to show him. And she did so with her mouth, her hands, her entire body, distracting him from any argument about why they shouldn't fi-nally consummate their relationship.

There was a slight resistance when she tugged on his hand, trying to lead him toward her bedroom, and she could see all the conflicted emotions pass across his face. Cupping his cheek, she whispered, "Craig, trust me, I know what you want to tell me. But there isn't a single thing you can say that would stop me from wanting you. Unless it's that you don't want me."

"Nothing could be further from the truth," he replied, his voice deep and loaded with desire.

"Then prove it."

Craig groaned as he lifted her into his arms and carried her the rest of the way to the bed. His mouth claimed hers and as he set her down, she slipped her hands into his undone shirt and yanked it free just as his body followed hers onto the comforter.

There was more kissing, more touching, more moaning as her bra came loose and her panties slid from her hips. Caroline was pushing his jeans past the rounded muscles of his rear end when his body stilled.

"I need to go get some protection," he murmured against her temple, then began to push off her, but she wrapped her legs around his waist and pulled him back.

"Don't leave," Caroline said, thinking she would die of humiliation if he came to his senses and rejected her now.

"Honey, I'm just going to the living room to get them out of my duffel bag."

Pleasure engulfed her as she realized that he must have known in the back of his mind that they would eventually make love. He'd prepared just as she had.

"That's okay," she replied, leaning toward her bedside drawer to retrieve the package she'd brought home from work. "I was too embarrassed to go to the drugstore in town, so I found these in one of the favor bags we had left over from a bachelorette party last summer."

When he rolled the condom on, Caroline knew with a certainty that this was the man for her. This was her destiny. He entered her slowly and Caroline gasped as the hard tip filled her.

"Are you okay?" he asked and she could hear the tension in his tone, as it must've taken him an extreme amount of willpower to hold himself back.

"I've never been better," she sighed. "Please don't stop now."

"I never can tell you no," Craig said, then thrust deep inside her, only to freeze when she winced in pain. "You...you're a..."

"I'm yours," Caroline said, using her calves to wind around him and draw him in closer.

She'd been a virgin, Craig thought, trailing his fingers along her spine as she curved her body next to his afterward. There was no turning back now. Caroline had unwittingly given him a precious gift and all he'd given her in return was false hope.

Unless...

What would happen if Caroline never regained her memory and went on believing they were engaged? Could Craig actually go through with their marriage? The past couple of weeks, he hadn't faked his attraction for her or even how much he cared about her. In fact, the more he'd gotten to know her, the more he could see that she was well educated and determined to live her life the way she wanted.

And apparently, she wanted him.

Caroline sighed and hooked her left leg over his thigh. His own arm under her shoulders instinctively pulled her closer, as though he could never get enough of her. And deep down, he knew that would be the case. How could he possibly let her go now?

If she really wanted that life to be on the ranch in Thunder Canyon, there was no way he would be able to tell her no. Besides, Craig was tired of being the voice of reason.

The truth of the matter was that the night she'd pulled out those matching Christmas stockings, he'd been terrified at first. But as he'd battled sleep all night on her sofa, he'd come to the conclusion that he could no longer imagine his life without Caroline in it. All he could hope was that, if she remembered nothing else, she knew that he'd always tried to do the right thing.

Her left hand was absently caressing his chest and Craig knew that if she continued, he would want her on her back again. Or on top of him this time. As great as their first time had felt, he didn't want to make her sore—or at least sorer than he'd probably already made her. Using his palm, he cupped her hand in his, slowing her motion.

After a couple of seconds, he found himself stroking her left ring finger, the one that had remained bare throughout all of this supposed engagement. Craig froze at the realization, wondering how both of them had overlooked something so obvious.

"Are you okay?" Caroline propped her chin up on her right hand. Her brown hair was thoroughly disheveled and hanging in messy waves around her face and she had never looked more adorable or more loved.

Oh, God. He'd fallen in love with her.

The realization should have made him go cold and sink into the bed with fear of the unexpected. Instead, Craig basked in the warmth of Caroline's heated body as a feeling of weightlessness and euphoria settled into a cocoon around him.

"Actually," he said, unable to stop the smile that played on his lips as he began tracing her ring finger again, "I was just thinking we should go to a jeweler to pick something out soon."

Caroline gasped before scrambling up to her knees, not bothering to take the bedsheet with her as she beamed a smile at him. "You mean an engagement ring?"

"Of course," Craig said, then chuckled as she rained kisses down over his face.

"I—" she kissed his cheek "—love—" she kissed his forehead "—you—" she kissed his chin "—so—" she kissed his other cheek "—much." She kissed his lips. Then she held her face over his and he saw the depth of her happiness reflected in her eyes. "I was hoping that you'd propose by Christmas."

Hearing her say that she loved him gave Craig the strength to take over the world. Or at least to flip her over and take his time covering her with kisses.

But then he heard her last sentence.

"Propose?" He braced his hands against her shoulders, holding her in place and preventing her from distracting him anymore with her full, sensuous lips. "But we're already engaged."

"Not officially, though."

"What do you mean 'not officially'?"

"Craig." Caroline opened and closed her mouth several times. "Look, I know you were a good sport to go along with all those things I said after I bumped my head. I can't imagine how crazy you must've thought I was. But we can stop all the pretending now, can't we?"

"Hold on." Something clawed at his throat and it took several attempts to swallow the shock down. "You got your memory back?"

Chapter Eighteen

"Technically, I've always had my memory." Caroline's smile was less dreamy this time and a bit more sheepish, and the hair on the back of Craig's neck stood at attention. "I just also had one additional memory that wasn't quite real."

"When did you realize we weren't engaged?" He had a million questions he wanted to ask, but that sensation that had clawed at his neck earlier was now throbbing near his ears and he wasn't sure he wanted to hear the answers.

Caroline sat up much less playfully than she had earlier and slowly tucked the bedsheet under her arms. "The first night you kissed me. I knew there was no way I could've forgotten something like that. Everything came flooding back."

"You mean, you knew for almost two weeks and never told me the truth?"

"I thought…" Her voice trailed off and two little creases appeared above her nose.

"No. Don't give me that confused, hopeless, please-rescue-me face," Craig said and could see by her recoil that his words had hit their mark. He stood up and snatched his jeans off the floor before continuing, "I'm the one who should be confused. I'm the one who looks like the hopeless fool. I'm the one who got played."

He heard her indrawn breath before he'd scooped up his abandoned dress shirt, shoving his arms through the sleeves as he stomped out of the bedroom. In the living room, he fumbled with his boots, anger blinding him and frustration making his motions erratic. He needed to get out of this house. He needed to get away from Caroline, away from all the deception.

It felt good to slam the front door behind him, until he realized that he'd forgotten his keys in the pocket of his winter coat. The coat he'd left inside, along with his hat and his dignity.

But there was no way he'd go back inside to retrieve his belongings. At least not now. He stared at his truck covered with at least two inches of snow, shivering when he realized the crew cab doors were locked and he couldn't climb inside for warmth. All he had on was jeans, a thin dress shirt and boots, minus the socks. He wasn't sure where those had ended up earlier in the evening when he'd been in a blinded hurry to shed his clothes and feel Caroline's skin pressed against his.

Crunching the fresh powdery snow under his heels,

Craig strode toward the street, refusing to think about the cold or about Caroline's warm naked body. His heartbeat pounded in time to each angry step he took. He should call someone for a ride, but he'd been so stupid in his rage, he'd also forgotten his phone and his wallet.

Had he ever been this upset before?

With no destination in mind, he thought about continuing down to the boardinghouse to get a room for the night, but Melba and Gene Strickland were pretty old-fashioned when it came to relationships and the types of people they allowed to stay at their place. They likely preferred a guest who didn't show up and disturb them in the middle of the night after a reckless bout of lovemaking with a woman who'd been pretending to be his fiancée.

Instead, Craig made a left at the corner and found himself walking down Rust Creek Falls's picture-perfect Main Street. As a kid, he'd remembered a pay phone in front of Crawford's General Store, but when he arrived, he saw that it was long gone. Just like his youth. Just like his common sense.

Caroline probably didn't even know what a pay phone was, Craig thought as he kicked through the layer of snow on the sidewalk. He should've known better than to fall under the young woman's spell. His life had been exactly the way he'd wanted it before he walked into that wedding planner's office. Before he'd rushed to save a pretty stranger from knocking herself out. Before it was *his* world that got knocked off its axis.

The twinkling Christmas lights along Main Street

mocked him, each blink reminding Craig of the holiday he didn't know he'd been looking forward to. The holiday he'd been starting to think of as his and Caroline's.

They were going to do the Candlelight Walk together and he'd envisioned the two of them wrapping presents side by side at the community center next week for Presents for Patriots. He'd even planned to take her home to Thunder Canyon and hang their matching stockings over the family's huge fireplace on Christmas Eve. The stockings he'd made fun of.

The life he'd thought he no longer wanted.

Originally, he'd wanted a partner for the ranch. A helpmate. Now, though, all he wanted was her.

His brain told him that there could be no love if there wasn't trust. Yet, at the same time, his heart told him that there could be no love if he wasn't with Caroline.

Craig's steps slowed and, as his anger cooled, so did the rest of his body. Shoving his hands into his front pockets, he arched his back, bracing against the cold wind pummeling him from behind.

"Craig!"

He whipped around to see Caroline rushing toward him, balancing a bundle in front of her as she navigated the icy sidewalk in faded jeans and cowboy boots. Bright turquoise ones and, judging by the worn leather, not exactly new. So she *did* own a pair after all.

He tried to tell himself that it didn't mean anything. It didn't mean that she belonged on his ranch or in his world. But then he saw what she was carrying and his breath left his body, his ribs squeezing against his lungs.

"When I noticed that you didn't take your truck, I

was worried about you being outside in this weather without your coat." Caroline handed him the folded sheepskin coat with his Stetson hat on top, then, without saying another word, she turned around and walked back toward Cedar Street. She didn't apologize or make excuses or try to convince him to come back to her house to talk things out.

Was she really just going to let him go?

Craig slammed the hat onto his head and began walking after her, tempted to ask about his truck keys. As he was shrugging on his jacket, something fell to the ground. He reached down and came back up with a wool scarf. This wasn't his. When had he ever worn a scarf?

Yet the sight of the red plaid pattern stopped him in his tracks. Her scarf.

She'd chased after him. On foot and in the middle of the night with snow barreling down on her, Caroline had trekked along the frozen sidewalks just to bring him a damn scarf. She'd given him her trust. She'd given him her virginity. She'd given him her love.

And he didn't even have the decency to say thank you.

Now it was his turn to chase after her.

"Caroline, wait," Craig called out as he quickly caught up with her at the corner. She didn't turn around, but at least she stopped. "Thank you for bringing my coat."

He saw the back of her head nod and his stomach clenched. She took another step and Craig suddenly didn't want her to leave.

"How did you know where I would go?" he asked,

burying his hands in his fur-lined pockets and rocking back on his heels. His bare feet slipped inside his boots and he cursed himself for forgetting his socks.

Caroline turned around and, in the dim glow of the old-fashioned streetlamp, he could see the dark sadness in her usually bright eyes. "I followed the footprints. Apparently, you're the only fool running around downtown Rust Creek Falls in the middle of a snowstorm."

"I definitely feel like a fool," Craig admitted.

"And you don't think I felt like a fool, too?" Caroline's face tilted up and he could see that the normally happy and composed wedding planner was also willing to fight some battles.

Originally, Caroline was only going to make sure Craig wasn't wandering the streets of Rust Creek Falls without a coat, his stubbornness exposing him to the bone-chilling elements. She'd anticipated him being annoyed that she hadn't told him about her memory returning earlier and she didn't blame him for that. However, she wasn't the only person who'd done some misleading in this relationship. In fact, if anyone had been played the fool, it had been her.

"*I* was the one who looked like an idiot when I fell off a stupid chair in front of a stranger and hit my head on the ground," Caroline started, the stiffness in her spine having nothing to do with the snowfall or the chill in the air.

"Just for the record," he said, shrugging as if the weather wasn't bothering him at all, "you hit your head on the bookshelf. I caught you before you actually hit the ground."

"Like that makes it any less embarrassing?" Caroline rolled her eyes before continuing. "*I* was the one who woke up in the hospital thinking I was engaged to that same stranger. *I* was the one who insisted you were my fiancé to the doctor, to Josselyn, to everyone who came into my office later that week, despite the fact that I knew all of you were keeping a secret from me. My mother, a national icon for women's rights who doesn't believe in marriage? Yeah, *I* told her we were engaged, while you stood there looking all sexy and shirtless in my kitchen. *I* gushed about our relationship that *you* knew was completely fabricated."

"You thought I looked sexy when I was shirtless?" Craig dipped his chin, lowering his voice.

But Caroline would not be swayed by her body's traitorous reaction to him when she still had things to say. "Yes, I got my memory back that night you first kissed me and didn't tell you. It was selfish of me to keep quiet this past week. But I did it because I fell in love with you and wanted to keep you."

"You wanted to keep me?"

"Of course I did. Craig, I wanted you from that moment you carried the donut box into my office. I never would have believed that we were supposed to be together or said any of those things if I didn't already know in my heart that I meant it. I meant every word I ever said. My feelings for you were never a lie. So, now, tell me your excuse."

"My excuse?"

"Why didn't you tell me the truth from the beginning?"

"Because the doctors told us not to upset you. They said you would eventually remember things at your own pace."

"But you *stayed* at my house. You willingly jeopardized my reputation."

"Dr. Robinson said they couldn't release you from the hospital unless someone could watch out for you. And you were the one insisting I stay with you when Josselyn invited you to recuperate at Sunshine Farm."

"But Dr. Robinson didn't say you had to take me to Thanksgiving dinner with your family." Caroline put her hands on her hips. "Dr. Robinson didn't say you had to go along with that engagement party at the Maverick Manor."

"Fine. Dr. Robinson didn't say that I had to like being around you either, but guess what? I did. I liked the way you were always positive and happy and made these wonderful home-cooked meals without any vegetables. I liked that you were patient with my bickering grandparents and that you were kind to my grouchy cat and that you slipped a roll of cherry Life Savers into my shirt pocket every afternoon when I picked you up from work. I liked that you knew so many random things about so many subjects and could count cards to come up with the best hand, but were still humble enough to fold and let Meemaw and Grandpac win the game."

Caroline shivered, not from the cold, but from his words. Craig unfolded the red plaid scarf, which was still in his hands, and coiled it around her neck, using the ends to pull her closer to him. "I liked being your fiancé because I like you."

"Just 'like'?" she prompted, walking her fingers up the lapels of his coat as she arched one eyebrow.

"Maybe a little more." Craig groaned when she pulled her hands away from his shoulders. "Okay, a whole lot more. But it took me a full two weeks to fall in love with you. How did you know so soon that I was the one? Would any cowboy who had walked into your office that day have been the man you wanted?"

Caroline's heart fluttered at his words that he'd fallen in love with her. "Have you ever heard of Winona Cobbs?"

"The old psychic?"

Caroline nodded. "Well, she predicted I'd be engaged by Christmas and then she gave me a few clues as to who it would be. The second you walked into my office, I was sure it had to be you. It was my last thought before I hit my head."

"I'll admit, there was something about you in the beginning that made me want to take care of you. I don't know if I agree with all that premonition and destiny stuff, but it's hard to deny that I was in the right place at the right time."

"Or maybe *I* was in the right place at the right time?" Caroline offered. "Maybe *you* were the one who needed rescuing?"

"Only time will tell." Craig smiled, cupping her cheek.

"Then why don't we start over from the beginning and take things slowly?" Caroline stuck out her hand

and said, "Hi. My name is Caroline Ruth. It's nice to meet you."

"Hi, Caroline. I'm Craig Clifton and I am completely in love with you." He pulled her hand up to his lips and giddiness bubbled in the back of Caroline's throat. "That should be all the time we need."

As his mouth landed on hers, all either one of them could think was...

Engaged by Christmas.

Epilogue

On Christmas Eve, Craig shifted in his metal folding chair beside Caroline as they watched the elementary school's performance of *A Christmas Carol* at the community center in Thunder Canyon.

"What'd Bob Cratchit say?" Meemaw whispered loudly down their row. She'd had to lean across Grandpac to ask Caroline since Craig's grandfather had been the first to arrive this evening and had used name-badge stickers to save seats for the entire family.

"Dammit, woman," Grandpac whispered back. "Get your hearing aid fixed. And you can't just move your chair and sit wherever you want. You're blocking the aisle."

"Well, seeing as how you conveniently saved my seat on the opposite end of the auditorium, I didn't really have a choice."

"I should've saved a seat for you in the dang parking lot," his grandfather muttered loud enough to draw the attention of the fifth-grade usher.

Craig rolled his eyes, hoping his grandparents didn't completely ruin the surprise he had planned for Caroline. Or worse, get them kicked out of Caroline's favorite holiday play.

"Cratchit is basically telling his wife that it's Christmas and she needs to set a good example for the children by toasting his horrible boss, Mr. Scrooge," Dr. Ruth whispered as he turned around from the row in front of them. Caroline's dad, who'd flown in with Caroline's mom from India late last night, held up the bright screen of his electronic tablet. "I have both the book, as well as the adapted script for the play, loaded on my iPad if you want to follow along."

"Did you know that Charles Dickens never even gave Mrs. Cratchit a first name in the original version?" Dr. Rodriguez put her arm along the back of Caroline's father's seat as she spoke to the entire row behind her. "Because women apparently didn't deserve any sort of notability or recognition in Victorian England."

While Craig had been excited to meet Caroline's parents for the first time, he was also now questioning his own parents' offer to extend an invitation for everyone to come to Thunder Canyon for the holidays. He shifted in his seat again, wishing he had brought Caroline here tonight alone.

"If you ask me, Mrs. Cratchit should tell ol' Bob to shove his brownnosing toast to Scrooge up his—"

"Shhh, Meemaw." Craig pointed to something going on offstage. "The important part is coming up."

The boy who was playing the role of Tiny Tim limped off the stage, trying to hold on to a wrapped gift box that was meowing as the rest of the audience murmured and giggled.

Dr. Ruth held his tablet closer to his face. "I don't remember this happening in the original."

Craig caught the young actor's eye and was about to lift his arm behind Caroline's back to point her out. But Grandpac beat him to it. "She's right here, kiddo. Next to me."

When the little boy set the squirming box on Caroline's lap, he announced in a proud voice, "A Merry Christmas to us all. God bless us everyone!"

The crowd hushed as they swiveled to watch Caroline remove the lid to her gift. Tiny Tim, the feline version, was inside, squatting on his two good hind legs and proudly meowing his normally grouchy head off.

Caroline giggled and lifted the cat out and Rob spoke up from behind Craig's shoulder, "I can't believe you put your poor cat in a box, Craig."

"It was my idea," C.C. said from where she was now standing next to the young actor in the aisle. "And look, Tiny Tim is loving being the center of attention."

The animal was in fact now purring in Caroline's arms, his tail slowly swishing back and forth as if he was ready for his encore. Craig's father hovered behind them, his video camera zooming in.

"Sit down, dear." His mother pushed his father's arm. "I can't see."

"I'm in the middle of something here," Craig reminded everyone and Caroline gasped when she saw him drop to his knee.

"Caroline Ruth," he started, and Dr. Rodriguez gave a not-so-discreet cough. "I mean, Caroline Rodriguez Ruth, would you do me the honor of becoming my wife?"

Tiny Tim let out another meow as Craig untied the ribbon attached to his collar and pulled the diamond ring free. "As well as my spoiled cat's adopted mom?"

A tear trickled out of Caroline's eye as she eagerly bobbed her head up and down while Craig slid the ring onto her finger. When he pulled her and Tiny Tim into his arms, the entire community center erupted in applause.

Two months later, Craig was knee-deep in overseeing the cattle breeding season, while Caroline was busy establishing the Thunder Canyon location for her and Vivienne's newest wedding planning office.

But both of them always made time to meet with the architect and builder they'd hired to create their dream home on the Clifton family ranch. There would be a small guest cottage for when Caroline's parents came to town—or for when Grandpac needed a space to cool off after having a big fight with Meemaw during holiday dinners—and there would be plenty of bookshelves for their memories and pillows for Tiny Tim.

Caroline and Craig still hadn't set a wedding date, but now that they'd been engaged by Christmas, fulfilling their destiny was no longer as important as the rest of their journey.

* * * * *

If you like this book by Christy Jeffries,
Don't miss

The Firefighter's Christmas Reunion

On sale December 2018!

And look for the next installment of the new
Harlequin Special Edition continuity
Montana Mavericks: The Lonelyhearts Ranch.

Bah, humbug! Bailey Stockton hates the holidays.
And romance. Until he meets Serena Langley, his
very own Christmas angel. Can she bring the gift of
happiness to the biggest scrooge in Rust Creek Falls?

Don't miss
Bring Me a Maverick for Christmas!
by award-winning author Brenda Harlen.

On sale December 2018, wherever
Harlequin books and ebooks are sold.

*And catch up with the rest of the
Montana Mavericks: The Lonelyhearts Ranch
in these great titles:*

The Maverick's Bridal Bargain
by Christy Jeffries

A Maverick to (Re)Marry
by New York Times *bestselling author*
Christine Rimmer

The Maverick's Baby-in-Waiting
by Melissa Senate

The Little Maverick Matchmaker
by USA TODAY *bestselling author Stella Bagwell*

Unmasking the Maverick
by Teresa Southwick

The Maverick's Christmas to Remember
by Christy Jeffries

Available now!

She rose from her seat of slab rock. "We'd probably better
be going. We still have one more hiking trail to cover before
we hit another set of campgrounds."

While she gathered up her partially eaten lunch, Sawyer
left his seat and walked over to the edge of the bluff.

"This is an incredible view," he said. "From this distance,
the saguaros look like green needles stuck in a sandpile."

She looked over to see the strong north wind was hitting
him in the face and molding his uniform against his muscled
body. The sight of his imposing figure etched against the
blue sky and desert valley caused her breath to hang in her
throat.

She walked over to where he stood, then took a cautious
step closer to the ledge in order to peer down at the view
directly below.

"I never get tired of it," she admitted. "There are a few
Native American ruins not far from here. We'll hike by
those before we finish our route."

A hard gust of wind suddenly whipped across the ledge and caused Vivian to sway on her feet. Sawyer swiftly caught her by the arm and pulled her back to his side.

"Careful," he warned. "I wouldn't want you to topple over the edge."

With his hand on her arm and his sturdy body shielding her from the wind, she felt very warm and protected. And for one reckless moment, she wondered how it would feel to slip her arms around his lean waist, to rise up on the tips of her toes and press her mouth to his. Would his lips taste as good as she imagined?

Shaken by the direction of her runaway thoughts, she tried to make light of the moment. "That would be awful," she agreed. "Mort would have to find you another partner."

"Yeah, and she might not be as cute as you."

With a little laugh of disbelief, she stepped away from his side. "Cute? I haven't been called that since I was in high school. I'm beginning to think you're nineteen instead of twenty-nine."

He pulled a playful frown at her. "You prefer your men to be old and somber?"

"I prefer them to keep their minds on their jobs," she said staunchly. "And you are not *my* man."

His laugh was more like a sexy promise.

"Not yet."

Don't miss
A Ranger for Christmas *by Stella Bagwell,*
available December 2018 wherever
Harlequin® Special Edition *books and ebooks are sold.*

www.Harlequin.com

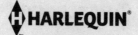